MORE
THAN
YOU KNOW

MORE THAN YOU KNOW

ANNE CANADEO

"Do one thing every day that scares you."

—Eleanor Roosevelt

Whether you're right,
Whether you're wrong,
Man of my heart, I'll string along
I need you so
More than you'll ever know

"More Than You Know,"
Billie Holliday version (released 1939)
Music by Vincent Youmans
Lyrics by Billy Rose and Edward Eliscu (1929)

Praise for More Than You Know

"A superb mystery…full of color and dripping with atmosphere. Canadeo's good-hearted but flawed characters are so true-to-life, it's hard to believe they aren't real."—**Donis Casey**, award-winning author of the *Alafair Tucker Mysteries* and *The Adventures of Bianca Dangereuse Hollywood Mysteries*

"A multi-plotted mystery that kept me intrigued throughout…nonstop action and dialogue that made the story come alive."—***Dru Ann Love***, Agatha, Anthony and Macavity Award-winning author and Raven Award-winning book advocate

Chapter One

"Your brother said you lost your job, but it wasn't your fault?"

Grace expected Harry Shaw to ask that question, but she wasn't sure how to answer. A waitress set a cup of coffee down in front of each of them. The scent was tempting, but she kept her gloved hands in her lap.

"There were a lot of rules in the typing pool, and I didn't follow most of them. So, I guess it was my fault."

"Always so honest, Miss Russo?"

"You'll find out anyway. Once you call my references."

If you call them. Joe made it sound like his army buddy would hire any female between sixteen and sixty who could roll a sheet of paper into a typewriter. They'd been sitting there long enough; she still had no idea what Harry Shaw thought of her.

"Where were you working again?"

"Pioneer Insurance. They don't say 'fired' there, they say 'dismissed.' Maybe they think it sounds more official."

"Possibly." He seemed to find her amusing, though she wasn't trying to be.

He'd asked her to meet him at the Schrafft's near Times Square. Which was fine with her. Schrafft's on Fifth had been Colin's favorite spot. She didn't need to be distracted by that right now.

She watched Harry Shaw light a cigarette; the heavy block of silver looked smart and expensive. At odds with the rest of him, a not-so-fresh white shirt, a wrinkled grey suit, and a stain on his tie that didn't blend with the swirling pattern. He was either single or his wife needed glasses.

"Sorry…would you like one?" He held out the pack, Lucky Strike. The smoke smelled strong and sweet.

"No, thank you."

She did smoke once and awhile and would have loved to now, if only to give her hands something to do. But smoking on an interview was almost as bad as chewing gum she'd been taught.

He took a long puff and tapped the ash on the edge of his saucer. He'd never removed his hat, a black homburg, tipped back. Even sitting perfectly still, he looked ready to bolt. A lot of men had come back that way, edgy and restless. That was the least of it.

"I catch a few cases from Pioneer. They do remind me of the army now that you mention it. What department were you in?"

"Claims. I started as a receptionist and was promoted to case manager during the war. But when Mr. Delaney came home—I was his replacement—they gave him back the job and found something else for me."

"They knocked you down a peg or two."

"They said the typing pool was the only opening I qualified for." There had been another for a case manager, but her supervisor had saved that for a man, too.

"Still, it must have stung." He took another draw on the cigarette, squinting against the smoke. The silence between them filled with the clatter of dishes and rising voices.

A group of women at the next table burst into laughter as one waved a flimsy negligee above a gift-wrapped box. Across the aisle, a young mother with a baby in her lap and a child on either side doled out bits of creamed chicken on toast, the cheapest sandwich on the menu.

Harry Shaw waited for her to say more. To vent some grievance. The demotion *had* stung, the pay cut, too. But Grace was not a whiner. A soldier like Bob Delaney deserved a good job after all he'd been through, and she wasn't the first woman to step aside for a G.I. It just didn't seem fair that his old job was hers, too.

"I was sorry I couldn't stay in Claims. I liked the work, and I was good at it. I have a letter from my supervisor if you'd like to see it?"

He didn't answer, but she passed it to him anyway. She'd found a fresh envelope that morning and hoped he didn't notice how the page inside was creased and handled.

He dipped his head to read the note, and her gaze followed a thin scar that curved down from his forehead, through his eyebrow, ending at the top of his cheek. Like a tear in a sheer curtain. Or maybe a question mark.

She doubted it slowed him down with the ladies. She'd say he was attractive, in a rough around the edges way. Rose wouldn't think so. Grace was sure her sister would ask about that first thing.

"Very nice." He slid the envelope back but didn't say more.

She heard the meter ticking. It wasn't the last job in New York, but she was so weary of the search, and saw no reason why she shouldn't have this one.

"Could you tell me more about your work, Mr. Shaw?" Grace tilted her head, careful not to overdo and give the wrong idea. She wasn't flirting. Though maybe it would take a little of that, too, to land this fish. "How did you get into this business?"

"The usual way, I guess." He drew on his cigarette. Wise to her ploy? That didn't mean it wouldn't work.

"I was a cop before the war. A detective. When I got home, I had to wait for an opening in the force. I hooked up with a P.I. to keep a paycheck coming in, and by the time there was a chance to go back, I didn't want to."

"So, you like working on your own more than being a police officer?"

"It suits me for now. There's no pension or paid vacations. But I make my own hours, and there's no one calling me on the carpet about rules and regulations."

He didn't seem the type who fell in line easily, though he must have in the service. He'd been her brother Joe's commanding officer.

"What would my responsibilities be?"

He seemed reluctant to reply. "Type, file, answer the phone. Keep track of the billing, not that there's much of it." He shook another cigarette from the pack. "I'm out a lot. I need someone who can handle themselves alone. Get the facts straight when people call. That part is important."

"I dealt with clients all the time in Claims, taking down information and asking questions, when I needed to."

"Good for you." He leaned back and took a better look at her. Threads of smoke curled between them. "Most people are afraid to ask questions. Afraid to sound rude or even stupid."

"Maybe they're afraid of the answers they'll get. But if they weren't, guys like you probably wouldn't have much business."

He smiled so quickly she almost missed it. "We'd get a lot less."

"What kinds of situations do you investigate?"

"It's not like in the movies, if that's what you think. It's pretty humdrum stuff."

"Like the insurance business, you mean?"

"Got me there. I look into claims from time to time, suspicious ones. Injury, theft. Arson isn't my area, but I've seen that, too. Companies that come up short on their inventory call me. I also work for defense attorneys and private clients. Matrimonial, mostly. Or someone skips out on a debt or a bail bond." He shrugged and met her gaze. "Not humanity's finest moments, Miss Russo. I can promise you that."

"I don't shock easily." She sat back and squared her shoulders. "And I can type, file, take dictation. Do whatever needs doing."

He met her gaze but didn't look convinced. "There's a lot of confidential information in my office. I need someone who's discreet."

"I'm extremely discreet. I had to be at Pioneer."

He didn't reply, just tapped his cigarette. Did he think she was pushy? Men didn't like that, especially a prospective employer. Her mouth worked faster than her brain at times.

A waitress swept past and refilled Harry's cup. Grace watched him stir in half the cream pitcher and two sugar cubes. She expected a PI to take it black. This one definitely had a sweet tooth.

"The job is only temporary. Did Joe tell you that?"

"He said your secretary is out sick?"

"Mrs. Pfeiffer. She had her gall bladder removed. There were complications. She'll be back in a month or so. You're probably looking for something permanent."

That was true. But she was willing to take anything.

"Listen, you're a nice girl. Smart, too. Just like Joe said. Nothing personal, but I think you'd be better off in a big office. Another insurance firm, or a bank? There are plenty of good outfits besides Pioneer. They'd take a sharp gal like you in a minute."

Grace had thought so, too. A few weeks ago. But all the openings went to ex-G.I.s, and a lot were still looking.

She caught his gaze and wouldn't let him look away. "Maybe so. But I really think *you* should hire me. By the time you decide if I'm working out, I can catch up on the filing and typing. I bet there's piles of it on Mrs. Pfeiffer's desk." She'd already said too much but didn't pause to take a breath. "Frankly, Mr. Shaw, I don't think you have anything to lose by giving me a try."

She twisted her gloves to keep from saying more.

Harry Shaw ground out his cigarette. Then just stared at her.

Chapter Two

"Did you get the job?" Rose sat at the dressing table, studying a picture in a magazine as she pinned up her hair. If her little sister had applied half the effort in school, she wouldn't be working in a paper box factory. But even with a mouth full of bobby pins, she was so pretty, Grace had to smile.

"He told me to come in on Monday at nine. I guess that's a good sign." Grace sat on her bed and unlaced her oxfords. The F-train had skipped Carroll Street, and she'd walked all the way from Bergen. She couldn't wait to pull off her panty girdle and loosen her bra.

"Doesn't that mean you're hired? I'd say so."

Grace reached for the buttons at the back of her blouse, pearl-shaped and slippery. "I'm not sure. He's a funny guy. Not what I expected."

Joe spoke about Harry Shaw with such respect; she'd pictured someone older. More dignified. A uniform did a lot for a man, and Shaw had lost that advantage in his rumpled civies.

Rose helped with the last button. "He's probably alright if Joe likes him. Is he good-looking?"

"It was an interview, Rose. I didn't notice."

She'd try to remember that one in confession. Once Rose got going in that direction, it was hard to change the subject.

"I bet you didn't notice if he was single, either. You can't find a man if you don't keep your antennas up."

"They didn't fit under my hat." She slipped out the pin and set the black tam on her dresser. "The job is only temporary. His regular secretary will be back in a few weeks."

"Think positively…By the way, I don't remember you asking to borrow that blouse."

Grace offered a sly smile. "I didn't expect you to catch me in it. I'll rinse it after dinner."

"For goodness sakes, it's Friday night. You should be out, having fun. Not home doing hand laundry."

Grace was unfazed by Rose's scolding, content with her plan of rinsing lingerie and starting a new book.

"I might play Bingo at St. Rocco's with Mama and Nona." She hated bingo but couldn't resist teasing.

"What's the use. If you're washing the blouse, can I give you a slip or two?"

"At your service, Ma'am."

Grace didn't mind; the favor was fair exchange for sharing her sister's wardrobe. They were nearly the same height, but nowhere near the same build or looks. Rose was petite with a pert figure. Grace loved her shiny, auburn curls, but Rose dyed her hair blonde lately, to please her fiancé, Frank. Grace hated to watch the long, painful process.

She was content with her brown eyes and dark hair and wouldn't change her looks, even for Cary Grant. Though she'd always been a bit curvier, there was rarely a garment or accessory exclusive to one of them. Grace would test the seams on Rose's skirts and stretch out her sweaters, though her sister rarely complained.

"It's not fair. You got enough on top for both of us," Rose would say.

"I'd trade in a heartbeat if I could, honey. This twin set is way more trouble than it's worth."

Grace meant it, too. Ever since adolescence, her feminine assets had been mostly a nuisance. She dressed sedately, avoiding styles that made her look like a floozy. But some men still thought a full figure signaled she was easy, or didn't have a brain in her head. An even worse insult in her book. She'd been chased around a few desks, too. Harry Shaw didn't seem the athletic type, but she'd been surprised before.

Rose watched her pull a cotton house dress over her head. "How's the pay? Better than Pioneer, I hope."

"Worse. But something's better than nothing."

Grace didn't need to earn much living at home, though before her exile to the typing pool, she'd been saving to find her own place, a studio or one bedroom in the city she could share with her best friend, Lucy Bianco. Lucy was studying to be a nurse at Flushing Hospital. She had to board there, and they didn't see each other much. But Lucy would graduate in a few weeks and was already looking for a job.

Grace hadn't said a word to her parents. She didn't want to start World War III before it was absolutely necessary. "Nice girls don't live alone. It gives men ideas," her mother would say.

As if men needed any special reason for those ideas.

The moving-out plan was shelved for now. She hadn't saved much, and Rose's wedding was only two months away. As the maid of honor, Grace wanted to give her sister a big bridal shower and a generous gift—"*a boosta*," her family called it. Working for the PI a few weeks should cover that much.

"Look what came today." Rose pulled a white box out from under her bed. "From Aunt Nina."

Grace summoned an eager expression. Watching her sister's wedding plans unfold was not always easy. She would have felt a lot different if Colin had come home. They would have been married by now. Maybe even had a baby.

There was little reason to keep hoping or checking the Red Cross list, but she couldn't help it. She heard stories all the time about men with memories wiped clean by shell shock or a head injury. Stuck in some distant place without I.D. The chance of that grew slimmer every day, but until there was absolute proof, she couldn't let it go. Not completely. It would feel like a betrayal.

The box was square and deep. Rose flipped off the cover and pulled her prize from layers of crisp, white tissue. "The cake stand from my pattern. Isn't it beautiful?"

"Very elegant. Perfect for your future dinner parties."

Rose didn't bake, but she was already a good cook. Their mother had insisted that they both mastered the basics—marinara, Bolognese, and meatballs. Sautéed vegetables that didn't turn to mush. Lasagna, of course.

Grace had little talent for cooking and even less interest. When her meatballs fell apart in the frying pan, her mother would stare down in dismay, looking as if she'd failed her older daughter in some important way.

Her mother was the type of cook who could make a good meal from next to nothing. Even when challenged by rationing and shortages. If there was olive oil and garlic on hand, the family ate well. Her father's vegetable garden had helped, too.

"Dinner's ready. Someone set the table," her mother called from the bottom of the stairs.

"Coming, Ma," Grace shouted back. Rose shoved the box under the bed, and they went down together.

Grace's mother stood at the stove; a flowered apron tied around her thick waist. The rich, warm smells that filled the kitchen reminded Grace that she'd barely eaten all day.

"What's for supper, Ma? Smells good." It was Friday, fish of course. The question was what kind.

"*Linguine con vongole.* Your brother asked for the clams this morning, but he's already out gallivanting." She stared at the counter, dicing a pile of parsley with quick, sharp strokes.

Out with his trumpet, she meant. Making the rounds at bars and nightclubs, where friends on stage might ask him to sit in. He was angling for a spot with a band that had a steady gig and steady pay. In the meantime, he sipped whiskey neat and tapped his foot, waiting to be called up to play a tune or two. If he got his wish, he'd drink too much to celebrate; if he didn't, he'd drink too much for consolation.

Grace heard the radio in the parlor; Murrow reporting the day's news. Her father dozed in his chair, *The Daily News* spread across his lap. He'd removed his tie, but still wore a suit vest over a starched white shirt, cuffs neatly rolled over his wrists. "A hand-stitched suit and well-pressed shirt is a tailor's best advertising," he'd always say, publicizing his shop every day in that way.

Her grandmother sat by the front window, watching the street as she hooked a lace tablecloth for Rose's trousseau. The white linen floated across her dark dress while her fingers plied the needle and thread.

Rose took plates from the cupboard. "How about Camille? Is she coming up?"

"She's been in bed all day, poor thing. The bad headache, again. Aspirin doesn't even help. She just lies in the dark with a cool cloth on her head. I hope she got some sleep."

Rose set the dishes on the table. "Maybe some fresh air would help. Or if she found a job and kept herself busy?"

A mean thing to say, but probably true. They both thought their sister-in-law was aptly named; her personality did tend towards high drama.

"Lower your voice, she'll hear you." Their mother gave Rose a look as she glanced at the stairway that led to the newlyweds' little apartment.

Rose replied in a harsh whisper. "Honestly, Ma. What does she do down there all day? I'd go out of my mind."

"She helps me with the house and the laundry. She visits her mother and goes to mass. What else should she do? They're trying to start a family. Your turn will come. You'll see."

Rose laughed. "Not that fast, it won't. We're going to buy a house before we even think about kids."

Rose and Frank had been going together since grade school but put off their wedding to save a down payment. Frank was an apprentice plumber, and Rose had her factory job.

Her mother peered under a pot lid. "It's what God wants. Meanwhile, your brother should be home with his family, not sitting in a bar all night. He's a grown man with responsibilities. He doesn't act like one."

Rose didn't defend Joe. Grace didn't try either. Not anymore. Her mother didn't understand. But Grace had never expected the Army's discipline, or even the horrors her brother had been through, to dull his ambition. If anything, those lost years had sharpened it. Music was his refuge, a sacred place where he shut out the roaring, off-key world. And blocked out the terrors that still burned in his head; fires, smoldering in a dark, distant forest.

Joe would disappear for days. They could never predict when. He could be on top of the world one minute, in a pit of despair the next. Since he'd come home, there was rarely any in-between.

Her mother's rosary beads would filter through her fingers, hidden in an apron pocket. She'd light candles to the Virgin Mother and consult Father Dominic, who would make a special visit to talk to Joe.

Grace's father would talk to Joe, too. Sometimes coaxing. Sometimes cursing. Joe hunkered down inside, like a boxer leaning against the ropes, wearing out his opponent. His stone-hard resolve untouched by appeals to common sense or conscience.

Grace wasn't sure what was worse—when Joe went AWOL or when he came back, full of apologies and promises. He lost job after job but didn't care. He worked for Camille's uncle now, painting houses, and Grace wondered how long that would last.

Joe was not ready to be a father. Grace doubted he even wanted to start a family. Camille had claimed she was expecting right before they got engaged, Joe had told Grace privately, but she had a miscarriage soon after. A convenient miscarriage? Grace could hardly blame her if she'd tricked him. Camille had waited a long time, and Joe had dragged his heels to the altar.

"I'll bring Camille some tea and toast," Rose said.

Grace placed the bottle of Chianti on the table, next to her father's place. "I'll go down after dinner. Maybe she wants some company."

Her mother nodded but didn't praise them for doing what was right. "Rose, slice the bread near the sink. The crumbs are falling all over the floor. And put the red pepper on the table."

She pulled a strand of pasta from the boiling water and nibbled the tip.

"*Andiamo.* Let's eat while it's hot."

Chapter Three

Grace wasn't due at Harry Shaw's office until nine. She knew exactly how long it would take to get there, the address just east of Times Square, and she was ready by half past seven.

She'd decided on a navy-blue suit, with a long jacket and a kick pleat skirt. Rose said she looked like Mrs. Miniver, which was possibly true. She brightened the outfit with a dark red skimmer and matching baby dolls she'd only worn once, on Easter Sunday. Mrs. Miniver never wore red pumps...did she?

There was hot, strong coffee in the kitchen, and she stood at the counter to sip from a tiny cup. Italian coffee, her grandmother made every morning in a battered pot that twisted together in the middle.

"Cara, mangiare qualcosa. Non si può andare fuori con lo stomaco vuoto." Dressed and ready for nine o'clock mass, her grandmother beckoned, offering slices of Italian bread toasted beneath the broiler and slathered with sweet butter.

"I'm fine, Nona. I can't be late my first day."

Nona made a disapproving face. She refused to speak English, though everyone knew she understood it well enough.

Grace placed her cup in the sink and kissed her grandmother's soft, dry cheek. "See you later."

"Addio, bella. Dirò una preghiera per voi."

Grace laughed. "Thanks, Nona. I can use a prayer or two."

She checked her purse for subway tokens, then left from the side door. The alley between the brick houses was damp and cool. She didn't notice

Joe until she stood right next to him.

He sat on the pavement, his back propped against the wall. His chin rested on his chest; hat tipped over his eyes. He was either still drunk or asleep. Maybe a little of both.

The battered leather case that held his trumpet sat beside him, and a bottle of milk he'd swiped from the box was balanced on top, half empty. She hoped it had sobered him up.

"Joe?" She called his name and waited. "Are you okay?"

He wore his best sports jacket, a flashy shade of yellow. A flamboyant silk tie she'd never seen before hung loose from his neck. The top buttons of his white shirt were open, and a dash of lipstick stood out on the fabric, like a blood stain.

"Come on, wake up." Grace nudged him with her toe.

He opened his eyes and blinked. "Ow…what was that for?"

"I know you heard me."

He grinned, and she knew it was true. "Look at you. Heading someplace special?"

"It's called work. Some of us think it's special."

"That's our Grace. Up and at 'em."

"You'd better get going, too."

"I will, Buddy. If you say so." He sighed and frowned. "Camille is going to give me hell. What else is new?"

"I'd act the same. Probably worse."

Joe met her glance, then took a sip of milk.

"Come on, Joe. You know it's not right. If you want to play your music, that's fine. Nobody's stopping you."

"Sure doesn't look that way from here."

"How about another trio? You did well with that."

Joe had been in a group before the war. The musicians had day jobs but played on weekends in the neighborhood, at the church hall, local bars, and restaurants. It wasn't the solution his heart was set on. She knew that. But it was something. You had to compromise in life, make the best of the cards in your hand. He should accept that by now.

"I'm into a different scene, honey. It's hard to explain."

Grace crouched to face him. "I wish you could explain it to me, Joe. I want to understand. We all do."

He didn't answer and stared straight ahead. Grace heard a door slam and felt a rush of air.

She stood up and smoothed her skirt. "Your friend Harry Shaw hired me. More or less." Grace decided not to add how she'd more or less twisted his arm, though she was sure her brother would laugh to hear it. "We're trying each other out."

Harry Shaw had decided that having her around to answer the phone and such was better than nothing. She didn't take offense since she felt the same about being there.

"He'd better give you a job if he's got one. Or I'll have a little talk with him."

Grace knew he was joking. Joe liked to sound tough. With his height and broad shoulders, he looked the part. Her brother could be hot-tempered and had earned his share of black eyes and fat lips, but Grace knew he never looked for a fight or threw more punches than he had to.

"It might work out. You never know. I've got to run, and you can't sit here all day. Nona's going to catch you next, and she'll use the broom."

Joe laughed and seemed to be gathering himself. "Don't worry, Gracie. I'm fine. Better than fine."

His groggy voice lifted on a bright note along with his expression. Grace couldn't tell if it was the liquor left in him or if he had a reason to feel so cheerful.

She hoped it was the latter. But nothing to do with the lipstick stain.

"Glad to hear it. Because you can't go on like this. You know that, right?"

His smile drooped, and he suddenly looked sober. "I know what I have to do, kid. I got this covered. Honest."

She touched his shoulder. "If you say so. But I'm waiting until you go inside. Even if you make me late my first day."

He tipped his fingers to his forehead and slowly stood. Then walked up the alley, rocking from side to side, before he pulled open the door and disappeared.

He'd left the milk and a few cigarette butts, but she didn't have time to clean up. There was something else where he'd sat—a dark, blue square.

She leaned over and picked up a matchbook with a silky cover. "The Starlight Room" was stamped in silver, surrounded by tiny stars.

She flipped it open and read the print inside—*Music, Dancing, Floor Shows Every Night! 8 pm & 11 pm*. Below that, an address in the mid-forties, on the west side.

One of Joe's hangouts. One of many. She tucked it in her pocket and headed to the street.

At least he'd come home. Her father had left for his shop long ago, but her mother would be relieved. She'd pour her son coffee and make him eggs. Camille was a different story. How long could the same drama play out between them?

Camille often threatened to move back in with her parents. Once or twice, she did. The Riccis lived only a few blocks away, on President Street. It wasn't the distance that was meant to teach Joe a lesson; it was the shame.

Joe would stoically take the blow. After a day or two, he'd make the long journey to bring her back. Sometimes Grace thought he secretly wished Camille would stay with her family, but he couldn't stand to watch their mother bear the brunt, facing down neighbors and church friends. Even the milkman knew of Joe and Camille's troubles.

By the time she returned to Red Hook, Grace hoped to see the table set for seven. Camille with an appetite and a smile on her thin, pretty face. Joe showered and sober, and too tired to wander after a solid day's work.

The music from his record player would float up from their apartment, Duke Ellington or Louis Armstrong. Ella Fitzgerald and Billie Holiday, singing songs that reminded Grace of wartime and happier days, before that.

Or the less familiar sound of Joe's latest heroes, Charlie Parker, and Dizzy Gillespie. Miles Davis and a piano player with an odd first name she could never remember, who Joe just called Monk. Sometimes Joe played along, rehearsing with the masters. He sounded as good as any of them, she thought.

But what did she know?

The rattling train dove beneath the East River. The lights flickered, and the car went black. Grace remembered Joe's somber expression when she'd said, "You can't go on like this."

His answer should have brought relief. It sounded as if her brother finally had a plan.

Now she worried what Joe's solution would be.

Chapter Four

Grace reached the address on Harry Shaw's card at a quarter to nine, a narrow, nondescript building with a crowded lobby. She fit herself into a packed elevator and wriggled out when the operator called, "Fifth floor," to find herself in a large waiting room.

Several couches and armchairs stood empty; magazines stacked neatly on polished end tables beside reading lamps and ashtrays. The décor, a little worn, though she'd seen worse.

A receptionist at a large, curved desk typed at lightning speed and did not spare Grace a glance. She wore cat-eye shaped glasses and a bright green twin set. Her sleek brown hair was parted in the middle, hair combs on each side restrained masses of curls. Behind her, a bank of operators, six or more, worked at a blinking switchboard. Headsets fit over hairdos and hats; they tugged out wires and plugged them back in.

Grace leaned closer, trying to catch her attention. "I'm here to see Mr. Shaw. Grace Russo. He's expecting me."

The receptionist yanked a page from the machine. "Room 32, on the left. I'll let him know you're here."

Carpeting muffled Grace's steps. Behind the closed doors, murmuring voices could be heard. Stenciled letters on plate glass identified the occupants–Webber & Nelson Publicity, The Schrader Group Investments, Featherstone Insurance.

She found Harry Shaw's office at the very end, across from a travel agency. At least, she found the number. The space where his name should have been was filled with cardboard. Before she could knock, the door swung open.

Harry filled the threshold, shirt sleeves rolled to his elbows. He looked bigger and taller than she recalled. Scars on his arms matched the one on his face, though darker in color.

"You found the place, I see." He opened the door wider and politely stepped aside.

"Yes, no problem."

They stood in a small outer office, large enough for a wooden desk that faced the door and two wooden chairs. Sagging shelves along one wall were filled with file folders. A few of the shelves had collapsed and spilled mounds of paper on the floor.

A small patch of sunlight filtered through a window on an airshaft. A plant on the sill drooped in its ceramic pot. There was a partition behind the desk, dark wooden paneling on the bottom, and frosted green glass on top. The door in the middle opened to the inner office; Harry's, she assumed.

"Sorry about the mess. A client flipped his lid last night when I showed him some photos of his wife in an unflattering pose. Ran out without paying the bill, too."

Grace nodded but didn't answer. She wondered if disgruntled clients tore the place up a lot. Which might explain why her interview had been held in a luncheonette.

She dropped her purse on the desk, then waded into the mess.

"Any special way you'd like this sorted, Mr. Shaw?" She did her best to sound calm and business-like. As if finding an office shaken like a snow globe was a typical sight.

"You can call me Harry. Unless a client is around."

"Thanks. Please call me Grace."

She'd never been on first name basis with a boss before, but this job was going to be different. She already knew that.

"Ida Pfeiffer, God bless her, has no rhyme or reason to the way she's organized things. Not that I can figure out. But if you ask that woman to find a scrap of paper from a case closed months ago, she has her hand on it in seconds. It's uncanny."

Grace forced a smile. The amusing explanation didn't help.

"The only folders you need to separate are the ones marked with an 'O' on the corner like this, see?" He held one up to show her. "That means it's still open. If the 'O' has a line through it, like this, the case is closed. I only need open case files handy. The rest can be organized any way you like."

Alphabetically, Grace decided. Even Mrs. Pfeiffer should approve of that.

"Just gather up the photographs. I'll know where they go." She got the feeling he didn't want her to see the photos, which piqued her curiosity. "I'll have a janitor fix the shelves."

Grace nodded. "I'm sure I can manage until then."

Harry headed for his office, and Grace waded into the paper sea, eager to start her first official task.

The phone rang. Luckily, she was near the desk but still felt the soles of her pumps glide over the mess the last foot or so, as if skidding on a patch of ice. She tried not to show a reaction as the desk luckily provided a backstop.

She hit the blinking button and lifted the receiver. "Harry Shaw and Associates. May I help you?"

"Is Mr. Shaw in? It's Richard Nolan, at Luxor Electronics."

"One moment, please." She couldn't find the hold button and covered the mouthpiece with her hand. "Mr. Nolan. Luxor Electronics."

"I'll take that in my office."

"He'll be right with you, sir." She found the right button and set the call blinking. Then watched Harry's shadow through the glass. He took a seat at his desk and turned to stare out the windows as he talked.

He looked settled, and she felt it was safe to slip off her shoes. She made her way to an empty carton and got to work, relieved to be alone, but unsure of where to start.

She matched up any names, locations, or dates she could find, fitting the far-flung pages into the correct folders. She'd never liked jigsaw puzzles, and this was a massive one.

Along with typed sheets, there were pages torn from notebooks and pocket-sized pads, covered with handwriting and even smaller, scribbled bits. All of it was dated, the time noted, down to the tiniest scrap. Harry Shaw wrote in a neat, square hand, mostly pencil. She felt that a person's handwriting said a lot about them, though she wasn't drawing any conclusions yet.

Grace didn't mean to read more than she had to, but each file told a story that drew her in, albeit written in a foreign language. She could already hear Harry Shaw's voice in the terse narrative:

Date: 3/30/1947 Time: 12:15 pm.

Osborn left his office at Edison Custom Shirts, 328 Madison Avenue, boarded the Madison Avenue bus, and disembarked at 79th Street, 12:27 pm. Headed north on foot, then west, stopped to buy a newspaper at a kiosk, corner of East 79th and 5th Avenue. Crossed 5th and entered Central Park. Walked to the children's playground, bought a hot dog, and sat on a bench at the east side of the reflecting pool. He ate and read the paper.

12:47: Osborn left the bench. Did not take the paper. Disposed of trash and took a path heading south, back to 79th and Fifth. Approximately two minutes later, a man seated on the west side of the pool (I will refer to him hereafter as Subject A) walked around the pond and picked up the discarded newspaper. Medium height and build, bald. Thin mustache. Gray pin stripe suit and black fedora. Refined looking, gentile type.

He followed a path north, away from the playground. About 500 feet down the path, he removed a white letter-sized envelope from the paper, placed it in the breast pocket of his suit jacket, then dumped the paper in a trash basket.

She turned to the next page in hand but found notes from a different case. She sighed and stared around. She wanted to find out what Osborn and Subject A were up to. Passing a wad of cash? Photographs? A document? Who had hired Harry to watch them? She sifted through some pages on the floor, but it was a wasted effort.

At least she had something to do. She could be sharpening pencils and waiting for the phone to ring. Her new boss didn't seem the type to give much instruction. Mrs. Pfeiffer had probably been here so long; he had no idea what she did all day.

There were not many photographs in the heap, and all related to open files, she noticed. She looked them over curiously, even though he'd told her not to. Grainy, black and white pictures shot at odd angles. A shiny car on a rainy street. A brownstone with lights on inside, a face at a window. A flat, low factory, a plume of smoke rising from a chimney. A crowd of people crossing the street. Grace recognized the arch in Washington Square. A man in a raincoat, walking towards the camera, was circled with waxy, red crayon.

She found several pictures clipped together. The man had thick white hair, the woman, much younger, a shapely blonde. Seated close in a restaurant, embracing in a doorway, silhouettes captured through a car window.

Did Harry take these pictures, or did he hire someone? She would ask some time. She'd handled photos for claims reports—mostly water damage from a leaky roof, or broken windows. These were more interesting and not at all shocking to her, as he'd assumed.

Grace hadn't dated all that much, but she wasn't a virgin. Though she knew she gave that impression and didn't try to dispel it. A single woman had to watch her reputation.

Colin wanted to get married before he shipped out—a quick service at City Hall. Grace feared that would bring bad luck. She wanted her father to walk her down the aisle at St. Rocco's, a church wedding with all the trimmings, and both families looking on. She didn't want to be a war bride. Or a war widow. As it was, the bad luck had landed anyway, and she'd been left in a shadowy place a lot like widowhood, but without the province.

She regretted now she hadn't agreed to City Hall. It wouldn't have given them a minute more together, but it would have made him happy.

No one knew she'd been with Colin before he'd left. Not even Rose. They'd taken precautions, but Grace had still worried for a few days when her friend was late. Just nerves, a relief at the time, but it made her sad now. At least she would have something, some part of him, to love. She would have found a way to keep a baby, too. No matter what anyone said. Even if she had to move somewhere where people didn't know her and call herself a widow.

It was hard to kill love. Real love. She knew that now. Sometimes she wasn't sure if she still loved Colin, or if she was frightened to face the hollow place not loving him would leave. She struggled to recall a clear image of his face or the scent of his skin. The memories had faded and would keep fading. Another kind of loss and mourning.

What would happen to these blurry, found-out lovers? Would they cling together, or would Harry Shaw's discovery tear them apart? Their file was still open, though hers didn't seem to be.

She came to her feet, pushed a heavy carton towards the wall, and started on another pile.

By the time Harry emerged, she'd cleared most of the floor. She thought he was impressed, even though he didn't say anything. He wore his suit jacket and held his hat.

"I'm going out. I'll check in for messages. You can take an hour for lunch. Tell Betty, the girl at the window up front. She'll watch the phone. Let her know if you need anything. She seems to run the place. I'd give you a key, but the lock is busted. The locksmith will come around three. Just tell him to leave a bill."

Grace nodded, trying to remember the instructions. He'd told her he was out a lot, but she suddenly felt abandoned. Had the client who flipped his lid managed to break the lock on the door, too? She hoped that guy wasn't coming back.

"If a Mr. Geiger calls, tell him you haven't seen me all day, and you have no idea when I'll return. Ronald Geiger. Got that?"

"I'll make a note," she replied, scribbling the name on a pad.

"By the way, from time to time, you'll have to bend the truth a bit." He offered a questioning smile. "Can you manage that?"

She matched his light tone. "Not a subject covered in secretarial school, but I'll do my best."

"It gets easier with practice."

"So I've heard. I'm almost finished with the files. Anything else I can take care of while you're out? Type letters, or look over the accounts?"

"There's a Dictaphone in my office. You can type up a few case reports. Don't forget to make a carbon. Leave both copies on my desk."

"Two copies, no problem."

Grace hoped she had the right supplies. She could always borrow what she needed from the all-knowing Betty. Or get directions to the nearest stationery store.

He put his hat on, a pale grey fedora today. It suited him better than the black homburg.

"I almost forgot. Eleanor and Franklin. They're fine for now. I'll introduce you tomorrow."

Grace had no idea what he was talking about. Her cousin had come back with a metal plate in his skull. He seemed perfectly normal most of the time, then would say the oddest things.

"The Roosevelts?"

"Goldfish. In a little bowl, near my desk."

"Sorry. You didn't mention that."

"Slipped my mind. No pun intended. A client gave them to me. He claims watching fish is relaxing."

Grace had never heard that before. "Is it?"

"Every time I stare at the bowl, I get thirsty and want a drink. That relaxes me."

Grace smiled at the joke, though he did seem the type who might be found in a bar during office hours. She once had a boss who checked messages from his favorite watering hole throughout the day. She hoped Harry Shaw didn't fall into that category.

He tugged the hat brim at an angle. To hide the scar, or look stylish? The touch scored on both counts.

"So long, Grace. Hold down the fort."

"Good-bye, Mr. Shaw."

She remembered too late he'd told her to call him Harry. The door had already closed, and he was gone.

Chapter Five

Grace didn't feel like going out Saturday night. She was worried about Joe. He'd left the house with his trumpet after dinner on Wednesday and hadn't been back since. Three nights was his record. It looked like he was shooting for four.

Rose hastily dried the dishes so she'd have time to do her hair and makeup. "Don't tell me you'd rather stay here than come with us. I won't believe you."

They both knew the routine: she'd barely be able to hear, "Your Hit Parade" over her mother's sewing machine, while her father kept switching to the ball game.

"Standing watch won't make Joe come home any sooner," Rose added.

Grace knew that was true. And it was easier to agree to another blind date than argue with her sister. Or, her mother, a vocal ally in the long-standing plan to fix Grace up with one of Frank's friends. Or a cousin, or co-worker. Or some guy he hardly knew but had button-holed to meet his fiancé's older sister. Preferably, from an Italian family, though Frank had exhausted that list. Not that Grace gave the qualification any weight, though Rose and her mother did.

Grace wasn't sure what category Don Rappley fell into. All she remembered from Rose's description was that he dressed well and had a car.

Sure enough, seven o'clock on the dot, Frank and Mr. Rappley appeared at the front door. Frank, in casual clothes, a loose khaki jacket, and patterned sports shirt. Rappley wore an expensive-looking plaid sports coat and burgundy bow tie with a matching pocket hanky. All smiles and affability as he led them to a dark green sedan.

"Town and Country. Nice." Frank circled the car. "You must be doing well, Don."

"Can't complain." Don looked at Grace as he answered and opened her door. Rose and Frank jumped in the back seat.

Don checked the side mirror and started the engine. "Let me know when you're ready, Frank. I'll get you a good deal."

Salesman. She should have guessed from the way he'd looked her over when they were introduced, as if sizing up a customer.

"We might just do that," Rose said. "We'll need a car on Long Island."

Frank nodded. "I hear the roads are empty out there. Women drivers can't do much damage."

The men laughed; Rose did, too. "I'll be a good driver once I learn. It doesn't look that hard."

"Sure, you will. And Frank will take out plenty of insurance." The men laughed again, and Don smiled at Grace. "How about you, Grace? Do you know how to drive? I could teach you sometime."

Was he flirting? Testing the waters, at least. Grace acted as if she didn't get it. "Thanks. Our family doesn't own a car, so I guess there isn't much point."

Don looked back at the traffic. They'd just passed Cadman Plaza and approached the bridge. "When you move to Long Island to live near your sister, your husband will teach you."

"Maybe." Grace already disliked him. It was going to be a long night.

She gazed at the skyline and the river, glittering like a long black ribbon. She wished Colin was driving. She would sit back and close her eyes and let him drive all night if he wanted. She wouldn't even ask where they were going.

"What movie did you girls pick?" Frank said.

Rose leaned forward. "A western at the Paramount with John Wayne. It has a romance, too. Dorsey's band is playing, and there's some comedian, I can't remember who."

"Sounds good to me." Don turned to Grace. "Are you a John Wayne fan?"

"He's all right."

"But not your favorite. Let me guess…Humphrey Bogart?" Before she could reply, he added, "I've got it. Gregory Peck."

She met his gaze, he'd guessed, and easily. She did like Gregory Peck. She liked his looks and serious personality, though she knew he might be very different in real life.

"How did you guess that?" Rose said. "He is her favorite. He's going to be in 'Gentleman's Agreement' next. It will be out soon."

"Right, that book about the Jews. Did you read it?" Don asked Rose.

"My sister did. She can't stop reading. Books, newspapers, cereal boxes. It's amazing she doesn't wear glasses."

Thank you, Rose. Why don't you tell him how I used to drape a towel on my head and pretend to be a nun?

Frank leaned over the seat. "A lot of Kikes bellyaching. Plenty of our boys died, saving their skin. They want their own country? Fine with me. I won't miss 'em."

Grace was about to reply, but Rose caught her eye. "Please, don't," her look said. "You're on a date, remember? We're not in the United Nations."

Grace ignored her. "Did you hear that story about Groucho Marx? He tried to join a country club that didn't accept Jews. They said they'd allow his family in if they didn't use the pool. Groucho said, 'My daughter is only half Jewish, can she go in up to her waist?'"

Everyone laughed, except Frank. "Funny. But it doesn't change my mind. A lot of people feel the same."

Grace was about to argue but stopped herself. What he'd said was ugly, but true. A lot of people did think that way. She was especially surprised when guys like Frank, who had fought on the front and seen everything there was to see, would say that and really mean it. The Jews deserved a jump to the front of any line after what they'd been through. Not shut out of jobs and housing, their kids bullied in school. How were we any different from the Germans when we did that?

"I like John Wayne," Rose announced, trying to smooth things over. "I like the rugged type, like Wayne or Ronald Regan. Or even Frank Sinatra."

Her fiancé looked stung. "What about Frank Stanco? Is he on your list?"

Rose kissed his cheek. "You've got a list all to yourself, silly."

Grace felt relieved when the lights in the theater dimmed, and the newsreel began. Don was the talkative type. Grace nodded and smiled and asked questions, then realized she wasn't listening to his answers.

The movie was boring, but Don kept her busy, slipping his arm around the back of her seat, then hugging her shoulder. She shrugged him off by searching in her purse for mints or pretending she'd dropped something. He eventually sat with his arms crossed over his chest.

When the music soared, and the credits rolled, Rose and Frank led the way out to the aisle. Grace and Don followed, quickly swallowed by the crowd that flowed towards the lobby. She felt his hand on her back, guiding her forward. He was a few inches shorter, and she would have chosen lower heels if she'd known. But he wasn't a small man, broad-shouldered with a barrel chest, and a pugnacious air to match.

They'd reached the lobby; moviegoers streamed in all directions under the huge chandelier, down the curving staircases, and in and out of the heavy gilded doors. The scent of popcorn and grilling hot dogs wafted over from the concession stand.

"Would you like a Coke or a bite to eat, Grace?"

"I wouldn't mind a cocktail. Can we skip the show and go somewhere?"

He looked at her as if she'd turned into another girl. "Great idea. Someplace nice. How about the Stork Club? They know me there. We'll get a table up front right away."

He was trying hard to impress her. Grace felt a twinge of guilt, tricking him. Maybe not tricking but surely manipulating. "What a nice idea. But I can't go dressed like this. I heard The Starlight Room is fun. And it's more casual."

"Never heard of it. I think you look perfect. I'd be proud to take you anywhere."

"That's sweet… but I'd feel out of place somewhere fancy."

"Okay, whatever you say. Is this club on Swing Street?" Grace knew he meant a stretch of 52nd between Fifth and Seventh Avenue, lined with nightclubs, one after the next, most no larger than a living room and filled every night. Jimmy Ryan's, Three Deuces, The Onyx, and many more that Grace didn't even know the names of. She'd made the rounds a few times with Colin. Once to see Joe play, though he didn't come on stage till well after midnight. She'd needed coffee to stay awake.

"No, just a few blocks up. We can walk from here."

It didn't bode well that The Starlight Room wasn't in the well-known row. She could tell Don thought the same. Still, he said, "Lead the way. Your wish is my command."

She felt relieved, then quietly horrified as he wrapped his arm around her waist. "There's my sister. I'd better tell her we're leaving."

She slipped away and met Rose, who held a soda in one hand and a box of Cracker Jack in the other. "We're going to skip the show and get a drink."

Rose looked delighted by the news. "Fine with me. Wait till I tell Frank he finally found a guy you like."

Grace didn't reply. Rose had no idea she was on a mission to find their errant brother. Grace was happy to leave it that way.

Chapter Six

Out in Times Square, Don took her hand and tucked it into the crook of his arm. Broadway was packed; she didn't mind his help making their way down the sidewalk. They sidestepped a cluster of tourists, taking photos of the Camel sign as the cowboy blew lazy smoke rings into the clear, dark sky. The theater goers weren't out yet, but the mild, spring night had coaxed many to roam the avenues.

When they turned down West 46th, the street was dark and quiet, and almost empty.

A blue neon sign for The Starlight Room glowed in the middle of the block. Steps from Hell's Kitchen, it wasn't the best neighborhood. Don seemed to be thinking the same thing.

"Who told you about this place?"

"A girl at work. She said it's nice, once you get inside."

How smoothly the lies tumbled out once you start. Grace was surprised at herself. But she was dissembling for a good cause, she reminded herself.

"We're here now. If we don't like it, we can leave," he said.

The entrance was on the ground floor, a shiny wooden door beneath a dark blue canopy. A placard on the sidewalk advertised Gem Washington and The Music Makers, and a singer named Lana Delmar.

Once inside, her eyes adjusted slowly to the low light. The decor was sleek and modern, but luxurious. The walls and carpeting, soft blue, with a silver rail around the dining area. She saw a bar near the entrance and tables, covered in white clothes, set in a U-shape around the polished wood dance floor and stage. A few steps up, curved banquettes, with pale blue cushions, circled the walls.

"Your girlfriend was right; it is nice inside."

Grace felt relieved and smiled. "Yes, I have to tell her."

A maître d' in a black tuxedo welcomed them. Grace nearly missed the neatly folded bill in Don's fingers; it passed so quickly. "Table for two. Something private, with a good view of the stage."

"Certainly, sir. Right this way."

They were led to the banquettes. The stage was set up for about seven pieces, typical these days. The big bands had faded, especially since the war. A lone musician sat at the piano playing a slow ballad.

A satin curtain shimmered behind the bandstand. The nightclub's name, projected from a spotlight, hovered over the fabric, as if the letters floated on a pool of water. Star-shaped points of light covered the walls, ceiling, and floor, slowly circling, making Grace feel as if the room was in motion.

She quickly searched the tables but didn't spot Joe. Was this a wild goose chase? Joe could be anywhere tonight. She was not only wasting her time but had put herself in a sticky situation.

"The booth in the corner, sir?" the maître d' said.

"Perfect." Don turned to Grace. "It's quiet. We can talk."

Grace thought it was perfect, too. If she did spot her brother, best to be out of view. She slid into the seat, forced closer to Don than she wanted to be. She picked up a menu and ordered the house cocktail, a Stargazer. Don asked for rye on the rocks and steak tartare.

The drinks soon arrived; hers, a faint blue liquid in a chilled martini glass. Predictably, decorated by a silver swivel with a star on top.

Don raised his whiskey. "Here's to blind dates. Like wishing on a star, right?"

Grace touched her glass to his. A corny line, but you couldn't blame him for trying. She took a careful sip, tasting rum and coconut syrup. The drink was stronger than she'd expected, and she blinked as she set it down.

"Too strong for you, honey? Would you like a sherry instead?"

Grace shook her head. "I'm fine."

He smiled, approving of her fortitude. Maybe thinking she'd get drunk quickly? He was right. She needed to be careful.

"So, you work for Chrysler Motors, Don?"

"That's right. National sales, not pacing the floor, though I trained there. I take business courses at night, too. A college degree will give me an edge over the other guy."

He acted as if he already had an edge. Or, thought he did. "I should take classes, too. I had a scholarship to a state university, but my parents didn't want me to live far away."

Don sipped his drink. "Frank said you were sharp. I can see you as a teacher. I'd bet you'd be a good one."

He meant it as a compliment, but she didn't think she was the type. Colin had been studying history at Fordham. He'd planned to get a Ph.D. He would have made a good college professor. She would have liked that life, too.

"If I ever go back, I'd study psychology."

"Psychology, huh? You've got a lot going on in that pretty head, don't you?" He laughed and rested his arm behind her shoulder. "I think it's nice for a woman to take a class or two before the kids come. But my wife won't have to work. I don't want her to. A woman needs to make a nice home and take care of the kids. That's her most important job, don't you think?"

"Probably. But women had some hard jobs and raised their children while their husbands were away. Sometimes, gone for years."

"The ladies did their part. No question. But the men are back now. Women can be women again. Unless they want to be career gals."

He looked at her as if she might belong to that suspect club; hard-edged females who'd rather work in an office than make babies. Women who felt no guilt taking a good job away from a man who had to support his family. It was positively unnatural. Even worse, maybe one who preferred the company of another woman instead of a man.

Grace had sipped the blue drink slowly but steadily. She suddenly noticed her scalp felt numb. Don's face looked big and rubbery in the soft light. Or maybe it looked that way in any light. She couldn't recall.

It was silly to argue. She'd never see him again if she could help it.

"Don't you want to get married and have kids?" he persisted. "I thought every woman wants that."

"What a question—proposing to me already, Don?"

He laughed and leaned back. "Not on the first date, honey. Though in your case, I could make an exception."

Grace met his gaze and looked away. Not soon enough. He squeezed her shoulder and moved in for a kiss.

The band had returned to the stage. Not a moment too soon. The bright, brassy notes of "A Night in Tunisia" blasted through the room.

"I love this song. Let's dance." Grace narrowly ducked his embrace and slid out of the booth.

"That's what we're here for." He sounded reluctant but rose and straightened his jacket.

Down on the floor, Don took command of her body as if she was a blow-up doll, placing one hand firmly on her waist and planting her hand on his shoulder. Before she knew what was happening, he set off at a fast pace.

She felt herself steered around the floor like a Chrysler in stilettos. He was holding her so tight it was hard to ease back. He rested his cheek on her hair, the difference in their height even more obvious.

"You're a good dancer. Most girls can't keep up with me."

"Don't pin a medal on me yet. I'm not sure I can either." She'd answered honestly, but he chuckled as if she was irresistibly clever.

She studied the stage each time they swept by but didn't spot Joe. The song ended and the players moved smoothly into the next number.

The band leader was a tall, dapper man, not that young but lithe and animated. He smiled and leaned towards the microphone, "Thank you so much, ladies and gentlemen. Are you ready to have some fun?"

The audience shouted back a boozy, affirmative reply.

"I'm Gem Washington and these my Music Makers, here to play all the songs you love, old and new. All night long." He winked and laughed, his glad-talking style reminding her of Louis Armstrong.

"I'm going to bring out a very special young lady to help us with the next tune. We just can't live without her, and you won't want to either once you hear her sing. Let's have a warm welcome for the beautiful, delightful, the one and only… Lana Delmar."

The singer had already stepped out from behind the curtain and moved gracefully across the stage. A coppery satin gown, covered with sequins, was the perfect complement to her rich brown skin and the waves of mahogany hair that fell to bare shoulders.

She smiled and nodded gratefully. Then seemed solemn and focused as she took the microphone and moved to center stage. Grace recognized the opening notes of "All of Me" as the singer waited for her cue.

Her voice was powerful, each note smooth and strong, as if she felt every lyric. Grace knew Billie Holiday's recording the best. Lana Delmar was brave to step up for comparison. Her version was just as sultry and soulful, sung with a style and confidence all her own. Her voice, jazzy and sexy, without overplaying the sentiment. She didn't rush. She made the audience come to her. She made them sit up and listen.

Something about her seemed familiar. Grace couldn't put her finger on it. Her head felt too fuzzy to figure out where and when. Had she seen the singer perform before? Perhaps, though she didn't go to nightclubs much.

The ballad drew a crowd to the dance floor, and Don slowed his pace. "Mind if we sit the rest out?"

"Of course not."

When they returned to the table, Don ordered another rye, neat this time. Grace asked for soda water.

"That one always gets me. My girl couldn't wait. She took up with some guy who was

Four-F. An extra kick in the teeth, right? I didn't find out till I got back. At least I had something good to think about over there, while I was getting shot at."

Grace felt bad for him. She wasn't sure what was worse, being dumped in a letter on the battlefield, or being deceived all that time. "That's awful. It must have been hard to handle that after everything you went through."

"It was rough for a while. I won't deny it…But she wasn't the one for me. That's all there is to it."

Grace felt sorry for him. He wasn't a bad guy. But she wasn't the one for him, either.

The song ended, and the singer bowed at the applause, then stepped back from the spotlight.

"Wasn't that lovely? Lana Delmar can have all of *this* guy, anytime." Gem Washington chuckled and strolled to the edge of the stage. He peered into the audience, a flat hand shielding his sight.

"Well, lookie, lookie, look. Who do I spy? A friend of the band is in the house, and we're in for a treat. I got to warn you, this fella's gonna burn the place down with that horn of his." Gem waved, beckoning someone forward. "Come on up here, you son of a gun…"

Don sat brooding over his drink. Luckily. He didn't notice her reaction when Joe jumped on the stage.

Chapter Seven

As much as Grace had hoped to find her brother, the sight of him stole her breath. He looked so different under the bright lights, larger than life. A big, dark-haired man she hardly recognized. Or maybe it was just because he was happy. Happier than she remembered seeing him in years. Certainly, since he'd come home from the army.

He leaned back and lifted the shining trumpet to his lips. A trilling introduction to "More Than You Know" brought a hush to the crowd.

The singer stepped beside him, and the house lights dimmed. A single spot circled the couple while points of starlight spun around the darkened room. Lana's voice melted and merged with the brassy notes from the horn, two melodies caught in an intimate tangle. The audience sat still and quiet; even the dancing couples watched, swaying from side to side on the floor.

"Whether you're right, whether you're wrong, man of my heart, I'll string along... I need you so. More than you'll ever know..."

The song ended on a long, strong note. Lana Delmar closed her eyes; one slim arm stretched above her head. The mellow coda from Joe's horn hung in the air. The room was silent for a heartbeat, then exploded in applause. She answered with a radiant smile and bowed gracefully. Joe did as well.

When he lifted his head, his face beamed. He turned to his partner and gazed into her eyes. Then waved and deftly left the stage.

"Lana Delmar and Joe Russo. Aren't they something else?" Gem Washington shouted above the applause. "Lana just recorded that tune with yours truly and the Music Makers. You'll hear it on the radio any day. She's the next big star, folks. Mark my words. And that Joe Russo—man, can he play. His mother should have named him Gabriel."

The audience chuckled. Grace smiled. She'd love to tell her mother that one.

"Sit tight, folks. They'll be back," Gem promised.

Grace clapped again, glad to be in the shadows. She felt sure Joe hadn't seen her.

Don swirled his drink. "I liked the singer. She's really got something. The trumpet player wasn't so bad, either."

"Not bad at all," Grace said quietly.

Her brother had played as well as any famous musician featured on a marquee. But she didn't want to talk about Joe. Don hadn't noticed that she and the "not so bad" trumpet player shared the same last name.

"It's sad in a way. He's got some talent, but only a handful of guys like that make it. I wouldn't bet my salary on those odds."

"Maybe he loves it so much, he doesn't have a choice."

Don replied with a small, tight smile. "Everybody's got a choice about what they make of their life, honey. Any guy who says otherwise is lying to you. And himself."

He held out a pack of cigarettes, and she pulled one out. He lit it, cupping her hand with his. Then shook out a cigarette for himself.

"You were right, this is a nice place. I hope you're having a good time?"

"I am," she assured him. "Thanks."

He sat back, enjoying his smoke and looking pleased by her reply. Grace felt quietly pleased as well that her plan to find Joe had succeeded.

Now what? Did she drag her brother home by his collar? Did she even let him know she was there?

Maybe it was enough to observe him in this alternate life. Like following Alice through the looking glass. She was beginning to understand what drew him to a place like this, night after night. But after witnessing his sheer and utter joy on stage, convincing him to give it up seemed hopeless.

Don leaned over and gently rubbed the back of her neck, making tiny circles with his fingertips. Grace willed herself not to flinch. "You're a million miles away, honey. Feel okay?"

She dropped her cigarette in an ashtray and turned to him. "Sorry... I have an awful headache. I don't know where it came from."

Likely, a combination of the blue cocktail, finding Joe, and listening to Don's chatter. Her mission accomplished, she needed to call an end to the evening.

"Really? I was just about to order another round." He leaned over to catch her gaze. "If you don't feel well, I'll just settle up."

"Thanks. I'll run in the powder room and meet you up front."

Grace set off, weaving through the tables. Then turned down a carpeted hallway with a telephone booth on the left and a door on the right marked, "Gents." She guessed that "Ladies" was a little further down, but the next said, "Storage."

Open a crack, she heard voices inside, hushed and urgent. A woman and a man. Her brother? She thought so but needed to be sure.

She crossed to the phone booth and stepped inside, then picked up the receiver. The door slid closed, and the light flashed on, but she wedged it open with her toe.

She couldn't hear the voices anymore. When she listened intently, she heard rustling fabric and soft moans. Sitting perfectly still in the dark, she held her own breath, not daring to make a sound.

A few moments later, a man stumbled out and smoothed his hair with both hands. She didn't want it to be Joe. She wanted to look away before she could know for sure. But even with his back turned, she knew. He took a few more steps, then stopped to wipe his mouth with a handkerchief. He stuffed the hanky in his pocket, straightened his tie, and headed towards the bar.

Lana Delmar emerged. She tugged the neckline of her gown and arranged a satin shawl around her shoulders. Her dark eyes were shining; cheeks flushed with a dusky glow.

Grace was about to step out of the booth when swinging doors at the end of the hall opened, and another man appeared. He called to Lana, and she stood stone still, her expression blank. When she turned, a smile graced her lips, though the rest of her posture betrayed her alarm.

"You were something up there tonight, baby." Close to her now, he grabbed the singer roughly, one arm hooked around her slim waist. "You sang that last one for me, right?"

"You're the only one in the room, Eddie. You know that."

Grace had noticed Lana's boyfriend before, moving around the club, talking to the waiters and bartender in a way that suggested he was the boss. He wasn't that old, and not bad looking from far off. Up close, his features seemed softened and smudged. Already slacked-jawed, with lidded eyes, and reddish-brown hair thin on top. A well-cut dinner jacket, with ample shoulder pads, hung from his slouching body. Midnight blue with satin lapels, it looked custom-made to match the club's décor.

"You know how to dish up the sweet talk, don't you?" His soft laughter mocked her. "Let's see if you can convince me later." He squeezed her close to nuzzle her neck and bare shoulder. Grace felt the pinch in her own ribs and had to admire the woman's composure.

He suddenly pushed the singer away, as if she was tethered on a string. "Get a drink. A quick one. Then back to work."

Once again, Lana didn't answer. Just before she moved out of reach, he slapped her bottom. She didn't even turn her head.

He chuckled and walked back toward the swinging doors. A waiter, balancing a tray of covered dishes, rushed out. He nimbly sidestepped in time to avoid a collision, but the wide tray brushed his boss's shoulder.

"Mr. Martone! I'm so sorry!" The waiter shook his head, struggling to balance his load.

"What are you, blind?" Martone stared down at his jacket. "Look at this crap! You dumb ass moron—"

The waiter stepped back. Grace heard the tray rattle. An older man, bald on top with a thick mustache, he wore a dark blue waistcoat and a cummerbund pulled tight over his belly.

"I'll have it cleaned, sir. No, wait… I'll buy you a new one. I'll order it tomorrow."

Eddie Martone stared back, then struck him across the face backhanded. The man's head slammed into the wall, and he slid to the floor, the tray, along with him, a clattering mess of silverware and broken plates. Kitchen helpers and other waiters rushed out the swinging doors, then stood frozen as Martone stood over his victim.

"Dump this pile of crap in the alley. All of it." Martone delivered his orders in a flat, bored tone, then strode away, fussing over his jacket.

Grace slipped out of the phone booth and stumbled to the powder room. She felt sick to her stomach and splashed her face with cold water. Then swiped on fresh lipstick with a shaky hand. She felt like hell and looked even worse.

Her brother was in a jam, his best jackpot ever. Grace pictured him being beaten to a pulp while the owner of The Starlight Room looked on with a thin, satisfied smile.

No wonder Joe had not been able to explain things to her.

Chapter Eight

It was half past four. Grace typed with one eye on the clock, eager to leave at five, whether or not Harry showed up. The way he'd greeted Grace at nine on her first day had turned out to be a fluke. Her new boss did not keep regular hours by anyone's clock. From the case notes left for her to type, she learned that most of his surveillance work took place at night. It only made sense he'd sleep in some mornings.

He'd called at ten to say he'd be out most of the day and gave no further details. He seemed to like it that way, which had irked her at first. Until she realized that as soon as he passed along his notes, she found out everything she wanted to know and more.

The phone rang, and Grace pushed the blinking button. "Shaw and Associates."

There were no associates. Harry had been frank about that. He liked the way it sounded, and he thought the idea of a team effort made a client feel more confident.

"Roger Ingersoll. I need to speak to Mr. Shaw immediately. Is he in?"

"Not at the moment, sir. May I take a message?"

"When will he be back? Do you know how I can reach him?"

"Perhaps this afternoon. I can't say for sure, sir."

Grace heard the slow, frustrated breath she'd come to know well. Mr. Ingersoll called often, his need always urgent.

"I want to know if there's any news about my… situation. Things are heating up. Just tell him that. He can reach me any time at the Murray Hill number."

Grace promised to relay the message, her tone calm and business-like, as if she had no idea what Mr. Ingersoll's "situation" might be. Though in fact, she knew everything. Mr. Ingersoll's mother was being wooed by a man many years younger, a gigolo, who was after her money. Or so her son claimed.

"A smooth-talking fortune hunter, who picked her up at the country club. Where else would a guy like that trawl for rich widows?"

He wanted Harry to dig up the man's past, which he was sure was sordid, maybe even criminal, so he could rub his mother's nose in the dirty details. The perfect tonic to snap Muriel Ingersoll out of her romantic daze, her son thought.

"A routine assignment," Harry told Grace. "But rarely as cut and dry as it looks. Especially to a guy like Ingersoll, who's only worried about sharing Mommy's piggy bank when she kicks off. Women of a certain age are far more clear-eyed about these arrangements than anyone credits them. And even gigolos fall in love once and awhile."

Grace thought of that now as she wrote out the message.

"Did you get that, honey?" Mr. Ingersoll said. The door opened, and Harry walked in. He stood at her desk, waiting for the call to end.

"Yes, I did, Mr. Ingersoll." Grace looked up at Harry. Wide-eyed, he gestured with his hand, as if slitting his throat, and Grace struggled not laugh.

"I'll give Mr. Shaw your message first thing when he gets back."

"Thank you, dear. Please do."

Grace hung up the phone, and Harry pulled off a yellow hard hat, the type worn on construction sites. He was dressed in one of his disguises—tan coveralls and work boots. A metal toolbox swung from one hand. She wondered if the stains on his knees and elbows had been added for effect, or if he'd really been crawling in the dirt somewhere.

A closet in his office held a wardrobe that could transform him into any number of identities—plumber, doorman, kitchen worker, taxi driver, milkman, plain old bum, even a priest.

When she'd asked him about it, he'd said, "These clothes make me invisible,

Grace. Like more than half the world. The rest of us, focused on our smug little lives, being served, driven around, waited on by people we barely spare a glance."

Harry set the toolbox down and leafed through his messages. He yawned and tossed the one from Ingersoll in the wastebasket. He looked in need of a shave and a few hours of sleep.

"Mr. Nightingale wouldn't leave a number," Grace told him. "He said you knew how to reach him."

"Tell Harry the package is on the way from Chicago. I'm not sure when it will reach New York. But it will be soon. Got that, sweetheart?" Mr. Nightingale had said.

Grace took down the words exactly, realizing later the caller's voice sounded a lot like a man who'd called the week prior, though his surname had been Robins.

"I checked with Betty. No deliveries for you today."

"Right. Thanks." He tucked the message in a pocket, then left the rest with her.

"Anything else?"

Grace shook her head. "Just a few pieces of mail on your desk."

He nodded, then went into his office and shut the door.

She sat up straight and took a breath. She hoped he didn't ask her to work late. She usually didn't mind. He always paid her for the overtime. But she'd figured out a plan to see Lana Delmar, and timing was all. She wanted to speak to the singer about Joe, the sooner the better.

Her brother had finally wandered home Sunday morning and gone straight to bed. Every few hours, raised voices were heard from the basement—Joe and Camille arguing, as usual. But neither of them surfaced, not even for Sunday dinner.

Grace knew her mother was concerned, but all she said was, "A young, married couple needs their privacy sometimes. I'll save them each a dish." If only good food could solve their problems, Grace had thought. What would her mother think—what would anyone in the family think?—if they knew the truth.

Grace had neither the energy nor the heart to confront her brother on Sunday. This morning, he'd left the house before she was out of bed. Just as well. When she finally pinned him down, her position would be stronger if she could talk to Lana Delmar first.

Harry was on the phone; his deep voice filtered through the partition. Grace typed the last page of a report. Several more sat on her desk, waiting to be filed in the new system she'd devised.

Mrs. Pfeiffer's haphazard shelves had been replaced by two wooden file cabinets. With the help of the all-knowing and ever-efficient Betty, Grace had located the cabinets in an empty room down the hall.

"Very nice, Grace. Very official. Looks like a law office in here now," Harry had said. "Minus the lawyers, thank God."

She'd just finished typing when Harry emerged. She felt, rather than saw him, watching as she proofread the page and pulled it out, careful not to tear the carbon.

"The Fleming case. You wanted it by the end of the day?"

"Right. Thanks." He ran a hand through his thick, straight hair, which he wore combed back from his forehead. When it was combed.

"Is there anything else? I'd like to leave by five. I have an appointment." Intentionally vague. The less said, the better.

"Sure, go ahead. I'll leave a note if something comes up."

Harry watched as she tapped the pages into a neat pile and covered her typewriter. She took her purse from a desk drawer and picked up the large bouquet she'd bought on her lunch hour. She'd left it on top of a filing cabinet so it wouldn't get mussed. The offering needed to look expensive without taxing her pocketbook. Lilies were in bloom and seemed a good choice.

"Nice bouquet. Did your boyfriend send you that?"

Grace laughed. "I bought them on my lunch hour. For a friend."

"How about that fellow you were dancing with the other night? I hope you didn't drink too many blue cocktails. It's just cheap rum mixed with food dye."

Grace had been working a pin into her hat and nearly stuck herself. "You were at The Starlight Room Saturday night?"

"I was there on a case."

Grace picked up her purse. "It's all right. I'll hear the rest on the Dictaphone."

He smiled and crossed his arms over his chest. "I was tailing a guy who claims to have a back injury. He managed a mean rhumba before I finished my first bourbon."

Grace laughed. She'd seen plenty of bogus back injury claims. The faker often spent the insurance payment before the check arrived.

"A miracle cure?"

"More like a miracle blonde. She'll hop right off his lap when the money doesn't come through. Your fellow looked like a talkative guy," he added. "A salesman, maybe?"

"Maybe." Grace slipped on her coat. She wasn't sure how Harry had figured that out. How long had he been watching them?

"We just met. My sister's fiancé introduced us."

"I see." She could tell what he was thinking, blind date. He seemed surprised. "Was that club his idea?"

"It was mine. What's the difference?"

He picked up the case report and paged through. "You should stay away from that place."

"Why do you say that?"

"I can't tell you more, sorry. You won't hear about it on the Dictaphone, either." He looked up at her again. "Why The Starlight? Did someone recommend it?"

Grace fished her gloves from her purse and snapped it shut. He might as well know. He was Joe's friend. Maybe he could help. "I was looking for Joe. He hadn't been home in a few days, and my family was worried. I thought I might find him there."

"What about your father? Why didn't he go look for him?"

His reply annoyed her. Her father was the last one to blame for Joe's problems. "My father's chased after Joe plenty. This was different. I didn't want anyone to know."

He was silent for a moment. Then said, "Miss Russo, you surprise me."

"I'll take that as a compliment."

"That's how I meant it. Did you find him?"

"He came on stage and played a song. But he never saw me. I didn't want to make a scene."

"Guess I missed him. If I get the chance, I'll tell him the same thing I just told you."

Grace knew that Harry and Joe were distant friends at best; army pals were often that way. Full of fond feelings when they met, and willing to do a favor if they could. But not necessarily in close touch. Perhaps their reunions revived more painful memories than happy ones.

Grace tucked the flowers in her arm. "I'd better go. Good night."

"Good night. I hope your friend enjoys the flowers." Harry had taken a message slip from his pocket and stared at it: the note about the package from Chicago.

"I hope so, too." Grace doubted he'd seen through her story but wasn't entirely sure. He was a champion at masking his feelings and thoughts. She'd never want to play poker with him.

Two crowded elevators passed before she hopped into the third. She held the flowers close, careful not to crush the petals. The sweet scent filled her head, along with Harry's warning.

It was impossible to tell if she should heed his advice when he wouldn't say more. His annoying discretion again. Which is partly what he's paid for, she knew.

She'd return to The Starlight just this once before the club even opened. There couldn't be any harm in that.

Chapter Nine

The Starlight wasn't far, but the streets were filled with nine-to-fivers, rushing to catch buses and subways. Grace made her way through the sea of bodies, the bouquet cradled in her arms.

When she reached West 46th Street, she crossed to the sidewalk opposite the club. Then pretended to search her handbag.

It was half past five, the club opened at seven. She wondered how early the singer arrived. Packing herself into that sequin dress couldn't be easy. Then there was hair and make-up. Lana might already be in her dressing room, but Grace needed to know for sure. She'd figure out something. She wasn't going to back down now.

Grace scanned the street, looking for a spot where she could keep the place in view without drawing attention. She'd read enough of Harry's reports to know the basics. As she considered her options, a burgundy Cadillac pulled up in front of the club. Grace stood beside a tree and watched.

A man got out of the back seat, on the street side. Grace didn't need to see his face. It was Eddie Martone. Lana Delmar slipped out the other side, looking very chic in a turquoise coat with a shawl collar, black gloves, and matching turban.

Eddie exchanged a few words with the driver, and the car pulled away. Then he took Lana's arm and led her down the alley next to the building at a clipped, commanding pace. After she went in the side door, he strolled back to the sidewalk and entered through the front.

Grace felt sorry for her. Then remembered why she'd come.

She leaned against the tree and took a deep breath. She didn't have to do this. Joe could sort out his own problems. Or not. She could walk back to Times Square and be home within an hour. Her mother would be delighted with the flowers.

Don't be such a chicken. At least try. For Joe. For Camille. For the family. What's the worst that could happen? Someone chases you away?

She crossed the street and headed down the narrow, dark alley to the metal door, where she'd seen Lana go inside. She knocked and knocked again. Finally, the door opened. A man in a stained white apron worn over an undershirt stared at her. Blurry blue tattoos trailed up his ropey arms. He was bald, with bulging eyes, and his nose looked like someone had taken a hammer to it.

"Flowers, for Miss Delmar."

The way he looked her over made Grace uneasy; a gold tooth glinted in a gap-toothed smile. "I'll take it to her, honey."

He reached for the bouquet, but Grace stepped back. "There's a song…It's sort of a singing telegram."

He stared at her, then waved his hand. "Back through the kitchen. Second door on the right. A singing telegram for a singer? Is that a joke?"

She slipped past and didn't answer. She made her way through the bustling kitchen, then down a narrow hallway. She found the singer's dressing room and knocked.

"Who is it?"

Her mouth was so dry she could barely speak. "Flower delivery."

"It's open."

Grace stepped in the room, immediately confronted by her own wide-eyed expression, reflected in a mirror framed by lights. The singer stood at a clothes rack, examining a creamy satin gown.

"Put them down anywhere. I'll get some water later…Oh, wait. Let me give you a tip, Miss." Lana Delmar took a black clutch off the dressing table.

Grace held on to the bouquet. She felt frozen and couldn't remember what she'd planned to say. "That won't be necessary," she managed.

"Don't be silly. Here, take it." Lana Delmar stepped closer, offering a generous tip, a shiny quarter, along with a kind smile.

"I'm not here about the flowers…" Grace's voice trailed off as the singer stared at her curiously.

"Grace? Grace Russo?"

Now it was Grace's turn to be surprised, as the singer's voice struck a distant memory. "Do I know you?"

"Don't you remember me? Mary Delmore, from Clinton High."

She waited for Grace to answer and smiled to herself. Grace could almost hear her say, "We all look the same, right?"

Grace was caught off guard. "Of course, I do. But you look so different. Not so much today," she added. "I saw you sing on Saturday night. You had on a lot of make-up and your hair was different. And your name is different, too."

Mary's expression softened. She looked wistful. "It's all right. It's been a long time. Seven, eight years? A lot of things have changed. For everyone. Wait, let me shut the door."

She glanced down the hall, left, then right, before snapping it shut. Then turned to face Grace again.

"Did Joe tell you to come?" Her tone was hushed.

"He has no idea. But I know about the two of you. That is why I came to see you."

"I want to talk to you, too. But not here." Mary checked a small clock on the dressing table. "There's a bar around the corner, on Eighth Avenue. McNulty's. Give me a few minutes. Take a table in the back. I'll find you."

"All right." Grace met Mary's glance and headed for the door, then remembered the bouquet. She dropped it on a wooden chair and stepped out into the hall, confused and off balance.

Her plan was not unfolding as she'd imagined. Not one bit.

Grace often met her girlfriends for cocktails, but never at a place like McNulty's. A huge jar of hard-boiled eggs floating in water set the mood of the decor, along with wooden bowls of unshelled peanuts, the kind she ate at ball games. Handwritten signs were taped to the mirror behind the bar. *Restrooms for Patrons Only. In God We Trust, All Others Pay Cash.*

Still, the place was filling quickly with a pre-theater crowd, a cut above their surroundings, looking for cheap drinks and thick sandwiches. A haze of blue smoke floated above their conversations.

Grace walked to the bar; nut shells crunched beneath her steps. She ordered a Manhattan, then found a table near the window where she could watch for Mary. An abandoned newspaper sat folded on a chair. Too nervous to read, she picked it up and skimmed the headlines.

Thomas E. Dewey, New York's Governor, would likely be the Republican candidate in the presidential election next year and had a good chance of beating Truman. It was Queen Elizabeth's twenty-first birthday and the steelworkers had won a fifteen-cent raise. Not bad. Maybe she should look for a union job.

She sipped her drink and browsed ads for dresses and shoes, then checked her watch. A little over a half hour had passed. Grace wondered if the singer would show up.

She doubted Mary had tricked her. She'd sounded sincere, and Grace hadn't missed the cautious, even fearful light in Mary's eyes when she checked the hall before closing the dressing room door. And it had been impossible to ignore the rough way Eddie Martone handled her.

No wonder Mary had turned to Joe. He'd always been the protective type, always finding a bird with a wounded wing.

Grace spotted Mary as she came through the door, and met her at the bar, glass in hand.

"Hello, Mary," the bartender said. "Rye and ginger, on the rocks?"

"That's right." Mary dropped a bill on the bar. "Need another?" she asked Grace.

"No, thank you."

"Let's go back. It's quieter." Quieter, and less chance of being seen, Grace knew she meant.

The back room had stucco walls and a low ceiling. The smoke was thick, and so was the smell of beer and whiskey.

Grace set her drink down and took a seat. Mary sat across the table, her long, graceful fingers resting on the edge of her glass. She looked contrite. Or maybe nervous? It was brave of Mary to come. Grace had to grant her that.

Mary sighed and lifted her gaze. "So, here we are."

"Yes, here we are," Grace agreed. "But where is that? You tell me, Mary. I'm lost. Dumbstruck, to be perfectly honest." Grace took a sip of her drink. "How long have you and Joe been seeing each other? It didn't start back at Clinton…did it?"

Chapter Ten

Mary didn't answer. Her former schoolmate looked more familiar in the shadowy light, though the gawkiness of their teenage days had vanished. Mary's cheekbones were high, her lips full. Carefully penciled brows framed luminous eyes, soft brown with golden lights. Her wide, dimpled smile had not changed one bit. A smile that always made Grace smile in return. Grace did remember that.

"It's hard to say. He sat near me in band. I played the French Horn. We'd talk sometime. And you know, we were always looking." She shrugged. "But he could never ask me on a date. We both knew that. Even if he wasn't already seeing Camille. I knew that, too."

"When did it change?"

"We were alone in the band room one afternoon. One thing led to another, and Joe kissed me." She looked at her drink and smiled. "It wasn't much. But it seemed a lot back then. And it was enough to spark things up. We started seeing each other in secret that summer, after graduation."

Grace thought back; those months seemed like a hazy dream, an endless string of sunny days. The news reels of war in Europe, a mild distraction, like flies buzzing against the screen.

Joe was eighteen and working for their Uncle Mario, her mother's brother, mixing cement and learning how to lay bricks. Though Grace already knew the dull, heavy trade wasn't for him.

Her father knew Joe had no interest in working in his shop, nor the temperament for it. He'd urged him to look for a union job, as a plumber or a welder. His friends at the Italian club would smooth the way. Joe agreed, but never set the plan in motion. Suddenly, there was no need to decide. Not for Joe, or so many young men his age.

That spring, he'd taken Camille to senior prom, and they seemed to be going steady. Apparently, he was also seeing Mary.

Grace shook her head. "I had no idea. Nobody did. He was good at hiding your relationship."

"We both were. I was seeing another fellow, too. Lester Holmes. I knew him from the neighborhood. My parents liked him for me. He's the pastor at our family's church now. I could have been a minister's wife if I'd played my cards right." Mary sounded amused by the idea. Maybe a bit regretful, too, for passing up an easier path than she'd chosen?

"Did you break off with him for Joe?"

"No, not because of Joe. Lester loved my singing. But he didn't want a wife who was out all night, working in a nightclub or a bar. He thought I should only use my gift in a church or a professional choir. I knew I'd never be happy if I agreed to that, always wondering if I could have made something of myself. I chose my music. And I never looked back." Mary nodded. "He took it hard. But he didn't stay single long. A nice church girl snatched him up, though she wasn't always so godly towards me. She thought I wasn't good enough for him. Maybe she was right." Mary shrugged. "I still go to a service at his church from time to time. It makes my folks happy. I sang with the choir on Easter Sunday. Lester asked me. He's still trying to reform me, I guess. 'Love the sinner, hate the sin?'" Mary rolled her eyes and smiled. "His wife is a soprano, too, and she was madder than a wet hen when I showed up. That was half the fun."

Grace could picture Mary leading a church choir, her powerful voice rising to the rafters, moving hearts and spirits. She was truly gifted. As Don Rappley had said, she really had something. Grace felt it the other night and saw it now, clearly. Some inner glow, magical and magnetic, that had nothing to do with makeup or fancy gowns, or even a spotlight.

But there was still a warm, easy way about her, even in this awkward situation. Grace remembered that from school days, too. The way they'd laughed together in Home Economics when their Angel Cake turned into a pancake. Mrs. McCormick had given them both a D. "For Deflated, I guess," Mary had quipped.

Mary sipped her rye and ginger. "Everything changed when the war came."

"Didn't it… For you and Joe, too, you mean?"

"He called me from Times Square after he signed up and asked me to meet him. He said he had to fight, but he'd come back for me. A little while later, I heard he got engaged to Camille. At least she thought so."

It still hurt Mary to recall that part of the story. Grace could hear it in her tone.

"He broke off with you when he went into the army?"

"I broke off with him. He promised he'd square things with Camille and asked me to wait. I said 'no,' but he kept writing. Letter after letter. Finally, I gave in. He claimed he didn't love Camille, but he didn't know how to get out of it. He kept reminding me that he'd never given her a ring."

Grace remembered that. Nobody was sure if they were engaged or not. Everyone thought Joe couldn't afford a ring. Camille wanted a diamond; a pearl wouldn't do. Grace's mother offered him a stone from a stick pin, passed down to her in the family, but Joe refused. They thought he was proud. Or maybe superstitious, waiting until he came home to make it official. But it hadn't been that at all.

Her brother had returned last February, in the wave of troops discharged a few months after the Japanese surrender. Camille and her family were already planning the wedding.

"He kept saying he needed time to let her down easy. I made him choose. I waited a long time. I needed an answer." She paused and looked down at her glass again. "A few weeks ago, we ran into each other in a club on 52nd, and it started up again."

"You knew that he was married?"

Mary nodded and looked down at her drink. "I knew. But we couldn't help it."

"You didn't help it," Grace corrected quietly.

She expected Mary to be angry, but she wasn't. "I know what I should have done, Grace. I know I should have sent him away. I was with someone, too, but it was nothing compared to Joe. I felt awful without him. He felt the same. We can't be apart anymore. We just don't want to be."

Grace didn't know what to say. She stared at Mary until the singer looked away.

"You hate me now, right? You think I'm a home wrecker. A whore. Even worse." Mary caught her gaze again, her eyes urging Grace to reply.

"I don't hate you." Grace was about to reach across the table and squeeze Mary's hand. But stopped herself. She felt confused; the script she'd planned was all muddled now. She'd pictured herself persuading the unknown Lana Delmar to break off with Joe. Appealing to her conscience, or even shaming her into it. She'd expected to feel angry with her. But that wasn't the way she felt at all.

If she and Mary had met again by chance with Joe out of the picture, she would have been happy to see her old school friend, in awe of her glamour and talent, and how well she'd done. Now it was all mixed up in her head, how she really felt sitting here and the mission she'd planned. Grace wasn't sure what to say.

"I don't hate you, Mary. I really don't. In a way, I understand. Or I'm starting to."

"Well, that's something." Mary met her gaze and looked away. Grace couldn't tell what she was thinking.

"I'm not judging you. I don't mean to," Grace said, knowing that was exactly what she'd done so far. "Joe is just as much responsible, maybe even more. People have affairs. It happens all the time. But Joe is married, and if he won't end it, you have to be the strong one. Camille thinks they're going to start a family. She might be pregnant again. She's already had a miscarriage."

"I know, and I feel bad for her. But Joe says he didn't go through so much overseas to be tied to a woman he doesn't love. And for both of them to be miserable the rest of their lives. He says he's going to leave her, whether we end up together or not."

Grace didn't answer. Her brother was far better at juggling women than she'd ever imagined. He did seem unhappy with Camille. Grace had chalked that up to adjusting after the army and living in that tiny apartment. Now she knew it was more. A lot more. Maybe Joe did plan to leave Camille. Or had spun a comforting fantasy about it, deluding both himself and Mary, imagining a life together in the spotlight, endless duets, and applause.

"He's been through a lot," Grace said in a softer tone. "We don't know the half of it. Joe acts tough, but he's more sensitive than other guys. He needs time to settle down and accept his responsibilities. You have to let him go, so he can do that."

Mary sat back and tilted her head. "With all due respect, I think I know what's going on in Joe's head a lot better than you do. I don't think settling down is his problem. Not the way you mean."

Grace wanted to argue, but she couldn't. Mary probably did know Joe better than she ever would, in some ways. This was a hard conversation, one of the hardest she'd ever had.

"Let's say he leaves Camille to be with you. What then? You two dance off into the sunset? You know how people will treat you. You know how hard it will be to stay together. Even if you find a justice of the peace who'll marry you."

Grace knew mixed marriages were legal in New York, but it wasn't that way in the rest of the country. Not by a long shot.

"I'm not saying it's right," Grace added quickly. "It's just the truth."

"You're not telling me anything I don't know," Mary said quietly. "It's hard enough to have a drink or a bite to eat someplace where people won't give us dirty looks, or worse. Or where the waiters won't spit into our soup. That is, if they let us in the door."

Grace felt embarrassed to hear that and ashamed. But she knew it was true. "It shouldn't be like that. It really shouldn't. But that's what you'll face if you stay together."

"Maybe now, but I hope not forever." Mary looked up at her. "Things are changing. Bit by bit. What about that ball player, Jackie Robinson? That's something, isn't it?"

"It's definitely progress," Grace agreed. But even if attitudes were changing in some circles, they weren't changing anytime soon on Sackett Street. And maybe, never would.

"My family will never accept you." It was hard to be so blunt, but she saw little choice left. "They'll be angry at him, too. Are you willing to cut Joe off from everyone he loves?"

When Mary didn't answer, Grace added. "It took them two years and a world war to warm up to my Irish boyfriend."

Mary looked up; she seemed surprised. "I have a family, too, Grace. A mother and father who have high hopes for me. And an older brother, who served just like Joe. He works moving furniture now, not able to get half the benefits white soldiers do, even though he's entitled on paper. You think my family wants to see me marry a white man? My mother told me, 'Never let a white man touch you.' She said, 'white men think colored girls are easy and will go with anybody. And if you don't go, they'll force you.' I know all white men aren't that way," Mary added. "But enough have reminded me of her warning."

Grace had never heard it laid out so plainly, but she knew what Mary said was true. "Joe was never like that, though, was he?"

"Joe?" Mary smiled, a softness in her eyes. "Joe was so shy, I didn't know what to think. That's how I knew he really felt something. He liked me for myself. Just for who I am, inside." She tapped her chest just above her heart. "He never seemed to see the color of my skin."

Mary sighed and stared into the chattering crowd and cloud of smoke. "What I'm trying to say is that my family won't understand, either. They're religious people. They were strict with me and my brother. Singing in a nightclub is bad enough in their book, no less marrying a divorced white man. Did you ask Joe if he's willing to make me lose my family? Why don't you ask him first, and see what he tells you?"

Grace felt her cheeks flush. "I'm sorry…I'm sorry about the way that came out. But we seem to agree that it will happen. You'll both be cut off from the people closest to you."

She waited for Mary to answer. When she didn't, Grace said, "Why set yourself up for such a hard life? Don't you wonder how your children will be treated? Or worry that these sacrifices will ruin things between you?"

Mary swirled the ice in her glass. "I'd be a fool if I didn't. But now you sound like you're wishing that on us."

Mary's tone was mild, not at all a rebuke. Something between wistful and curious. Grace hadn't meant her words that way, but Mary's observation hit a nerve.

"I know what your people think of us," Mary added. "What is it you Italians call colored folks? Multano?"

"Moulinyan," Grace said the word softly, avoiding Mary's gaze.

"I know what it means. Joe told me."

Grace felt relieved. Admitting it was said was bad enough. The direct translation was eggplant, an insulting reference to skin color and even the shape of a Negro's head.

"Did you ever look at a map?" Mary asked. "You could spit at Africa from Italy. You could swim from Sicily. I bet you've all got some eggplant in you. Maybe that's why you make such a fuss."

Grace knew that was probably true, though she'd never heard anyone before Mary say it.

"Joe said when you found out, you'd be on our side. He said you were different from the others and had your own mind about things. I thought you might be on our side, too. I remembered you that way, Grace. You were nice to me in school. The only one at the table who would even speak to me. The other girls acted like I was invisible. Or worse."

Mary smiled to herself, remembering. But when she lifted her gaze, the disappointment in her eyes stung.

Grace had been nice to her, partly in defiance to the girls who shut Mary out and demeaned her, but mostly because she truly liked Mary. Something between them just clicked. But they weren't really friends, not beyond the Home Ec. room. They didn't eat lunch together in the cafeteria or whisper in the library. They didn't sip ice cream sodas side by side after school.

There were lots of cliques in high school, a highly defined pecking order. It was just the way things were. Grace knew that wasn't the real reason. Maybe she hadn't even been conscious of it, but still, she'd never pushed herself to step over the invisible line drawn between her and Mary or challenged the unspoken rule.

Grace remembered how she'd sliced open her finger one day in the classroom kitchen. Only Mary had kept her head, wrapping the cut in a dish towel, while their teacher had nearly fainted at the sight. Then Mary walked Grace down to the nurse, squeezing the makeshift bandage tight.

The school nurse was surprised to see Mary deliver a white girl to the health office, but Mary pretended not to understand her dismay. "A little blood doesn't bother me, Mrs. Newton. Mine's the same color," Mary had said in a cheerful way.

Grace took a sip of her drink, almost gone now. She wasn't sure what else to say. Part of her wanted to assure Mary she was on their side. She had no doubt that Joe and Mary loved each other. And she did agree that people should be free to be with whoever they loved, without scorn or opposition.

But a logical, realistic voice insisted that wouldn't help. She'd be fooling herself to think her approval could change anything. No one could make this path easier. Or persuade her family to accept Mary as Joe's wife.

"I'm sorry for what you and Joe have been through, I really am. I know it's not right," she said finally. "I'm just being realistic. I'm trying to keep you both from making a mistake. Think of what's ahead. How hard it will be."

Mary twirled the bits of ice left in her drink, staring at the glass as if she expected a message to appear. A mystical solution to their debate.

"I know you think you're doing the right thing, Grace. But who's to say what's wrong and what's right? I thought I knew. I'm not sure now." She lifted her head and pinned Grace with her gaze. "Who gets to make these rules? Who is it, exactly? Can you tell me? If I need to mind them, I just want to know who it is. That's only fair, don't you think?"

She stared across the table, waiting. Grace stared back but had no reply.

"My grandmother always says, 'If you keep doing what you always do, you'll get what you've already got,'" Mary continued. "How can anything change if people don't start acting and thinking differently? People like me and Joe. People like you. It's got to start somewhere. Do you understand what I mean?"

"I do." Grace wanted to believe it could be that simple but still didn't see how.

"I'm sorry. I don't mean to go on about it," Mary spoke softly again. "But no matter what you or anybody else thinks, I can't make something dirty out of Joe and me. Something ugly and unnatural. We're just like everyone else, two people who love each other. We tried to shake it loose, but it won't quit. We see that now, and we stopped trying. We don't want to hurt anyone, but we want to stay together. We have to. Joe said we need to go away, someplace where we'll be treated better. There's a music scene in Paris now. We can find work and be in on something new. It will be easier for us there, too. If you don't understand, there's nothing I can do."

Grace did understand—that was the problem.

Mary took a quick, final sip from her glass and stood up. She tugged her turquoise coat over her shoulders. "I'd better go. They'll send the hounds out after me in a minute."

Spoken with a smile, her manner offhand. Though some faint, dark note left Grace unsettled, an image in her mind's eye of Mary chased like prey.

"Thanks for talking to me. I know it wasn't easy. For either of us," Grace said.

"That's all right. I did want to tell you my side." Mary picked up her purse and gloves and offered a dimpled grin, her bright eyes teasing. As if no harsh words had passed between them.

"Thanks for the flowers, Joe's sister. That's some bouquet. How did you know I love lilies?"

"Lucky guess." Grace shrugged and smiled back. She almost came to her feet to hug her old school friend goodbye but felt ashamed after all she'd said.

She couldn't help imagining how it might be if things were different. Mary and Joe happily married. She'd drop by their apartment on her way home from work and help put their kids to bed. They'd eat and drink, and laugh, and Mary would be like another sister.

She watched Mary disappear into a cloud of smoke and high-pitched laughter. Could the world ever change that much? Bit by bit, like Mary said?

Maybe someday. But not in time for their happiness.

Chapter Eleven

Grace came in the side door. Joe's overalls hung from a hook on the wall, his paint-splattered boots on the floor below. That didn't mean he was home, but at least he'd made an appearance.

She walked into the kitchen, dimly lit and spotlessly clean. The scent of cooking lingered. Her mother's sewing machine thrummed in the dining room, and Grace didn't feel like shouting over it.

Her mother had been a seamstress in a dress factory on the Lower East Side when she was young. That was how she and Grace's father had met. Her mother had never stopped sewing, working on orders from her husband's shop, and custom-made dresses and coats for her own steady customers. She'd been overwhelmed during the war, with everyone pressed to make their wardrobe last. The shops were full again, but she still had plenty of work. It was the season for frilly white communion dresses and even fancier wedding gowns.

Grace opened the oven and took out a dish that had been kept warm. She set it on the table, where her mother had left a napkin and place setting, then sat down and poured herself a glass of wine. She lifted the lid to find a large saucy square of eggplant parmigiana. She sat back and sipped her wine. What were the chances?

"Grace, you're home. I didn't hear you come in."

Her mother stood in the doorway; a tape measure dangled from her neck; her work smock studded with straight pins.

"I didn't want to interrupt you."

Her mother poured a cup of demitasse, set a biscotti on the saucer, and sat across the table. She wouldn't allow anyone to eat alone, no matter what time they came home.

"Nona made her eggplant."

"It looks good." Grace took a forkful. There'd be questions if she didn't show an appetite.

"How's your girlfriend? Did you have a nice time? I'm surprised you didn't have dinner together."

It took Grace a moment to recall the excuse she'd given for coming home late. "We met for a drink. It was long enough to catch up."

"I tried to keep up with the girls I used to work with, but you get married and have kids. You get too busy after that. You look tired, honey. Did you work hard today?"

"Not especially. But I do feel tired. I might go up early."

"How do you like your new job? It must be lonely, the only one in the office."

"It can be quiet. My boss is out a lot. But if I want to chat, I visit the girls at the switchboard. They've been nice to me."

"That's good. As long as you have some company." Her mother dipped the tip of the hard cookie in her coffee and avoided Grace's gaze. Grace knew what she really meant—left alone to think too much about Colin.

"There's always plenty to do. But my boss doesn't watch every little thing. I mainly work on my own. I like that."

Harry did not shower her with praise, but she could tell he was pleased with the job she'd been doing. He trusted her to carry out his instructions and knew she was smart enough to figure out the rest.

"So, you like the boss? You were worried about that."

"He's nothing like the managers at the insurance company. He's not stuffy and formal. And he listens to what I say."

"Don't speak your mind too much, *bella*. You don't want to lose this job, too." She brought her cup and saucer to the sink. "And don't get familiar. Men take liberties, alone in an office with a pretty girl. Married or not."

"He's not married." Grace had never asked but felt sure of that.

Her mother shrugged. "Even worse. You make sure he treats you with respect. It's up to the woman."

To guard her virtue, her mother meant. "I know, Ma. Don't worry." Grace struggled to hold a serious expression. "Where is everyone? It's so quiet."

"Rose is out with Frank, and your father went to bed early with the hot water bottle. His back again. Nona is at church, the Holy Name Society. Camille had to see her family, someone's birthday over there."

Grace knew her mother wished they had a better relationship with Joe's in-laws and were invited to birthdays and such, like her friends with married children. But as long as Camille ran home crying every few weeks, that wasn't going to happen.

If the Riccis and the rest of the neighborhood ever found out about Joe and Mary… Grace felt her stomach knot at the thought.

"Did Joe go, too?"

Her mother wiped the counter with a dishcloth. "Sure, he went. They should be back soon."

Grace set her plate aside. Walking Camille to his in-laws' house was no guarantee that Joe had gone inside. For her mother's sake, she pretended otherwise.

"Some fella called you. Dan Ripley?"

"Don Rappley." After an awkward parting, Grace assumed she'd never hear from him and certainly not this soon. His eagerness put her off even more, though it didn't feel fair.

"That's right. I took down his number if you want to call back." Her mother watched Grace's reaction. "That's the fellow you went out with Saturday night, right? Rose said you liked him."

"He was alright." Grace chewed a piece of bread and stared straight ahead.

"So, you'll see him again?"

Grace shook her head. "He's not my type."

"That's too bad. He sounds like a nice fellow."

Her mother seemed about to say more. Who are you waiting for, sweetheart? Joe Di Maggio? But it had all been said before.

Her mother tugged the tape measure from her neck. "There's ice box cake," she said, heading back to the machine.

The treat was tempting, but Grace decided to pass. Her stomach was queasy.

She washed her dish and glass and went up to her room.

She was relieved to hear Joe would be home soon. Partly relieved, and partly anxious about confronting him. She'd tell him straight out; she knew about Mary and had tried to make her see reason.

He'd be angry. But maybe the shock of someone in the family knowing about his secret life would shake some sense into him. And dissolve the sweet, airy daydream he and Mary shared. They could never live happily ever after. Not in Paris. Not anywhere. Somewhere deep inside, they knew that. They had to.

Grace showered and changed into loose, wide-legged slacks and an old cotton blouse, then sat on the living room sofa with a book. She'd been reading *All The King's Men*, on loan from the library, but needed a break from the heavy plot and cynical view. She'd also borrowed *The Hollow* by Agatha Christie which had been published last fall. The country-house-murder-plot was distracting without demanding too much concentration.

She'd once read that even Christie found Poirot a conceited bore and liked Miss Marple best. Grace agreed, but she'd read anything by the queen of mysteries, some books more than once. She found the stories even better when she knew the villain's identity and could see how the author hid the clues, usually in plain sight.

Her grandmother came in, passed along a few bits of church gossip, then went to her room. Rose came home a short time later and went straight to bed. She had to punch in at six thirty.

The phone rang at a quarter to eleven. Her mother picked it up in the kitchen and spoke quietly. She came into the living room, the sewing smock folded over her arm. "That was Bella Ricci. Camille doesn't feel well. She's staying over with her parents tonight."

Grace put her book down. "Another migraine?"

Her mother shrugged. "It's probably just heartburn. They must have had a big meal."

"What about Joe? Is he on his way back?"

"He'll be home soon. Shut the lights when you go up. The electric company doesn't need any more of our money."

"I will, Mom." Grace returned to her book, determined to wait for her brother.

She woke hours later, a cramp in her neck from the sofa arm. The weak glow of a lamp on the end table was no match for the sunlight that slipped between the damask curtains.

She stood up and stretched. Had Joe come home, and she hadn't heard him? She checked the passage by the basement steps. His overalls and boots sat just as she'd seen them last night. The door to the apartment was closed.

She walked down and knocked. Softly, then harder. Then opened the door a crack and called his name. She sensed the shadowy rooms were empty and stepped inside. Had he come and gone? Left early for his job? Why would his work clothes still be by the door?

She looked past the small sitting room, into the bedroom at the back. The bed was neatly made with a white satin coverlet. A heart-shaped pillow with a ruffled edge, carefully placed at the top of the bed. A handmade gift from one of Camille's aunts, given at her bridal shower. How happy she'd been that day. How much she'd been teased by the older women.

A statue of the Virgin Mother sat on the night table with two pink roses in a small vase beside it. Next to that, a photo of the couple on their wedding day. Joe, in a black tux, stood behind his bride, one arm stiffly circling her waist. Camille posed with a small smile, her dark eyes bright, her slim body lost in a sea of white lace.

Grace stepped back. The scene felt too private. She suddenly felt very sorry for Camille and very angry at her brother.

She headed upstairs to get ready for work, her knowledge about Joe and Mary like a bag of stones on her back. She would talk to Joe and soon. She started the shower and turned the water on colder than she liked, wondering how she'd make it through the day without falling asleep at her desk.

* * *

Grace continued to wonder all morning, blinking away sleep as she typed the final report about Roger Ingersoll's mother. Apparently, the country club pro, Chet Atkins, had easily led Muriel from the tennis court to his bed.

"My mother is too old to play tennis. Or anything else that huckster has in mind. She's fifty-three, for God's sakes. She'll have a heart attack," Ingersoll shouted in Harry's office one day.

But Harry had observed that Muriel displayed a talent for the game. She'd quickly progressed under Chet's caring tutelage.

Despite the salacious details, Harry's deep voice on the Dictaphone made her drowsy. More than once, she felt her eyes close, even as her fingers moved over the keys.

Luckily, Harry was out. Grace pulled off the headphones and yawned. The shiny wooden desk looked like a comfy pillow. She could rest her head on her arms, and no one would be the wiser.

The impulse was tempting, but Grace wouldn't take the chance. Even if Harry didn't catch her, a client might.

She grabbed her purse and pushed her chair back. Harry needed the report by five for a meeting with Ingersoll. If she ate lunch at her desk, she could finish in time. First, she needed to stretch her legs and clear her head.

Grace ducked into a sandwich shop a few doors down and came out minutes later with a chicken salad on rye and two cups of coffee, packed in a paper bag.

When she got back to the office, the door was unlocked, and Harry stood near her desk. He held a newspaper in one hand, the pages fanning at his side like a bird's wing.

"Hello, Harry." She smiled and set the bag down. He didn't smile back. Or even answer. Was he mad at something? She'd never seen him lose his temper and didn't want to know what that looked like.

"I just ran down to get lunch. I should have left a note. Want some coffee? I have two—"

"Have you seen the afternoon paper?"

She was about to take out the cups, but something in his manner drew her full attention. "I didn't get a chance."

"Remember when I warned you about The Starlight Room? A woman who worked there was murdered last night. She called herself Lana Delmar, but her real name was…"

"Mary? Someone killed Mary?" Grace crossed the short distance between them and grabbed the newspaper. The item was on the second page, but the headline was bold enough. NEGRO NIGHT CLUB SINGER STABBED TO DEATH.

Grace pressed her hand to her mouth. The room spun, and the newspaper fell to the floor. She grabbed the desk to stop herself from following.

She felt Harry's steadying touch on her shoulder. He spoke quietly. "Did you know her?"

Grace nodded and could barely speak. "We went to high school together. I just met up with her again."

Harry handed her a clean, white handkerchief. She wiped her eyes and swallowed back her tears.

"At the club the other night? On stage, you mean?"

"I didn't recognize her Saturday night. But I saw her and Joe together, so I went back last night to talk to her. And found out Lana Delmar was Mary Delmore. She and Joe have been seeing each other on and off for a long time."

"She was the friend you went to visit with the bouquet?"

"I pretended to have a delivery to get inside the club." Grace shrugged. "You do that sort of thing a lot."

He looked annoyed but put it aside. "So, you spoke to her about Joe. In her dressing room?"

"She didn't want to talk there. I got the feeling she was worried someone might overhear. We met at a bar a few blocks away. McNulty's."

"I know the place, go on."

"We talked for a long time…About Joe, mostly. And high school. We weren't close friends, but we got along well, and she'd always been nice to me. She was a good person. She had a good heart. And such a wonderful voice." She looked up at him. "Did you ever hear her?"

"I did. She could really sing, that's for sure."

Grace remembered the very last note Mary sang, eyes closed, her arm raised. The deafening applause. Mary's bright, warm smile. And how, even after the way Grace had tried to wear her down and chase her away from Joe, Mary had managed to smile and say, "Thanks for the flowers, Joe's sister."

"How can she be gone? How can that be?" Shock and sadness broke over her like a wave. She covered her face with her hands and cried, her body shaking.

Harry stood beside her, waiting. She felt his hand on her shoulder but didn't look up. "I shouldn't have told you that way. I'm sorry, Grace."

She took a deep breath. "I'm glad you were the one to tell me. I'm glad I wasn't alone. Or with my family. At least, with you, I don't need to hide how I feel. And what I know about her and Joe."

He glanced at her, then stared out the window at the air shaft and the flat, black roof below. "The police are going to question everyone Mary knew. Joe is at the top of the list. It won't take them long to find out about their relationship. Was he home last night?"

Grace felt her chest tighten. "He and his wife went to visit his in-laws. Camille didn't feel well and decided to stay. We expected him around eleven. I waited, but I don't think he came back. The bed in their apartment hadn't been slept in."

She was rambling, even she could hear it. She knew what Harry was trying to say; the police were going to question Joe about Mary's death.

"Joe didn't kill Mary. Even if he was stringing her along and didn't really plan to leave Camille. He cared for Mary. I think he really loved her. He's mixed up and has a temper at times. But he could never kill anyone... Not that way."

Joe knew what it was to take another life. But he'd been a soldier, fighting the enemy. The police understood the difference. Didn't they?

"I just want to prepare you." And people murder people they profess to love every day, she almost heard him add. "The coroner will estimate the time of death, give or take a few hours. If Joe can prove he wasn't near Mary's apartment within that time frame, he should be fine."

"I hope he sat at a bar and drank until he fell off the stool. Or maybe picked a fight and spent the night in jail." She stood up and straightened the papers on her desk, hardly aware of what she was doing. "But if he was wandering around the city and got so plastered, he can't remember…"

"A list of 'what ifs' never helps. Don't worry. It will be all right."

She knew Harry meant well, but he had no way of knowing that for sure. "I'm glad you think so. But what if the police decide Joe killed Mary? My brother is such a hot head. I'm afraid if he's questioned, he'll provoke them." She looked up at Harry and grabbed his arm. "You'll help him, Harry. Won't you?"

He looked surprised, then nodded. "Of course, I will. He won't need my help. He'll alibi out. End of story."

She wished he could convince her. Inside, a sense of dread slowly spread, like a dark stain on a white cloth.

Chapter Twelve

The red-faced Mick was in charge. He stood behind the chair and banged Joe's head on the table so that he fell forward like a round-bottom toy, the kind that tips over and bobs up again. This time, Joe rested his cheek on the scarred wood, pain shooting down both arms to the cuffed wrists in his lap.

Mahoney pulled him up by his hair. "I'm talking to you, Russo. Sit up straight, damn it. Like you learned in the army, remember?"

Mahoney's partner, Kruger, thin face, slick black hair, stood on the other side. "We're making it easy for you, thick head. She was just a colored girl. The D.A. hardly gives a shit. The bitch came at you with the knife. Just say it."

Joe tasted blood. He wanted to spit in Kruger's s face. "The hell I will. Don't call her that."

"Or what?" Kruger's fist tightened ready to fly. Mahoney touched his arm and sat facing Joe. He smelled of sweat and coffee, and under that, stale beer.

The leather holster cinched around his shoulder creaked. Joe stared at the black handle, then dropped his gaze. He'd love to shoot the fat bastard between the eyes, and the other one, too, for the things they said about Mary. Then blow his own head off. That would make a few headlines.

How many saps sat here before him and swallowed this crap? How many heads got slammed on that table till they played ball? He was no pushover. He'd never sell Mary out to save his skin. He'd never degrade her memory the way these bastard cops wanted him to. They'd could beat him senseless.

He wouldn't do it.

Mahoney picked a bit of tobacco from his teeth. "You like the dark meat, Joe? Some fellas do. Never tempted, myself."

"I'd rather stick it in a monkey at the zoo." Kruger hovered over Joe. "I'd rather stick it in a pig."

Joe lifted his gaze. "I bet you love to make those little piggies squeal, too. Oinky-oink, big daddy—"

"Wise guy, huh? You piece of—" This time, his fist struck the mark. Joe's head jerked back, pain bursting in his nose and mouth. He felt the chair tip backwards until a uniform stepped up and caught it right before he hit the floor.

Then cast a guilty look at the detectives. "He was going to hit his head."

"And save me the trouble of cracking it open." Kruger rubbed his knuckles. "That mouth isn't going to blow a trumpet any time soon. Or swap spit with some—"

Mahoney cut in. "Okay, boys. Enough fun," He lit a cigarette and blew the smoke in Joe's face. "You're just annoying us now, Joey, my boy. You got one more chance to save your stubborn dago arse. Here's how it went between you love birds last night. You got there around one. You had a fight. Money, booze, whatever. Pick one and stick to it. You'd both been at the bottle, and it got ugly. She came at you with the knife, and you tried to take it away, the gentleman that you are. Next thing you know, she's stabbed in the gut, poor thing. Maybe even stabbed herself."

"It happened fast. A big stinking accident," Kruger added.

"That's right. Plain and square. But you panicked and left the scene. Down the fire escape, to the street. You dumped the jacket and weapon in a trash pail a few blocks away. End of story." He raised his hand, flat-palmed, like a priest at the end of mass. "Unintended homicide. Manslaughter, second degree," he repeated for the umpteenth time.

"You get off light, a few years in the clink. You might even walk on account of killing your share of Krauts. And her being a nigger slut." Kruger stood behind Mahoney's chair, too edgy to sit. Or maybe seeking protection.

Joe's body stiffened. He stared at Kruger, blood pounding in his head, and no way to get at him.

Mahoney leaned forward, his hot breath in Joe's face. "You plead not guilty; the D.A. goes for murder one. We've got enough to nail you three times, son. Like Jesus Christ, his holy self. You need to see the photographs of the murder scene again? Or the letters you wrote? I don't know what a jury loves more, photos or letters. The D.A. doesn't need to say a word. They'll have a verdict before their fat behinds warm those jury room chairs. Don't be noble, son. The world's got more heroes these days than it knows what to do with."

He pushed a pad and pen at Joe and sat back, like a teacher in detention hall, waiting for Joe to write down a hundred times, "I will not cuss and fight in the corridors... I will not cuss and fight in the corridors..."

"Put it down in your own words, soldier. Just like I told you. I bet your little wife Carmen is worried sick. Remember her?"

Camille. Her name is Camille. A wise guy reply welled up but didn't get past his fat lip. The bastards were right about one thing. He couldn't play his horn with this mouth. He'd be lucky if his aperture wasn't ruined for good. Not that it mattered. He didn't need a trumpet where he was going.

They waited for Joe to respond, but he wouldn't lift his gaze from the table.

Kruger leaned forward and nearly whispered. "Your little colored gal was a hop head. We found her stash of pills in the nightstand. She was loaded and came at you with the blade for money, right?"

"Dirty junkies." Mahoney made a sorrowful sound. "They'd shake down their own grandmother for a buck."

"God damn it, stop calling her that. She was clean as a whistle. Eddie Martone left the pills. He killed her, too. Or had some stooge do it. Why don't you bang his head on the table? See what he has to say?"

"Not that again. Martone was nowhere near the scene. But he was banging your gal plenty, we hear." Kruger wore a spiteful smile. "Who else was she giving it to, Joe? In your letters, you said it made you crazy. I guess a guy puts up with a lot if he falls for a whore. Then one day, he blows his stack. He can't take it anymore. Is that what happened?"

Joe stared back, then jumped up and lunged at Kruger, aiming his head at the cop's gut like a battering ram. They fell to the floor, Joe on top. He fit his forearm under Kruger's chin and pressed so hard the bastard gasped, red-faced and choking while Mahoney and the uniform struggled to pull him off.

Mahoney nailed him in the jaw, and Joe fell back against a wall. He shook it off, dazed for a moment.

He tasted blood in his swollen mouth when he spoke. "My grandmother punches harder than that, you fat bastard."

Mahoney yanked him up by his collar, like a fish on a line. "You greasy piece of crap. You're one hot-headed wop, aren't you?" Joe braced himself but felt no fear. "I'm warning you, hot stuff. Start talking, or you'll wish to God you had."

"You can bust a gut. I want a lawyer. I know my fucking rights."

He didn't really. Only what he'd seen in the movies. He'd been disciplined in the army, but never brought before a military judge. The chaos had helped, and Harry Shaw, who'd saved his ass more times than he wanted to tally.

Mahoney dropped back into the chair. He swept up the photos and shoved them in a folder. "Time for a break, sonny boy. To piss your pants and think things through. You'd better whistle a different tune when we get back, or you're looking at life. Even the chair."

Kruger pushed his shirt sleeves down. Joe guessed his neck hurt bad, but he be damned if he showed it. "I'll be ringside for that show. I'll toss some peppers and onions on you, Russo. Like the sausage stand at the Feast of Saint Genaro."

Mahoney paused in the doorway and laughed. He strolled out, and the others followed. The heavy door slammed.

There was a glass of water on the table, but he couldn't reach it. He stared at the walls, then the ceiling, afraid of what he'd see. Mary laying in a pool of blood. Her beautiful eyes staring up at him, blank and sightless.

His Mary. His love. His heart and soul.

He pounded his forehead with his shackled fists, the pain building until he thought his skull would crack. He grit his teeth, soundlessly calling her.

His left eye was already swollen shut. He finally closed the other, too.

They stumbled through the brush over frozen ground, silent to a man, no light but a sickle-shaped moon that hung in the black sky. Dampness seeped into his bones, the bite of the frigid night in every breath. They moved north through some forest in France. He could hardly remember where or why. To kill more Germans. Wasn't that always the reason? Clouds of mist drifted through the branches like ghosts who had lost their way.

In the darkness ahead, something crashed through the trees, the sound coming closer. The enemy. Had to be. It was moving in the wrong direction to be their own.

He heard the order to seek cover and dropped belly down in the dried leaves and bits of snow. He raised his rifle and waited, one shoulder braced against a tree. Heart pounding, like it always did this inning of the game.

Branches snapped, and a shape appeared on a rise behind the trees. He took aim, waiting for the order.

"Hold fire!" Shaw shouted.

The shadowy form moved forward, and Joe made out horns, sharp and wide. Eight-foot span? Wider? Bigger than any he'd ever seen in the woods upstate.

The huge head swayed from side to side, eyes rolling like big black marbles. Blood streamed from his neck and chest as he galloped, then stumbled. Hit by scattered fire up the line. Or some jerk had taken a potshot. He would have been screaming if he could.

Joe had already dropped his gun as the pitiful sight galloped past. He could never be sure afterward if it was a true memory or just his mind's way of filling in the blanks. He could swear for one second, the beast stood stone still and met his gaze, full on.

Terrified, shocked, trying to outrun Death. All the while knowing there was no winning that race. The wild, bewildered eyes begging, if not for an explanation, then simple mercy.

Joe stepped from cover and stretched his hand, without knowing what he meant to do or say.

"Russo—down, you idiot! That's an order!"

"Jesus Christ. Finish him off, somebody," another soldier shouted.

Before Joe could find the heart, a single shot sounded. Front knees buckled, as if in prayer before the stag listed and dropped to one side. His last bellow, a dreadful sound.

"Rest in peace, poor bastard," from behind a tree.

"Lucky bastard, you mean," another said. "Do me the favor when my turn comes, buddy. Will ya'?"

Maybe Mahoney would do him the favor. Pull the gun from the holster and put a bullet in his head.

But that would be too lucky. He'd never had much of that.

Chapter Thirteen

They walked up Manhattan Avenue towards the subway at 125th, even though trains were few and far between at such a late hour. Her father walked ahead, looking for a cab. It would cost a fortune, and who would drive them all the way from Harlem to Red Hook? But he seemed determined. Or maybe needed time alone.

Grace walked with Harry and spoke quietly. "Joe was in there so long without a lawyer. God only knows what they made him say." Harry had already told them that the police can tell a suspect like Joe anything. They could lie about evidence or witnesses. Her brother was gullible enough to believe them, too. "They didn't bring anyone else at all in for questioning. They're too lazy to look for the real killer."

"You heard what Mr. Kramer said." He meant the attorney, Martin Kramer that he'd found to represent her brother. He came to the station quickly, but Joe had been alone with the cops for hours. "There's a lot of physical evidence, and Joe has no alibi for the time frame of the murder. And a strong motive, from the detectives' point of view. They have no reason to suspect anyone else."

"Is it really that hopeless, Harry? That cut and dry? Joe did not kill Mary. Doesn't that count for something?" She hadn't meant to raise her voice, but heard it grow louder. It was very late, and she was more than tired.

"I was about to say, a jury has to be convinced beyond a shadow of a doubt. Kramer is good at muddying the water. I've seen him shake guys lose who didn't have a prayer." Like Joe, he might have added. "And we still haven't heard Joe's side."

The way the police had kept them from Joe nearly made Grace scream. Her brother would offer some explanation for this nightmare. He'd tell them something that would prove his innocence.

"I'm sorry I lost my temper."

He glanced at her and met her gaze. "A little moxy isn't a bad thing. You'll need a lot to get through this, Grace."

She was glad he hadn't taken offense. Harry didn't have to stick around and help them. He could have given her Kramer's number and left it at that.

"I keep feeling as if this can't be happening. But it is."

Harry nodded; hands thrust in his pockets; his hat slid back on his head. "That's how it goes sometimes. You're strolling along, doing fine, and life lands a sucker punch out of the blue. Knocks you clear off your feet." He shook his head. "Nothing you can do but get up and keep going. One foot after the other."

She tried to meet his glance, but he was gazing at some distant point down the empty avenue. She got the feeling he was thinking of some troubles he'd faced of his own.

Harry pointed across the street. "Looks like your father found a cab. That's a good sign."

A minor miracle, but still not enough to cheer her. Her father stood by a yellow taxi and pulled open the back door. He turned to Grace and waved.

She didn't want to ask, but she couldn't help it. "I know Joe's got a temper and screws up a lot. But you believe he's innocent. Don't you?"

Harry looked down at her. "I do, Grace. But I'm not going to lie to you. It will be hard to get him out of this mess. Maybe Joe has to weigh his options."

She knew what he meant; Joe should take the plea deal.

"Thanks for being honest. And for everything."

"Get some sleep. Tomorrow will be another tough day."

Joe would go before the bench and plead not guilty. Kramer would appeal to the judge for bail, citing Joe's war-time service and practically clean record. But he'd already told them bail was highly unlikely after a charge of first-degree murder. They should expect Joe to be moved to Rikers Island, where he'd wait for a trial.

Bail. A trial. A judge. Prison. How would her brother ever get through this? How would her family?

She said goodnight and ran across the street, hugging her coat against the dampness. In the back of the taxi, her father patted her shoulder, then turned to the window. Crying, the silent way he did, moisture at the corners of his eyes, wiped with the back of his hand. She turned to offer him comfort but finally stared out her own side.

The taxi sped downtown, weaving around trucks collecting trash and making deliveries, the city as empty as she'd ever seen it. They crossed the river, towards Brooklyn, a stain of morning light on the horizon.

Grace said a silent prayer. Tomorrow was already here.

* * *

It felt as if someone had died. Or, the darkest days of the war, when heavy combat was reported in places where Joe and Colin fought. Nothing to do but carry on the small, dull acts of living, moving as if underwater.

Her mother was stoic, but quietly weeping when she thought no one could see. She stood at the stove, cooking scrambled eggs. The aspirin and Brioschi on the counter, a warning to give her wide berth. Her father sat at the table; clean shaven, thin, grey hair combed back with tonic. He might have been going to a wedding or a funeral, dressed in his best suit and tie, the jacket draped on the back of his chair.

She saw a manila envelope on the counter, which she guessed held the deed to the house and maybe her father's bank book. The chances Joe would be granted bail were a million to one, but her father was prepared to stake everything he owned on freeing his son.

Grace watched him unfold the newspaper, holding it at arm's length with an expression of disgust. He turned a page or two, then squashed it in his hands and put it in the trash.

"Did you hear from Mr. Kramer about Joe's hearing, Pop?"

"This afternoon, he says." He sat down again. "He's not sure yet the time exactly. I'll go to the courthouse and wait."

"I'll come with you."

"You stay, *cara*. You done enough last night." He offered a warm look. Any other time, he would have smiled. This morning, he couldn't manage it.

"It will help Joe to see us there. We should all go." Her mother didn't turn, but Grace knew she was listening.

"Your mother can't see your brother like that. It's too much for her."

Her mother pushed the eggs into a dish with a spatula and shut the gas. "Joe might get the bail and come home. Right, Anthony? You told me last night that's what the lawyer said."

Her father looked uneasy. "He said he'll ask the judge. Don't get your hopes up, Theresa. It's complicated."

Her father had spared her mother the bare bones truth about the judge granting bail. If Joe took the D.A.'s deal and pleaded guilty to manslaughter, he'd be transferred immediately to a different prison to serve his sentence. Either way, Joe would not be home for a long time.

"Did Joe change his mind about the plea? Did Mr. Kramer mention it?"

"He don't see Joe until right before the hearing. But he'll ask him again."

Maybe she was naïve, but she didn't want her brother to admit guilt to a crime he hadn't committed, even if they'd let him say it was an accident. And even if the chances he'd be acquitted by a jury were slim.

Her mother took her dust rags and the carpet sweeper from a cupboard and headed to the living room. Grace knew she was about to start cleaning with a vengeance, the way she did during her worst days. Grace followed but knew her mother didn't want any help. Once the dust was gone, her mother and Nona would take out the horn and holy water to cast off *maloloccio*, the malevolent force that had brought on this calamity.

This morning, her mother had good reason. The police had searched the house from top to bottom yesterday, pulling books from shelves, peering under mattresses, going through closets and drawers. They'd torn Joe and Camille's place apart.

"I'm not sure what to do about the apartment. Maybe Camille doesn't want me to touch her things."

"We should call and see how she's feeling." Grace wondered what Camille had told the police. She'd probably suspected Joe's infidelity. Women sensed these things, but still felt pushed off a cliff faced with the truth.

Her mother shoved the carpet sweeper under the coffee table until it growled in protest. She turned it over and pulled a thread from the brush.

"I doubt she'll speak to us. None of them will now. They're not real family, those Riccis. Alta-Italia, noses in the air. They always looked down on us. On Joe. Like he wasn't good enough. We're dead to them. You'll see."

She pushed the sweeper around the rest of the room. Then dusted the lamp tables, the pleasant scent of lemon oil, at odds with their distress.

Father Dominic would be back. He'd stayed with her mother, Nona, and Rose all night. Frank had been with them, too. Though not quite that long.

Grace rescued the newspaper from the trash and brushed off some coffee grains. The story was on page three, *Suspect Held in Stabbing of Colored Night Club Singer.* Pictures of Mary and Joe were set side by side. Hers, a glamorous, publicity shot. His, a mug shot taken last night. Unshaven, bleary-eyed, he looked like a homeless bum.

She skimmed the article, unable to read it word for word. The report made Joe look so guilty.

Rose walked into the kitchen, still in her pajamas and pin curls. Grace could not fathom how she'd managed to put her hair up in the midst of the crisis. But that was Rose.

"I'm going with Pop to Joe's hearing. Want to come?"

Rose poured herself coffee and sat at the table. "I don't think so."

"Why? Don't you feel well?" Rose had called in sick, but only because she'd gone to bed too late to get up for her shift.

"I'm all right. All things considered. I have to meet Frank when he gets his lunch break."

You could see Frank anytime, this is important, Grace wanted to say. But she doubted it would persuade her.

"What does Frank think?"

"He feels sorry for Joe and all of us. He really does." Rose paused and glanced at the kitchen door. "But he said Joe had it coming."

Grace wasn't surprised and felt sure he'd said more.

"What did you say?"

Rose sipped her coffee. "It's hard to defend a guy who cheats on his wife. Even if he's your brother. And with a colored girl. She must have been a slut. They're all like that."

"Don't you dare say that." Grace could have slapped her sister across the face. "Mary was a good person. You don't know a thing about it, and Frank knows even less."

Rose looked surprised. "And you do?"

"I knew Mary in high school." Grace paused, not sure of how much she should tell her sister. "And I saw her Monday night. We had a drink and talked about Joe."

Rose was shocked. "You knew about her and Joe?"

"Only since Saturday. Don't tell Mama and Pop. And don't ever let me hear you say she and Joe deserved this. Nobody deserves to die that way. Least of all Mary." Grace could easily see Mary's dark eyes wide with fear at the end. The image would not leave her head.

"Tell that to Frank Stanco when you see him. Or I will."

Her sister looked mollified but also annoyed. "Frank has his opinions. You know that."

Grace knew. More than she wanted to. Her sister had always held her own opinions, too. Until she signed the job over to Frank. She could have grabbed Rose's shoulders and given her a shake. But it wouldn't change anything. Rose still wouldn't understand.

No one could understand the sadness she carried today. For Mary, as much as for her brother. Sadness and guilt for the things she'd said and could never take back.

The doorbell rang with rude insistence, the chimes echoing through the house like church bells. Hard knocks on the front door followed. She heard her parents shouting but couldn't understand what they said.

"The police again?" Rose stared at her.

"Reporters," Grace realized. She ran into the living room as her mother pulled the drapes closed and her father yelled at the door.

"Go away! *Vamos!* My son is innocent, for Christ sakes. Go away, or I'll call the cops."

Rose ran in from the kitchen. "They're at the side door, too. Make them go away, Pop. This is horrible."

Rose ran upstairs while their parents ran back to the kitchen. Grace followed, repulsed by the sight of a stranger's face, pressed to the window. He banged on the glass, shouting when he saw them. "Hey, Russo—give us Joe's side. The cops say he's going to the chair. Tell us it ain't so. There's dough in it for you, Pop. You can get your son a good lawyer…"

Grace took a step towards the window, about to tell the reporter where to shove his dough. Then felt frozen, as if in a nightmare where she knew she should act, or even scream, but couldn't.

Her parents pushed past her. "Find the newspaper, Anthony," her mother said. "We'll cover all the glass."

Grace turned and headed to her bedroom. Not to hide under the covers, like Rose. She'd dress for the hearing. If her father insisted that she stay home, she'd wait until he left and find her way to the courthouse on her own.

She would be there for Joe.

Chapter Fourteen

"Where's Pop? Why didn't he come? What the hell, Grace? This is no place for you."

Joe's greeting stung, but her heartache at the sight of him stole every rebuke that might have crossed her lips. "I'm not here as family, Joe. We came to talk about your case."

"So I can start the inquiries," Harry added.

They'd signed in at the prison entrance as officers of the court. Harry mentioned the visit after Joe's hearing, and Grace had been surprised—and relieved—when he'd asked her to come.

Her father couldn't have joined them, even if he'd wanted to. He was boarding his shop on Court Street and sweeping up the glass inside. Bricks had been tossed through the windows last night, and vile words painted on the storefront—nigger lover, filthy wop, and worse.

The police woke the house at five a.m., but her father took the news without emotion, as if he'd expected it. He shook a few pills for his heart from the brown bottle he carried in his pocket, tossed them in his mouth, and left.

Joe bowed his head in apology. "Sorry, Grace. This place has me jumping out of my skin."

A prison-issued crew cut showed his pink scalp and a scar on the top of his skull. Not a wound from the army, a childhood souvenir, collected after making a playground swing flip over the frame and circle all the way around. On a dare and because he'd felt no fear, no consideration of the consequences. Of course, he'd landed on his head.

Just the way he'd landed here.

Harry offered him a cigarette. Grace had brought him two cartons, a few magazines, and money for the commissary. Visitors were not allowed to give the inmates much. Rat traps were not on the list, but would have come in handy, from what she'd seen.

Harry had prepared her during the ferry ride, but the sight and smell of the place was still a shock. They sat in a small room with a wooden table and chairs. Dampness seeped from the cement walls. One high, narrow window was covered with wire mesh, bars, and spider webs. Fluorescent bulbs on the high ceiling offered little light.

The guard who had delivered Joe stood just outside the door, somehow looking bored and vigilant at the same time.

Harry took out a notebook and pencil. "We don't have much time. Take me through Monday night. Every detail you can recall. Even if it doesn't seem important."

Her brother took a shaky breath. "I told Mr. Kramer everything. He wrote it down, word for word."

"Humor me. I didn't come all this way for nothing, did I?" Harry's tone took on a harder edge.

"Tell us, Joe. I need to know, too." Harry had seen the police report, including witness statements, photos of Mary's body, and other physical evidence, but she had not. The attorney's office was sending a photo-stat copy, and Grace was already strategizing how to get her hands on it .

"Eddie Martone killed Mary and fit me up for it. What else is there to know? So what if his alibi holds up? He has a gang of dopes who'll do anything he wants, even swear the Earth is flat, if he wants them to. Who knows how many cops he has in his pocket?"

"Did you see Martone talk to any of those dopes privately that night? Or in the days prior? Did any money change hands?"

"Money's always changing hands in that place." Joe stared at them with bloodshot eyes. "Mary is gone. I wish I was, too. They can lock me up forever. I don't give a damn except Martone gets away with it. I could kill him with my bare hands."

Harry didn't reply, though she guessed what he was thinking. Emphatic declarations of wanting to kill someone were probably not a good idea right now for Joe.

"I saw her, Joe. We had a drink Monday night. Did she tell you?" Her admission snagged his attention.

"I heard all about it. The flowers. Everything you said, too." Grace knew he was angry. "You rattled her good, Grace. She was having second thoughts about our plans. It nearly broke my heart. That's what you wanted, right?"

Grace felt sad to hear that, even though at the time, that had been her intention. "Was she mad at me?"

"She was upset. But she always liked you, Grace. Despite what you said. She liked you a lot. That was Mary. She could never stay angry for long, no matter what anyone did to her. Not long enough to make a difference."

Harry leaned forward. "Did you tell the police that you and Mary had words?"

"I'm not that stupid. Besides, it wasn't a real argument. Not a screaming match like when me and Camille go at it."

Harry looked relieved. "What time did you get to the club Monday night?"

"About a quarter to twelve. Second set was winding down."

"You were in Brooklyn earlier, with your wife's family. How did that go?"

"I wanted to leave at ten, but Camille wanted to stay. We had a fight in the kitchen. Everybody heard. Camille's got a mouth on her. She knew I was headed to the city after I walked her home." Joe took a drag on his cigarette. "She said if I didn't stay, she wasn't coming back to the apartment. Ever. Then her parents chipped in with their two cents, saying how bad I treat their daughter and what a bum I am. So, I walked out. She's happier with them anyway, in her old bedroom like a little girl. I don't know why she ever married me."

Joe rubbed his mouth with his hand. His knuckles were battered and raw. From fights, more than one. He already looked as if he'd lost weight. Or maybe it was the gray uniform, hanging off his wide shoulders. He looked wary and diminished, shrinking into himself.

Bruises around his eyes and mouth had turned a greenish brown. Like rotten fruit. Or the rainbow in a gasoline puddle. Most of all, he'd lost his cocky attitude. The brash, irreverent grin he'd been born with.

Harry looked up from his notes. "Let's get back to the club. What happened when you got there?"

"Not much. The place was empty. I waited at the bar, but Gem didn't call me to sit in. I didn't mind. I was tired and edgy. I would've played like crap."

"What about your jacket? You told the police that you lost it?" Grace asked.

"I wore it Saturday night. But I was loaded when I left and forgot it there. At least, I thought I did. Mary looked around the club on Sunday but couldn't find it."

"What did the police say when you told them?" Grace asked.

Joe laughed, a bitter sound. "They said I needed a better brand of bull shit."

"Did you see Martone Monday night?" Harry asked.

"He was playing poker in the cellar when I got there. There's always a game going on, high stakes. The cops look the other way."

"I've heard," Harry said.

"He runs girls in a house a few blocks west in Hell's Kitchen, too." Joe caught himself. He glanced at Grace. "Sorry, Grace. This isn't for ladies' ears."

"You'd be surprised what we ladies hear. Go on."

"He came up around midnight, with two mugs. Sharp suits, lots of cuff. Mobbed up types. They sat at his usual table. Looked like a business meeting. He's got his fingers in a few pies. He called Mary over after the set, showing her off like a piece of sirloin to a pack of dogs. Then he walks her to the bar."

"What did you do?" Harry paused from jotting notes and looked at Joe.

"I felt like my head might explode. But I kept my cool. I maybe said hello and kept drinking. I barely look at her in front of him. That's what we did, to keep him off our trail. Guess it didn't work. Or someone tipped him off."

"Who knew about you and Mary?" Grace asked.

"Just Gem Washington. But Mary trusted him. After that, what the hell do I know? Did I know that was the last time I was ever going to see my baby girl?" He rubbed his forehead, his eyes glazing with tears. "I should have dragged her out of there. I should have told Eddie Martone and the whole frigging world that I loved her and that was that."

He covered his eyes with his hand, and his body shook. Grace hadn't seen her brother cry since they were kids. She'd never seen him heartbroken.

"Easy, Joe." Grace reached to touch his sleeve.

The guard opened the door halfway and shouted. "No contact with the inmates."

Grace quickly sat back, her hands in her lap.

"Go on, Joe. What happened next?" Harry prodded.

"Mary went to her dressing room. I stayed at the bar and had another drink. Gem and a few guys from the band left for an after-hours club uptown, The Indigo Room. They asked me to come, but I made some excuse. The bartender, Arty, was still closing out and planned to catch up with them. I acted like I needed the john, but I slipped back to see Mary." He glanced at Grace. "We agreed to meet at her place and talk things out."

"Did you see her leave?" Harry asked.

"She has to leave through the side door. That baloney. She already had her coat on when I went back to the bar and settled my tab. I was about leave, too, when Eddie asks me to drop off an envelope, a few blocks downtown."

"The opposite way you were headed," Grace said.

"That's right," Joe replied.

"Do you make deliveries for him often?" Harry asked.

"Never. Though a hell of a lot of envelopes are coming and going around Eddie Martone. The guy should run the frigging post office. He usually sends one of his stooges, like Dante or Bernard."

"Dante Fiori, his body man, and Bernard Gervasi, the boxer?" Harry checked his notes.

"Ex-boxer. Those flat feet and slow hands don't matter now. Most of his opponents are tied to a chair."

"Where were Martone's men, guarding the game?" Harry asked.

"I thought so but can't swear to it. I never saw Bernard. I did see Dante prowling around, but he disappeared, too. Now I'm figuring Eddie sent one of them to knock Mary off while he sidetracked me." He lit up again and blew out a plume of smoke. "He's got another lug head in the kitchen, an ex-con named Hubie."

"George Huebner, you mean," Harry cut in. "He's been around a long time. Did hard time for Eddie's father, Leo. Never ratted out his boss, either."

"Then he's as loyal as he's ugly," Joe said. Grace realized they were talking about the tattooed man who had opened the door when she brought Mary the bouquet.

"I doubt Eddie would tap him for the job," Joe continued. "He's dumber than he looks, and that's saying something. Anyways, I should have told Eddie I didn't have time to be his errand boy. But Mary and I were set to sail to France tomorrow night. I didn't want to stir the hornet's nest. To tell the truth, I dreaded an argument with her. The bastard even slipped me a fiver for my trouble. I didn't want to take it, but he stuffed it in my pocket."

"Where did Eddie go when you left?" Harry asked.

"He said he was going downstairs to win back his money. Judy, the house manager, had already left. Arty had settled his cash drawer and was about to leave to meet the guys."

Before Harry could ask another question, Joe said, "Who knows where Eddie really went? Maybe he did the dirty work himself. Maybe he wanted to see the look on her face. Anyone at the club would give him an alibi. They're all scared to death of him."

Harry kept writing in his book. "You made the delivery?"

"The fellow was waiting at the meeting spot, took the envelope, and shoved it in his jacket. Barely said a word."

"Then what?"

"I should have used the five bucks for a cab since I was running late. I may have got there in time. But I saved it for our first night in France. A nice dinner somewhere." He stared at a spot somewhere on the wall above Grace's head. "I took the 2 train to 125th. Mary's place is a few blocks up, on 127th."

Harry nodded. "How did you get into the building? Do you have a key?"

"The door to the street is always open. But we had a code with the buzzer in case Eddie was there. I buzzed a few times, but she didn't answer. I thought she was in the shower."

"Did anyone see you on the stairs, or in the hallway?" Grace asked, hoping Joe might remember a witness who had not come forward yet.

"Not that I noticed. Unless they were peering out their peepholes. When I reached her door, I heard the record player, stuck in a scratch, the same three notes over and over. It was the tune she recorded with Gem's band. It set me off. The door was unlocked, which also rattled me. I walked in, and the place was a wreck. Then I saw her. On the floor."

The last few words came out on a choked sob. Joe stopped speaking and stared blankly. He blinked and rubbed his eyes again. "I knelt down, I felt her pulse…It was hopeless. She was already gone."

"What time do you think that was?" Harry asked.

"One, maybe later. I didn't know what to do. I lost my head. I couldn't stand the sight, her lying there. All that blood. I couldn't breathe, I thought I might pass out. It felt like I was back on the field. I knew what it would look like if anyone found me there. I ran up to the roof and crossed to the building next door. It's a short space; I used a plank of wood. Then I ran down and found my way to the street. I had to get away."

"Did you meet anyone on the staircase in that building?" Grace asked. "Did anyone see you come out?"

"I don't know. I wasn't thinking straight. I could have knocked someone down, and I wouldn't remember."

"Did you ever think of calling the police?" Grace did mean to berate him. She just wanted to know.

"Sure I did. But I knew they'd point the finger at me. I was right, too. Never mind I'm the last person in the world who'd lay a finger on her. Mary was the only reason I woke up in the morning. Martone set me up like a ten-pin. I'd laugh my head off if I didn't want to bang it on a wall even more."

Grace lowered her gaze. It was hard to see her brother like this. She had no words of comfort or even hope to offer. Hope that wasn't pie in the sky.

He was in a jam, worse than she could ever imagine.

Harry sat back, nonplussed. "You ran. Then what?"

"I bought a bottle and rode the subway all night. Around six or so, I found a mission downtown. The ladies gave me coffee and some clothes. I told them I'd been in a fight. I figured the cops would look for me, but I went back to Brooklyn anyways and showed up at the job. Like I had nothing to hide. Because I didn't. Except for not reporting her body."

They already knew that's where the police had picked Joe up.

Harry paged through his notes a moment, then looked back at Joe. "Was Mary using pills or cocaine? Take your time. Lying to protect her won't do any good."

Joe answered in a heartbeat. "She never touched that junk. She'd barely take an aspirin. Ask me again, and I'll bust you one. Never mind you're helping me."

"Understood. There were no drugs in her blood according to the autopsy."

"But the cops will lie about that in court, too, because it fits their story," Joe finished for him. "It makes her out to be trash. Martone's the trash. He's the pill popper, among his other charms. Uppers, downers, whatever he can get his hands on. He wanted Mary to use, but she wouldn't touch it. He'd have his high, then crash in her bed. Better than him being sober and on top of her, we both thought." Joe glanced at Grace. "Sorry, Grace. This isn't good for you to hear."

Harry glanced at her, as if he had regrets now, too, about letting her come with him.

"Do I look the least bit shocked? Just tell us what we need to know. Pretend I'm not even here."

Joe took a breath and squared his shoulders. "I hated sharing her with Martone. That's what you're going to ask next, right? Mary made her bargain while we were apart. She thought she'd never find anyone she loved as much as me, and Eddie was nice to her. At first. He bought her things and made a lot of promises. She already wanted to get away from him before we met up again, but she was afraid of what he'd do. When we got together a few weeks ago, there was no way around it. She managed to keep him away from her. Just like I was staying away from Camille. We had our plan to skip town and focused on that."

Harry nodded. "How did her bargain with Martone work exactly?"

"He paid her rent, bought her clothes, and bobbles. What she needed to look good on stage, to get ahead. Gem helped her first. He taught her about using her voice, how to put a song over, how to act on stage, and all that. Though even he admits she's a natural. He put her forward with his band. But it helped him, too. People were coming in to hear Mary, not the Music Makers. Even though they're good, don't get me wrong. Mary was loyal to Gem, too. She had offers to sing at better venues but wouldn't go without him. Mary caught Eddie's eye, and he convinced her he could do more. He said he knew people in the business and paid for a recording, finally. Then held on to it, just to torture her."

Joe drew on his cigarette and tapped off the ash. He had more to say, and Harry didn't interrupt him. "The only way to protect her was to take her so far away, he couldn't track us down. He's a cruel, shrewd bastard. Mary was afraid he'd find a way to make her pay, no matter where we went. He'd said as much, plenty of times."

Grace remembered the fear in Mary's eyes, the night they'd met, and her heart ached. Fear she hadn't understood at the time. Mary walked around the world looking as free as anyone, but she'd been a prisoner as much as Joe was now.

Some might blame her for the deal she'd struck with Eddie Martone. Grace didn't. What power did women have in this world? Sure, some women could get where they wanted, without a man's help. But not many. Especially a colored girl.

Mary had almost broken free, too. Almost, but not quite. Grace thought she might cry hearing the whole story.

But not in front of Joe and certainly not, Harry. He was letting her work on Joe's case. She wouldn't give him a reason to exclude her.

Chapter Fifteen

They left the prison in silence, the same way they'd come in, passing through checkpoints where they signed registry books and collected belongings that weren't permitted inside.

It had been raining on the ride over, but the clouds had cleared, and they stepped into the cool shadows of a spring evening. A violet haze lingered on the horizon; the jagged outlines of the prison buildings lit by the setting sun.

The putrid smell was worse outside, much worse. Like rotten eggs, wafting up from the rough earth.

"Until the mid-1930's, a fair amount of the city's garbage was dumped here, just beyond the prison walls," Harry had explained. "LaGuardia cleaned it up, but the trash returned as landfill when other politicians decided to expand the island and the prison. They didn't realize the methane and stench would never stop rising from the ground."

"Or they just didn't care?" Grace had asked.

"That, too," Harry had agreed.

She couldn't stand thinking of Joe stuck in this place for months. She worried about his moods. He'd already said he had no reason to live. What if he tried to harm himself? Who would stop him? She didn't know how he'd manage to stay sane. Especially without his music.

They had to get him out. They had to find out who killed Mary and get him home before something awful happened to him, too.

She glanced at Harry as they followed a path to the landing. "What now?"

"We jump on the next ferry and get the hell out of here."

They found a place on deck at the rail and watched as the hands untied heavy ropes. The ferry set off at a slow chug, and Grace felt relieved to breath the fresh air over the river and watch the island drift away.

Harry managed to light a cigarette, cupping his hand around the flame, and barely managed to save his hat when a stiff breeze caught it.

"What do you think?" he asked finally.

She was surprised he was interested in her opinion, though she certainly had one. "Joe is convinced Eddie ordered one of his thugs to kill Mary. I can believe that. But I don't think it was because of their affair. If that was the case, why not kill Joe? I saw Eddie with Mary," she continued. "The way he spoke to her and handled her. As if she was his wind-up doll. It wouldn't make sense to destroy a favorite plaything, and one he invested money in, too."

Harry puffed his smoke and nodded. "One way to see it. Though I wouldn't credit Martone with too much logic or self-control. Why do you think Martone wanted her out of the way?"

"Because she knew about something he's up to, maybe something going on at the club." Her hair blew across her cheek, and she pushed it back with her hand. The damp breeze would whip it into a mass of curls by the time they docked. No help for that. "More than the poker games and prostitutes. I think Mary knew about something bigger, and it was too dangerous for him."

"Maybe she tried to blackmail Martone. Sounds to me like she and your brother needed cash for their new start."

Grace gave him a look. "It'd be a miracle if he saved enough for a ticket. Mary probably picked up that tab. Still, I don't see her as the blackmailing type, and it would have been a huge risk. She truly feared Martone. And she was going away with Joe in a few days. Someplace where Martone couldn't find them. Like Joe said, 'why rattle the hornet's nest?'"

He took another drag on his cigarette. "You've got this all worked out, Grace. I don't know why you even took me along."

His sarcasm irked, but she couldn't help smiling. Then he smiled, too. "I haven't thought of anything else since Joe was arrested. I even dream about it."

"I'll bet." His voice softened with a note of sympathy. "What you say makes sense. It's a valid line of inquiry. But one the police checked off their list. Eddie's ties to Mary surfaced quickly. But he alibied out, and the cops didn't see a motive. Not to say there isn't one. They just like Joe better and built a strong case against him. Despite his denial, they have no incentive to look further."

"But you do," she pressed.

"My job isn't finding the guy who really killed Mary and dragging him into a police station, like some hero detective in a comic strip. Kramer pays me to dig up dirt, enough to create doubt that Joe did it. To show a jury there were other people in Mary's life who might have killed her. Beyond Joe, or even Eddie Martone."

Grace already knew that. But she still didn't think that was the best way to help her brother.

"I'm sorry, Harry. I know you're taking on this work as a favor." When he could be earning easy money with clients like Roger Ingersoll. "But it sounds like you're giving up before you even start."

"I'm being honest, Grace. And realistic. I'm telling you fair and square how these things pan out." He glanced at her. "I thought that's what you wanted. To be on the inside."

"You know I do."

He leaned on the rail and tucked his tie under his jacket. "The bottom line is Eddie Martone might be hauled into court now and then for show. But he's out like a ping pong ball. His father, Leo, shook all the right hands. He had plenty of cops and even a judge or two in his pocket. When Leo was sent up, all Eddie had to do was keep up the payroll. He's not going down for this, even if we hand over a photo finish."

"I get your point. But I'm not talking about his usual bad behavior. I think there's something a lot worse going on. Too big for Eddie's protectors to shove under the rug. He can't own every cop and judge in the city."

Grace knew that she sounded desperate. Maybe even naïve. Something a hysterical woman would say. But she couldn't hide her feelings and saw no reason to. Harry remained distant and cynical. She hated that. He had to see Joe's future was hanging by a thread.

He and Joe had both seen men die every day, blown to bits before their eyes. Death was a familiar face, just a few stools down the bar, sipping a whiskey neat, bidding his time.

Perhaps from Harry's point of view, Joe's fate was cast, no matter how hard they tried to save him.

"Mary had relationships besides Eddie and Joe," he said. "She had secrets. We all do. Once I dig a little deeper, it should help Joe's case. It usually does."

Grace didn't like the sound of that. "I didn't think Mary was on trial here. That doesn't sound fair. Or respectful."

He took a last puff and flicked the butt into the murky green river. "Mary's gone; may she rest in peace. We're fighting to save Joe now. Aren't we?"

"I know my brother. That's not the kind of help he wants. If he was willing to toss Mary under the bus to save himself, he would have taken the plea deal."

"He still could," Harry pointed out.

"You think he should. Even though he's innocent."

"It's not right or fair, but innocent may not be enough. I'd never push him to take it if that's what you're asking."

"I don't think you would. But is that what you'd do?"

"If it would take twenty years off a jail term, or keep me out of the chair, I might say I took a life by accident, or even in self-defense. I admire his noble stand. But poor Mary is gone. It won't help her now."

"It's funny that you should say that, Harry." Grace tried to catch his gaze, but he kept his eyes fixed on the low brown skyline of Greenwich Village, drawing closer. "You talk like a guy who looks for the easy way out. According to Joe, you're anything but. He told me what you did to save your men. He said it was a miracle you survived."

Harry looked uncomfortable. She wondered if he was angry that she'd brought up his battlefield heroics.

"I'm sure by the time Joe was done, I'd beat back the entire Third Reich."

"It sounded like there were enough of them."

"At a moment like that, you don't have time to think. Joe and the rest depended on me. You take your chance and hope for the best. Over there, it always seemed better to die trying."

"Maybe it's the same for my brother. Maybe he's willing to die trying to prove his innocence, instead of confessing to a murder he didn't commit. And smearing the reputation and memory of a woman he loves with all his heart and soul."

"I think that's exactly how he sees it." Harry sounded unhappy to agree.

The ferry glided into the slip, then rocked a bit when the hull hit the pier. As the crew hopped out and tied up, Grace and Harry moved with the flow of passengers down to the dock.

When they reached the street, Harry said, "Care for a drink? I know a bar nearby."

"I can't remember when I needed one more."

He smiled and put his hat on. After they crossed, he said, "I know you won't like this, Grace, but I'm going to close the office. I'll be out most of the time, who knows where, and you should be home with your family. They need you right now."

The announcement blindsided her. Grace had a feeling something else was going on, but knew it was pointless to ask. "I can still answer the phone and all the rest. I'd think you'd want me there if you're out so much."

"The front desk can handle it. It should only be a few days."

Grace felt her temper rise. Considering what had happened in the last twenty-four hours, a few days felt like forever.

"I thought I was going to work on Joe's case. Be on the inside. Isn't that what you just said?" She was angry and couldn't help showing it. "Now you're shutting me out?"

"You can help, Grace. Down the line. You asked good questions in there. And I knew you wanted to see Joe." He glanced at her as they walked. "It will only be a few days. I'm not sure how long exactly. I'll pay you in advance for the week. I'm sorry, but this is the way I have to play it."

His expression tightened. He'd obviously expected she'd be "nice" and not argue with him. The truth was, she had no choice. If he didn't want her involved, she was out. Period.

"You have enough on your plate, without doing my job, too." His tone was conciliatory, but Grace couldn't let go of her anger.

"I'm supposed to wait at home and do what exactly? Say the rosary all day with my grandmother?"

"I know you don't understand. There are reasons. Good ones."

She didn't ask him to clarify. She knew he wouldn't.

Her thoughts flew ahead, picturing the long days and nights with her family, doing nothing. She already felt smothered and frustrated.

Damn Harry Shaw. She'd figure out some way to help Joe, with or without his blessing. She stared straight ahead, secretly calculating and so mad she could spit.

They'd come to a red light and waited to cross. "I'm going to pass on that drink. It's getting late."

"Sure. I'll walk you to the subway."

"That's all right. I know the way." The light had turned green, and she left him on the corner. "See you, Harry," she called over her shoulder.

"Good night, Grace. I'll be in touch."

She heard his reply but didn't answer. Or look back.

Chapter Sixteen

Fort Greene was only a few miles from her neighborhood, two or three stops from the Carroll Street Station, but Grace had rarely ventured there. She emerged on DeKalb Avenue and decided to ask for directions.

An old, colored woman walked towards her, pushing a baby carriage. Her directions to the church were brief and clear. Grace was nearly there.

"I heard there's a funeral today. That girl from the neighborhood, stabbed up in Harlem."

"Mary Delmore," Grace said quietly.

"I don't know the family. But people say she sang like an angel." Her hand flitted down light as a bird's wing to smooth the baby's blanket. "She's singing on a cloud now, rest her soul."

Grace pictured Mary in a sequined gown, harmonizing with an angelic choir. Would she follow their celestial score, or lead them in a jazzier riff?

"I'll say a prayer," the woman added.

Grace thanked her and moved on, down a tree-lined street of brownstone buildings, some in disrepair but most well cared for, humming with life. A big orange cat sat between lace curtains, licking its paws. Spring flowers spilled from window boxes and bloomed in sidewalk gardens.

Three men worked around a pile of bricks and a wheelbarrow filled with wet cement. Further along, a flock of little girls in cotton dresses jumped rope in a school yard, singing "Miss Mary Mack." Braided plaits bounced in rhythm with the rhymes.

A woman appeared in a doorway; a yellow kerchief tied over her hair. She stared at Grace, unsmiling. But waited for her to pass before she tossed a bucket of soapy water on a flight of steps, then swept her way down with short, quick strokes.

Grace had been uneasy coming here but felt foolish now. The cars and clothes looked a bit poorer perhaps, but the street was more alike than different from Sackett Street.

A block or two further, the church came into view—white clapboard, with a narrow steeple rising from the peaked roof. Set back from the street on a long, narrow plot, it could have been plucked from a country road and dropped on the city lot by some unseen hand. A sign in front read, Bethel AME Church, and on the next line, Reverend Lester Holmes. Under that, the hours of Sunday service, bible school, and choir practice were listed.

On the sidewalk in front, solemn men in dark suits and bright white shirts stood near a long black hearse, waiting to carry Mary's coffin inside. A stream of mourners in their Sunday best walked up the path to the large wooden doors. Grace followed, relieved that she was not late.

The sanctuary was small, too small for the crowd that continued to swell. The church was as simple inside as it was out. None of the ornate plaster moldings, stained glass, and gilded touches she was accustomed to. No shadowy alcoves with statues of the Virgin or martyred saints, encircled by smoldering candles.

Still, it was a holy place, perhaps more so for its humility. A wooden pulpit on one side, choir rafters on the other, an altar table covered with a white cloth in between.

The singers stood ready, in long black robes, music sheets in hand. Just in front of them, a man seated at an organ played a simple hymn as the mourners filed in.

The large wooden cross that hung on the wall behind the altar table was empty, she noticed. Missing the sculpture of Jesus that always met her view; bloody head and hands, eyes rolled up, gazing to heaven in pious confusion. Grace found its absence a surprising relief.

Rows of benches lined each side of a center aisle. She recognized Gem Washington, the band leader from The Starlight Room. He sat with a few men who looked like musicians.

She didn't intentionally search for a spot near a white face. There were some, though not many. A voice on the aisle whispered, "Room for you here, honey. I can scoot over."

A woman about her own age caught Grace's gaze. Her mouth outlined in coral lipstick matched bright, wavy hair, a small black fascinator pinned on the back of her head. Grace thanked her and sat, placing her purse in her lap.

She looked around for Eddie Martone but was not surprised at his absence. She wondered if he'd sent the grandest flower arrangement, a spray of white gladiola and long-stemmed pink roses. The one she'd sent from Joe was modest but elegant, a bouquet of white lilies in a tall vase. She was pleased to see it placed at the altar along with the rest. Perhaps because his name was not on the card. "Forever loved, never forgotten." was all that the message read.

Her neighbor leaned closer. "I hate these things."

"It's never easy, but much worse for her family," Grace said.

"I'll say. Especially the way she went out. How did you know Lana, if you don't mind me asking?"

Grace wasn't sure how to answer. She hated to lie in a church, no less. But if anyone knew she was Joe's sister, she'd probably be thrown out.

"I knew her in high school. We sat together in Home Ec."

"That's nice. I don't keep up much with my school friends. I didn't know her long, but she was one sweet gal. Heart of gold. People always say that, especially when someone dies. But it was true about Lana. She was the type who would always help you out if she could, whether you needed a safety pin to fix a garter or a few bucks till pay day."

The redhead smiled but seemed sad, remembering. "My name is Suzie, by the way. Suzie Kurtz."

"Grace." She offered a smile in place of her last name. "You work at The Starlight?"

"Just the cigarette girl. I'm really an actress, but you need to pay the rent till Hollywood calls, right? I quit last night. My boyfriend made me, because of what happened to Lana. It spooked him. It spooked me, too, to tell you the truth."

"It was awful. But the police say they caught the guy who killed her. What does the club have to do with it?"

Suzie smoothed her gloves. "I don't know exactly. And I don't want to know. Let's leave it at that."

Grace ached to ask more, but a piercing organ note signaled the start of the service. The mourners rose as the choir began to sing, "Precious Lord, Take My Hand."

A choir member stepped forward to lead the group. Her hair was gathered in a tight bun, emphasizing a pretty face and large, dark eyes. Her long robe covered a full figure, but she moved with grace, gesturing with her hands as she sang in a rich, soulful soprano. The choir joined again, the organ notes rising, as the vibrant sound filled the sanctuary to the vaulted ceiling. Grace felt the notes to her bones. She'd rarely known such a thing.

All heads turned as the pallbearers appeared at the back of the church. Mary's shiny coffin rested on their shoulders. They walked to the altar in slow, measured steps, followed by Mary's family. Her parents, side by side. A sheer black veil from her mother's hat covered her face, but Grace could still discern a striking resemblance to her daughter. Mary's father, stoic but weary-looking, supported his wife by her arm.

Behind them, a grandmother and other relatives, aunts, uncles, cousins. This was the family Mary had described, with high hopes for their daughter. Mainly, that she'd settle down and marry a respectable man, have children, and lead a happy life.

Would they ever have approved of Joe? Nobody would know now.

A minister in a black robe, a black tippet draped over his shoulders, stood at the top of the center aisle. Mary had spoken of him, too, her former boyfriend, Lester Holmes. He met Mary's family as they took their seats in the front row and embraced each in turn. A tall man with broad shoulders and a strong jaw, his expression was solemn, his demeanor dignified as befitted the occasion, though Grace got the sense such was his temperament.

Grace's heart went out to Mary's family. Especially her mother, with her head bowed and shoulders shaking as she quietly wept. It wasn't right for parents to outlive their children. It was positively unnatural.

The choir began a second hymn, *"There is a balm in Gilead to make the wounded whole. There is a balm in Gilead, to heal the sin-sick soul..."*

Grace had never heard the song before, certainly not in St. Rocco's. She found the melody and lyrics comforting. When the hymn ended, Reverend Holmes led the congregation in the Lord's Prayer. There were scripture readings at the pulpit by Mary's Aunt Lottie and her brother, Cyril, a big man with broad shoulders that strained his suit jacket. Grace recalled that he'd fought overseas and now worked moving furniture. This morning, he'd help carry his sister's coffin into the church.

The reverend took the pulpit again. He stared down a moment to gather his thoughts, though Grace noticed he spoke without notes.

"We're gathered in the Lord's house today to bid farewell to our dear sister, Mary Delmore. A joyful farewell. Mary's gone home now, bless her soul. To the Lord's everlasting mercy, care, and love."

The first few shouts startled her.

"Amen, brother!"

"Hallelujah! She's gone home."

Grace glanced around to see who'd called out, then realized no one found the interruptions disrespectful or untoward.

"It was just a few weeks ago, on Easter Sunday, that Mary came home to us. She took her place with our choir and lifted our spirits with her remarkable singing, bringing joy and beauty into this world. That's what Mary did. That was the gift Mary gave so freely."

He paused; his head bowed. "She was taken from us much too soon. Most especially and painfully, from her family: her dear mother, Adelaide, her father, James, and brother, Cyril. We pray that God enfolds their grieving hearts in his love and grants them acceptance for what they cannot change or understand.

"Who understands the mystery of God's ways? Or his plan for our lives? I'm not afraid to admit I'm often baffled. That's when I fall back on my faith and remember God's outstretched hand is there to catch me, lest I sink into despair.

"My heart is heavy this morning, thinking of Mary and the tragic end to her short life. Almost too heavy to deliver these words. But scripture tells us, there is a plan and a purpose to everything under heaven. All that befalls us, good and bad. God had a purpose for calling Mary to his side. And in such a way."

He paused; his gaze swept over the sanctuary.

"I hear tongues wagging, and I pray for those who judge her. *Judge not, and ye shall not be judged.* God doesn't need us to do his job. Our job down here is to lift each other up. There are more than enough folks out there ready and eager to knock us down." He pointed to the doors at the back of the sanctuary with a sweeping gesture. "More than enough."

He stepped back and took a breath, then squared his shoulders again.

"Mary stands before him now to answer. Just like I will, and all of you sitting under this roof right now. And out there, too, beneath the roof of the blue sky. Mary will answer to our Lord, and only to Him, for her good deeds and misdeeds. For her triumphs and missteps. He alone will judge her.

"Here and now, we can only give thanks to God from the depths of our hearts for the gift of Mary Delmore, for allowing her to walk among us on this green earth for even a short while. For her light, that made the world so much brighter. For her kind heart, beautiful voice, and gentle spirit. That is how I will remember our sister, Mary. May she rest in eternal peace, in His love. Amen."

There were more shouts of affirmation as the choir began to sing, *"Amazing Grace, how sweet the sound, that saved a wretch like me....I once was lost, but now am found, was blind but now I see..."*

When Reverend Holmes stepped down from the pulpit, Grace noticed tears in his eyes.

The coffin was carried out and the aisles filled with mourners, following Mary's family. Grace followed Suzie out of their row, then outside to the fresh air and sunlight. She watched Mary's coffin loaded into the hearse. The Delmores climbed into an old gray Ford to follow.

Grace looked around for Suzie, but the redhead had disappeared into the scattering crowd. Grace retraced her path to DeKalb Avenue. The shade had deepened, and the cool breeze felt refreshing. The orange cat was gone from the window, as well as the housewife washing the steps. But little girls—a different group, she guessed—were still jumping rope in the school yard. Their rhythmic chant blended with the slap of the ragged rope as it struck the ground.

The funeral had left her feeling sad and unfocused. She wanted to help Joe but had no idea what to do. She felt annoyed again at Harry for leaving her high and dry.

She had not known Mary well, but felt certain the last thing Joe's true love would have wanted was to see him unjustly punished for her death. To see the love they'd shared degraded and defamed, twisted into an ugly picture.

She trotted down the subway steps but couldn't head home to Sackett Street. She pushed through the turnstile that led to the westbound trains instead, into the city.

A headlamp appeared down the tunnel, and a train rushed up with a dank-smelling gust and came to a screeching stop. Grace stepped into a car that was nearly empty and took a seat.

Placards above the windows advertised Budget Pest Control and the Miss Rheingold contest. Last year's Miss Rheingold looked a little like Suzie Kurtz, Grace thought. Which gave her an idea.

A good one, too.

Chapter Seventeen

"I heard there's a job here. For a cigarette girl?"

Grace had tried the club's front entrance, but when no one answered, she walked down the alley and knocked on the side door. A colored girl appeared, about Rose's age, a long white apron was tied around her slim waist, the white cloth on her head, edged with black curls. She met Grace's gaze a moment, then let her in, unsmiling but still somehow friendly.

"You need to see Judy. Miss Stemple, I mean. She manages the front of the house. Come in, I'll show you." The girl waved a slim hand, and Grace followed.

The cook and his helpers moved about the kitchen in a well-choreographed dance, complete with the music of clanging pots and cooking sounds. Grace recognized the man who had opened the door when she'd come to see Mary. The lumpy head, jutting jaw, and tattoo-covered arms were hard to forget. He chopped meat on a wooden block, his apron splattered with blood. Luckily, he was focused on his task and didn't notice her.

Grace followed the girl down the narrow hallway that Grace knew led to Mary's dressing room.

"The dining room is through the double doors at the end. Judy's out there, somewhere. Don't let her scare you," her guide added. "She can be moody and gets her back up, like a cat."

Before Grace could answer, the tattooed man shouted from the kitchen, the bloody cleaver hanging from his hand.

"Cut the chatter, Sylvie, and bring up those damned onions. You didn't even peel the frigging potatoes yet."

"The potatoes are peeled and boiling, Hubie." Under her breath, the girl added, "You better watch 'em, before they turn to mush and you blame me for that, too."

Grace tried to catch her gaze, but the girl ducked her head. She pulled open a door and disappeared, like Alice down the rabbit hole. The scent of a damp cellar wafted up the stairwell.

Grace continued down the passageway; the door to Mary's dressing room stood open a crack. She spotted the rack of elegant gowns and could almost smell Mary's perfume. A sign in front of the club advertised a new singer, Dolores Hayes. Grace was surprised and saddened to see how quickly Mary had been replaced. She doubted any singer could.

But the girl applying for this job had never known Mary Delmore…or Lana Delmar, she reminded herself. Only what she'd read in the newspapers.

The club looked different in the daytime, without the camouflage of spinning stars and glistening satin. Like an aging actress, bare of make-up and glamorous trappings.

The room was empty, except for a blonde who stood at a table, sorting wooden coat checks on the cloth. Tall and slim, her thick, shiny hair was parted on the side, and her figure rivaled any movie star.

"Miss Stemple? Suzie Kurtz told me that you need a new cigarette girl?" Grace's words came out in a rush, punctuated by the sweetest smile she could conjure.

A cigarette dangled from red lips. She tapped it on an ashtray, taking her time before she looked up. "Are you a friend of hers?"

"Not exactly." Grace took care with her reply. "We're in the same acting class. She told me that she quit her job here last night."

"Just what I need, another actress." Judy rolled her eyes, pale blue, shaded by thick lashes and penciled brows. "You girls don't get it till it's too late. Then you wake up one day, and you've wasted your whole life, hanging up some other dame's fur coat."

Grace got the feeling she'd just heard Judy Stemple's life story. She wasn't sure what to say.

"What's your name?"

"Lucille Bianco. Everyone calls me Lucy." Grace had decided to use her best friend's name as an alias. Russo was out of the question. "I have some sales experience. I worked in a department store on Fifth Avenue, Bergdorf Goodman." That part at least was true. "I'm sure I could do a good job for you."

"Fifth Avenue, huh? *La-di-da.*" She puffed her cigarette and squinted at Grace through the smoke. "Ever wait tables, princess?"

"I was a waitress at a luncheonette in Red Hook, on Court Street. And a place in the same neighborhood called Mario's."

Grace hoped the references would not be checked quickly, or at all. Grace Russo had waited tables at those places, but no one would know Lucy Bianco.

Judy frowned, and Grace watched as the last wooden chip was matched to its mate, a strange version of solitaire. Judy stepped closer and looked Grace over, as if she was a leg of lamb hanging in Funicello's window.

It hadn't made sense to go back to Brooklyn to change from the somber black suit and silk blouse she'd worn for the funeral. She'd ducked into Woolworth's, picked out an armload of accessories, and done herself over in the restroom there.

A red, polka dot scarf was tied around her neck, the collar of the blouse flipped up. Her sedate pearl earrings replaced by cheap gold hoops that would certainly leave green marks by the end of the day. She'd removed a demure black hat and fluffed out her hair. The crowning touch was new lipstick, Havana Nights, applied with a heavy hand. As Judy looked her over, Grace wondered if she'd gone too far.

"Wait here." Judy disappeared into the check room and returned with a shimmery blue dress. The strapless bodice, cinched waist, and flared skirt, lined with rustling crinoline layers, reminded Grace of the Cupie dolls given out as prizes at St. Rocco's bazaar.

"See if this fits. And don't bust the zipper trying." Judy glanced at Grace's hips. "Powder room is up that way." She pointed with a coat hanger.

Stripped to her panty girdle and stockings, Grace felt like Cinderella, facing the glass slipper. She pulled the dress over her head and sucked in a breath as she inched up the zipper.

The hook at the top wouldn't catch, but she found a safety pin in her purse and made do. If she held her left arm straight down, maybe Judy wouldn't notice?

Her breasts spilled over the heart-shaped neckline, and she tugged the fabric up. "If the nuns at St. Rocco's could see you now. They wouldn't know whether to hit you with a wooden ruler or pray for your lost soul."

A few moments later, Judy inspected her appearance. A navy-blue shirtwaist dress, with big black buttons and a patent leather belt, suited her air of authority.

Grace waited for the verdict, still holding her breath.

The cigarette tray sat on a nearby table, the fresh packs arranged in neat, colorful rows. Judy picked up a blue satin sash and clipped the ends to the tray.

"Put this on. Let me see you walk with it."

Grace slipped the sash on, then balanced the tray across her middle just below her chest. She took a few tentative steps. It was hard to look straight out and not down at the tray. She gripped the edges, trying to keep the tray level.

"For goodness sakes, you walk like a longshoreman. Didn't anyone ever teach you how to move across a stage?"

Grace turned, the tray spinning with her. She caught it just before the packs spilled to the floor.

"I didn't get to that class yet."

"You're kidding me, right?" Judy sounded unconvinced. Was her cover blown already?

Judy slipped the strap off Grace and put it over her own shoulders. Then strolled about the dance floor as smoothly as a swan gliding over a pond. At the stage, she turned on her heel and retraced her path between the tables, chin up, shoulders back, long legs swinging out from her hips. She was tall, as tall as a man but moved with fluid ease.

"This is how it's done." Before Grace could answer, she added. "I know these days they say acting is all about your pathetic little feelings. All that psychological mumbo jumbo. But you still need to sing and dance and walk a straight line without falling on your face."

Grace had never been compared to a dock worker, though as a teenager, she'd been scolded about her posture.

Grace met Judy's gaze and smiled. "That's good advice. Are you an actress?"

Grace caught herself just before phrasing the question in the past tense, which surely would have been an insult.

"I was a dancer. A professional. Not some two-bit contest winner. I danced in Broadway shows and at Radio City."

"A Rockette?"

"That's right. Four shows a day, six on Sunday. Not so long ago, either."

Grace was impressed. Her stage struck, alter ego, Lucy was, too, even more. "Wow, that's really something."

"Yeah, sure. That and a nickel gets me on the subway. Now I have metal pins in my back. But I can still walk across a room like a lady. Which is more than I'd say for some people."

Grace bristled at being chided again and by a stranger, no less, but held her tongue.

"I'll practice at home. With a book on my head." She and Rose had once run races across the living room that way after reading an article in a beauty magazine.

One corner of Judy's mouth turned up in a begrudging smile. Grace already thought she was pretty, but she was more than that, even though she was no longer young. In her mid-thirties at least, though her glamorous looks belied that number.

"A book on your head, huh? You'd better use the yellow pages. Can you start tonight?"

Grace was surprised, but quickly nodded. "Absolutely. I'd love to."

Judy almost smiled again, more of a sneer. She thought she was getting the upper hand on Lucy Bianco. Grace let her think so. Even when Judy named a pitifully low wage, Lucy didn't bargain.

"You'll make it up in tips with that figure. Be polite, but don't flirt. No drinking on the job. Even if Rockefeller's buying. You're not here to find a sugar daddy, understand?"

"Of course not."

Judy looked doubtful, as if she'd heard that denial before. Judy had found her sugar daddy, Grace noticed; one who'd given her a large, square-cut diamond she wore on her left hand. A real rock, Rose would say.

"If a fella gets fresh, don't fly off the handle. You be nice. Bernard will take care of it. Mr. Martone, the owner, doesn't like a scene."

Grace doubted she'd be "nice"—she'd be anything but. But didn't interrupt as Judy reviewed the rest of the employee rules, including her hours, which were long, days off, which were few, and punching the time clock, which was required if she wanted to get paid.

"I'll show you how to set up the tray tonight. Get here early. Arty, the bartender, will change the big bills. He flirts with anything in a skirt. Don't take him seriously."

"I won't. I have a steady."

"Good. What's his name?"

Colin, Grace nearly replied. But it felt disrespectful to his memory. "Harry," she said as the name popped into her head.

"Tell Harry not to visit. No free booze here. He'll only distract you. Pauline runs the check room. Be nice to her. She's Mr. Martone's third cousin or something. You know those Italians." She pronounced the word, eye-talians. "She's not very bright. If you have any questions, ask me."

There was a free meal each night for the staff, and there might have been more. Grace had stopped listening. She couldn't wait to take off the Cupie doll dress. How would she wear it for six or seven hours at a stretch?

When Judy was finished, Grace said, "Thank you so much for the job, Miss Stemple."

"You can call me Judy. Don't thank me yet; Mr. Martone has to meet you. Think of the first week as an audition."

"I understand. I'll do my best."

With any luck, a week was all she'd need.

* * *

Late-day sunlight filtered through the trees as Grace made her way up the side street. She turned on Broadway and walked towards Times Square.

She slipped into the first phone booth she saw to shed her costume. Like Superman, she realized. The gypsy earrings and scarf were saved in the shopping bag. With the black suit jacket and hat back in place, she felt herself again.

The entrance to the B train was in sight, but Grace still wasn't ready to return to Red Hook and the drama waiting there. She wondered if Harry had made any progress with Joe's case today. Was he even working on it?

He'd probably be impressed that she'd talked her way into a job at The Starlight Room but would insist she didn't follow through. Just as well he wasn't around to tell her what to do.

She slipped a nickel in the phone and dialed the office, wondering if he was carrying on as usual and ducking her for some reason.

The line rang twice. A switchboard operator picked up. "Harry Shaw and Associates."

"Hello, Dora, it's Grace. Was Harry in today?"

"I haven't seen him. We were told to take all calls. Do you want to talk to Betty?"

A moment later, Betty's crisp tone greeted her. "Harry left you a check. I'm holding it up front."

He'd mentioned something about paying her for the week. Grace had been so angry, the gesture had barely registered.

"Did he say when he'll be back?"

"Not to me." Betty sounded confused, as if Grace should know the answer to that. "Not many calls, but a package came by messenger. From a law office. It's marked 'Confidential.'"

"From Martin Kramer?"

"That's right."

The police report and photographs, all the evidence collected against Joe. "I'd better look at that. I'm in the neighborhood, I'll be right over."

Grace was out of the booth before her nickel dropped. She rushed down Broadway, weaving around slow walkers.

From conversations with Martin Kramer and Harry, she already had a rough idea of what she'd find in the package. But maybe she'd spot some small detail the police had missed. Not missed, but had intentionally ignored or brushed aside, hellbent on proving her brother guilty.

Would Harry have willingly shared the information? She couldn't say. But she was glad now he'd gone AWOL, and she didn't need to ask him.

Chapter Eighteen

He found her in the usual place, sitting on a bench in the shade of a tall oak. Oblivious to the view, the majestic Hudson, edged by soft brown cliffs. A crochet hook and strand of yarn in her hands, she frowned over the task like a child. The nuns said it kept her calm, though she looked anything but to Harry. She'd never been the type of woman who liked handwork. She could barely darn a sock or sew a button on his shirt. Or iron one, for that matter. That was not why he'd married her.

Dappled light outlined the curve of her cheek. He missed her long hair, the way it fell across her face when she dipped her head. She'd fret at the bathroom mirror, rolling it up in all sorts of contraptions, though it would never hold a curl for long. He always told her it was wonderful, but she never believed him.

The nuns had cut her hair short as a boy's. They didn't even ask him. "It's hard to keep her clean and tidy, Mr. Shaw. I'm sure you understand." The mean one, Sister St. Ignatius, always went the extra step to make him feel ungrateful. And guilty. As if he was to blame that she was there.

She didn't blame him. She didn't remember anything of her life before. Or their life together. She barely recognized him from week to week and didn't even remember that he was her husband. Or, what the word meant.

"I know it's hard, Mr. Shaw. But it's a blessing in a way," the nun had once said.

"If this is the way your God blesses us poor suckers, send me straight to hell," he'd almost answered. He was headed in that direction anyhow. It was pointless to argue.

He usually came on Sunday, the designated visiting day. Safety in numbers, he'd always felt. But Dr. Conklin had wanted to talk in person. A brief but devastating consultation, complete with x-rays, a short, blunt diagnosis, and the doctor's sympathy. Harry felt sick to his stomach. More so, facing her now.

"You have a visitor, Laura." Sister Bernadette announced in a mild tone. She was a nice one, Harry recalled.

Laura lifted her head, her expression curious. "It's your husband," the nun added.

He didn't wait to see if she remembered his name. It was too hard. "Hello, honey. How are you doing?"

He forced a smile, and she glanced at him briefly, then down at the yarn and hook again. He walked closer, hat in hand. "May I sit with you awhile?"

Laura shrugged and looked at the nun.

"Of course, you can, Mr. Shaw," Sister answered. "I'll be on the porch if you need me."

The reassurance was as much for Laura's sake as his own. She could explode with rage over nothing. Violent and irrational. It was hard to settle her when she got that way.

Sometimes she'd have a real fit. Epilepsy. The head injury caused it. Even with the drugs, it wasn't controlled completely.

"A storm in her brain," the doctor said. "She's lucky to be alive."

The textbook definition, he should have added. This wasn't a real life. It seemed the very opposite to Harry. Worse than death in a way.

Her face looked thin; her complexion sallow. She'd once had such beautiful skin, a real Irish rose. But it could have been the shadows in the shade, or the brown cardigan they'd dressed her in. She hated that color. It broke his heart a little to see the round white collar that folded over the top of the sweater's edge, like a school uniform. Broke his heart a little more if that was possible.

She used to read him like a book, the slightest frown or sigh. She always knew when something was eating him. She didn't have the slightest notion now. Barely met his gaze. Even if he told her, she wouldn't understand.

He sat on the other side of the bench and set his gift between them. "This is for you."

She glanced at the paper bag but continued stitching. Did she remember what was in it? Fruit, every time, the same kind, too. They said that would help her remember him.

Once he'd brought her a box of chocolate-covered cherries, so sweet they made his teeth ache. She'd always kept a box hidden in the pantry and ate them secretly. She hid Hershey bars all over the house, too. Maybe they tasted better that way. A guilty pleasure. As if she'd ever had anything to feel guilty about. He was sure she missed her chocolate more than she missed him.

The nuns said he couldn't bring sweets. "She eats too many at once and makes herself sick."

"Aren't you going to look inside?'

She took the bag and opened it. "Oranges. Right?"

"That's right." He lowered his voice. "And something else you like more."

He sat back and watched her face as she searched. She pulled out a Hershey bar and slipped it in her pocket.

"I'll save this."

"Good idea. Just don't show sister or I'll get in trouble."

"Don't worry." She met his gaze and nodded. As if he was the one that needed care and protection.

Her eyes were so blue, like the sky in late July. He could lose himself there, out of time and space, forgetting everything that had gone wrong, feeling like he used to feel. Like he yearned to feel but never would again.

She stared at the needle and yarn. "I have to do my work. Sister needs it."

"What are you making?"

She shrugged. "A square. Sister needs a lot of them." She showed him a few rows of stitches that could possibly end up as part of a quilt or a lap robe.

Like the one that covered her legs, despite the spring weather. Legs that once ran up and down the subway steps in high heels and anticipated his every move on a dance floor. Legs that crossed and uncrossed, with a swish of silk stockings. Long, smooth legs that wrapped around his body in the middle of the night.

Her feet, covered in brown oxfords, peeked out from the blanket's edge. They seemed to belong to another woman.

She pulled a length of yarn from the ball that sat on the bench between them. "When this is done, I'll make another."

And another. And another. Until…?

The doctor said she was losing ground. Her damaged liver and remaining kidney were wearing out. It was hard to say how long the battered organs would hold up.

"Dialysis might help for a while. But you'll have to move her to another facility. That would be confusing and upsetting for her, to say the least. And likely cause a setback in her cognition. Eventually, even that treatment won't be enough." He paused, letting the harsh facts sink in. "I'm sorry, son. There's no cure."

Harry already saw a yellowish cast to her complexion and the whites of her eyes. Was that his imagination? How long could she last? The doctor didn't know. Or didn't want to say.

The first time he'd set eyes on her must have been a Friday. Friday was pay day, and he'd gone into the bank near the station to cash his check. She sat behind a teller's window. Waiting to start his life for him. He'd line up at that window every Friday after, along with every other lug he worked with.

Tellers were watched closely. She wasn't allowed to make small talk with the customers, just "please" and "thank you." But he had a feeling from the way she looked down and smiled when he spoke that she liked him.

One day, he stood outside the bank and waited. She didn't look surprised to find him there. She let him walk her to a bus stop and ride with her to Queens, where she lived with her folks and her older sister. The next night, he took her to dinner. And that was that.

Two weeks later, they were married at City Hall. They knew he was going to be called up, and they didn't want to wait. The registry office was full of couples in the same boat, most of the grooms in uniform. She wore a pale pink suit and a hat with a floppy brim and carried a bouquet of white roses in her gloved hands. Her sister Kay was the maid of honor, and his partner from the force, Charles Byrd, the best man.

They drank a bottle of cheap champagne on the Staten Island Ferry and called it their honeymoon. Then went home to a three-room apartment, empty, except for a bed, and didn't leave all weekend.

Her mother had a fit. "You aren't really married without the blessing of the church. You're living in sin."

"That sounds like fun, Ma. Why is there so much cooking and laundry?"

His wife could make him laugh and even had a sharp tongue now and then. They'd argue, but it didn't mean much. They were happy for the short time they had together before he shipped out, even happier when he came back in one piece.

They thought the war was their biggest hurdle, the big question mark. And they got through it. Living in a fool's paradise, with no idea of what was barreling towards them.

She could be stubborn and didn't like it when she didn't get her way. Like taking the car to see Kay when she'd only got her license the week before. They'd had a row about it. He'd been out all night at Byrd's stag party and crawled in at five with a world-class hangover. He needed to sleep, not drive up to Tarrytown for no good reason. At least, that's what he'd thought at the time. He gave up arguing and went to bed.

"Suit yourself," he'd said. Or something like that.

The brake lines had been cut for him. Not her. Any way it played out—him, her, both—Leo Martone couldn't lose that bet.

The message came through, loud and clear. A message he'd ignored. Not ignored exactly; one he'd stood up to, defied. He'd made it through the war, for Christ sakes. Some two-bit mobster from Hell's Kitchen didn't scare him.

He found out he was wrong. There were consequences to telling the simple truth. Especially in a courtroom. The news that only she'd been hurt, and he'd been spared, had probably pleased Martone more. The bastard had stuck it to him even deeper that way. They both knew it.

He picked up the ball of yarn and wound the strand around his wrist. "I'm tied to you, Laura. You can't get rid of me now."

She looked surprised. "What did you do that for?"

He forced himself to smile, feeling he might cry. "Because…" He didn't know what else say. "Because I love you."

He did love her. More than ever, but in a different way than before.

She looked confused. And frightened. She dipped her head and stitched. "The bell will ring for dinner soon. Sister will come for me."

He slowly took the strand off his wrist and set the yarn back on the bench. "I'll wheel you in. What do you think?"

She shook her head and stared at her hands. "Sister will come. She'll come when the bell rings."

He'd expected that reply, but he had to try. Their visits usually ended this way. He pushed too hard, and she retreated beyond his reach.

He sat back, lit a cigarette, and watched her work. When the bell rang, Sister Bernadette walked across the lawn towards them. He rose and dropped a kiss on his wife's head. Her body tensed at the small, swift touch.

"Good-bye, sweetheart. I'll see you Sunday."

"Good-bye, Harry." She looked up and smiled, finally.

He smiled back but wouldn't fool himself. It was only her relief to see him go.

Chapter Nineteen

The nun had given him a list of things Laura needed—a new toothbrush, a full slip, socks, and underwear. White cotton, she'd instructed, like little girls wear. The sisters bleached everything. He passed the list to Kay with some bills. "And buy her something pretty. A new blouse or a dress. The clothes they make her wear look straight from a poor box."

Kay slipped the money in her apron pocket. "I'll make sure she looks nice next time you see her, Harry."

He appreciated Kay's help but always had mixed feelings about stopping here. It was exactly the sort of home Laura would have made for them, right down to the cup and saucer in front of him—creamy white China with pink roses, from a set the sisters had split after their mother died.

He would have found a job with regular hours, for an insurance company or a bank. They would have had kids by now. At least two. They'd already decided. Now, Laura's half of the china was in a box somewhere, and the life they'd imagined nowhere to be found.

"What do you think will happen, Harry? The doctor said, with that one kidney, it's just a matter of time and ..."

"I know, Kay. I had a long talk with him, too." Harry didn't mean to be sharp and felt sorry at the pinched look on her face. "I'm sorry... It's been a rough day."

She set a plate of cake by his cup and sat across from him. He didn't want the cake but took a bite to be polite and because he'd negotiated down from a meatloaf dinner.

"It's all right. I keep thinking it will get easier to see her, but it never does."

It only got harder. She didn't need to say it.

For a long time, he thought Laura would come back to herself bit by bit. Maybe not all the way, but enough for him to take her home. He'd find a woman to watch her during the day, and they'd sit together at night and talk, the way it used to be.

That was never going to happen. She wasn't going to get better, only worse, and faster than he'd expected. Day by day, she faded, like a chalk drawing some kid scrawled on the sidewalk. One day, he'd come to visit with his sack of oranges and the chocolate bar, and she'd be gone.

Kay sipped her coffee. She spoke quietly, as if Laura was nearby, listening. "I didn't notice any jaundice. Did you?"

"Not really." That wasn't true, but he didn't want to talk about it anymore.

"The nuns are good to her. They keep her comfortable and clean."

"I hope so." One day, he'd found a bruise on Laura's arm. Sister St. Ignatius explained that Laura had fallen during one of her spells. It didn't look like that kind of bruise to him; it looked like a handprint. There was no way to know what was going on there. Even if Laura could complain, she'd be afraid to cross her keepers. If his suspicions were ever confirmed, he'd wrap those beads around that nun's neck until her eyeballs popped out.

"I'd have her here, Harry. You know I would. Especially now." At the end, she meant. "But I couldn't manage when she gets in a state."

It wouldn't be a visit if Kay didn't say that. She felt as if she'd failed her little sister, and that meant he'd failed Laura, too. Even more.

Then he had to answer as he always did. "I know you would, Kay. I know you really want to. But you're not a nurse, and no one faults you. I certainly don't."

Kay seemed about to answer, then covered her mouth with her hand. Phil walked in the door, still in his green coveralls, hands stained with grime.

"Harry, old man. Good to see you." He washed at the sink, then grabbed a beer bottle out of the icebox. He offered one, but Harry declined. "Thanks, pal. I'm fine with the coffee."

He could have used a shot of whiskey but didn't want to ask. His brother-in-law was off the hard stuff these days. Though he did well enough with his Budweisers. A guy could be a lush drinking beer as soon as hard liquor. Not that it was any of his business.

It was just as well to skip the shot. It would be a long night, and he needed a clear head.

Phil slapped the cap off on the edge of the counter. "How's Laura? Kay said you came up to see the doctor."

"It's not good. Her kidney is failing. There's not much they can do."

"That poor girl. What she's been through." He took a long pull on the bottle and shook his head. "You, too, Harry. It's a damn crime the way that guy walked. It must eat you alive."

"Can't say I don't think about it." Harry knew it wasn't smart to admit even that much. Even to his in-laws. Especially tonight. But saying he didn't care or didn't think about it wouldn't sound right either.

"That bastard better get what's coming someday. I hope he burns in hell."

"Phil, please. Isn't Harry upset enough?" Kay gave her husband a look.

"Sure, he is. We all are. If there's no justice in this world, there's got to be in the next. Or what's the point? Right?"

Harry lit a smoke. He didn't want to debate theology tonight. But he didn't count on the scales being balanced in some sweet hereafter, where Laura would be put whole again. Laughing and beautiful, the way he'd known her. That was a fairy tale. A painting on a holy card, rays of light streaming out from behind the clouds.

There was nothing behind those clouds. How could there be? Not after what he'd seen on the battlefield. The camps. Hiroshima. How could any God worthy of the title let the train run so far off the rails?

Maybe He put the whole mess together on a whim and got bored. Like a negligent parent, going out for a drink while the little ones were left to fight it out on their own. To run with scissors, play with matches, cry themselves to sleep, believing some grown-up would creep into their bedroom sooner or later, and whisper, "Hush now, I'm back. Everything will be all right."

The truth was those children would wake to a cold, quiet house, all alone.

Justice for Laura would be dealt in the only game he was sure of. Here and now. Soon, and by his own hand.

He stubbed out the smoke and pushed back his chair. "It's getting late, folks. I don't want to hold up your supper."

Kay checked a pan in the oven and wiped her hands on her apron. "Sure you won't stay? I bet you haven't had a home-cooked meal in weeks."

"Not since the last time I sat at your table." Harry touched her arm as he headed for the door. "It smells delicious, but I have to get back to the city and work on a case. An old army buddy is on the hook for murder. I'm trying to help him get off."

It wasn't a lie. Not really. It was the work he should have been doing and would resume soon. When his business up here was done.

"That the guy who stabbed the nightclub singer? You know him?" Phil had sucked down his first beer and started on another. "The papers make him look guilty as sin."

"He says he didn't do it, and I believe him. But it will be tough to prove."

If Eddie Martone was behind the murder, Harry meant. He felt bad for Joe's family. Grace especially. She was as hard-headed as her brother, no question. Just like Joe, loyal to the core. Ten times smarter, too. That was for sure.

Harry put his hat on and pulled open the door. "Night, folks. Thanks for the coffee. I'll be in touch."

"Good luck, Harry. Don't be a stranger," Phil called back.

"Let us know if you hear from the doctor again," Kay said.

"Of course, I will." He waved goodbye and stepped into the cool spring night, relieved to close the door behind him.

His car was parked at the curb in front of the tidy bungalow. A crescent moon hung just above the horizon, behind the treetops. The blue-black bowl of sky arched above was studded with points of light.

He tipped his head back and looked up. You could see a lot of stars up here. He'd forgotten that. Even more, where he was headed. It would be even quieter, too. And darker.

He pulled the map and flashlight from the glove compartment. White Lake was about a two-hour drive north, on Routes 9 and 6, but he had to backtrack first.

Make a scene at a toll booth in the southbound lane, spill all his change on the road so the collector would remember him. And stop at a diner in Mount Vernon for good measure, to overturn his coffee and leave the waitress a memorable tip.

Then he'd swing north again, taking back roads once he got closer. His neighbor, Lenny Klinger, would let himself in and manage the rest. He'd turn up the radio, order a few bottles from the liquor store, and make it seem like Harry was in his apartment all night. Lenny owed him one, and this put them square.

Byrd had given him directions to the farmhouse, landmarks mostly that would be tough to spot on the pitch-black mountain roads. The gun was under an empty milk can behind the barn. A .38 caliber that would be traced to a gas station stick-up in Port Jervis two years ago. Harry didn't ask Byrd how he'd come by the weapon.

The last time he'd driven to the Catskills, Laura sat beside him. She'd begged, cajoled, and threatened until he took her on a "real" vacation.

She'd booked a room at a big old hotel where they'd sat by a square, blue pool and read magazines, under the glaring sun. Or watched other people play shuffleboard and toss horseshoes.

In the late afternoon, they floated on the lake in a dark green rowboat. He did all the grunt work while she sat in the prow like Cleopatra on the Nile.

He'd been bored to tears and mocked the place mercilessly. He'd give everything he owned to spend one more hour with her there, to watch her dangle her hand in the water. And close her eyes against the sun.

It figured Tedesco would hide out in Monticello. The racetrack drew more low-lifes than a pile of manure drew flies. Half the horses were hopped up, and more than half the jockeys.

Byrd would be first on the scene. Harry guessed he'd already written the report. Two shots to the head, two in the gut. Mob hit. These animals cannibalized each other every other day. No one would shed a tear over the sad end of Raymond Tedesco.

Some fresh-faced detective with time on his hands, who still believed in the job, might connect the dots. But Harry's alibi would hold up. Ninety-nine per cent of the cops he knew would look the other way. And might even tip their hat to him.

Chapter Twenty

Two tables in the dining area had been left bare of the club's fancy linens and place settings. A handful of employees sat eating their free dinner. Grace didn't recall a rule about whites and coloreds eating separately; maybe Judy thought she didn't need to include one.

Three musicians from Gem's band sat at the first table, sheet music spread between them. They hummed different sections, debating how the tempo should go. She'd hoped to get them talking about Mary, but now felt awkward choosing the company of the colored men over the two white faces at the other table. Add to that, the musicians did not spare her a glance. Only one looked up with a quick, shy smile, then back at his food.

She chose a seat at the other table, across from Clara Trento, the restaurant's cashier and bookkeeper. They'd met earlier in the kitchen. A small velvet hat arched over a mixture of brown and gray strands, pinned in a tight knot. Her plaid dress and round glasses reminded Grace of a librarian but suited the older woman's serious duties just as well.

Clara met Grace's gaze and nodded, then continued reading. The book cover was protected by a jacket made of butcher's paper, but Grace had checked the running heads at the top of the page as she'd passed; *Forever Amber*. Clara, you naughty girl, Grace secretly admonished.

Next to the cashier, a man about her age studied a scratch sheet and jotted notes in the margins of the newspaper page. A blue satin bow tie hung loose over his white shirt. He noticed Grace and jumped up to pull out her chair.

"Pardon me. You must be the new cigarette girl."

She didn't like the way he looked her over but forced a smile. "It's the dress, right? Dead giveaway."

"No disrespect to Suzie, but that frock never had it so good."

"I bet you say that to all the new cigarette girls."

He laughed. "Arty Pulaski, behind the bar."

Grace had already guessed. "Lucy Bianco."

"Pleased to meet you, Lucy. Have you worked in many clubs?"

"I've done some waitressing, but this is my first job in a supper club. I'm really an actress. Studying to be one, I mean."

"You're certainly pretty enough. The spitting image of Ava Gardner. But you hear that a lot, right?" His expression was sincere as he tested his charm.

"No, I don't. Not ever." He was shameless. Clara thought the same. She closed her book and came to her feet.

"You need to sign out your cash drawer, Arty. It's late."

"Didn't you hear, Clara? Eddie wants me to give out the liquor for free tonight."

The older woman lifted her chin and left. Arty winked at Grace. "I love to tease her. I don't mean any harm."

Grace wasn't so sure of that. He folded the newspaper and lifted a white waistcoat from the back of his chair.

He wasn't as attractive as he thought, but not bad-looking. A cock's comb of dirty blond hair topped brown eyes, and a sharp nose and chin. His quick movements and supple hands reminded Grace of a magician. She could easily imagine him draped in a black cape, pulling a martini from a top hat.

"Catch you later, Ava." His wink made her shudder, but she answered with a smile. A bartender saw a lot, heard a lot, and was trusted with secrets. It was worth her while to stay on his good side. He was a horrible flirt, as Judy had warned. But it was smart to play along and deal with the consequences later.

Alone at the table, she looked down at a mixture of overcooked vegetables and grisly meat. Her mother would have slapped the dish from her hand. It was inedible, and that was just as well. Any more than a sip of water and Grace feared she'd burst the Cupie doll dress, an unscheduled opening of the floor show.

She considered talking to the musicians, but the table had gone silent. The trio sat up alertly, and Grace followed their gaze. Gem Washington was headed their way.

Tall and broad-shouldered, his smooth, dignified gait satisfied even Judy's high standards. He was a showman and dressed the part in a three-piece suit, dove-gray with chalk pinstripes and a burgundy bow tie. His black shoes were polished to a glassy sheen, jacket sleeves edged by the perfect length of white cuff, studded with black onyx links.

Beneath the brim of a classic black derby, his gaze swept over the men. His expression held no hint of the toothy, good-natured grin he'd worn on stage.

"Finish up that slop. We need to warm up. The new arrangement sounded like crap last night."

"We're just going over the changes, Gem." A band member at the end of the table gathered sheet music as he stood up. The rest rushed the last bites of their meal.

"Where the hell is Dolores?"

"In her dressing room," the same man answered.

"She should be out here by now. Tell her I'm waiting, damn it."

"I'll go, Gem." Another fellow jumped up. He wiped a last dash of gravy from his plate with a crust of bread and stuffed it in his mouth. He was very young and looked as if all the stew in the world couldn't fill his tall, lanky body.

"Make it snappy. And don't choke in the bargain, Floyd. You'll be even less use."

The others grabbed their jackets and followed Gem to the stage. She'd heard about demanding band leaders from her brother. But Gem's disposition surprised her, his offstage personality the antithesis of the easygoing chap who bantered so pleasantly with the audience. Maybe it was just a bad mood, but she had a feeling that was not the case.

A busboy cleared the dirty dishes, and another set the tables for paying guests. Judy stood at the check room and beckoned Grace with a crook of her finger.

"You're on time. That's something." The cigarette tray sat on a table. Grace guessed she was about to hear more instructions. "Pay attention. I won't go through this twice."

The band was rehearsing a loud, lively number, and Grace could barely hear how to arrange the tray and where to find more cigarettes when she ran out. She'd carry bills and change in a glittery wallet attached to a belt around her waist. And keep track of what she sold with a tally sheet, kept on a clipboard in the check room. It was due each night before she left, and it had to balance.

"Got that?" In a flowing blue gown, golden hair studded with star-shaped clips, Judy might have been a powerful goddess. The kind that could turn a cigarette girl into a croaking frog if her tally didn't match her wallet at the end of the night.

"I think so." Grace nodded again, more emphatically.

"You think so, huh? I guess we'll see." Judy checked a slim gold watch. "Doors open in five minutes. You have time to freshen up and put on more lipstick."

Grace thought she was wearing plenty of lipstick but didn't mind an excuse to slip away. Judy sailed into the dining area to reprimand a busboy.

Pauline, the check girl, had been hiding in the coat room, rattling hangars, and trying to look busy. Short and round, her smooth dark hair was cut blunt to her chin. She wore a plain navy-blue dress with a bit of hand-embroidered lace at the lace neckline, where a small gold cross hung. The type of girl who looked middle-aged before she was twenty. Who might marry early in a match engineered by family. Or grow old in the house where she was raised, a favorite aunt, left to care for aging parents. Either way, she looked woefully out of place at the glittering nightclub.

Grace smiled when Pauline peeked out. "Is she always like that?"

Pauline looked reluctant to speak against their boss. "You'll get used to her."

Grace knew she wouldn't be there long enough. "I guess we'll see." Grace mimicked the formidable Miss Stemple so perfectly, even Pauline dared to smile.

***

By nine o'clock, nearly every table was filled. Grace was surprised. She remarked to Arty when she needed to break a twenty. "Some crowd. Is it always like this?"

"Hardly. Poor Lana put this place on the map. I guess a nice juicy murder is good for business."

His casual joke upset her. "People can be ghoulish, that's for sure."

Grace gathered the bills and stuffed them in the wallet. She couldn't deny what he'd said was true. But it disgusted her and made it harder to act her part.

The job proved more difficult than it looked. Customers expected her to jump when they beckoned, to light a smoke, empty ashtrays, even bring more water or bread. Her bottom was patted and pinched so many times, she'd lost count.

Eddie Martone arrived after ten. Grace had begun to wonder if he'd show at all. Suddenly, there he was, waltzing in as if he owned the place. Because he did, she reminded herself.

Judy and the maître d', Oscar, trotted over to greet him. Pauline took his coat, and Arty mixed the boss's martini as if his life depended on it, the shaker a silver blur in his hands.

The waiters and busboys were tense and watchful, like woodland creatures sniffing a predator's approach. Gem Washington's voice grew louder, his repartee sharper. He raised his baton and whipped the band into a frenzy.

Judy hovered by Eddie's barstool like a golden lioness, guarding a king. A dissipated monarch, reptilian in his slack body and sallow skin. A man his age certainly could have served, but Grace guessed he'd never worn a uniform. Unless at a costume party. A con man like Eddie could pay a dozen doctors to write ten letters each, claiming he was unfit. Myopia, hearing loss, fallen arches, or even bone spurs were the usual trumped-up diagnoses. She could easily see it.

Grace was selling cigarettes at a table near the bar when she noticed Judy and Eddie confer and glance her way. A cold sweat slipped down her back, but she held a straight face and focused on her customer.

Eddie finished his martini and slid his glass forward for another. After a few more words with Judy, he headed for the hallway that led to the phone booth and restrooms and eventually, the swinging doors.

She breathed a sigh of relief that she'd dodged closer scrutiny. This time at least. Grace had noticed a few men come in, well-dressed, without female company. They'd throw back a quick drink, then disappear in the same direction as Eddie.

She guessed they'd gone down to the basement to play poker, the high-stakes game Joe mentioned. Still, she was curious to know for sure. When she spotted another lone wolf finish a short whiskey and take the same path, she followed.

It was awkward to maneuver through the swinging doors with the tray. Her appearance drew curious looks from the passing wait staff. Clara marched out of the kitchen and met her head on.

"You're not allowed back here. You need to stay up front."

Grace held both sides of the tray and sidestepped a waiter who pushed a clattering trolley.

"I need to ask Judy something. I thought I saw her come this way." She cast Clara an innocent look and peered over her shoulder.

"She's not here. Get back in the dining room. Go on now." Clara shooed her away like a farm wife scolding a rebellious chicken.

Grace held on to her wares and turned, then walked back towards the dining room. But not before she spotted the customer from the bar. He opened the door that led to the basement and disappeared.

There was definitely something going on down there.

Chapter Twenty-One

By the time Judy sent her on a break, Grace's feet ached, and her head pounded. She pushed through the side door and stepped into the alley, eager for fresh air. But mostly inhaled the scent of garbage and gasoline.

Handling cigarettes all night had made her crave a smoke, and she'd bought a pack of Chesterfields out of her tips. She'd just lit up when the metal door creaked open.

It was Sylvie, the kitchen worker, who'd let her in the club the other day. She was tugging a trash pail through the door. About a head shorter than Grace, with slim legs and arms, she was stronger than she looked. But the door was still winning.

Grace stepped over and held it open, and Sylvie looked surprised.

"Thanks." She bumped the pail down a few steps and looked Grace over. "I guess you got the job."

"I guess I did."

"You don't sound so happy about it. If you don't mind me saying."

"I'm not sure yet. It is harder than it looks." Grace meant more than Sylvie could guess. "And the tips aren't nearly as good as Judy promised."

"Yeah, I'll bet." Sylvie smiled. "Every job is harder than it looks if you do it right. That's what my father used to say."

"Sounds like something my father would say. In Italian," she added. "I bet neither of them ever squeezed into a dress like this and toted a cigarette tray all night. On spike heels, no heels."

Sylvie laughed. "That's for damn sure. But wouldn't we love to see it?"

Grace laughed, too, and offered the pack. Sylvie took a cigarette, and they leaned against the brick wall, smoking side by side.

Grace tipped her head back to gaze at the blue-black strip of sky bracketed by the rooftops. "I can't find a single star tonight. Must be too many streetlights."

Sylvie flicked some ashes to the pavement. "Real stars never shine over this place. You have to make do with the fake ones, spinning around the dance floor."

Grace glanced at her. "What makes you say that?"

"I don't know." Sylvie shrugged, seeming curious that Grace would take anything she said seriously.

"I nearly didn't take this job because of that singer who got murdered last week. Lana something?"

"Lana Delmar." The good humor drained from Sylvie's expression. "Her real name was Mary."

"Did you know her?"

"Not very long, but long enough. She gave me a dress. Wine red with a black velvet collar. I had to meet my boyfriend's family and didn't have anything nice to wear. She made me keep it, too."

Grace didn't doubt it. Mary probably gave Sylvie a hat and gloves to match. "That was sweet of her."

"She was always like that. That's what makes it worse. The way she died, I mean. I keep expecting her to walk out of her dressing room or see her up on the stage."

"I know." Grace had been feeling the same all night. Then she caught herself. Lucy Bianco had never known Mary. "I know how it is when you lose someone suddenly."

Sylvie drew on her cigarette. She turned to Grace and nodded. She had lovely eyes, wide set in a perfectly oval face.

The metal door flew open, and they turned to see who was coming. Grace prayed it wasn't Judy.

"How long does it take to dump a friggin' pail of garbage?" Hubie staggered towards them; Popeye arms arched at his sides. Grace could smell the sweat and cooking grease on his body three yards away. "Get your ass in here, you lazy slut. Before I drag you by that woolly head."

Sylvie lifted her chin. "I'm just having a smoke. Cook said—"

"I don't give a crap what Cook said. I'm your boss. When will you get that through your thick skull?" His expression twisted, pale skin splotched with red. Grace heard Sylvie take a breath and felt her own body tense as he moved towards them.

Grace was closest and blocked his path. "It's my fault for keeping her. We just got talking. "I'm new here. My name is Lucy. I don't think we've met." Grace offered her hand, as if at a garden party.

He frowned, looking confused.

"It's Hubie, right?"

Sylvie slipped around them and ran inside. He turned just in time to see the door close behind her. He looked back at Grace.

"You think I'm stupid or something, and I don't know what you did? Stay out of my way if you know what's good for you. Smart ass bitch."

Hubie followed his prey with heavy steps. Grace released a breath she didn't even realize she'd been holding. She hoped the bustling kitchen and Cook offered protection when Hubie caught up.

Chapter Twenty-Two

I t was almost noon when Grace made her way downstairs Saturday morning, still in her nightgown. She was relieved to find the house empty. Rose had left at dawn for the factory to make up lost wages, and her father was at his shop. There was a note on the kitchen table from her mother. She'd gone out with her shopping cart to Court Street and added that Nona was visiting Mrs. Costello.

Grace retrieved her files and notebook and set them on the kitchen table. She'd typed a copy of all the documents that had come from Kramer's office and made detailed notes about the photographs. The yellow sport coat stained with blood. The silver handled steak knife; identical to the knives she'd seen at The Starlight Room. The fingerprints and footprints found around Mary's apartment. The open window that led to the fire escape.

Other photos had been upsetting, even gruesome and hard to examine, but she forced herself to examine them objectively. The signs of a struggle near Mary's bed. Mary's body in a pool of blood, staring up with a stunned expression in her dull, lifeless eyes.

She fixed herself coffee and toast, then read the pages of the police report, logged, and signed by Detective Patrick Mahoney. She read the witness statements and everything else, jotting notes in the margins and in a notebook she'd found in her bedroom. The type with a marble cover that she'd once used to write essays for history and English classes.

You're playing at this. You know that, right? You have no idea what you're doing, a voice taunted.

Last night it did seem so. For all her effort, she'd learned nothing, except to confirm Martone ran an illegal poker game in the cellar of the nightclub and employed a man who was a pig with a cruel streak. And that she was lucky to have enough office skills to land a better job than selling cigarettes or washing dishes like Sylvie.

At the end of the night, she handed in the change purse, which matched her tally sheet perfectly—after the addition of a few tips. Grace steeled herself to talk to Judy.

"There's a man in the kitchen, Hubie. I heard him bullying the girl who washes dishes. He said some awful things."

Judy seemed confused. "What do you expect me to do?'

Grace was surprised by the question. "I think you should speak to him."

Judy offered a blank look and puffed her cigarette. "I don't have much to do with the kitchen staff. Hubie works for Cook. That girl probably deserved it. They're all lazy as sin."

"No, she didn't." Her name is Sylvie, she almost added, but realized Judy probably knew that.

Judy frowned, a deep crease between her brows marred her perfect features. "You'll last around here longer if you mind your business, Lucy. And your mouth. Pauline would be a good friend for you. If you even have time to socialize. Stick with your own kind. You get me?"

"Loud and clear." Grace struggled to tamper her anger. One more word and she'd be fired.

The exchange with Judy was the last in a list of the night's frustrations. Harry would have laughed, watching her. She could picture his smug look.

She wanted to believe he was hard at work on Joe's case, but the abrupt way he'd closed the office had set her nerves on edge. She'd never forgive herself if Joe ended up in jail while she sat on the sidelines, leaving it all to the contrary P.I.

She'd never forgive herself, or Harry Shaw.

She thought of all the reports she'd typed for him and the monologues on the Dictaphone. She had to start with Mary. It couldn't be more obvious.

* * *

135

It was a long, rattling ride from Red Hook to Harlem, but the subway car was nearly empty and quiet. Grace took out her notebook and filled the pages with everything she knew about Mary and the night she was murdered. All she could remember from their conversation at McNulty's, the bits and pieces Joe had mentioned at Rikers, even memories from school days, and what she'd observed at the funeral.

Still, except for the long shadow Eddie Martone cast over Mary's life, and her secret affair with Joe, no other relationship seemed significant enough to motivate her murder.

She needed patience. This was a long game, nine innings or more. Harry once told her most of his work was watching and waiting. And that he usually didn't know if what he observed was significant. Not until the end.

She changed at Houston Street for the D, and eventually emerged on 125th and St. Nicolas Avenue. The police report had noted Mary's address, and Grace headed up the busy street, towards 127th. The route was lined with shops, the sidewalks crowded. She felt conspicuous in the sea of dark faces, a well-dressed white woman who'd wandered too far uptown. She ducked her head a few times to ignore surprised and questioning glances.

She turned down Mary's street and found the address, a five-story building, with a long flight of steps from the sidewalk to the entrance. A shoemaker's shop stood on the street level to one side, a hair salon on the other.

The façade was impressive, and must have been even more so in its day, lacking the fire escape that zig-zagged up to the roof. Ionic-style columns and carved stone molding framed the front door.

The paint was peeling, a rusty shade of brown, and the window frames looked rotted, a few panes covered with cardboard. Still, cement urns near the steps overflowed with pansies, hopeful and persistent, predicting better days.

She'd read somewhere that Harlem had been planned as a suburb for affluent white families, but when the grand buildings could not be filled, the landlords began renting to Negroes. White neighbors had fled to points north and East, Westchester, and Queens. Since the thirties, waves of colored families had migrated there from the south. The spacious apartments had been chopped and chopped again to meet the need. And not accidentally, to multiply the rent yielded by each building.

A heavy glass and wood door stood ajar, and she stepped into a dark foyer, the white and black tile floor damp from a recent mopping. A slip of paper on an apartment door beside the stairwell read, "Superintendent—Fredrick Beale." She heard a radio on inside and knocked, but no one answered. She stepped forward and knocked harder.

The door opened a crack, and a colored woman about her mother's age stared out. She had a thin face and large, questioning eyes. A white apron covered a floral dress, and the scent of cooking wafted into the hall.

"Mrs. Beale? I wonder if I could speak with you a minute or two, about Mary Delmore?"

"Are you a reporter? We already told the newspapers all we know. We have nothing more to say, Miss."

She began to close the door, but Grace pushed back with her shoulder. "I'm not a reporter. I work for a private investigator, Harry Shaw. Maybe he's already been here?"

Mrs. Beale shook her head. "Nobody by that name has come by."

Grace was unhappy to hear that and felt even more reason to press on. "We work for the attorney who represents the man accused of Mary's murder. We're sure he's innocent. We need to find out what really happened."

The super's wife pursed her lips. Grace could tell she accepted Joe's guilt as a proven fact. But she took the card Grace offered and read it.

"They let women do this sort of work now?"

Grace wasn't prepared for the question, though she should have been. "Mr. Shaw is out of town. I'm helping out."

"I barely knew the girl. Though it's a shame what happened. I feel for her family. No parent should ever go through that. Still, I don't know anything about it. I need to get back to my cooking…"

Grace felt her chance slip away. Two photographs stood in gold frames on a polished wooden table that faced the doorway, a vase with fresh flowers set between them. Portraits of smooth-faced young men in uniform. One had a medal on a ribbon draped over the corner, a Bronze Star. Not as high an honor as the Silver Star or Purple Heart, Grace knew. It probably should have been one of those instead, from what Grace had heard about colored soldiers being overlooked for any honors or recognition.

"Are those soldiers your sons?" Mrs. Beale stared at her and turned to the portraits. Her expression tightened, and Grace worried that the question had angered her.

"Our boys, Lyle and August," she finally answered. "They both served. Only August came back."

"The man accused of killing Mary served, too. His mother prayed every day that he'd return. Right now, she's praying he doesn't spend his life in prison for a crime he didn't commit."

Mrs. Beale wiped her hands on her apron. "I'm sorry for her. Honest, Miss. But whether he is, or he isn't—"

"Anything you can tell me about Mary, or the day she died, could help. Anything at all."

Mrs. Beale paused and finally unfastened the chain. She led Grace to a tidy sitting room and offered her a seat on a stiff green velvet couch. She sat in a matching armchair; hands folded in her lap.

"Like I told the police, I didn't know the girl very well. But she was friendly and polite. Sometimes she'd play her records or practice singing, but otherwise, the place was quiet. No arguing going on, or anything like that. Like some of the tenants." Mrs. Beale paused, and Grace waited. The super's wife had more to say about Mary than she'd realized.

"Did you see anything unusual the day Mary died, or the days prior? Did she have any visitors?"

"She never lacked for company. Men, mostly."

Mrs. Beale didn't seem to be judging Mary, just stating a fact. With little prodding, she described a regular visitor that fit Eddie Martone's description, and one that sounded like Joe.

"White men, both of them. I guess that was a sign of trouble brewing right there."

Grace met her glance but didn't reply. Mrs. Beale added she hadn't seen either the day of Mary's murder, or for at least a week or so before. Grace guessed both men visited late at night, after the Beales went to bed and were no longer watching who came and went.

"—Come to think, her brother stopped by. He knocked on my door when her buzzer wouldn't answer."

"Her brother, Cyril?"

"Didn't give his name. Tall, slim man. Nicely dressed."

Grace had seen Cyril Delmore at the funeral. He was tall, but muscle-bound, a big man. He'd been wearing a suit at the funeral but was not particularly well-dressed.

Mrs. Beale's description sounded like Gem Washington. Why would he call himself Mary's brother?

"We only spoke a minute or two. It was late afternoon. I told him she was likely at the nightclub where she sang, rehearsing. He asked if he could leave a note at her door."

Grace recorded the detail, though she doubted the note could be found. And Gem would have known if Mary was rehearsing. Then again, maybe there was no rehearsal that day, and he expected to find her in?

"Can you remember when this was? Last week? The week before?"

She pursed her lips and stared at the ceiling. "About a week after Easter. I was putting up a pot of split pea soup with the ham bone from Easter dinner. We'd finished the leftovers by then."

She pressed her hands together. "Which reminds me, I have to get back to the kitchen. The family will be here tomorrow after church. August and his wife have two little ones."

Mrs. Beale beamed, mentioning her grandchildren.

"Thanks for your time." Grace rose and tucked the notebook in her purse. She paused, wondering if she dared ask the next question.

"Before I go, could I see Mary's apartment? I promise not to touch anything."

Mrs. Beale was already at the door. "There's not much to see. The police left it a shamble. We haven't had a chance to clean it up."

"It would still be helpful."

She sighed. "I'll get the key. But only for a minute."

"I understand. Thank you."

Grace followed Mrs. Beale with quick steps, into the narrow hallway and up four flights to the top of the building. The stairwell smelled of cooking and trash, with an overlay of ammonia. Roach powder, sprinkled along the bottom of the walls, followed their path. Once or twice, a shadow scampered at the edges of her sight, but by the time she turned, the phantom had disappeared into the woodwork.

They approached the last landing, and Mrs. Beale glanced over her shoulder. "Watch your step. The light up here keeps going out. Something in the wiring. My husband has to fix it."

She opened the apartment door to the right of the stairwell and stepped back. "The rent is paid to the end of the month. Her family needs to take what they want. I'll bring some to church, and we'll put the rest on the street."

Grace walked into the apartment, but Mrs. Beale didn't follow. The photos in the file had given her some idea of what she'd see. Still, it was different to stand between the four walls where Mary had lived. And so recently died.

The single room had space for a large bed, which was not far from the door, and a small table and kitchenette on the opposite wall. Two narrow windows faced the street. The few pieces of furniture were mismatched but selected with taste. Art posters were tacked to the walls. In the middle of the room, a Japanese screen stood behind a satin loveseat, a tear in the upholstery hidden by a fringed shawl.

"She had a lot of fine dresses," Mrs. Beale said. "So many, she was selling some and giving a lot away, too."

"Why was that? Did she say?"

"She was going on a trip. She couldn't take much. Not all those clothes." Preparing for her escape to Paris with Joe. Of course, she couldn't take much and selling her belongings raised some money for their new start.

Coats, shoes, and hats to match, Mrs. Beale might have added. A metal rack dipped under the weight of Mary's wardrobe. Day dresses mainly, her fancy gowns were at the club. A rainbow of shoes lined up neatly below, and hat boxes above.

Mary must have made good money singing at the club, maybe even fifty dollars a week. But the wardrobe was more plentiful than even those wages would allow. Eddie Martone had paid the shopping bills, Joe had told them. Her brother may have brought Mary gifts from time to time but could barely support Camille on his erratic wages.

"Make sure you lock up, Miss. You can slip the key under my door. Just don't take long. I'm not even sure if this is allowed."

Mrs. Beale seemed to be having second thoughts. But it was too late to do anything about it.

Chapter Twenty-Three

Grace raised the shades; the room flooded with light. Her heart, with sadness. The gritty, grey powder the police spread to search for fingerprints covered the windowsills, a dresser top, and most every surface.

They'd found Joe's prints all over, though it didn't prove much since he'd often visited.

"No signs of forced entry. There appeared to be a brief struggle," Detective Mahoney had noted.

The mess that remained told the story of Mary's final minutes: a China lamp knocked sideways; the shade torn. The contents of an ashtray and fragments of blue glass scattered on the floor.

Mary had died next to her bed on the bare wooden floor. Reddish brown stains showed at the edges of a plaid wool blanket someone had tossed down to cover the spot. Mrs. Beale or her husband? Grace had seen photos, too many, of Mary's lifeless body lying in a pool of blood. Different angles and sections, close-ups of the knife wounds.

One hand pressed to her chest, her dark eyes staring blankly at the ceiling. Her expression, stunned. Surprised that she was dying? Or, that the person she'd welcomed into her home had attacked her?

Grace turned to the dresser, where open drawers spilled over; Mary's slips and underwear pooled on the floor. The scent of her perfume rose from the silken folds.

Grace doubted anything important was left to find. The police had taken plenty—more than they needed to build their case. They'd found letters from Joe, the bundle tied with a ribbon, stuck behind her gloves and scarves.

There hadn't been time at the office to copy the letters or even read them closely. But she'd skimmed a few and taken notes. Her brother had always struggled with words, preferring his trumpet or his fists to express himself. But there it was, line by line, his heart laid bare. His hopes for their romance and desperate declarations of what he'd do to himself if Mary ever left him. Passionate and even poetic words that would have played well in a movie but would be twisted in a courtroom to prove a love-sick obsession.

In the nightstand drawer, the police had found a stash of pills in a cigar box. Uppers, downers, and everything in between, including a vial of cocaine. Eddie Martone's personal pharmacy, Joe said, and Grace believed him. The prosecutor would twist that around, too. Even though the autopsy had found no trace of drugs or even alcohol in Mary's blood.

A pile of books was scattered on the bed where the police had tossed them after rifling through. She picked up a small white Bible, opened the cover, and found an inscription.

To Mary, with sincere appreciation for leading our choir on Easter Sunday, April 6th, 1947. Thank you for sharing the gift God so generously bestowed upon you with our congregation.
Your brother in Christ,
Reverend Lester Holmes

Was Reverend Holmes the man who'd introduced himself to Mrs. Beale as Mary's brother? The police had not interviewed the minister. Why would they? Most likely, no one knew that he and Mary had once been romantically involved. Grace had already considered talking to him. Now she definitely would.

Another caught her eye. *The Street* by Ann Petry, the first best seller written by a Negro. Grace hadn't read it yet, though she'd meant to. She glanced at the jacket copy, then slipped the book in her purse. She knew it was wrong to remove anything from the apartment, but she couldn't resist taking one of Mary's small possessions.

A portable record player was set up on a wooden cabinet near the door, stacks of 45s piled around and below, on the floor. Grace opened the doors and found more inside. Practically all female vocalists—Billie Holiday, Ella Fitzgerald, Anita O'Day, and Dinah Washington. Alberta Hunter and Ma Rainey. A full collection of Edith Piaf's recordings as well.

This was Mary's university, the library of her higher education. Grace could imagine Mary in this room, listening and studying, testing a certain phrase or pause, making it her own.

She lifted the cover of the case, which had been dusted for prints, and found a disc on the turntable. "MORE THAN YOU KNOW (Youmans-Rose-Eliscu)," the orange label read. And on the next two lines, "Vocal by Lana Delmar, Gem Washington and The Music Makers."

Was the record playing when Mary's visitor arrived, or did the killer set this tune on the turntable? The black disc and the arm of the player had not been dusted for prints, she noticed, and she couldn't recall if the police report addressed that question.

She lifted a few of the other records and glanced at the jackets. Most showed a glamor shot of a famous vocalist. A shorter stack to one side was uniform, the same plain brown paper jacket and orange label showing through a hole in the middle of each disk. Copies of Mary's recording.

She didn't see the empty jacket for the disc on the turntable and searched around the cabinet. She'd nearly given up when she spotted it stuck between the cabinet and the wall. She carefully eased the cover out and looked it over.

Household dust clung to the paper. Nothing unusual there. But along the opening where the record slipped in and out, she saw two smudges, rusty brown. Above them, curved shaped marks.

Not smudges, she realized. They were bloody fingerprints.

* * *

"Esther? Is that you?"

Grace had just locked Mary's apartment. An old man stood in the doorway across the landing. Bent at a painful angle, he worked two canes as he moved towards her. He squinted behind thick lenses, the eyeglass frame mended in one corner with first-aid tape. High waist pants were fastened to leather suspenders. His grey shirt looked as if it had once been part of a work uniform, the fabric worn thin but clean.

She took a few steps towards him. "My name is Grace, sir. You must be Mr. Robillard?"

The report had described Mary's neighbor as a retired hotel porter, age seventy-one. Bald on top, a fringe of soft silver curls matched a full, thick beard. His body worn down by decades of work, he looked more like one hundred and one.

He seemed surprised she knew his name. "That's right. Who wants to know? You a reporter?"

"No, I'm not. I'm not with the police department, either." She offered the same explanation for her visit she'd given Mrs. Beale; she worked for the attorney who was defending the man accused of killing Mary.

Louis Robillard knew who that was. He nodded; the tip of his beard grazed his shirt. "I recognized his picture in the paper. Big, tall fella. Dark hair. I've seen him here. Mary was a sweet flower; she had all the bees buzzing around her."

Grace tried not to smile at his comparison. "You told the police you saw a man in a yellow jacket knock on Mary's door. Was it him, the same man you just described?"

"I only saw the fellow from the back. Through the peephole. I heard the steps and the voices, so I looked out."

"You didn't open the door?"

"I meant to. Mary sometimes brought me a hot dinner from the club where she works. She brought me one that night—roast beef, potatoes, and peas. And a big slice of pie. She was something. Always had a thought for an old fella like me." He looked away, his voice thick. "I had the clean plate in my hand to return. But her caller went in quick, and she shut the door. I didn't want to bother her."

"You never saw the man's face?"

"No, Ma'm. There wasn't much to see. The light was out on the landing, and his back was turned. Tall guy, in a wide-brimmed hat and a yellow sports coat. Gloves on his hands, though the weather didn't call for it."

"Did you hear anything they said?" Mr. Robillard hadn't mentioned overhearing the conversation in his statement, but she asked anyway.

"Not really. Mary laughed when she opened the door. She seemed surprised. She said something like, 'Oh, it's you.'"

Mary had been expecting Joe. Why would she sound surprised?

"Did you see anyone else up here that night? Did you hear any sounds or footsteps?" Maybe Louis Robillard had seen Joe go in or out a short time later, but the police had omitted that from his statement.

"No, Ma'am. I did not. A little while after the visitor went in, the music got turned on loud. I suppose somebody could have come up without me hearing."

"The record player wasn't on when Mary answered the door?"

"If it was, I didn't notice. Mary wasn't like that, playing loud music late at night. She was respectful of folks who didn't keep her hours."

The next question was harder to ask, but she had to. "Are you sure you didn't see the man's face, even a glimpse? His profile, maybe?"

Louis tilted his head and peered at her through his thick glasses. "Or his skin, you mean? White or brown? Why don't you ask me straight out? The police did."

Grace couldn't deny that had been the purpose of the question but winced at his reaction. "I'm just trying to find out what happened, sir."

"Sure, sure. And while you're at it, find some colored man to take the place of the white guy the police threw in jail. Should be easy. The cops won't care, one way or the other. Might even sit better with them."

Grace was thrown off balance and didn't know what to say. Though she understood why Louis Robillard would assume that was her intention.

"I apologize if I offended you. You did say the light in the landing wasn't working that night." And Mr. Robillard's glasses had not been mentioned in the report.

He tipped his head back to meet her gaze. "The light in the landing has nothing to do with it. Mary and this fellow in the newspaper were sweethearts. I saw him here all the time. Fire like that burns two ways. Just as strong when things go wrong. Sometimes stronger… If you'll excuse me, Miss, that's all I got to say."

Before Grace could reply or even thank him for his time, he ambled back into his apartment, and the door snapped shut.

Chapter Twenty-Four

Grace arrived at the club with more than an hour to kill before she could punch in. Recalling the free dinner, it seemed smart to fortify herself with a sandwich. She ducked into a coffee shop across the street. The place was nearly empty, and she found a table with a clear view of the street.

The shade in the club's front window was drawn, and the placard advertising the band had not been set up on the sidewalk yet. She ordered a grilled cheese sandwich and a cup of coffee, then took out her notebook.

She'd made notes at the apartment house, but there was more to record, about what she'd seen and the comments of Mrs. Beale and Louis Robillard.

Before leaving the building, she'd found her way to the roof and saw the wooden plank stretched between Mary's building and the building next door. Just as Joe had described.

The gap between the rooftops was less than a yard, though the drop was five stories straight down. Risky to cross in daylight, no less in pitch darkness.

She'd climbed up and stood on the wood. She was far from the ledge but still swallowed back a sour taste as a breeze tugged her hat. She took a step, and the plank bounced, like a diving board.

She lost her nerve and climbed down, imagining her brother's desperate state.

She'd borrowed a camera from the office, one of many Harry kept handy. She took photos of the rooftop and the plank but doubted it would matter.

If only Joe had walked down the steps and out the front door. Someone may have seen him, hatless and coat less, presenting a piece that didn't fit the investigators' carefully crafted account.

The police had searched the roof but didn't mention the plank. Perhaps it had been noted but struck out of Detective Mahoney's report since it complicated the narrative that law enforcement wanted to sell to a jury.

It also conflicted with a witness account of a man running down the fire escape who fit Joe's description. Joe's bloody prints were all over the apartment, but none had been found on the iron railings outside. A small point, but it did seem unlikely, if not impossible, that someone could race down the narrow steps without holding on.

There was so much to put in order, so many small details. Grace felt overwhelmed. Two days in, and she was almost ready to concede the job was beyond her.

Across the street, a large black box truck pulled up to the club and backed into the alley. The driver jumped out and knocked on the metal door. Hubie appeared, along with Bernard and Dante. The Three Stooges, if ever she'd seen them. When Judy appeared, Grace sat up sharply.

The men waited as the tall blonde sauntered to the sidewalk. She lingered a moment, watching the cars and pedestrians stroll past. Grace sat back, afraid to be spotted.

Judy turned and clapped her hands as she walked back down the alley. "Chop, chop," Grace could almost hear her say. The men began to unload a delivery of cardboard cartons. Stationed at the door, Judy checked each box and made notes on a pad.

The driver stood by smoking. When the last carton was carried in, Judy handed him a thick white envelope. He peeked at the contents, then climbed into the cab.

Grace leaned forward as the truck pulled into the street. She looked for a name or emblem on the side, but there was only a big square of gray paint where one had been covered over.

The truck roared down the street, and the alley stood empty. Grace sat back and sipped her coffee. She'd seen produce and meat delivered to restaurants. Most of it, in open crates. The cartons could have held canned goods, or even dishes and other supplies, but she doubted it.

She had noticed printing that might be a company name on a few of the cartons, but she was too far away to read it. She scribbled notes in her book and finished her coffee. There was just time for a cigarette before Lucy Bianco had to report for duty.

Grace dreaded another night as her alias but reminded herself why she was doing this. A hope that the delivery would shed some light pulled her forward.

The club filled quickly, even faster than the night before. She wondered if Gem Washington felt gratified for drawing a full house or saddened by the reason.

She'd hoped to talk to him, but there had been no opportunity. He arrived after the staff dinner was cleared and went straight to the stage where the musicians and his new vocalist, Dolores Hayes, were warming up.

She doubted Gem would reveal anything worth knowing in a passing conversation with a cigarette girl, but she had to try. Maybe there was something to be learned by what he didn't say.

Customers kept her running until the lights dimmed for the first show. Pauline needed a break, and Grace was covering the check room when Eddie arrived. Once again, Judy, Oscar, and Arty fussed over him. Dante followed his boss like a dark shadow.

Once Eddie was set up with his martini, Judy stood by his chair. Heads close together, he asked questions, and she whispered brief replies. When his cocktail glass was drained, he waved off a refill. He left the bar, and Judy followed like a loyal pet. They disappeared down the hallway toward the kitchen.

To look over the boxes. Grace would have bet on it. She considered following, but she couldn't abandon the check room and the cigarette tray. She'd be fired on the spot.

By the time Pauline returned, Eddie was back, glad-handing customers at tables near the stage. Judy stood at the bar, surveying her bailiwick.

She looked even more glamorous tonight, in an off-the-shoulder gown, black satin, and form-fitting to mid-thigh, where the skirt flared out, trumpet style. Her thick hair was parted and combed to the side, very Veronica Lake. Large sparkling earrings and black, opera-length gloves were her only accessories, along with the huge diamond ring, worn over a gloved hand.

She seemed wound even tighter than Friday night, when she'd watched the staff like a circling hawk. So far, she stuck to the front of the house. Grace chalked up her nerves to the delivery until a better reason appeared.

A tall, fair-haired man walked in; his smooth looks enhanced by a well-tailored tux.

"Mr. Brooks, how good to see you." As Oscar took his hat, Judy headed toward them like a torpedo aimed at a U-boat.

Diners at a table near Judy and her visitor waved Grace over, and she eagerly complied.

"Carter, you're late. I thought you stood me up." Judy's sharp greeting to her beau wasn't surprising, but Grace found the little girl pout totally out of character. Clearly, the former Rockette had more range in her repertoire than Grace had given her credit.

"Midtown was hell. I had to leave the cab and walk most of the way." He leaned down and kissed Judy's cheek. "God, you look beautiful. I should have run."

She made a face, but kissed him back, then wiped a smudge of lipstick off his cheek. She took his arm and led him to the bar. The attractive couple, so elegantly dressed, seemed surrounded by a golden light, as if they'd stepped off a movie screen, or off the pages of a magazine.

Grace had pictured Judy's fiancé as an older man, distinguished but a bit paunchy. Definitely gray-haired, or maybe even bald. One who would enjoy showing off his gorgeous trophy. She hadn't expected such a fresh-faced fellow, years younger than the former showgirl. But Judy was beautiful, and maybe Carter wanted mothering? From a chilly, severe mother, albeit.

You never could say what drew two people together, or what went on between them privately. Grace had learned that long ago. The truth was, even the parties involved didn't know the half of it.

Carter chatted with Arty in a familiar way as the bartender mixed a

Manhattan. Judy was drinking champagne. They touched glasses, gazing into each other's eyes. Grace had seen enough and headed for the tables near the dance floor.

Judy was breaking all her own rules. Grace was pleased to see it, and her boss's handsome distraction created an unexpected opportunity.

Eddie held court in the same booth he'd sat in Friday night. Three men she'd noticed earlier at the bar had joined him. They laughed too loud, shouted at the waiters, and smoked so much a blue cloud hung over the table. Veiled in shadows, they huddled together from time to time for confidential conversation.

So far, she'd only seen Eddie from a safe distance. She knew that had to change sooner or later. But when he caught her eye and snapped his fingers, she wasn't ready.

She'd just sold a pack of Lucky Strike and waited as the customer sorted through the coins in his palm, deciding on a tip. A few pennies would look cheap to his date, but he seemed pained at the prospect of parting with a whole nickel.

Martone caught her gaze and held it. "Some smokes here, honey? Before the war is over, if you don't mind?"

The other men laughed. Grace skipped the tip and headed to the table, purposely moving at a stately pace. The band was on a break, and she sensed she was about to provide entertainment for Eddie's entourage.

Martone curled his lip, making a face he thought was a smile. His eyes were bloodshot. His skin looked waxen. He was not a healthy man.

"Come a little closer, doll. I don't bite. At least not until we've been properly introduced."

His buddies laughed. Grace stepped closer. The tray was nearly under his chin. "Lean over, honey. Let me see what you're selling."

Grace met his gaze and looked away. She felt blood rush to her head. With a blank expression, she gripped the tray to keep it steady and leaned forward as little as she dared.

Eddie's friends snickered like schoolboys. One let loose a low whistle.

"See anything you like, fellas?" His question made them laugh louder.

"She's got a nice rack of merchandise. Very tempting."

"We only carry top quality here, boys," Eddie replied. "Judy must have found this one in a burlesque house."

Grace stood up abruptly, her expression blank, cheeks burning.

"Easy, doll. What's the matter? Can't take a joke?" Eddie grinned, baring small yellow teeth. He plucked a pack of Gauloises from the tray and tossed down a five-dollar bill. "Keep the change."

The tip amounted to double her salary for the night, but it could have been a hundred for all she cared. It was hard to quash the impulse slap him across the face.

"Thanks," she said quietly. She backed away a few steps, hoping he was done.

"Hey, not so fast. You forgot to light me up." He'd torn open the pack and pulled out a cigarette with his lips. Then nodded at a slim silver lighter on the table near his glass.

Grace picked it up and struck the flint, then held out the flame.

He held the cigarette in his teeth, like FDR. But instead of drawing closer, he jerked his head from side to side, taunting her. More entertainment for his pals, who laughed even louder. She stretched her hand to catch his cigarette and missed.

"Sorry, honey. No more fooling around. Scout's honor." Another burst of laughter at his apology.

He held his head still, and she tried again. One of his buddies nudged his neighbor as she felt Eddie's hand slide up her leg and under the petticoats. Before she could move away, his hand closed around her bottom and squeezed as if testing a melon in the market. His cold, glassy gaze challenged her to react. She took a quick step back and dropped the lighter, still aflame.

She'd aimed for his lap, but for better or worse, the lighter missed the mark and landed in his plate. The flame flared a moment, then sizzled, a smoky thread rising in the air.

His audience roared. He stared at her, his mouth hanging open like a red wound. Sweat slid down her back as she stared back.

Then he laughed, loud and ugly, along with his pals, who slapped his back.

"Son of a bitch, wish I had a camera. You should have seen your face."

"What a tiger. I'd like to get her in the sack."

If she said a word or took one step away, he'd fire her, just to show he could. Any chance of helping Joe and finding out the truth would be gone.

She froze, not knowing what to do.

Two waiters rushed up to clear Eddie's place. One fished out the lighter and wiped it on a napkin.

Grace felt a hand on her bare shoulder. "Table five. They're waving at you. Chop, chop." Judy pointed to a table near the dance floor. "After that, leave the tray with Pauline and take your break."

Judy, her unlikely savior, looked annoyed. As if she'd caught the new cigarette girl coming on to the boss. There must have been a rule about that, too.

Grace felt like dumping the tray and running out the front door, a streak of cuss words in her wake. She forced herself to walk away as if nothing unusual had happened, knowing Judy and maybe even Eddie were watching.

She didn't glance back. Or give a thought to her posture.

Chapter Twenty-Five

You don't look well. You better sit before you fall down." Sylvie dragged a crate towards Grace, where she stood leaning on the brick wall. Then held her arm as Grace's legs gave way.

A cigarette dangled from Grace's hand. She'd just lit up but let it drop to the ground. "I'll be okay. Just a little lightheaded. I didn't have much to eat today."

"You want something from the kitchen? A sandwich? A glass of water?"

"That's okay." Grace touched Sylvie's arm, moved by her concern. "I'm just a little queasy. It will pass."

She couldn't shake off her run-in with Martone. The moment clung, like a foul smell. She felt ragged and drained. Doubting herself and the impulse that had driven her here. Naivety and bravado were a bad combination.

"Maybe you should go home and get to bed at a decent hour. These late nights can wear you down. Judy won't fire you for feeling sick. Pauline can sell the cigarettes."

"I'd love to, but it's only my second night. I just need a minute before I get back in the ring."

Sylvie looked amused. "Okay, champ. Take your time. When you're ready, I'll point you in the right direction."

Grace met her gaze and smiled. It felt good to have an ally, even if Sylvie didn't know the real reason Lucy Bianco needed one.

* * *

When Grace returned to the dining room, the second set had just begun. Judy and Carter sat at Eddie's table. A few of Eddie's cronies were gone, but the group was still large enough to fill the booth. Judy was in high spirits, laughing wildly when her fiancé filled her glass with more champagne. As the foam spilled over the top, she leaned forward to sip it up.

"I love the bubbles, Carter. That's the best part. You know how much I love them."

The men at the table chuckled, all except Carter. Judy didn't notice. Carter put his arm around her, but she didn't seem to notice that either.

Grace waited at the check room, watching for customers to call her over. The dance floor was filled as Dolores and Gem sang a lively duet of "Jeepers, Creepers." Dolores had a pleasant voice, but nowhere near Mary's caliber. Her talents were more suited to light, breezy tunes. Not the soulful ballads Mary could put over so well.

The next number in the set was always a solo by Gem at the piano. Usually a light, upbeat tune, like "Ac-Cent-Tchu-Ate The Positive" or "Swinging on A Star." The musicians left the stage, and a spotlight picked up the band leader on the bench.

He took the microphone and said, "I think you all know this next song. An oldie but goodie, and one of my favorites."

He turned to the keys and paused, staring at some distant point in the darkness. Then began a slow, deliberate version of "I'm Gonna Sit Right Down and Write Myself a Letter." But nothing like Grace had ever heard it performed.

The tempo was reduced to a painful crawl. His usually mellow voice straining and a bit off-key as the phrasing took erratic dips and turns. His touch on the piano grew heavy, even frantic at moments, pulling the audience under.

"—I'm gonna write those words so sweet, they're gonna knock you off your feet…"

Except for low chatter and the distant clink of plates and silverware, the room was exceptionally quiet, the audience sensing they were privy to an intimate performance.

Gem had put aside his mask to reveal his true pain, his true soul. In the final bars, his hands stroked the keys tenderly, as if gliding over a lover's body. The notes slowed and quieted, the last lyrics not so much sung, but spoken, his voice low and rough.

"—and make believe…it came from you."

Head bowed, both hands resting on the keyboard, he looked beaten. Undone and emptied. Fragments of poetry came to Grace's mind. Or maybe it was a verse from the Bible. *I am poured out like water. My heart, like wax, melted within me.*

The audience responded with a smattering of applause. Far less than he deserved, Grace thought. He nodded and blinked, as if they'd woken him from a deep sleep. And he didn't care a whit if they'd liked it or not.

"Thank you, folks. Thank you kindly," he murmured as he rose off the bench.

A moment later, the lights went up, and his usual, cheery expression dropped like a curtain over his face. He swung the baton, kicking the band into the bright intro of "Personality," and couples streamed back to the dance floor.

Grace was at a table near Eddie's banquette when she heard voices rise. Judy came to her feet and swayed on unsteady legs. Carter got up, too.

"Come on, honey. Let's get you home. It's late." Carter reached for her, but she pushed him away.

"Get her out of here. She's making me sick." Eddie's voice was low and vicious. "There's nothing more disgusting than a drunken, sloppy broad."

Judy leaned over him, a tilting blonde tower in black satin. "Shut up, you. You make *me* sick. God damn hop head know-it-all…that's what you are…" She laughed, a harsh sound and pointed at him with one gloved finger while her tall body swayed. "I know how to get you where it hurts, big shot. I can fix your wagon for good, too."

He stared up at her. The color drained from his face. He grabbed a knife off the table, knuckles clenched around the handle. "Get her out. Now. I mean it."

Carter wrapped his arms around Judy and pulled her away. Dante appeared and took hold on the other side. She struggled a moment, but soon gave in. At the front of the house, Oscar had already hailed a cab. Carter draped his tuxedo jacket over her shoulders and swept her out the door.

A few of the patrons watched the drama and commented in hushed tones. Except for the brief but threatening moment with Eddie, Grace realized a drunken woman at a nightclub, even one who was shouting, was not a shocking sight. Unless you knew the players.

Had Judy narrowly escaped Mary's fate? Had Mary been trapped alone with Eddie, without a Carter Brooks to save her?

There was a deep, intimate connection between Eddie and Judy. She'd always sensed it. Tonight, it popped its head out of a dark hole, like a hissing weasel. A vicious beast, bearing sharp teeth.

Grace waited as Arty changed a ten-dollar bill. His hands moved swiftly, dealing out the singles in a neat pile. "Judy tied one on. I was surprised. She strikes me as the type who can hold her liquor."

"It's the pills. They don't mix well with champagne."

Grace picked up the bills and answered with a curious look.

"Pain pills. For her back," he added.

A customer tapped the bar with his empty glass. "Another one over here, buddy?"

"Coming right up."

She lingered, watching Arty drop some bitters into a frosty mixing glass. He dropped in a sugar cube and splash of water and muddled it with a long, shiny spoon.

"I almost forgot," she said, "I'm out of Chesterfields. There aren't any more in the check room. Do you know where I can find some?"

He dropped in a jigger of Burbon and a few cubes of ice. "Are you sure? There should be plenty."

Grace feigned an innocent look as he stirred the concoction, poured it in a glass, twisted an orange peel, and set it on top. "I checked everywhere. So did Pauline. I wouldn't bother, but a guy at Eddie's table wants them."

"Give me a minute. I'll get some from the storage closet." He served the drink to his customer—first sweeping an empty glass away and setting down a clean cocktail napkin.

"Thanks." Grace turned, hiding a smile. She set off with her tray, one eye on Arty as he served the drinks he'd mixed, then searched the register drawer for a key ring.

He left the bar and walked to the hall that led to the swinging doors. Grace gave him a head start before she followed. She dropped the tray at the end of the bar and hoped none of the customers helped themselves to free smokes. She hadn't made enough tips to cover too many losses.

She saw Arty about halfway down the hall, standing at the door to Eddie's office. The door stood open a crack, enough to see a desk against one wall that overflowed with mail and piles of paper. It was flanked by two tall, black metal file cabinets. Next to that, an armchair placed by a torchiere lamp, newspapers scattered on the floor all around it.

The rest of the space was filled with boxes stacked high against the walls. An electric cord dangled from an open flap. Grace could finally read the printing on the side.

Luxor, the name of Harry's client on Long Island, an electronics factory that had hired Harry to investigate missing inventory. It looked like she'd found it.

Past the boxes, a closet door stood open. She couldn't see Arty, but heard him inside, moving things around. When she saw him coming out, she backed down the hallway with quick, soft steps. By the time he emerged, she was far enough away to act as if she'd just come to look for him.

"Arty...what took you so long?"

"I said I'd be right back. You shouldn't have followed."

She shrugged and took the cigarette cartons. "Thanks, I owe you one."

Arty looked pleased by her offhand remark. "Really? I'll take you up on that, Ava. How about a drink after work?"

An excuse was on the tip of her tongue, but instead she nodded. "Sure, that would be fun."

She headed off to pick up the cigarette tray and pictured Judy stretched out on a bed with satin covers, a cold compress on her forehead. Judy's night was over, but Grace knew she still had plenty of work to do.

* * *

Grace changed into her street clothes and hung the despised dress in the check room. The last customers had left, and the lights in the dining room were turned up, revealing the shabby truth. Bus boys yanked soiled linens off the tables and stacked the chairs. The bandstand stood dark and empty, the piano closed and covered.

She looked for Arty, but the bar was empty. Except for Gem. He sat at the end, sipping a glass of whiskey, straight up, and smoking a thin, sweet-smelling cigar.

This was her chance to speak to him, but she was exhausted and doubted she could break through his cool reserve.

"Have you seen Arty around, Mr. Washington?"

He lifted his head and met her gaze. "He's in the kitchen with Clara, counting out his drawer. That could take a while."

Arty seemed to be a trusted employee, but she didn't doubt that Clara watched every penny that dropped into the till. Heaven help the fool who stole from Eddie Martone.

"Guess I'll wait." He returned to his drink, and she took a seat a few stools down.

"I been wanting to tell you how much I enjoy your music." She meant it, too. The band was good and made the night's ordeal a lot more bearable.

He managed a small smile but didn't meet her gaze. "Thanks, Miss. That's kind of you to say."

His voice sounded tired. And a bit insincere?

"It's Lucy. I started working here last night."

"Too soon to be sick of the show," he noted with a small laugh. "Give it a night or two."

"I doubt that. You make it different every time."

She wasn't trying to flatter him; it was true. Gem didn't follow a strict set list, like most band leaders. He read the mood of the crowd and mixed it up. According to his own mood, too. His repartee was always fresh. That couldn't be easy either.

"I was here a while ago on a date. There was a different singer, Lana Delmar. She was wonderful."

His expression tightened. "Yes, she was."

"I read about what happened to her. What an awful thing. Had she been with your band a long time?"

"You could say that. I found her in a church choir. I brought her along. A lot of good it did either of us." He finally looked at her, then away, seeming surprised he'd admitted so much.

"I'm sorry," she said sincerely. She wasn't sure if she should ask anything more, but doubted she'd have another chance. "The newspaper said the police got the guy who did it."

"Joe Russo."

"That's right. Do you think it was really him?"

Gem shrugged and drained his glass. "The police think so. What do I know? It had to be somebody."

The scent of hair tonic announced Arty's arrival. Grace almost didn't recognize him out of his bartending outfit. He wore a tweed sports jacket and a flashy print tie, a brown fedora in hand.

"Sorry to make you wait. Clara counts the take like it's her life savings."

Gem quietly chuckled. "She wouldn't care half so much if it *was* hers."

Arty grinned. "Good point."

Someone knocked on the door, and Arty stepped over to answer. He recognized the late visitor and let him in.

"Any seats at the table, Art?"

"Vinny G. just tapped out. They'll be thrilled to take your hard-earned money."

"Great." The latecomer smiled, despite the dig. He headed for the game, which was still going strong, Grace surmised.

At the end of the bar, he turned back to Arty. "Coming?"

"Not tonight, pal. Good luck."

She'd noticed how Arty studied the scratch sheet. It seemed he played poker, too. Expensive hobbies on a bartender's salary.

The visitor's gaze settled on Grace. "Sure, I get it. Good luck to you."

Arty laughed and shook his head. "Ready to go?" he asked Grace.

"Sure." Grace turned to Gem. "We're just going for a nightcap. Want to join us?"

She ignored Arty's frown, though he had a perfect right to be annoyed. Gem gave her a curious look; she thought he might agree.

He shook his head and stared at his glass. "No thanks. I'm going to finish this stogie and head straight to bed. You young folks have fun."

Arty looked relieved. "Another time then. See you, Gem."

"Sure, man. See you."

Grace said goodnight, wishing she had more time to talk to Mary's former mentor. She had a feeling there was a lot he could tell her if he wanted to.

Chapter Twenty-Six

Once they were outside, Arty said, "I know a little after-hours place downtown. I'll find a taxi."

"Sure, that sounds fun."

Grace forced a smile. The night felt chilly and damp, and she was suddenly exhausted. She smothered a yawn and watched Arty flag down a cab.

When he joined her in the backseat, she turned her head toward the window to hide another yawn.

"I think you should save a few of those for later. I didn't even get to my life story."

"I'm sorry." Grace laughed. "I'm not used to these hours yet. I'm more of nine to fiver."

"Really? I thought the acting crowd kept worse hours than club rats. Don't you drink at Sardi's all night, waiting for reviews?"

Grace grinned to hide her nerves. She was so tired she'd forgotten about her alias. "Only on opening night. When I'm the leading lady. So, basically… never."

"Never say never." He gazed at her a moment, the passing lights flashing across his face. He wasn't bad looking. He had kind eyes. "What do you say to a raincheck on the drink? I can take you home. Or we can grab breakfast. It's late enough and saves time in the morning."

Grace had to smile. He was more fun to be with than she'd expected. "I wouldn't mind a bite to eat. And I promise to stop yawning."

"I hope so. My delicate ego can't take much more of that." He made a face and touched a hand to his heart. Grace laughed again.

They ended up at a little restaurant on the Lower East Side, far enough down Second Avenue to be halfway to Brooklyn and open around the clock. The usual breakfast combinations were offered, along with Polish specialties.

All the waiters seemed to know Arty, and he ordered without the menu—fried eggs over easy, pierogi with kielbasa and potatoes on the side.

Grace chose cheese blintzes with cherry sauce and sour cream. She'd tried them once and recalled they were a lot like manicotti with sweet filling.

She was surprised to see so many tables filled so late at night. Mostly men eating alone: cabbies, bus drivers, policemen on a break. But there were several other couples, and a fair amount of Polish conversation in the air.

The waiter brought coffee, and she quickly took a sip, hoping it would wake her up. "I'm sorry if it seemed out of line asking Gem to come along. He looked like he needed company."

Arty shrugged. "That's all right. I like Gem. We get along fine. But he looks like that a lot. He's a moody guy."

"I've seen him get impatient with the band and Dolores."

"That's nothing. He can really blow. The musicians handle him with kid gloves. Though he has his favorites."

"He seems to treat Dolores nicely." Grace paused. "We were talking about that singer who was killed, Lana Delmar. Maybe that made him sad. He told me he discovered her. They must have been close."

Arty caught her gaze and looked away. "You could say that. The feelings were all on his side, from what I saw. He was grooming her, bringing her along. Taught her how to dress, how to do her makeup, and her hair. How to put a song over. She was bringing a lot of attention to his band. Lana was definitely going places. Some big shot heard her one night and asked her to sing on the radio. But she wouldn't do it without the Music Makers."

"Really?" Grace wasn't surprised at Mary's loyalty but wondered if Joe knew that story. He hadn't mentioned it.

"She looked up to Gem and was grateful for his help. Until Eddie came into the picture."

"Eddie stole her away?"

"Lana and Gem were never together that way, as far as I know. You can't lose something you never had, right? But I guess you could say, in a way, Gem lost Lana twice. First to Eddie, who pulled her in, like a spider snags a fly. He convinced Lana he knew people in the business and could help her get ahead. More than Gem ever could. Eddie can be charming when he turns it on. You'd be surprised."

"I would be," Grace said bluntly. But it made sense that Eddie persuaded her he could boost her career, Eddie being white and Gem being colored. Once Eddie decided that he wanted Mary, who was going to argue with him?

"How did Gem take it? I can't imagine it sat well, from what I've seen of his temper."

Arty took another sip of beer. "You sure ask a lot of questions about characters you don't even know, Ava."

His remark made her nervous, but she decided he wasn't suspicious. "I guess I do," she admitted with a laugh. "I am nosey about people. But hearing what goes on in other people's lives helps with my acting."

"Sure, I get it. 'All the world's a stage,' and all that?" She could tell from his smug grin he enjoyed surprising her.

She had to smile back. "I never took you for a guy who goes around quoting Shakespeare."

"I wasn't sneaking cigarettes in the boys' room the whole time in school. Whatever you want to call it, jawing about the other guy usually makes me feel better about my own problems."

"I know what you mean," she agreed. "So how did Gem take it? Losing Mary to Eddie?" He sipped his beer, and she hoped he'd answer her question without more prodding.

"He seemed to take it in stride. Who knows what he was really thinking? Gem can close down tight as a drum when he wants to. The guy was between a rock and a hard place. He couldn't go up against Eddie. That would have been plain crazy. If Gem was ever mad at Lana, I never saw it. But it must have hurt his pride. Even more reason he'd hide his true reaction."

"Did Eddie ever help her?" Grace knew the answer to the question but was interested in Arty's take.

"He footed the bill for a recording, but nothing came of it. Maybe in time something would have. I heard the records were cut but never sent out to radio stations and promoted. Who knows what happened to them?"

Grace knew. Boxes of the recording were piled in Mary's apartment. "I saw her sing once. I think she could have been famous. A real star."

"Everybody loved Lana. Even guys who don't give colored girls a second look." Grace wondered if Arty included himself on that list. Was he in love with Lana, too? Of course, she couldn't ask him that.

"Enough about her," he said. "Let's hear Lucy Bianco's story."

"There's not much to it. I don't want to make *you* start yawning."

"Just kick me under the table. Where are you from?"

"Brooklyn. Red Hook to be exact."

He continued with the usual questions, and she relaxed a bit, answering with the real facts of her life, slightly disguised.

"Why did you decide to be an actress?"

Grace was suddenly on guard again. "Don't I seem the type?"

"If you mean shallow and vain, then no. You don't seem that type at all."

Grace smiled. "Come on, we're not that bad."

The waiters arrived with their food, saving her from saying more.

"Cheese blintzes, cherry sauce, sour cream." Grace's order clattered onto the table. "Breakfast special for the gentleman." A few more dishes landed in front of Arty. "Anything else, folks?

They both declined. Grace tasted her dish; it was sweet but surprisingly good. "What about you? You said you were in the Navy?"

"I signed up right after Pearl Harbor and did my duty on a carrier in the Pacific. Before that, I just wanted to find a good job. Meet a nice girl, have some kids. Now I dream about owning a bar on a desert island, where no one can bother me."

His tone was half joking, half defeated. Grace forced a smile. "Won't the customers bother you?"

"That's just it, in my daydream, there aren't any." He lifted a forkful of potatoes and put it in his mouth.

"Sounds like you won't be in business very long. Aside from being lonely."

"No less than I am now. Slinging booze all night for people who don't even look me in the eye." He tried the kielbasa next, slicing off a chunk with his knife.

"The customers at the club can be rude. Not rude exactly. It's almost as if you're invisible. Part of the décor?"

"Exactly." He pointed at her with his fork. "You're a smart girl. Too smart to be an actress, Ava."

She grinned at his nickname for her. "And you seem too sharp to be behind a bar mixing cocktails."

"I appreciate your kind words." He nodded graciously and dabbed his mouth with his napkin. "I won't work there forever. But I'm sort of stuck." He paused and continued eating. "I always thought I'd be further along by now. I think about finding a real job. Or even going to college. Then worry I'm too old."

"You're not too old. Not at all. You shouldn't be so hard on yourself. You're not the first guy who didn't have it all figured out five minutes after you got back."

"When I look around, it sure feels like it."

Grace thought of Joe. Mary would have helped him settle down and get a grip. Her love gave his life meaning, even more than his music. She could see that now.

The blintzes were tasty but filling. She could only finish one. Arty ate quickly and nearly cleaned his many plates. It was hard to see where he put all that food. But she imagined his bachelor fridge with a few beers and a carton of curdled milk.

The waiter refilled her cup. "Do you think Judy will make it to work tomorrow night?"

"Tonight, you mean," he corrected. Grace hadn't checked her watch in a while but guessed it was after two. "Don't worry, the Iron Maiden will be there, come hell or high water. Even if her head is too big to fit through the front door."

Grace laughed. "I don't know why I'm laughing. She'll probably be in a terrible mood."

"She'll make The Bride of Frankenstein look like Loretta Young. But to be forewarned is to be forearmed."

"Thanks for the tip…I think. I guess I'm not sure how to act. I mean, she'll probably be embarrassed if she remembers the show she and Eddie put on."

"To the contrary, she'll sail in like the Queen Mary. As if it had all been a swell party. Eddie will act that way, too."

Arty had seen their performance before. "You said she takes pills that don't mix with alcohol?"

He didn't answer, and Grace wondered if he'd explain that, too. "I'm not giving away any secrets. She tells everyone about the accident, sooner or later."

"She did mention something about her back the day I came for the job. But she didn't go into details."

"She fell down a flight of steps, and the doctors had to use metal pins to put Humpty Dumpty back together. She still takes pills for the pain. Or she's been taking them so long, she can't stop." He paused and sipped his beer. "Long story short, that's why the great Judy Stemple, high kicker extraordinaire, left the bright lights."

The story was surprising and maybe explained a few things about her boss. "When did it happen?"

"About four or five years ago. I heard she was at the top of her game and had an audition in Hollywood lined up. I'm not sure that's true. You know how people exaggerate."

"Even so, what an awful thing to go through. And to lose your career like that." Grace felt sorry for her and forgave her sharp edges…a little. "How do you know all this?"

"Clara told me. She's been with the Martones forever. Eddie and his father, Leo, before that. She saw the whole thing."

"It happened at the club?"

He nodded and lit a cigarette. "Back when Eddie and Judy had something going on. I'm not sure what you'd call it. Madly in love one minute, at each other's throats the next. We've all met those special couples."

"Yes, we have." Grace could easily picture it.

"This one night, they were going at it hammer and tong. Clara claims Judy was pregnant. She wanted to keep the baby and get married, but Eddie wasn't buying. Who knows if that's true? Judy ended up at the bottom of the cellar steps. That part is undisputed."

"Eddie pushed her?"

"Clara never said, and I never asked. Knowing what a sweet guy Eddie is, I'd be shocked. Wouldn't you?" Arty held her gaze until she looked away. "When Judy recovered, Eddie gave her the job at the club. She's set for life, or as long as the place stays in business."

That was probably true, but Grace thought Judy had other plans. "She won't need to work once she marries Carter."

"You mean Carter Reed Whitney Brooks the fourth? Heir to the Brooks fortune? Did you know his Aunty Gertrude started up one of those big museums up on the avenue? But that's another story." Arty stubbed his cigarette out in his dirty plate. "I don't think Carter Brooks the third has signed off on the match yet. An aging ex-showgirl is probably not the type of brood mare the lad's folks have in mind to carry on the family line. Though Judy must stand out from the usual flock of debutante fillies. Maybe that's why Junior fell in love?"

That obstacle to Judy's happily after had never occurred to Grace. "I see what you mean. But maybe Carter really loves her, and what his family says won't matter."

"You're sweet." He smiled at her, and not in a sardonic way. "We won't bet on this one, honey. I don't want to steal your money."

Grace wasn't sure about that but didn't argue.

"If you follow the gossip columns, like I do," he added, "you'd know that Carter has a weakness for showgirls, and a bad habit of proposing to them. So far, he's never married any. The odds don't seem to be riding with our Judy."

Sweet Carter, totally adoring of his ice princess and affable as a puppy. Was he just acting out a rebellious fling? But Arty's explanation was convincing. Carter could afford to give out ice cube-sized diamonds, as if they were prizes in a Cracker Jacks box.

For the second time that night, and to her great surprise, Grace felt sorry for Judy Stemple.

"I said you were sweet, and I mean it. Take my advice, stick with your acting classes. Don't get sucked into the riptides at The Starlight Room. Eddie has a way of getting his hooks into people. Nice people, too. Before you know it, you're not so nice. But it's too late."

She sensed that he spoke from experience and wondered what hold Eddie had on him. Probably debt, linked to his gambling. Is that why he was stuck at the club?

"Thanks for the warning. But Eddie Martone will never get close enough to hook me."

"That's what all the pretty little fish say. Until they smell the bait."

* * *

The house was dark, and Grace took care to open the front door as quietly as she was able. She'd slipped in almost as late the night before, but no one had noticed. Tonight, she found her mother asleep in an armchair, glasses askew, a pile of sewing in her lap.

Grace had made it to the staircase when her mother woke with a start. "Where have you been? What time is it?"

"Just past three, I think… I'm trying to help Joe, Ma. I have to stay out late to talk to people. Go to places he likes to go."

Her mother rose and walked towards her. "Bars, you mean. Nightclubs. Where he met that woman."

Grace didn't know how to answer.

"You don't go all alone to those places, do you? You're with your boss, Mr. Shaw, right?"

Her mother looked tired and frightened. Less than a week had passed since Joe's arrest; her mother had aged ten years. Or maybe it was just the way a person looks when their well-ordered world shatters, and nothing makes sense anymore.

Grace came back down the steps and rested a hand on her mother's shoulder. "Please don't worry, Ma. It's only for a few more days. It will help Joe. I promise."

Grace wished she felt even half as sure as she sounded.

Her mother pressed her lips in a tight line. To keep from saying more, Grace guessed. Then turned away. Grace climbed up the steps again.

"Good night, Mama," she called down softly.

The small lamp in the living room switched off, but her mother didn't answer. Grace heard her sigh in the dark.

Chapter Twenty-Seven

Grace could have easily slept past noon, but Rose wouldn't let her. She stomped around the bedroom, opening and shutting drawers, tossing clothes, and dropping shoes.

Grace rolled over and covered her head with a pillow. Which was all the encouragement her sister needed. Rose grabbed her foot and gave it a shake.

"Get up, Grace. You don't have much time."

"Go away… I need to sleep." Her grumbled protest was muffled by the bedclothes.

"It's your own fault. I woke up at two, and your bed was still empty. Where were you all night?"

"None of your business," Grace mumbled.

"Okay, save it for confession. Mama wants us all to go to nine o'clock mass. She says we have to stop skulking around the neighborhood like we have something to be ashamed of."

Grace wholeheartedly agreed with her mother's decision, but it still didn't inspire her to open her eyes. She rolled over and pushed a wad of hair off her face. She'd dropped into bed without even a hair net and needed a wash and set today. Or tonight at the club, she'd look like Gravel Gertie.

"I'm too tired for church. Ma will understand."

Rose sat on the end of Grace's bed and purposely made it bounce. Then put on her shoes, sedate brown oxfords with laces and a stack heel.

"Better not let Frank see those." Grace knew how her sister's fiancé liked to see Rose dressed as stylish as possible, at all times. Even at Sunday mass.

"My new heels gave me a blister. And Frank's not meeting us at church."

Rose's eyes were glassy with either anger or hurt feelings. Maybe both. "He has to help a buddy move some furniture."

A thin excuse, Grace thought. Rose saw through it, too. She walked to the dressing table and sat down with a sigh. Grace gave up and pushed herself up against her pillows.

"You'll see him later. He'll come over for dinner."

"I don't think so." Rose's back was turned, but Grace saw her reflection in the mirror. "He said the job might take all day, and he'll be too tired to come by tonight."

She looked about to cry, but picked up a lipstick, smeared it on, then pressed her lips with a tissue. The color wasn't right for her complexion, but Grace kept the beauty advice to herself.

Instead, she said, "You can borrow my kid gloves if you like."

"Thanks. I will." Rose picked up the pair and pulled one on. Then stared at her hand.

"Are you and Frank having problems, honey?"

Rose nodded. Her chin trembled. "He wants to postpone the wedding. Until we know what's going to happen to Joe." She spun around to face Grace. "But the case might not go to trial for months. That's what the lawyer told Pop."

"Maybe Frank thinks it will be hard to hold a nice wedding while Joe's in jail. We'll all be focused on him instead of the bride."

"That's not why. I wish it were. He never says it outright, but what Joe did, sleeping with that colored woman and who knows what else—it disgusts him. When he looks at me now, he's thinking about that. I can just tell."

Before Grace could reply, she added, "I know he doesn't mean to blame me. But he looks at me differently now, Grace. I feel it. I really do."

Grace knew Frank's faults better than anyone. She knew he was small-minded and rife with prejudice. Fearful of anything unfamiliar, and everything he didn't understand. Which was plenty. But she never thought he'd hurt her sister this way. She wanted to knock on his door and punch him in the nose, no questions asked.

"I'm sure he's shook up. We all are. It's barely been a week since Joe was arrested. Give him a little time," she said quietly.

Rose shook her head. "I wish that was so, but he won't get over it. I know the way he thinks. The worst part is, I want to be mad at him. I *am* mad at him. Mad as hell sometimes. But I still love him, and I'm afraid. He's pushing me away, and I don't know what to do."

"Oh, honey. I'm sorry." Grace got up and hugged Rose close.

"I know you don't want to hear it, but I'm even madder at Joe. This is his fault. If he wants to ruin his life, it's his own business," Rose stammered into her shoulder. "He didn't have to ruin mine, too."

Grace felt her body tense, ready to defend their brother. What about Frank? Isn't he the one who's ruining things? But pointing that out would do little good.

The baby of the family, Rose, always got her way. Ever since her mother had placed the swaddled, pink infant in Grace's arms, she'd always indulged her. Protected her. Smoothed her way as much as she could. Joe did, too. As well as their otherwise strict parents. Rose hadn't been spoiled with material things; the family's modest means would not allow for that. But in other ways, sooner or later, Rose always got her way.

All she'd ever really wanted was to be a bride. She'd played wedding with her dolls endlessly and dress-up, as well. She was well rehearsed for the shining day when she'd walk down the aisle for real, in a white satin gown and flowing veil, with everyone looking on. A princess in a fairy tale. For a few hours at least.

Almost in her grasp, her prize was slipping away, melting like cotton candy in her hands. And there was nothing she could do. Of course, she was angry and upset. But in her heart, she knew the truth. It was too hard to admit Frank Stanco was such a shallow, ignorant man. Of course, she blamed Joe.

Grace hugged Rose tight, then let her go. She smoothed her hair with her hand. "It's going to be okay, honey. Joe's going to get out of this, and Frank will come around. He'll be sorry for the way he's treating you. You'll see."

That final note was wishful thinking, for Rose's sake. Grace thought Rose would be well rid of Frank. Her sister could do a lot better, though Rose obviously didn't see it that way.

Rose forced a smile. "I'll light a candle to St. Jude this morning, just in case."

The saint of impossible causes, Grace's favorite. "Good plan. Light one for me, while you're at it."

* * *

"I don't believe half of this. You're pulling my leg, right?"

Grace shook her head, her mouth filled with a bite of hot dog she'd bought from a cart. She sat on a bench in front of the Brooklyn Botanic Gardens, alongside her best friend, the real Lucille Bianco. On a rare weekend off, Lucille had come back to Brooklyn to visit her parents and called Grace while the family was still at church. They quickly made plans to meet on Court Street and take the subway to the gardens and Prospect Park.

On the ride over, Grace had filled Lucille in on the days since Joe's arrest and what she'd been doing to help him.

"I barely believe it either." Grace wiped her mouth with a paper napkin. "I know Joe's innocent, but I don't know if he'll get out of it. This is major league, Lucille. Not like his fist fights in the school yard."

Her friend grabbed her hand. "You'll get him out of it. He's damn lucky you care so much."

"He's my brother. What else can I do?"

"Act like Rose." Lucille had heard all about Rose's reaction and Frank's, too.

"Rose and I are different. We'll always be. I don't know how I'd act if I was the one getting married."

"I don't think that would make any difference to you." Lucille tipped a bottle of Coke back to catch the last drops. "It's probably not a good time to ask, but I see you so little. Have you heard from the Finnerans?"

Grace watched a pigeon peck the sidewalk and tossed a few crumbs from her roll.

"We said hello at church on Easter. But they didn't mention anything."

About Colin, she meant. Whenever she ran into his parents, it was so hard to even say his name. She knew if there was any news, they would tell her right away. It seemed pointless and even painful to ask.

"I feel guilty for saying this, but I haven't thought about Colin much this last week or so. Not the way I used to."

She could admit that to Lucille, of all the people she knew.

"I think that's good. It shows you're moving on, finally. You don't have to feel guilty, Grace. You should be going out and having fun. Colin would never want you to molder away like a nun or something."

Grace laughed. "I'm hardly moldering. Rose and my mother make sure of that." As they strolled into the garden, she told Lucille about her disastrous night with Don Rappley, embellishing the amusing moments.

"The funny thing is, I just about puked all over his leather upholstery, and he won't stop calling me."

Lucille could hardly answer; she was laughing so hard. "I keep telling you, men love it when you play hard to get."

The cherry blossoms were in bloom. They took the path to the Promenade and stood speechless at the top of the long corridor of trees. Countless clouds of pink petals swayed in the breeze, suspended on fragile black branches. Some floated down like confetti as they walked beneath, making her feel unexpectedly lighthearted and hopeful.

For the first time in nearly a week, Grace felt peaceful. She walked beside her friend as if transported to a heavenly place, far from all her worries.

"I'm graduating in a few weeks. Can you believe it?" Lucille sounded relieved and excited.

"I'm so proud of you, Lu. Envious, too," Grace admitted. "I wish I was doing more with myself than working for Harry Shaw."

"It's not your fault you got fired. Maybe it worked out for the best. You wouldn't be able to help Joe this way if you were still at Pioneer."

"I've thought about that. But after this mess is all over, I should look for a better job. Or start night school. Or both." She shook her head and threaded her arm through Lucille's. "Look at you. Your work is meaningful. You're really helping people. I'm just treading water. Waiting for some Don

Rappley to put a ring on my finger and give me babies. Is that when my life is supposed to start? The rest of it, just 'sitting on the shelf'?"

Lucille's boyfriend had been killed on Omaha Beach, and she had not been serious about anyone since. At twenty-five, Grace knew that people start to wonder why women their age weren't married. But it was different for Lucille. She had a career now, a place in the world. Grace felt jealous and frustrated.

"I understand, and I think you could be or do anything you set your mind to, Gracie. But you can't solve everything at once. Right now, you need to do your best for Joe. Keep working for this investigator, who I hope didn't disappear on you. After things settle down, you can figure out what you really want to do. And go after it. The way you always do."

It was good advice. Advice Grace would have given herself, but even more encouraging coming from a friend who knew her better than anyone.

Lucille met her gaze. "What do you think about our plan now? Sharing a place in the city after I graduate? I still want to do it, but if you've changed your mind, I understand. I can ask a girl from school."

"Don't you dare. Don't even think about it, Lucille Therese Domenica Bianco. Count me in. All the way."

If nothing else, the last few days had shown Grace she was ready to leave the house on Sackett Street, no matter what happened to Joe. Or what her family said.

"We'll be old maids together and take in stray cats," Grace added.

Lucille looked puzzled by the prediction. "Stray cats? For pity's sake, Grace. How about stray *men*? I'm just getting started. Let's have some fun."

Lucille had to get back to Flushing Hospital for a shift and left the park at two o'clock. Grace knew if she went home for Sunday dinner, her family would make it impossible for her to go back into the city. She called the house, and Rose answered, sounding disappointed that it wasn't Frank.

Grace told her she was out with a friend, taking in a movie and eating dinner afterward. Rose sounded unhappy to be left alone with their parents and grandmother. Grace felt sorry for her, but there was nothing she could do.

She found a bench on a quiet walkway near the Daffodil Hill. She'd brought along her notebook and set down recollections from her conversation with Arty.

"Mary had a lot of men in love with her besides your brother, didn't she? What a juggling act," Lucille had said.

"I don't think she thought of it as a juggling act. I don't think it was intentional. Men just…fell for her. Does a flower think about juggling bees? No, the bees just buzz around it," Grace said, remembering the words of Louis Robillard.

Lucille had been amused. She'd been eating an ice cream cone, which was rapidly melting. She licked a few chocolate jimmies off her fingers. "Jealousy. The kind that makes you see red. Any one of those Romeos could have lost his head and killed her. And framed your brother, which would have made the deed doubly satisfying, since it seems he'd won Mary's heart over all the competition."

Grace had already thought of that. "But which of them did it? That's what I can't figure out. Whoever it was planned carefully. They lifted Joe's jacket and hid it somewhere. They knew he'd go to Mary's and what time he'd get there."

"It had to be someone from the club," Lucille concluded.

Grace agreed. "Joe is convinced Martone killed her or paid someone do it. I've seen Eddie's temper. I could easily imagine him stabbing Mary for far less than cheating on him. Never mind plans to run away to Paris with Joe. But I can't dismiss the idea that Mary knew something that put her in danger."

It felt good to talk out her theories with Lucille. Though she should have been hashing them out with Harry. She hoped he'd pop out of the hole he'd been hiding in. It had only been three days since she'd left him on a corner in Greenwich Village, but it felt a lot longer.

She bought another Coke and took out the novel she'd found at Mary's bedside. She wasn't sure why she'd walked off with it. The apartment was a crime scene, and everything in it was possibly evidence. Even if it was of no interest to the police, it belonged to Mary's family now and should be returned. She'd find their address and mail it to them soon.

It wasn't like her to have sticky fingers. But the small, solid possession in her hands made her feel close to Mary, and a small part of her hoped some secrets would appear between the lines.

She opened the book and turned a few pages. There were notes jotted in the margins, and Grace wondered if the hand was Mary's, marking moments in the story that had moved her. Grace flipped to the jacket copy and quickly read it through. The story was about Lottie Johnson, a young colored woman who aspires to be a singer, but "meets a tragic end." The details were not given away, though she could imagine the rest.

She studied the author's photo, Ann Petry, who had somehow managed to write and publish a best-selling book. How many Negro writers, men and women, poets, painters, musicians, all kinds of artists, had created wonderful books and songs and art, but would never find this level of recognition in the world at large? Or anything close? In the white world, she should call it. Their work was hidden. Buried. Much like Mary's amazing talent and the stardom she should have achieved someday. A talent the world would never know now. The thought made her feel hollow inside and incredibly sad.

The book jacket slid, and a sheet of paper folded in a small square slipped out from beneath the back flap. Grace smoothed it open, expecting to find more of Mary's notes about the story.

She unfolded a single sheet of stationery, dated late March, and covered in a neat, even script.

Dear Mary,

I know you hate it when I get "all preachy," but my heart overflows to know you'll lead our choir on Easter Sunday. You might say my prayers have been answered. Your beautiful voice aside, to see you back in His house will bring me joy.

Spring is the season of new beginnings. Especially on Easter, when out of cold ashes and dashed hopes new life rises. I pray this day marks a new start for you, as well.

I know your life does not easily allow early rising on Sunday morning and a long subway ride, just to sit on a hard bench and listen to a windbag like me. But I humbly implore you to return to some church of your choosing. Most of all, to return to a Christian life. To the path you know is right.

God is waiting to be part of your life again. You and He were close companions once. As another former friend, I do know that about you.

I make this request of Mary Delmore, not Lana Delmar. I promise you, if Mary puts Him back at the top of her list; everything will fall into place. Most of all, she will find peace in her heart. That brilliant smile might fool the world, but it never fools me. The last time we spoke, you seemed troubled. I can only guess what weighs so heavily on your heart. And no conjecture sits well.

Do you remember what we meant to each other once? Etched on my heart, those moments are a part of me. For those lost days and memories, I beg you, let me help you. I fear you're drifting down a dangerous path, beyond the reach of my aid, or anyone's.

If you can no longer confide in me, give your troubles to the Lord. He will guide you, though his advice may not be what you want to hear.

I will meet you anytime, anywhere. Please let me help you, Mary. Until then, I hold you in prayer.

Always,

Lester

Grace sat back, the note in her hand. Reverend Lester Holmes was suddenly added to the list of buzzing bees. Right at the top.

Chapter Twenty-Eight

"Late nights agree with you, Ava. You're looking lovelier than ever." Arty had just locked the office and strolled beside her, cigarette cartons tucked under one arm and bottles of whiskey in each hand. He was as full of baloney tonight as usual. Or maybe it was kielbasa. Either way, his flattery fed her ego, she had to admit.

"It's the extra make-up. Otherwise, I'd look like a cadaver."

He laughed. "I hope our date was worth losing a little beauty sleep?"

"Oh, it definitely was." Hearing the history of the club's principal players made the time more than well spent.

Belying his reputation as a wolf, there'd been a mostly chaste kiss goodnight before Arty put her in a cab and insisted on giving the driver two bucks for the fare.

When they reached the bar, he handed her the cartons. "This should hold you for the night. Plenty of Chesterfields. If you need anything else, just whistle."

Grace ignored his wink and headed to the check room for the tray. The last few days, she'd pushed aside worries of being found out. Fooled herself into believing she was in control. But her good friend Lucille's shock and concern about this adventure had hit home. Now she wasn't sure how much longer she could string out the charade. The risk grew higher by the hour.

"Where's your change purse, Lucy? It's almost seven." Judy's greeting snapped Grace to attention. She'd just set up the tray and nearly tipped it over.

"I was just about to put it on." Lucy produced the annoying accessory, which made her feel like a bus conductor, and buckled it around her waist.

Just as Arty had predicted, there was no evidence in Judy's appearance of last night's overindulgence, or the least chagrin about it.

Outfitted tonight in a topaz blue suit of silk shantung, the club manager looked as if she'd stopped by on her way to a cocktail party on Sutton Place. Her long hair was pinned in a smooth French roll. A pearl necklace and earrings completed the elegant outfit, along with her usual aloof attitude.

It might have been a dress rehearsal for meeting Carter's parents. Grace couldn't help but think of the wrinkle in that romance.

When the house lights dimmed for the first set, there were far fewer tables filled than Friday or Saturday night, but the poker players still came in. Some sat at the bar for a quick shot of Dutch courage, some went straight to the basement. She already recognized many faces.

The band was halfway through the first set when she saw him. He sat at the end of the bar, his head down, reading a newspaper. Or pretending to. He called Arty over and ordered a drink, Bourbon straight up, sidecar of soda.

Did Harry know he'd find her there? That was impossible. He'd come to investigate. She felt relieved to see it.

She waited on customers, wondering when he'd notice her. A woman at the bar beckoned, and Grace walked over, chin up, shoulders back. Harry's glance took her in and returned to the paper. When he slowly looked up again, his mouth twitched at the corner for just a moment.

Grace sold a pack of Kools and two packs of Parliaments at the next table.

"Miss? Some cigarettes, please."

She walked over and held out the tray. "What brand would you like, sir?"

As if she didn't know.

"Luckys will do."

She picked out a pack and set it on the bar. "Thirty cents, please."

"Here you go. Keep the change." He reached into his pocket and gave her a quarter and a dime. "What's your name?"

"Lucy." Her smile was swift and impersonal. "I'm sorry, sir. I'm not allowed to chat with the customers. Enjoy the show."

"I'm enjoying it already…Lucy." He watched her walk away. "Hey, you forgot something." When she turned, he tapped the pack. "These aren't much good without matches."

Grace took a book from the tray and placed it next to his drink. "Sorry, sir."

"Fellow down on the end needs some smokes, Lucy." Arty had drifted towards them, polishing glasses. He gave Harry a sizing-up look as he spoke.

"I'm on it. Thanks, Arty." She took hold of the tray and quickly walked away.

Arty followed, walking behind the bar. About halfway down, he said, "That guy at the end of the bar bothering you? I can call Dante."

"He's harmless. You should see what I put up with." She smiled and headed to the tables.

She kept an eye on Harry as she moved about the room, but he barely glanced at her again. He watched the stage and ordered another drink. A couple sat down next to him who both had "Tourist" stamped on their foreheads. They seemed intent on drawing him into a conversation. She smiled to herself, knowing how much he was enjoying that.

At the end of the set, she walked to the check room to refill the tray. Harry was suddenly beside her, in front of the Dutch door. He looked past her and offered Pauline his hat check.

The girl disappeared into the closet, and he turned to Grace. "I think you dropped this. Miss."

He held out a matchbook, his expression blank. She glanced at him, then folded the matches in the palm of her hand.

"Thanks. They fall off left and right."

"You need to be more careful." His expression was grave.

She didn't answer. Pauline appeared with his black Homburg. Harry nodded his thanks and dropped a few coins in her jar. He fit the hat on his head and strolled out.

"Mind watching the tray a minute?" she asked Pauline. "I need to powder my nose."

"Sure. Just leave it."

Grace dropped the tray and headed for the restroom. Once inside, she opened the matchbook and found Harry's square handwriting. A single word, "McNulty's."

She freshened her lipstick and fluffed her hair for good measure, in case Pauline noticed. When she came out, the hallway was filled with card players. They looked confused and annoyed as Dante and Bernard herded them towards the bar.

"What the hell is going on? I was holding a full house. Aces high, for once in my goddamn life—"

"Shut up and move," Bernard growled.

She slipped along the wall like a bug, against the flow of irate gamblers. Then, through the swinging doors and down the narrow corridor that led to the kitchen.

The door to Dolores's dressing room stood open and dark. She slipped in and peered out. She could see into the kitchen, a bit beyond the frame of the doorway. It was enough.

The side door framed a view of the alley, the cool night air cutting through the steam and cooking smells. A truck was parked outside, and a delivery was being unloaded. Hubie, Bernard, and a few kitchen helpers carried in wooden crates.

Eddie was supervising. Grace had never seen him in the kitchen before. She'd never seen him talk directly to the help except for Judy and Arty.

"Down the basement. The cold box. Move it. Bernard, get the key."

Cook, a quiet man with a thin mustache named Constantine, turned from the big stove and handed Eddie's man a key ring.

The crates were carried to the basement as if a column of ants were transporting their treasures. Ice dripped from the slats, and she smelled the unmistakable odor of fish.

A driver stood at the side door. Eddie grabbed his collar with both hands and lifted the man off his feet. "What the hell took you? If this load is short, I'll crack your head open like an egg."

Eddie bounced the man's skull on the metal door; his hat flew off, and his chin bobbed. "I already told you; we broke down. The truck was leaking oil.

Swear to God, I called this place ten times. Nobody picked up."

"The hell you did." Eddie tightened his grip, and the trucker's face turned red.

He flailed, trying to grab Eddie's arm. "Knock it off…" The driver's words were choked. "I get the point."

Eddie pressed harder, and the trucker gasped, unable to speak. Just before the man was about to black out, Eddie let go.

The driver slid to the floor, coughing and gripping his throat. Grace swallowed hard, relieved to hear him breathe.

What was this about? Martone, flipping his lid over a fish delivery? Despite the price of oysters and even factoring in his explosive temper, there had to be more going on.

A crate crashed to the floor. Hubie and Dante jumped aside and cursed as cigarette cartons spilled in all directions. Gauloises. All of them.

"Pick that up, god damn it! Get it out downstairs." Eddie shouted and waved his arm.

The men kicked aside the slats of wood and gathered the scattered bounty. Then stuck it all in a burlap sack that Hubie held open, one that usually held potatoes. As they headed for the basement, Sylvie appeared and picked up the pieces of the broken crate.

Grace stepped back into the darkness. She wasn't sure what she'd witnessed, but it seemed a good time to return to the front of the house before anyone noticed she was gone.

The corridor was empty, but Eddie was still in the kitchen, and she was afraid to be spotted. Two waiters and a busboy pushed through the doors, carrying dirty dishes. She walked out of the dressing room and headed for safety.

She'd almost reached the bar when Judy appeared. "I've been looking for you, Lucy. Where the heck have you been?"

"I'm sorry. I had to use the ladies'. Something I ate. I'll get right back to work."

"You'd better." Judy watched her walk away. "I'll tell you when you can leave the floor. Do that again, and you're fired."

"I understand." Grace nearly squeaked her reply.

***

"How about a real drink tonight, Ava? It's not even that late."

The club had closed a little earlier than Saturday night, but it was late enough. Grace was at the bar, counting the coins from her tips so Arty could give her bills. She'd changed quickly; her coat and purse sat on a stool beside her. She was eager to meet Harry but didn't want to seem in too much of a hurry.

"Maybe some other night. I need to memorize some lines for a class tomorrow. I don't want to be embarrassed."

"I'd love to see you on stage sometime." Arty caught her eye as he wiped off a liquor bottle. "Before you hit it big and leave the little people like me behind."

Grace ignored his flirting and tried not to smile. "You can say you knew me when."

She pushed the greater part of the coins toward him. "I'll take a buck and a half for this pile, please."

Arty swept the change into his hand without counting, then gave her the bill and two quarters. A busboy approached with the Hoover, cutting off their conversation. Grace grabbed her things and waved goodnight. Then left by the front door.

She stood in the alley slipping on her coat when Sylvie appeared, dragging a trash pail to the sidewalk. She wiggled it in place, then stood up straight and rubbed her back.

Grace called and walked down to meet her. "I couldn't get out for a smoke. Judy caught me without the tray, and after that, she wouldn't let me out of her sight."

"Yeah, I saw you."

Grace wasn't sure if Sylvie meant that she noticed Judy's scolding. Or that she saw Grace hiding in the dressing room during the commotion in the kitchen.

But Sylvie would not give her away. Grace felt sure of that.

"Let's have a smoke tomorrow. She usually gives me time off around ten."

Sylvie smiled. "If you can stay out of trouble till then."

The side door opened, and Hubie peered out. "Get back in here, Sylvie. You're not done yet. Time to mop up."

Sylvie said goodnight and walked back up the alley. Grace waited until the door closed, then pulled off her gloves and turned to the trash pails. She gingerly lifted the first lid. Holding her breath was little defense against the pungent, fishy smell. She hoped the effort would be worth it.

Slats from the broken crate were in the third pail. She sifted through, looking for any piece with a label or stamp. She found a few marks burned into the wood and fragments of stenciled letters, impossible to decipher under the streetlamp. It wasn't a good idea to linger. Someone could come out of the club at any minute.

She stuck her plunder under her arm and headed to McNulty's. She had a lot to tell Harry.

Chapter Twenty-Nine

She hadn't noticed him waiting outside the bar until he stepped out of the shadows. "There you are. I was starting to worry."

His patronizing attitude annoyed her, though she should have expected it. She'd been doing fine the last few days on her own. But she wouldn't win any points with him on that question. Probably just the opposite.

"I don't know why you would. I'm just Lucy Bianco, aspiring actress. The only thing she's suspected of so far is being clumsy."

"As if you'd know if Martone sussed you out." He finished his cigarette and flicked the butt to the curb. "I guess you're not interested in hearing what a stupid, dangerous stunt you're pulling."

"There are more important things to talk about."

"How long have you been working there?"

"Not very long, since Friday. I've heard some interesting stories. And seen things. More than the poker game Joe told us about."

Harry looked unconvinced. "If something had happened to you in there, I'd be responsible."

Grace laughed. "You're my boss, Harry, not my keeper, or even my C.O. I'm the only one responsible for where I go and what I do. Not you, or my family, or anyone else. If it's any consolation, I would have wormed my way into the club given half a chance, even if you had been around. Though your absence did make it easier."

Harry squinted at her, his jaw set, and she braced herself for another round. But he didn't say more.

"Where were you all that time, anyway? You told me you were going to work on Joe's case, but I have a feeling that's not the whole story." His expression darkened, and she wondered if she'd gone too far.

"It's actually none of your business, Grace… If you must know, I had to take care of some loose ends for another client. That's all I'm going to say about it."

Grace met his gaze and took a long breath. She sensed that whatever messy business had drawn Harry away was as serious as it was confidential. Most likely, she'd never know.

"I hope the ends were tied up to your satisfaction," she said.

"More or less. I'm still waiting for the final verdict. But I can tell you this—I'm one hundred and ten per cent focused on Joe now. It's time for you to step aside and let me do my job."

"I had a feeling you were going to say that, too." Grace met his gaze and summoned a calm, polite tone. "What if you table your objections until you hear what I found out?"

He sighed and shook his head. Giving her this round, at least. "Fine… consider them tabled. For now." His gaze rested on the wood. "Can I at least ask why you're carrying around that bunch of…what is that anyway?"

Grace held the slats closer. "Pieces of a crate. It could be important."

He shook his head and stepped back politely so she could walk ahead. "Let's get a drink, Sherlock."

* * *

They found a table in the back room. The bar was much emptier than the last time she'd been there, but it was late on a Sunday night. Harry ordered a Bourbon straight up and a sidecar of soda. Grace had the same.

When the waitress left, she said, "I sat back here with Mary. It's hard to believe that was only a week ago tomorrow. It feels like a lifetime. I felt like the world was crashing down because Joe and Mary were in love and about to run off together. If only they had." She took a breath and looked up at him. "Now I know what a real disaster is—Mary murdered in such a cruel, senseless way, and Joe sent to jail for it. Maybe, if I'd acted differently, if I'd tried to help them, none of that would have happened."

Harry met her gaze, his expression softening. "Nothing you could have said or done would have changed things, Grace. Someone was out to get Mary and frame Joe. Period."

She wasn't so sure of that. She didn't answer. She set her notebook on the table and laid her hand flat across the cover.

"This is everything I've learned the last few days. Including my thoughts about the people I've spoken to, and what I've seen and heard. I've written it all down. Like the case notes you give me to type."

She waited, wondering if Harry was going to laugh. Or worse, demean her efforts in a humoring but condescending way. His expression showed only curiosity. Mild curiosity, she had to admit. But that was better than the alternatives.

"All right, let's hear what you've got." He took a sip of bourbon, and she did, too. The whiskey burned the back of the throat, but in a good way.

She flipped open the book and began with her visit to Mary's apartment building. Harry had been there, too, earlier today. He hadn't found Louis Robillard at home and was interested in what the old man had to say.

As she spoke, she noticed Harry's expression and attitude change, from curious to interested and even, seriously interested. When she came to the conversation with Gem Washington and the information Arty had related, he looked impressed. Even surprised.

Harry sipped the last of his drink and waved for another. "Who do you think did it?"

"I can't say yet. Or why she was killed. There's a lot going on at the club. Maybe more than you know about."

She flipped the pages to her notes from Saturday and told him about the delivery of cartons, the boxes from Luxor Electronics, among them.

"The place is a clearing house for hot stuff. But no one's been able to catch him. Martone moves the goods too quickly."

"Where does it go?"

"Overseas, probably. To be sold on the black market. All kinds of little luxuries can be sold for big profits there right now. Not even luxuries, really. Things we take for granted, alarm clocks, clothes, shoes, and purses. Liquor and cigarettes."

"Cigarettes. Right." She nodded. "I've heard they're used for money in Germany."

"More widely accepted than Deutschmarks," he replied. "Pretty soon, no one in the U.S. will be able to send cigarettes as gifts to servicemen. Seems to be fueling the problem."

"Which brings me to something strange I saw tonight. And the wood."

"Go on." Harry took a long draw on his cigarette.

"Right after you left, there was a racket in the kitchen. I hid in the singer's dressing room and watched."

She told Harry about the late delivery and the broken crate, and the chaotic scene that followed.

"Cigarettes are not stored in the basement, in the cold box. They're kept in a special closet in Eddie's office, with the liquor. Eddie grabbed the truck driver by the throat and nearly strangled the guy. It didn't make sense, even for him. And why would a crate of Gauloises be delivered with fish? That doesn't make sense either."

"None of it does. I could see if the brand was American. Eddie would be sending it to Europe with the rest of the loot. But a French brand would be traveling in the wrong direction."

She picked up the wood from the chair beside her. "I found these pieces of the broken crate in the trash. Maybe the marks will tell us something."

He met her gaze. "You catch on quickly. I'll grant you that."

His compliment was sincere, but half-baked. She laughed. "Thanks, but it's not exactly rocket science."

He looked about to reply, but let it pass. "Let's spread this stuff out and see what fits."

A few minutes later, they'd deciphered the stenciled letters, like the word jumble at the bottom of the funny pages. Their puzzle said, "Blue-Fin Seafood, Montauk, N.Y."

Harry examined the other marks, fragments of a red seal and letters burned into the wood. "The crate came through Marseilles, from what I can see. The city is a hub now for illegal drugs that flow from Turkey and Morocco. Heroin mainly. Cannabis, too. There was always a trickle, but since the War, business is booming and so is the demand on this side, sadly."

"Who's managing all this? French gangsters?" she asked.

"Some. I'm ashamed to say there are a lot of ex-GIs with a criminal bent involved, too. Most of them were deserters. They stayed behind and found easy money dealing in the black market. And now, drugs. Stateside, the Mafia figured out that pushing drugs is even more profitable than their usual rackets, protection, and gambling. The demand just grows and grows."

Grace was surprised to learn former U.S. soldiers were involved in such a dark, sordid enterprise. "So, Eddie has ties to the Mafia? I know he's awful, but that's major league. Isn't it?"

"You might say he inherited the connections. Eddie's father, Leo, was never very high on the chain of command, but he was part of the Bonanno family. It took four years and a mistrial, but Leo finally went up for thirty to life, for extortion and conspiracy to murder. Whatever rackets he had going were split up among the Capos. Eddie was left a few Tinker Toys. The poker game and some working girls. I'm sure he kicks back up and resents every penny. No way is Leo's little boy sanctioned to deal heroin. He'd have to be doing it under the mob's radar. Very risky for him, but high profit, too."

"Do you think that's what came in the crate?" Grace had not suspected drugs were in the mix, but it was starting to make some sense to her.

"From what you've said and the marks on the wood, it seems likely. And it's a strong motive for him killing Mary if she'd found out. She may have threatened to tell the cops if he didn't let her leave with Joe. Or maybe she threatened to tell the mob. Who'd fix his wagon even faster. And permanently."

Grace didn't think Mary had it in her to blackmail anyone, even Eddie. Not for money. But she could see Mary using the knowledge as a bargaining chip to gain her freedom.

"The bottom line is, if Mary knew, it put her in danger; whether she was shaking down Eddie or not." He paused for a long, thoughtful drag on his cigarette. "I'd love to blow the whistle on Martone. You don't know how much. But all we have now is a story about a row in a restaurant kitchen, and a bunch of broken sticks."

Grace hated it when Harry played devil's advocate. It only made her resolve stronger. "There's one way to be sure. I'll get a pack of Gauloises from the cold box tomorrow night." She braced herself for his reaction.

"You're pulling my leg, right? No way in hell are you going back in there." His voice was low and unyielding. He squinted at her through a thread of smoke.

Instead of her temper rising to meet his, she felt distant, detached. It wasn't just the late hour or the liquor dulling her senses. She felt as if a switch had flipped. She was finished with anyone telling her what she could and could not do. Especially a man.

"I told you before, Harry, it's not for you to say." She looked at him squarely and answered in a calm tone.

He sat back, his jaw tight. "Be reasonable, Grace. You've done some good work the last few days. No question. But you need to let me handle it now."

"I can get into the cold box. I don't see how you could get within a hundred feet of it. You don't even know where it is. Maybe you'll put on one of your fake uniforms and claim someone called about a gas leak?"

He smiled. "That's actually not a bad idea."

"And Eddie will send Dante or Bernard to hold the flashlight. How does that figure into the plan?"

His expression acknowledged her point. He tossed back the rest of his bourbon and washed it down with the soda. "It's late. I'm bushed. I bet you are, too. My car is right outside. I'll drive you back to Brooklyn."

"I am tired, too." Grace had left the club excited and alert, but suddenly felt deflated. "Red Hook is out of your way. I can find a cab."

He rose and put his hat on, glancing at her from beneath the brim. "We can talk more on the way. If it's really drugs, it might be moved out of the club any minute. Tonight, for all we know."

She knew that was true. She braced herself for another round of sparring as Harry led her to an old black Nash, parked in front of McNulty's.

At least he'd used the word "we." That was some progress.

Chapter Thirty

The silence in the car made her nervous as Harry drove downtown, but it was also a relief. She glanced at his profile, illuminated by the passing lights.

Finally, she said, "Were you working on Joe's case over the weekend?"

"Enough to know you were a few steps ahead of me." He glanced at her. "You seem to have a knack for it."

"Don't try to flatter me, Harry. I'm not that gullible."

"I mean it." His tone was flat, matter-of-fact. "I'll borrow that notebook if you don't mind. I'll give it back tomorrow."

"Keep it as long as you like." She was surprised that he'd asked. "I'll start another."

"That's just it. You need to leave the heavy lifting to me, Grace. I know how you feel. You've made that clear. But this is serious. You're no good to Joe if something happens to you. Something so bad you can't even imagine it."

Trouble was, she could. Especially when she recalled how Eddie had pushed Judy down the stairs. Or the sight of him, with blood in his eyes, gripping a steak knife. But she still wasn't willing to give in to Harry's demand. She stared straight ahead and didn't answer.

"You want to know how the Martones operate when someone crosses them? I'll tell you a story about this cop I knew. Young, idealistic type who came up the ranks fast and made detective early. Arrogant, too. The way young guys can be. This was a few years ago. Leo Martone was on trial for ordering a hit on some businessman in Queens. The guy ran a trucking company and wouldn't pay protection. Leo had to make an example of him and had the fellow beaten to a pulp, a few of his trucks set on fire.

"This cop had been undercover in the trucking yard. He was a material witness. Everybody warned him what might happen if he testified. Threats from Leo's gang. Even the D.A. warned him. This kid was cocky. Nobody was going to tell him what to do. Nobody was going to scare him off. He gets up on the stand and says his piece. First trial ends in a hung jury. Bought off or scared off is more like it. The cop goes into the service, comes back just in time to testify at Leo's second trial. The D.A. nails Martone, and everyone calls the cop a hero. Couldn't have won the conviction without him. Leo goes away for a long time, no chance of parole."

Grace had a feeling she knew where this story was going, but she didn't want to interrupt. He seemed in a trance as he steered the car down the empty, misty avenues.

"A few months later, the cop's wife wants to see her sister in Westchester. He's been out all night. His head is bigger than a Thanksgiving Day float, and he tells her he'll take her another time. They argue, and she gets in the car alone. She's driving crosstown from Murray Hill to the West Side Highway and sails through a red light. Garbage truck plows right into the driver's side. Because she's a bad driver? Nope. The brake lines were cut. Meant for the hero cop, of course."

He stopped speaking but didn't turn to look at her.

Grace was afraid to ask the question but had to. "Did the woman die?"

"She might as well have. It would have been kinder."

Grace's mouth went dry. She drew a deep breath. "How awful for them… How horrible for your friend to have that hanging over him."

"He's not a friend. Not really. I haven't seen that guy in a long time," he added quietly. "I'll tell you something else. The punchline to the story. He's sorry as hell now that he stuck his neck out, trying to do the right thing. He told me once it wasn't worth it. Not one damn bit."

They'd come to the bridge. Grace stared out her window at the lights along the Promenade and the long, gray warehouses along the river.

She knew what Harry was trying to say. But the risk would be worth it if it saved Joe from a lifetime in jail. Or worse. She didn't feel as if she had a choice.

"I'll go to the club tomorrow night for the last time. If I can't get into the cold box without drawing attention, I won't even try."

She could tell by the set of his jaw that he didn't like that plan. When he didn't reply, she added. "I won't do anything stupid, Harry. If anyone even looks at me funny, I'll walk right out. How can they find me? They don't even know my real name."

These people have their ways, she expected him to say. But he didn't have to.

Headlights from cars in the opposite lane slipped across his face. "I know how it is when you're so close to getting your hands on what you came for, and it's just out of reach. You can taste it. And you take stupid chances. Even a seasoned hack, like me."

She did feel that way but knew admitting it would only bolster his objections.

"I trust Lucy Bianco. She has good instincts. She's a natural at this job." She meant it as a joke, but he didn't smile.

They drove past Cadman Plaza and down Court Street. Grace told him where to turn, and they soon pulled up in front of her family's house. The light over the front door was still on, but all the windows were dark. He gazed at the narrow, two-story brick building, nearly identical to the rest on the street. She wondered what he was thinking.

"Will you be in the office tomorrow?" she asked.

"Just to pick up messages and check the mail. I don't expect you to come in if that's what you mean."

"I'm going to Fort Greene to visit Reverend Holmes. He and Mary were once sweethearts. They even talked about marriage. She told me it wasn't Joe that broke them up. She made a choice between her singing career and being a minister's wife."

"Mary probably had a lot of men in her past. I think we need to concentrate on the plates she was spinning recently."

"I see it just the opposite way. Mary was the plate being spun, with every man in her life wanting something different from her. Each with their own idea of what she should be." Before he could answer, she added, "I have to include Reverend Holmes on that list. I found a letter he wrote to her a few weeks ago. It sounds like he never got over her. He pleaded with her to give up the path she'd taken. He sounded upset."

Grace opened her purse and took out Mary's novel. "I found this on her dresser. The letter was tucked in the back."

He stared at the book, then back up at her. "You took evidence from a crime scene. Do you realize that?"

She could tell he was angry, but also tired, and wouldn't go on about it. "I didn't think of it that way. Mrs. Beale said the police were finished with the apartment."

She'd also said not to touch anything. The record jacket with the rusty smudges came to mind. The marks were probably to blurry to identify a fingerprint, so maybe it wasn't really evidence? But he wouldn't like hearing about that either. When she got around to telling him.

"Talk to the minister if you really want. I won't tell you how play it. You seem to do fine on your own without my advice. Try to find out where he was last Monday night. I don't recall his name from the police report."

"The police never spoke to him. Once they picked up Joe, they didn't look an inch further. How do we know the police really checked any of the other alibis? Eddie's men and Gem?"

"We don't. But I've already started. What about the bartender? I'd better add him to the list." He glanced at her again, then back at the street.

"Arty Pulaski?"

"Arty, right. The one who gave me the stink eye when you sold me cigarettes. Isn't he in tight with Eddie?"

Grace shrugged. "Oh, he's all right."

"Because he fed you after hours breakfast with a side order of juicy gossip? If he was angling to win your trust, he succeeded. You say this guy's a gambler. He might be in deep with Martone and can't afford to refuse his boss a favor. Any favor."

Grace felt blindsided. She should have thought of that. But she just didn't see Arty as a cold-blooded killer. "That could be why he's stuck at the club. But playing the horses is a far cry from murder. I don't think he's the one."

"Someone put on Joe's jacket and knocked on Mary's door last Monday night. Either for their own reasons, or because they were paid to go there. Or pressed into service. I don't think we can eliminate the bartender yet."

Wearing a hat and the jacket, Arty could have been mistaken for Joe. He was tall enough. Grace couldn't deny it. But the same could be said for Dante or Bernard. Even Gem. Or Reverend Holmes.

"Joe said Arty planned to meet up with Gem and a few guys in the band at an after-hours club uptown. The Indigo Room, I think it was."

"That's right. I'll check on it." Harry pulled a little pad from his pocket and made a note, then turned to her. "I'm still worried about you going back there."

He sounded different, his words coming from a different place. He wasn't bossing her around. Just stating a fact. From his heart. If he had one.

"I'll be all right."

"What time do you get to work?"

"Around half past six. Judy opens the door at seven."

"I'll park on the street and wait until you come out. If for some reason, you don't see the car, or something unexpected happens, call this number and leave a message." He scribbled a number on the pad and tore the page. "Find a safe place to wait, where there are a lot of people."

He put the slip of paper in her palm and closed his hand around her own. "I hope to hell Joe appreciates what you're doing for him."

"It's not that much. Not yet anyway."

"I think it is."

She felt as if they'd arrived in a new place. She'd always felt she could speak her mind with him, more than most other men. Certainly, other bosses. Now she felt like a real partner.

"I'm not doing it just for Joe. It's for Mary, too. And myself, in a way. And we haven't saved his neck yet. Let's not jinx it."

He sat back. "I wouldn't have said this a few days ago. But I'm starting to think we might."

"Thanks, Harry. Really." She leaned over and kissed his cheek, surprising him. And herself.

He sat very still. She felt the stubble of his five o'clock shadow on her skin and breathed in the scent of him.

Then she opened the car and ran to the front door.

* * *

Grace undressed in the dark, her clothes puddling around her feet. Rose woke up and spoke without opening her eyes. "What time is it?"

"I don't know. And you shouldn't either." Grace answered quietly, afraid to wake the rest of the family.

"Out with your boss again? I think you like him."

"We're working on Joe's case."

"Both things can be true."

"This is the first time I've seen him in days."

"That's not what Mom says."

"Mom doesn't know the half of it. And you're not going to tell her, either. Shut up and go back to sleep."

Rose rolled over and curled into a ball. "Now I know it's true."

Grace padded into the bathroom without bothering with the light. She stared at her shadowy reflection and splashed her face with warm water.

Her feelings for Harry had changed. She'd noticed it the moment she'd spotted him at the bar, but told herself it was just relief at seeing a familiar face. Now she wondered if she'd always been attracted to him.

She'd kissed him. Just on the cheek, but still, it was a stupid thing to do. She wondered what he thought, then decided it didn't matter. It was more important to clear her head and focus on getting into the cold box tomorrow night.

It had just been nerves. That's what she'd say if he brought it up, though she knew he wouldn't.

She was far from Harry's type, if he even had one. And he wasn't for her. Not in the long run. Or even a short run. It was just the adrenaline rush of the role she played. She'd be careful to keep a lid on her emotions and her eye on the ball.

She walked back to her bedroom, sensing the household asleep around her. She would never admit it to Harry, but she was afraid to return to the club, even for one more night.

If she backed out, he'd never blame her. He'd be relieved. But Mary's killer might go free, and she'd always blame herself.

Chapter Thirty-One

Reverend Holmes was not hard to find. Grace had noticed a sign for the parsonage when she'd come to Mary's funeral. She found his number in the White Pages and tried to phone, but no one answered. Which was just as well. He may have made some excuse not to see her.

The white clapboard house stood beside the church, with a peaked roof and covered porch in front. The yard was enclosed with a picket fence. She passed through the gate and walked up a bumpy brick path.

There were flower beds in front of the house. Clumps of tulips and daffodils that had bloomed the past week or so, now drooping under the weight of faded heads.

It was an old house, built at the turn of the century, she guessed. The clapboard was peeling, but the front door and shutters were glossy with a fresh coat of black paint. She tapped the brass knocker and stood back. Harry had confidence that she'd know how to handle the conversation, but she still wasn't sure what to say.

She didn't recognize the minister when he opened the door. Not for a moment or so, dressed in a slate grey shirt and matching pants, the word "Lester" embroidered on the pocket in red thread. She couldn't help but compare the rough uniform to the long robes he'd worn to lead the funeral service. Did he feel bitter, dressed this way for the world, every day but Sunday? Or did he offer it up as an act of humility, the way the nuns at St. Rocco had taught her?

"Can I help you, Miss?" His tone was polite but curious.

"I'm sorry to bother you, Reverend. If you have a few minutes, I'd like to speak to you. About Mary Delmore."

"Mary? What about her?"

"I work for a private investigator. We're gathering information for the attorney who's defending the man accused of Mary's murder."

"Joe Russo, you mean." He drew back, and she wondered if he was about to shut the door.

"That's right." Grace felt her mouth go dry. Of course, he'd read the newspaper articles and knew Joe's name. He'd loved Mary once. Maybe he still did.

"I'm not sure how I can help you…I'm sorry, I didn't catch your name."

"It's Grace." She left it at that. "Anything you can tell me might help, sir. We believe Mr. Russo is innocent."

"That very well may be. The Delmores have been members of the congregation for a long time, but Mary hasn't attended in years. I'm not sure I can tell you anything you don't know."

"She was here on Easter Sunday to sing with the choir. And you knew Mary well before you became a minister. Isn't that so?" He stared out at the street, avoiding her gaze, his expression uneasy. "It's just a few questions, Reverend. It won't take long."

"All right, come in. But I need to leave for work soon." He opened the door and stepped aside as she entered. "I was making coffee. Would you like some?"

"I would, thank you." She followed him into the house and walked down a short hallway, past a stairway on the right and the entrance to a sitting room on the left.

The room was small and neat, with a tufted sofa and a worn, brown armchair. An upright piano stood against one wall, the top covered with a cloth runner and family photos—a chubby baby crawling on a blanket, a solemn-looking couple standing side by side in front of a wide field, and a photo of Lester Holmes in uniform.

Further down, she passed a framed piece of hand stitching on the wall. "God bless every corner of this house."

At the end of the hall, she walked into a spacious kitchen. Large, clean windows framed the back of the property. He walked to an old-fashioned stove and lit the flame under a coffee pot. She sat at a wooden table painted white and watched him set cups and saucers.

Children's drawings were tacked to the far wall. One with a cross on a hill and a stick figure in a long robe with a beard, a halo, and outstretched arms. Jesus, she guessed, though his lollipop head was colored in with a brown crayon.

She'd never thought of Jesus any other way than fair and pale, with soft flowing hair and blue eyes. The version depicted in countless paintings, statues, and holy cards. But as Mary said, if you ever look at a map, highly unlikely. The Catholic church and everyone else, for that matter, ignored the geography.

He set their cups on the table and took a bottle of milk from the refrigerator, the shelves, mostly bare. He set the bottle on the table, and she poured a small amount in her coffee.

"Where do you work, Reverend?"

"I'm a janitor in a hospital. The night shift, mostly."

"It must be hard to work a full-time job and lead a church."

"It is hard but not uncommon. In some neighborhoods," he qualified. "It's a fine congregation, but a small one. They can't support a minister and his family. Not yet anyways."

"How many children do you have?" She glanced at the drawings.

"Just one boy, Isaiah. He's in first grade. My wife works in the cafeteria at his school, down the street. They come in when I go out. She says we should install a revolving door, but it's not so bad as that."

He smiled, and she did, too. And felt a twinge of guilt about imposing on him with her questions, and even worse, suspecting him.

He was a tall, strong-looking man. With even features and large dark eyes that held a gentle, intelligent light. Mary must have had a hard time giving him up for her music.

"Now, what did you come to ask me?"

"We're learning that Mary had a complicated life. Did she ever confide in you about something troubling her? Or someone she was afraid of?"

"One of the men circling around her, you mean. I'm calling them men. They were more like hyenas." His mild tone yielded to a sharper edge.

"So, she did speak to you about her private life?"

He paused to sip his coffee. "Even if she had, I'm bound to keep any conversation of that kind confidential. I think you know that."

"I do. But does that mean you can't shed any light at all on her problems or worries? Or who may have wished her harm?"

She had a feeling he knew more than he was admitting to.

When he didn't reply, she said, "I attended her funeral. I knew Mary in high school, and I wanted to pay my respects. Your sermon was a wonderful tribute to her, Reverend. It captured her beauty and grace, and her gifts so well. You asked the gathering not to judge her. What did you mean by that? Why do you think anyone would judge her harshly?"

He sat back. She didn't think he would speak. Except to ask her to go.

"God blessed Mary with many gifts. More than most," he said finally. "But she squandered them. She lost her way. I knew something was troubling her when she came to the church to rehearse with the choir, a week or so before Easter Sunday. I thought that was part of the reason she'd accepted the invitation. She'd come for comfort. For respite from a life that was treating her harshly."

"Did you find out what was bothering her, specifically? Did she mention anyone? The man she worked for maybe, Eddie Martone?"

He shook his head. "I tried to draw her out. I didn't learn much. Enough to know she was tired and confused. She seemed frightened of the future, of choices she had to make. I wish she had confided in me. She might be alive today."

"You thought you could persuade her to change, is that it?" She knew that he did, but she wanted to hear him say it.

"I knew who she was. Mary Delmore. Not some grotesque, Halloween version, Lana Delmar. Up on a stage in a tight dress and all that make-up. Like a painted doll."

"You saw her perform at the club?" Grace hadn't expected that and now worried she'd interrupted, and he wouldn't say more.

"Just once. And I didn't stay long. It was hard to watch her debase herself," he said quietly. "I wasn't exactly welcome there, either. Barely waited on, then told to drink up and get moving. Seems it's fine to have Negroes prance around for entertainment, but sitting in the audience is another thing."

What he'd said was true, but she'd never heard anyone spell it out so clearly. She took a breath, unsure what to say.

"When did you go to the club, do you recall?

"Not long after Easter, when Mary visited church. I thought if I saw her sing at that place, I might understand what kept her there and help her change. It was a Saturday night. I got off work early and stopped on my way home."

"Did you understand any better?" She was getting off the track, but the question just came out.

"Not at the time. But I think I do now. Now that she's gone." He suddenly seemed sad and even angry. "I'll tell you what happened to Mary. It's very simple, really. *'Give not that which is holy unto the dogs, neither cast ye your pearls before swine, lest they trample them under their feet, and turn again and rend you.'*" He met Grace's gaze. "*'Rend you,'*" he repeated. "Tear you limb from limb."

He spoke quietly and distinctly, not from a righteous height, but brought low by sorrow and even secret mourning.

"Now, if you'll excuse me, I really do have to get to work."

"Of course." Grace stood and picked up her purse. "Where do you work, Reverend Holmes?"

Before he could answer, Grace heard a key turn in the front door. She turned to see a little boy fly down the hallway, oxfords slapping the wooden floor.

"Daddy…why are you still here?"

Lester crouched to receive him, like a catcher setting up for a fast ball, his face bright with joy as his son landed in his arms.

The boy patted his father's cheeks. "Can you play with me in the yard?"

"Sorry, son. I need to go." Lester rose and lifted his boy in his arms as his wife walked in the room. She glanced at Grace with a curious expression.

"This is my wife, Charlotte," Lester said to Grace. "Charlotte, this is Grace. She's investigating Mary Delmore's death. She stopped by to ask a few questions."

"From the police?" Mrs. Holmes looked alarmed.

"A private inquiry. I work for a defense attorney." It took a moment, but Grace recognized Lester's wife from Mary's funeral service. She'd led the choir's first hymn as the casket was carried into the church.

"I see." Charlotte Holmes seemed disturbed and turned her back to slip off her sweater and hat. She picked up an apron and tied the strands around her waist. "Don't let me interrupt you."

She was attractive with a pretty face and dimpled smile, but not nearly as beautiful as Mary. She also had a lovely voice, Grace knew, but was not in Mary's league on that field, either.

Grace recalled Mary's description of her rival, the girl who had caught Lester on the rebound—a good churchwoman. One who had no great love for Mary. She'd probably been jealous, and still was.

Grace picked up her purse and gloves and offered a weak smile. "It's getting late. I'll be going."

Reverend Holmes walked her down the shadowy hallway to the front door. "I'm sorry I couldn't help you. As I mentioned, she hasn't been to our church for years, except for this past Easter Sunday."

"So you said, Reverend. Thanks again for your time."

Grace guessed his apology had been crafted for his wife's benefit. But even a minister was entitled to a few white lies.

* * *

Grace arrived at the club at six, though she didn't need to punch in until six-thirty. She scanned the street but didn't see Harry's car. He'd be here, like he promised, she told herself. If he isn't, what of it? She still had to go through with this last gambit.

She considered grabbing a drink to settle her nerves. Instead, she ducked into the coffee shop across the way and took the table near the window again. She ordered a cup of coffee and a slice of chocolate cream pie. She always craved sugar when she felt anxious, even though it made her even jumpier. At least after tonight, she didn't have to worry about fitting into the silly dress.

A copy of *The New York Post* sat on the table, and she paged through it. Several pages in, a photo of a charred building caught her eye. The short article reported a house fire in upstate New York, near the town of White Lake. A bullet-riddled body had been found in the rubble. The police were trying to establish the victim's identity.

A black car cruised slowly down the street and caught her eye. Harry's Nash. There was a space across from the club, not far from the shop where she sat. The car parked, and Harry cut the engine but didn't get out.

She left the coffee shop and crossed to the club. The car's headlights flashed once, she nodded to herself, but didn't turn her head.

* * *

Dressed in her costume, she arranged the cigarettes in the tray while the band members and Clara ate dinner. There was no sign of Judy, and Grace was relieved to have some time to think without the officious blonde pecking at her.

Pauline was in the check room reading a magazine, and Arty was stocking the bar. He'd winked when she'd walked past. She forced a smile but didn't stop to chat.

It was Monday and likely to be slow, which would make it harder to be in the wrong place at the wrong time. She had to manage somehow and had a vague plan of hiding a pack of Gauloises in her change purse and substituting it for one she'd lift from the cold box. The basement would be open for business as usual for the poker game. Another land mine to navigate.

She'd lied to Harry, and very boldly, insisting that she knew the basement's layout. He'd been right; it was important and could mean the difference between being caught red-handed or escaping with her prize.

She planned to meet with Sylvie for a smoke around ten when Judy usually gave her a break. Sylvie was the only one she could ask about the basement. There was a risk for Sylvie in answering the simplest questions. But Grace would never get her truly involved, even if she was willing.

Sylvie might even know if the contraband had been removed. If that was so, Grace knew she was off the hook. It also meant she had little to zero chance of nailing Eddie Martone and finding out why Mary was killed.

Chapter Thirty-Two

"Take your break, Lucy. Fifteen minutes."

Grace met Judy's cool gaze and nodded. She finished with a table near the stage and handed the customer some change, then quickly walked to the check room to drop off the tray.

"That guy wants some butts." Pauline pointed to a man waving at them.

Grace turned her back. "I have to get to the powder room. Or else. He'll figure it out."

A pack of Gauloises was already squeezed in the wallet on her belt. She wished she had a weapon in there, too, a pair of scissors or even a knife. But that was silly. She'd either get in the cold box or she wouldn't. She couldn't let her imagination run wild. Not now.

She walked through the kitchen and caught Sylvie's eye. Her friend answered with a small nod. As Grace pushed through the metal door to the alley, Sylvie grabbed a trash can and told the cook she was having a smoke.

Sylvie left the pail at the back of the alley and met Grace where she stood, close to the street.

"It's so slow tonight. That can wasn't even half full. Luckily, nobody noticed."

Grace had already lit a cigarette and offered Sylvie the pack. "I don't know why they even open on Monday. The dining room is like a graveyard."

"For the card game. Eddie's making plenty, even if nobody upstairs is eating steak and drinking champagne."

"I never thought of that way. You're right." Grace had to smile, despite her nerves. "I have to ask you something about last night when that crate broke, and the cigarettes fell out."

"Right, cigarettes. They must have got caught in the net. I hear that happens to fishermen all the time. What a darn nuisance." Sylvie tapped the ashes off her smoke and stared out at the street.

"Eddie told his men to put the cartons in the cold box. Do you know if they're still there?"

Sylvie glanced at her. "Why do you want to know that?"

Grace didn't answer right away. "I want to tell you, Sylvie. But I don't want you to get into any trouble."

"Are you in trouble?"

"Not yet, but I could be. There might be a lot of questions, and I don't want…" Grace shook her head. "Forget I mentioned it. We never had this conversation, okay?"

"This is about Lana, right?" Sylvie fixed her with large, dark eyes.

Grace was surprised by her guess. "Am I that obvious?"

"I just had a feeling." Sylvie took a drag on her cigarette. "What if you tell me the truth and let me worry about ducking trouble?"

Now she knew how Harry felt last night, trying to dissuade her from coming back to The Starlight Room.

"To start with, I'm not an actress trying to make rent money." As quickly and briefly as possible, Grace explained what she was really doing at the club. "Those cigarettes in the cold box might be the reason Mary was murdered. I need to get a pack so we can find out."

Sylvie met her gaze. Grace couldn't tell what she was thinking. "You called her Mary," she said finally.

"I knew her years ago in school. We weren't close friends, but we could have been. She was involved with my brother."

"Joe Russo is your brother?" Now it was Sylvie's turn to look surprised.

"That's right." Grace watched Sylvie, trying to gauge her reaction. Would she pull away now because she thought Joe was guilty?

Finally, she said, "She was my friend. She had a kind heart and never hurt a soul. I believe your brother didn't kill her, like you said. And the man who runs this little corner of hell probably did. Or had something to do with it.

I'd love to help you nail his behind."

Grace wanted to hug her. "Do you know if the cigarettes are still there?"

"I saw the sack there just before the club opened. Cook sent me down for butter. In the back of the box, left corner. Just past the sides of beef, hanging up. Most nights, the box is open till Cook goes down and checks what he needs to order for the next day. But he kept it locked tonight. He's got the key, and if he sends someone down, they give it right back."

Grace's spirits fell. "Sounds like I'm spinning my wheels."

"I once saw a spare key hidden down there. It might be gone. But worth a look?"

Grace moved closer. "Where do you think it is?"

Sylvie picked up a sharp stone. She turned and drew on the brick wall behind them. "This is the stairway. There's a rack of metal shelves filled with cans when you come down. On the bottom shelf, all the way in back, look for a little bottle. The key should be in there."

Grace nodded as she memorized the drawing. "Where's the card game? Not near the cold box, I hope?"

Sylvie showed her, making an X. "The game is in a room at the back. They keep the door closed unless a player comes out."

"Let's hope nobody runs out of money while I'm down there." Grace checked the time. There was barely five minutes before Judy would miss her. "I'd better go."

"Wait…what if I get it? No one will notice if I go down."

Sylvie's offer made sense, and Grace was tempted. But only for a heartbeat. She couldn't let Sylvie take the risk. She'd never live with herself if something happened to her.

She touched Sylvie's shoulder. "Thanks, but this is my brother's mess. I've got to keep it in the family."

"Alright, I get your meaning. I'll watch for Judy. You'd better hurry."

Grace was already at the metal door. "I'll work until closing so no one gets suspicious. I'll wait for you down the street. Just walk west, I'll find you."

Sylvie nodded and scratched her treasure map with the stone until it was a blur. "Good luck, Lucy... If that's even your name."

Chapter Thirty-Three

Grace threaded her way through the busy kitchen and down the narrow hallway. A waiter hurried past, balancing a tray laden with dinner plates under silver domes. She waited until he disappeared, then ducked through the basement door.

The stairwell was dark, the dim light at the bottom just bright enough so that she didn't trip on her heels. She waited a few steps from the top, listening. The muffled voices of the players could be heard at a distance. There was no other sound, and she began to walk down.

The metal rack stood just where Sylvie had described. She crouched down and felt around behind the rows of cans on the bottom shelf. Something crawled across her skin, and she bit back a shout. She didn't find the bottle and got down on her hands and knees to move the cans aside.

She was nearly crying with frustration when she felt it, stuck between the shelf and the wall. She pulled it out and stood up, her knees gritty and stockings ruined. The lid wouldn't budge. The key rattled inside, taunting her. She rubbed spit on the edges and twisted with all her might, but the metal had rusted and stuck to the glass.

The cold box stood nearby, the humming motor like the steady breath of a sleeping grey giant. The metal walk-in was six feet high and at least ten-foot deep. The big silver handle on the door, secured by a chain and heavy square padlock. The crowbar she'd seen used to open crates stood tilted on the box. She could use it to break open the lock but wondered if she was strong enough. There wasn't much time to find out.

Grace put the little bottle on the floor and smashed it with a can, hoping the sound wouldn't reach the poker room. She quickly picked the key out of bits of glass and pushed the rest under the rack with her shoe.

A roar of voices erupted from the players. She stood stone still, listening. Men were laughing and cursing. "You son of bitch. I thought you were holding a full house. I went out with a pair of Jacks…"

She ran to the box, twisted the key in the padlock, and pulled out the chain. The door was heavy, and she feared it would close and trap her inside. She picked up the crowbar and propped it open.

The acrid smell of raw meat hung in the cold air. A side of beef swung from a hook in the ceiling, beside a pile of barely plucked chickens. Blood dripped on the sawdust-covered floor. A crate of eggs stood in the middle of the mess, and she nearly knocked it over.

She quickly found the fish crates in the back corner, just as Sylvie had described. She searched behind them, then beside them, for the burlap sack. But it was not there.

She pulled open paper cartons and found more food, bricks of butter, bottles of milk and cream, mounds of green vegetables. She searched the entire cold box, but the sack was gone. She felt so frustrated, she nearly cried.

Feeling heavy and defeated, she walked out, quickly threaded the chain, then closed the lock, leaving everything just as she'd found it. She walked to the metal rack and kicked the key underneath.

The door at the top of the stairs opened, and a beam of light shone down. Grace jumped back, looking for a place to hide. But it was too late. She'd been spotted.

Heavy steps sounded, and Hubie appeared. "Judy's looking for you. Hiding down here, huh. What are you up to?"

"Nothing." Grace backed away but bumped into the metal rack. He reached out and snagged her wrist before she could get any further.

"Let me go, you idiot, or I'll scream my head off." She tried to pull away, but he laughed. Then twisted her arm back so hard she felt her shoulder burn.

"You snotty little bitch. I asked you a question."

"A few of the players wanted cigarettes. Dante said to bring some down."

"The players, huh?" Hubie pushed his face into hers. "You give them what they wanted? How about you give me some?"

He yanked her closer, twisting her arm so hard she thought it would snap. "Stop! Help! Help!" Grace called out.

The gambling room erupted in another roar of laughter and shouts. Grace heard someone pound the table and poker chips clinking.

A big, dirty hand pressed down on her mouth as her body was shoved against the metal wall of the cold box. Hubie pushed against her with all his weight. She tried to scream and struggle, but he was too heavy and strong. She bit at his hand and kicked his legs. He jeered and pushed her legs apart with his knee, one hand clawing at her underwear.

"Go on, fight. You little WOP bitch. You asked for this. You won't forget it either."

He pressed his arm against her throat, and she heard a zipper go down. She gasped for a breath, feeling choked and suddenly lightheaded, her limbs going weak as water.

Hubie shifted against her, seeming frustrated. "Keep still, God damn you. Before I…"

Suddenly, his eyes went wide, and he staggered back and groaned. She quickly moved aside as he dropped to the floor with a dull thud.

Sylvie stood before her, holding the crowbar. Her thin arms flexed, ready to strike again. Her expression blank with shock.

"Is he dead?"

Grace staggered forward to check. Blood seeped from his head, but his chest rose and fell. "The bastard's still breathing."

Sylvie dropped the bar and turned to her. "Did he get you?"

Grace shook her head and swallowed back a bitter taste. She felt so lightheaded, she thought she might pass out. She shook her head and took a deep breath, then grabbed Sylvie's hand, and squeezed. For a moment, she had no words.

"He would have, if you hadn't stopped him. I'd love to kick his balls up his throat, but we better get out of here. Go back to the kitchen, act calm as toast. Walk to the door and get out. Grab a trash pail or something. If somebody tries to stop you, make an excuse. Just leave as fast as you can. Walk west, up the street. Look for a black Nash parked about two doors down. My boss is in the car. His name is Harry. Tell him Grace sent you and you need help."

Sylvie stared at her. "What about you? You can't stay here either."

"I'll be out. Very soon. Don't worry. Tell Harry that, as well."

Sylvie nodded but seemed reluctant to leave her. Grace touched her arm. "Go ahead, Sylvie. We better go up separately."

She nodded again and ran up the steps.

The voices from the poker game rose again behind the door. A player yelled and banged the table. He sounded angry, and Grace waited, worrying that Dante or Bernard would appear, dragging out a sore loser. It happened almost every night.

She felt shaken and ached all over, but forced herself forward, her knees nearly buckling. She smoothed out her dress and climbed back up.

As the light approached, she considered her escape. The side door was closer, with fewer land mines to navigate in the busy kitchen than the front of the club. No one would notice her tattered appearance either.

But that choice was quickly eliminated when she heard Judy's voice from that direction.

She trotted up the passageway to the dressing room and tried the knob. It was unlocked, and she slipped inside. The room was dark, but light from the street filtered through a window. She frantically searched the clothes rack and found a black coat. Luckily, Dolores was bigger than her, and it fit over the dress. Grace felt bad that the singer would miss her coat tonight. But she'd return it, somehow.

A black hat with a short veil sat on the dressing table. She set it on her head and pulled the veil down over her eyes. Then found some pins to squash her hair into a bun. She picked up a dark red lipstick, coated her mouth, then buttoned the coat nearly to her chin.

The hallway was empty as she slipped out and made her way to the swinging doors, her head down, hugging the wall. A waiter with a loaded tray looked at her but continued on his way.

She pushed through the doors and into the club, her gaze straight ahead. She wondered if Hubie was rousing. Sylvie had landed a mighty blow on the monster, but he'd wake up sooner or later. Or someone would find him. It was hard not to race to the front door, but she somehow managed a normal pace.

Behind the frosted window on Eddie's office door, a light glowed, and voices murmured. He was conducting business. Important business. Grace could practically see the burlap sack through the wall. She would have given anything to know for sure.

Almost anything.

Up on the stage, Gem and Dolores stood at the piano, performing a frantic duet of "Jeepers, Creepers," mugging silly faces and forced smiles as they wound up the set. The tiny stars from the projector swirled around the room, gliding over the band, dance floor, and the sparse audience.

Behind the bar, Arty shook a silver mixer with all his might and didn't spare a glance as she walked by. Steps from the front door, her hand itched to push it open, but Oscar rushed forward and blocked her way.

His expression was confused and distressed. She drew in a breath and stared back, then averted her gaze. Was he about to call Judy? Or even Dante? She braced herself to make a run for it.

"Madam, *please*…Allow me." He swept past to pull the door open for her, sounding offended to be deprived of the privilege. "Shall I call a taxi for you?"

Grace smiled politely as she sailed out into the fresh air. "Thank you, but that won't be necessary. My driver is waiting."

Harry's car was double-parked in front of the club. Her legs nearly gave way as she ran toward it. She pulled open the passenger side door and saw his overcoat and hat piled in the backseat, but no sign of Sylvie.

"Where's Sylvie? Didn't she find you?"

Harry started the engine. "Get in and calm down, Mata Hari. Our friend Bernard is right across the street."

Grace glanced in that direction and saw Eddie's Cadillac. Bernard leaned on the hood, gazing at the treetops as he finished a smoke. She slipped into Harry's car and closed the door.

"We can't leave yet. I told my friend to look for you. We need to make sure she gets out, too."

"I got out fine." A voice in the back seat, from beneath the topcoat, said. Grace turned as the car pulled away, and Sylvie raised her head.

"Thank God. I thought you were still in there."

Harry turned onto Broadway. "You can come up now, Sylvie."

He waited until Sylvie sat up and put the coat aside. Then looked at Grace. "What happened back there? Sounds like it got messy."

Sylvie glanced at Grace. Grace knew she wouldn't tell and silently thanked her.

"It's a long story. I'll tell you later," Grace promised, though she had no intention. For one thing, he wouldn't let her work with him anymore.

She turned back to Sylvie again. "I don't think you should go home, Sylvie. It may not be safe. Is there any place you can stay for a while?" Where Hubie or even Eddie won't find you, she meant.

"I can go to my sister and her husband up in Harlem. But I don't think anyone will come look for me. I'm small potatoes."

Sylvie was no small potato in Grace's book. But perhaps it was true that Eddie and even Hubie wouldn't bother much about a "colored gal."

"You can let me out here. I'll catch a train uptown on the next corner," Sylvie said.

"We'll drive you to your sister's house. It's no trouble," Harry caught her gaze in the rear-view mirror.

As they headed towards Columbus Circle, Grace sat back, comforted by the bright lights. Horse-drawn carriages were lined up along Central Park South, across from the row of elegant hotels that stretched down to the Plaza.

They flew up Broadway past Columbia University, and Sylvie gave directions. Her sister lived on a street not quite as nice as Mary's. She told them to stop in front of an old brown tenement with small, narrow windows. Grace imagined the rooms cramped and dark inside.

Grace walked with Sylvie to the door so they could speak privately. She suddenly realized she wasn't going to see Sylvie anymore. It had only been a few days, but Grace knew she would miss her.

"I wish there was some way to thank you for what you did tonight. If you hadn't come looking for me, I hate to think—"

"You helped me, too," Sylvie cut in. "Now we're even."

"I'm still on the owing side. I made you lose your job."

"I'm glad to get out of there. I'll find something else."

"Something better. You're meant for better things, Sylvie." Grace knew that was true. "How can I reach you? Is there a phone I can call?"

"You can leave a message with my sister's neighbor, Mrs. Jefferson." Sylvie found a pencil and bit of paper in her purse and wrote the number down. She held it out but didn't hand it over. "Who's going to be asking for me?" she added with a smile. "I noticed how your boss calls you Grace?"

Grace laughed. "That's my name. Grace Russo. I almost forgot to tell you. I'll be in touch in a few days. When all of this is settled."

Grace leaned over, and they hugged. Grace hung on for a moment, her heart too full to speak. The scene in the basement flashed in her head and she shivered, overwhelmed again with gratitude for what Sylvie had done.

"Take care, Sylvie."

"You, too, Grace," Sylvie said as she stepped back. "You find out who really killed Mary. I think you can do it."

Grace nodded and blinked back tears as she ran to the car. It was just nerves, after all, she'd been through tonight. And hadn't even accomplished what she'd set out to do. She dreaded admitting that to Harry.

She slid into the front seat and shut the door.

"She's a sweet kid," Harry said as they drove off.

"More than that. She's smart and brave. And deserves a lot better than she's gotten so far, that's for sure."

Harry glanced at her. "What happened at the club? Sounds like you had trouble."

She knew what he was asking but ignored the question. "I didn't get the cigarettes. The sack wasn't in the cold box. Sylvie saw it there when the club opened. But I have a feeling Eddie was handing them off while I was down in the cellar. Scampering around like a bewildered mouse."

One that almost got caught.

"I'm not surprised he's moving the stuff quickly. Don't blame yourself. It took a lot of guts to try."

He didn't know the half of it. Grace knew he was right but felt deeply disappointed. After all she'd gone through, leaving the club empty-handed seemed a crushing defeat.

She stared out her window as they cruised downtown again. "What now?"

"A few ideas came to me."

She glanced at him. She wondered if he was trying to make her feel better, though she knew he wasn't the type.

"Should we consider Gem and the others again?"

"I'm not counting out that line of inquiry. I did check on alibis. Gem Washington went to the Indigo Room with a few of the band members, like Joe said. But he left almost as soon as they got there. A bartender heard him say he wasn't feeling well and was going home. And that club is only a few blocks from Mary's apartment."

"I guess that puts him back in the running." Grace felt a small spark of hope.

"I think so. Eddie's men, Dante and Bernard, are harder to pin down. I'm still working on those loose ends."

He didn't mention Arty, and Grace didn't ask. She was about to tell him about her visit with Reverend Holmes when he pulled over and parked.

"Let's stop here. It's pretty good. I haven't had a bite all day."

Grace glanced out the window at a small restaurant. A neon sign in the window said, "Betty's on Broadway—Home Cooking." Appetizing aromas wafted out to the sidewalk, but Grace wasn't hungry. The sights and smells in the cold box, and what had come after, had quelled any appetite.

They quickly found a table and ordered. When Grace only asked for a Manhattan, Harry gave her a look. "You better eat something. You'll fall on your face."

She added a bowl of soup, and he asked for a steak dinner, well done.

When the waiter left, he said, "It's probably just as well you didn't get into the box."

"Really? How's that?" Was he just trying to cheer her up? That wasn't his usual style.

"Let's say you were successful, and we found out for sure that Eddie is funneling drugs through the club. We pass the evidence along tonight, and you give a statement. A judge issues a search warrant, and there's a raid tomorrow. Even if Eddie isn't tipped off by then, there's a strong chance the goods are gone. You said it yourself; the cigarettes were probably handed off by now. The cops come out empty-handed, and Martone is all the wiser. He'll either lay off for a while or divert the next shipment in a way that would be impossible to find. No less, in time to help Joe."

She understood his point but still felt frustrated. The waiter brought their drinks, and she took an eager sip.

"It's silly to debate since I have nothing to show. But we could have handed the police solid proof of what's going on there and a clear motive for Eddie killing Mary. Even if they didn't find the rest of the drugs. Wouldn't that count for anything?"

"It would have been your word against Martone's. The sister of a guy who's locked up insists Eddie killed Mary and framed her brother. Which undermines your credibility, to say the least. By the time Martone's crooked lawyer twisted things around, you could be charged with possession of an illegal substance."

Grace sat back and sipped her cocktail. Considering how Joe stood charged with Mary's murder, the outlandish suggestion seemed possible.

The chicken soup she'd ordered to placate Harry was thin and cold. "Sick food," her mother would call it. She did feel a little bit lightheaded and nibbled on a Saltine.

"You said you had some ideas?"

Harry sprinkled half a shaker of salt on his steak and the other half on a lump of mashed potatoes. A pile of grayish-green peas, doubtlessly from a can, rounded out the plate. If this was what he called "pretty good food," she'd hate to see what he normally ate.

"I had some time to catch up on the news while I was waiting for you. The shipping news, mainly." He pulled out a folded square of newspaper from his breast pocket.

"This is the list of freighters that docked today." He handed it over, and Grace read the listing of ship names and points of origin. One was circled in pencil.

"The *Marie Louise*, from Marseille." She looked up at him. "Do you think Eddie is expecting another delivery?"

"I think he already got it." She could tell he'd quickly read her confusion. "This paper was a few days old. I bet the cigarettes you saw delivered Sunday night came off that boat. To evade the customs' inspection, the drugs are passed off out at sea, past the twenty-mile limit. That likely happened Saturday night or early Sunday morning, just beyond Montauk."

"And the boat delivers its catch to Blue Fin. And they deliver to The Starlight Room."

"That's right." Harry pushed another scrap of newspaper towards her. "There's a freighter from Marseilles due to dock in New York on Wednesday. My guess is another nice catch will be unloaded at Blue Fin Tuesday night. I'll get out there and see what happens."

"We'll get out there, you mean." She looked at him squarely over the edge of her cocktail glass.

He pushed his plate aside and lit a cigarette. His expression suggested he'd expected her reaction.

"I don't think that's a good idea, Grace." He raised his hand before she could object. "Not that I need to give you a reason. But there's a list of them."

Grace was about to argue, then sat back. "I can get there on my own. There are trains to Montauk Point. And taxi cabs once I get there, I bet. I can find Blue Finn Seafood just as easily as you can."

"Come on, Grace. That's ridiculous. This is real surveillance. I need to work alone, like I always do. You know that."

"And you know that you'd be nowhere right now if it wasn't for me. You wouldn't know about freighters from Marseille or Blue Finn Seafood, or any of this stuff."

That wasn't entirely true, but she wasn't going to be shaken off like a pesky fly. Not after what she'd been through.

He took a breath and stared at her. The same stare, she recalled, from their first meeting, when he'd tried so hard to discourage her from working for him.

"You won't let go of this, will you?"

She took another sip of her Manhattan and didn't answer.

He stubbed out the cigarette so hard he nearly knocked the ashtray off the table. "I'll pick you up at noon. I doubt anything will happen before the sun goes down, but it's best to get a look at the place in the daylight."

Grace nodded. She didn't want to interrupt and risk him changing his mind.

"We won't be back until Wednesday morning. Maybe even that afternoon. That won't be a problem for you?"

"No problem at all." Did he think she had to ask her mother's permission to go away overnight? He was almost right, but she wouldn't give him the satisfaction of admitting it.

"Wear vacation clothes. Bring some sunglasses and magazines. You know what I mean."

"I can do that." Could he? His idea of leisure wear was probably loosening the tie in his starched collar.

The waiter asked if they wanted dessert and coffee. Grace shook her head.

"Just a check, please," Harry glanced at Grace. "I'll drive you home. Get a good night's sleep. We have a long ride tomorrow, and important work on the other end of it."

"Yes, we do." It was hard to hide her satisfaction at the small victory, hearing him say "we." But she tried.

Chapter Thirty-Four

"What do you think our chances are of seeing a delivery tonight?" They'd been driving almost two hours but were not quite halfway. Grace calculated their progress on a map in her lap. She didn't like long car rides. She got too restless. As if the purpose of the trip didn't make her nervous enough.

"It's hard to say. The flip of a coin, probably. Sorry if that disappoints you."

Grace leaned back in her seat. "I just want to know."

"Joe won't go to trial for months. There's time."

"I'm glad you feel that way." She felt as if time was running out. As if each day they failed to figure out who really killed Mary, the trail went colder and colder. And Mary's killer sunk deeper and deeper into the shadows.

The sun had disappeared behind a patch of low grey clouds. She wore her sunglasses anyway, black rimmed, cat-eye shaped lenses that she'd borrowed from Rose. Without asking. The red and white polka dot scarf she'd bought at Woolworth's for fake Lucy Bianco was tied over her hair.

"Mind if I turn on the radio?"

"Not at all." Harry kept his eyes on the road. She got the feeling he was happy to see her distracted by something, so she'd stop asking questions he couldn't answer.

She twisted around the dial to find a station. Choices were few in this neck of the woods. Billie Holiday's voice broke through the scratchy static, singing, "Ain't Nobody's Business If I Do." Her sassy, bluesy style brought Mary to mind. Grace pictured Mary on stage in her dazzling sequined gown, singing the song just as well.

That was the last thing she remembered. Until she woke up, her head pressed against the window.

She sat up and rubbed her neck. "I'm sorry."

"For what? You've been up all hours the last few days. I'd give a hundred bucks for a sleep like that."

"Don't you sleep well, Harry?"

"Not much lately, to be honest."

She felt sorry for him but didn't want to say. Did memories of the war keep him up? That seemed likely, but she felt the question was too personal.

They were cruising through another village. The shops and churches looked old and pristine, the streets quiet, with few people to be seen. A sign said Water Mill, and as promised, they soon passed a large stone mill on the village square.

"How much longer do you think?"

"About an hour or so? I did some research last night with the Yellow Pages. There are cabins on the same road as the warehouse open year-round. If it's not a good spot for surveillance, we'll find something else. Or leave the car somewhere, approach on foot, and find a sheltered spot to keep watch."

The country roads were so deserted, a parked car sitting on the roadside all day, or even circling the same location, would stick out like a seagull wearing a top hat. Grace hadn't thought of that.

She watched out the window. Behind stone walls and barriers of leafy trees, she glimpsed white mansions and green lawns.

At a certain point, the landscape emptied into dunes and patches of scrub pines. There were few signs of civilization on either of the roads, except for an occasional seafood shack or a gas station. The sandy dunes were empty and endless, the way she imagined it must look on the Moon.

Grace sat up, sensing the ocean before she saw it. The road narrowed, the car taking dips up and down small hills.

Her view was suddenly filled with the wide horizon—a brilliant blue stretch of sky above and a blue-green swath of churning ocean, as far as the eye could see. Ragged white caps rolled swiftly to the shore.

She cranked down her window, and a sea-scented breeze filled the car, along with the echoing thunder of waves striking the shore.

"I forgot how spectacular the ocean is." She smiled at Harry, her kerchief flapping, then looked back at the sea. "My folks brought us to Coney Island now and then. We even took a bus to Atlantic City once and stayed in a big hotel on the boardwalk. But this place is different. The ocean looks so much wilder and bigger. If that's even possible."

Harry met her glance, then looked back at the road. She suddenly felt silly and self-conscious. If he'd begun to take her seriously, she'd certainly reminded him not to. Going gaga over the scenery like a "silly woman."

"I know what you mean," he said finally. "Though I could never put it into words as well as you do."

He glanced at her with a rare, brief smile. He'd opened his window, too, and the breeze blew his thick dark hair back against his forehead. He was a handsome man. She thought so now.

They passed makeshift shacks that offered hot dogs and fried fish, clusters of cottages, and a yellow Victorian that advertised rooms to let on a placard by the roadside. Most of the businesses were shuttered with signs that read, "Closed For The Season."

There were a few private houses, most hidden by hedges, rooftops peeping above the ragged rows of privet. And a rustic-looking inn on the edge of the ocean called Gurney's.

Grace could see from the map that a drive straight through town would bring them to the lighthouse and the very tip of Long Island.

Instead, they turned north, down a narrow lane that ran along the edge of an inlet, Cranberry Hole Road. A worn, arrow-shaped sign nailed to a telephone pole pointed the way to Blue Fin Seafood. A few moments later, the large, box-shaped wooden building came into view, set beside an inlet and a short beach edged by jagged rocks.

Harry drove by slowly. Large metal doors stood open on the roadside, and a black truck that bore the company name stood in the driveway.

It was dark inside the warehouse, except for a square of light where the building was open to the dock. Grace couldn't see much but heard echoing voices as men moved about in the shadows.

A short distance down the road, across from the inlet and rocky strip of beach, a green and white sign for Seaview Cottages swung in the breeze. A handful of white cottages studded a grassy hillside, like grazing sheep. Each had a square picture window that faced the water and a small porch with two Adirondack chairs painted dark green.

The building closest to the road was marked, "Office." Harry parked and put on sunglasses and a baseball cap. He began to get out of the car, then paused and reached into his pocket.

"I almost forgot. Put this on." He handed her a gold band, and she stared at it. "I don't have a flowery speech for you. Sorry."

She smiled at his joke. "You're not the type. I didn't expect one."

She slipped the ring on the proper finger, and he did the same.

"I know it seems silly. But I don't want to take the chance the proprietor is a prig. Though it's easy enough to buy these in the dime store."

"I've heard that." It wasn't the first time she'd checked into a motel with a man, but it still felt odd, waiting for Harry to return with a key. As well as seeing the fake ring on her finger, in a spot long reserved for the real thing.

A beat-up suitcase sat in the back seat, tan with brown trim and a worn leather handle. She wondered what was inside. She hadn't been sure what to pack, if anything, and had settled on her toothbrush, hairbrush, and a spare pair of underwear, squashed into her largest handbag.

She doubted Harry had brought more than that, or even a change of clothes. Perhaps it was just a prop. He was careful about his stage craft, which she found both amusing and instructive.

A few minutes later, he opened the door to Cabin 3 and stepped aside to let her walk in first. "Mr. Quigley asked a few questions but was happy to rent the place. Looks like we're the only ones here. The Baxters, Janet and Fred, from the Bronx. Your mother is babysitting junior so we can have a little getaway. Spoils him rotten, but it's only one night."

"I hope I can remember all that."

A waft of musty air mixed with pine-scented cleaner greeted them. She walked in slowly and looked around the small square room; a sink and hot plate near the door, and a round table by the window with two captain-style chairs. The lumpy double bed was covered by a pale blue chenille spread and pushed to the back wall.

Harry carried in his suitcase and tossed it on the bed. He flipped the locks and opened it. His selection of newspapers sat on top, and underneath that, a black binocular case, a camera case, and one that held a lens for long-distance. There was also a small metal coffee pot, a can of coffee, and a brown paper bag with the top rolled up tight.

At the very bottom, she saw a tan leather holster with a silver-handled gun tucked inside. He left that in the suitcase and closed it again.

"I brought the usual supplies." He set the coffee pot and can next to the hot plate, along with the paper bag. She hoped there was something to eat inside, though the packaging wasn't promising.

He picked up his camera and slung the strap around his shoulder. Then handed her the binoculars.

"Janet is a bird watcher. Loves her feathered friends."

"I'll remember that."

"Let's walk on the beach. Don't forget your kerchief and sunglasses."

He held the door open, and she walked through, sliding her glasses on and tying the kerchief under her chin.

They crossed the road and found a sandy path that threaded through the boulders, down to the shoreline. Grace rolled up the hem of her slacks and slipped off her shoes, then carried them in her hand. She liked wearing flats. She didn't care if the low heels didn't show off her figure. She liked feeling free enough to walk quickly, or even run if she felt like it.

She felt sure she looked the part of a woman on vacation. Less sure about Harry, though he'd tried. He wore a short khaki jacket over a white shirt, collar unbuttoned. No tie, of course, but she felt sure his grey pants belonged to a suit. Canvas shoes and the sporty cap hopefully distracted from that oversight.

She walked beside him along the shore, their backs to the warehouse. "Let's get a decent distance down the beach. Then you can scan the horizon for birds. When you're facing the warehouse, call me over to look."

Grace followed his instructions. She did see a few birds, mainly seagulls. She called Harry over and handed him the binoculars. He took a brief look out at the opposite shore, then at the warehouse. Then handed them back to her.

"Interesting. I might join the Audubon Society." He picked up his camera and checked the setting. "Stand near that rock. Act as if I'm taking photos of you."

Harry had her sit on a large boulder with her back to the warehouse. He stood nearby with the camera but was actually scanning the dock and building with the long distance lense as he gave her direction.

"Very nice, dear. Tilt your shoulder a little more. Big smile now, like a movie star."

Grace forced a smile. She sat up straight, her knees together, toes pointing at the sand as she'd seen in magazines. "Will this take much longer? This rock is hard."

"You wanted to come, remember? This is how it's done. Look out at the water. Smile as if you see your ship coming in. Quigley is peeping through the blinds. Let's hope he's just a busybody and not a snitch for Blue Fin."

Grace hadn't thought of that. The prospect inspired her. She turned to Harry with a dazzling smile and rested her hand on her waist.

"Very nice." Harry walked closer, pretending to take more photos.

"Is he still watching?"

"Uh-huh. Nosey bugger." Harry put the camera down. He lifted his hand and cupped her cheek. "Let's give him his money's worth."

He leaned down and kissed her. Grace was so startled; she nearly lost her balance. She clung to his shoulder and felt his arm slip around her waist.

Then it was over. He stood up and wiped her lipstick off his mouth.

"Are you alright?"

"I'm fine." She forced an even, unaffected tone. The sun had dropped close to the horizon, and she didn't need the sunglasses anymore, but kept them on to hide her reaction.

"He closed the blinds. Good. Take my arm in case he's still watching."

Grace didn't mind the offer, though she didn't make anything of it. Or the kiss.

Definitely not that.

Chapter Thirty-Five

Harry set the mysterious paper bag on the table and opened it. Then doled out the contents: two ham and cheese sandwiches, two apples, and a Hershey's bar that he carefully divided in half. There was also a pint of whiskey. She added a dollop to her coffee, and he did, too.

After the food was gone, he tore the cellophane off a fresh deck of cards, removed the jokers, and began to shuffle. "Know how to play gin rummy?"

"A little." She was good but liked to catch an opponent off guard.

"Let's put the radio on. That's what a real couple would do, right?"

Grace didn't disagree, though she thought a real couple with one night away from their toddler would finish the whiskey and go to bed about now.

An hour later, she fanned out another winning hand.

"I'm glad there's no money changing hands. You're a hustler, Russo."

She liked the compliment and his surprised expression even more. "You're lucky I'm not. You're an awful card player."

"I'm getting off easy. Except for the humiliation."

She took the cards and shuffled. "Your secrets are safe with me."

"I think they would be. If you knew any." He sounded as if he meant it, too. He lifted the edge of the wooden blind and checked the warehouse.

"Is it dark enough?"

"Just about. One more hand should do it."

She dealt and rearranged her cards. Harry took a card from the pile and dropped the deuce of hearts. She picked it up, and he winced.

"Is Mrs. Pfeiffer ever coming back?"

He laughed, low in his chest. "What made you think of that?"

"I don't know." It felt as if she'd been working for him for months, but it had barely been two weeks.

"Don't worry about Mrs. Pfeiffer. We'll cross that bridge when we come to it."

She wasn't sure what he meant, or if she even wanted to keep working for him. He took a card and left the Queen of Diamonds. She picked that one up, too.

It didn't take long for her win the last hand. Harry surrendered with a shake of his head.

She made a neat stack of the packs and stuck them back in the box while Harry peered through the blinds again.

"The spotlights are on at the back of the warehouse. That's a good sign."

They'd already worked out a plan. They'd pack up the car and park on the road, near the warehouse. Grace would wait while Harry crept up on the beach to watch for deliveries.

Harry stood at the bed, tossing things back in his suitcase: the cards, the empty coffee pot, and the whiskey. Everything except the camera and the binoculars. And the gun, she noticed. He left the holster and tucked the gun in his jacket pocket.

She followed him to the car and took her heavy sweater from the backseat. It was chilly, but the crisp air cleared her head.

When she closed her door, he said, "It's still quiet over there, but there are plenty of men on hand. I don't think the boss would pay for all those guys to stand around doing nothing."

He spoke softly. The lights were off in Quigley's cottage. But he still could have been watching.

A crescent moon hung above the glistening water like a silver ornament on a string. The black sky was coated with stars. Grace couldn't remember the last time she'd seen so many.

Harry handed her the binoculars, and she took a turn. There wasn't much to see. Burly men moving past the warehouse doorway and windows. She handed them back and huddled into the warmth of her sweater.

"Well, here we go. I won't start the engine. It will make too much noise. Hang on. We may hit a few bumps."

Harry put the car in neutral and gently steered as it rolled down the hill in reverse and then onto the road. The headlights were off, and Grace held on to the dashboard as they bounced along, feeling a bit of vertigo when he finally hit the brake and pushed the transmission stick back into Park.

The car had landed on the shoulder of the road, across from the cottages, not far from the path they'd taken to the beach. Large spotlights illuminated the back of the warehouse and most of the dock. Though the view was soon blocked by a truck that pulled up alongside the warehouse.

"I had a feeling that would happen. I just guessed the wrong spot," Harry murmured.

She was about to answer when she heard an engine out on the water, and the men in the warehouse call out to each other.

"A boat's coming in." He lifted the binoculars and followed the vessel's path. "It's a fishing boat."

Without another word, he opened the door and slipped out. He crept around the car without standing to his full height. When he got to her window, he said, "I'll be right back. But if anyone gets close, start the car and take off. Wait at the railroad station. I'll meet you there sooner or later."

Grace didn't answer. She didn't like that plan. For one thing, she didn't want to leave him here alone. Even if he did have a gun. And for another, she didn't know how to drive.

She tried to follow Harry's movements on the beach, but soon lost sight of him. Which was a good thing, she realized. If she couldn't spot him, neither could anyone at the warehouse. Harry had told her earlier that the bright lights on the dock would make it harder to see anyone approach from the beach. The way it's hard for actors on stage to see the audience.

The logic reassured her a bit as her gaze moved from the clock on the dashboard to her wristwatch and back again. Five minutes passed, then ten. She considered stepping out of the car to look for him but didn't want to risk being spotted. She still heard voices and could see the front half of the fishing boat, which was tied up at the dock.

But she couldn't see what was going on behind the truck.

Harry suddenly appeared, scuttling around to the driver's side like a crab. He slipped back behind the wheel. "It was a real boat with a real catch. They hoisted it on the scale. I waited, but nothing else was unloaded."

"False alarm."

"Seems so. But they're still open for business." Harry checked his watch. "Maybe they expect more customers."

A short time later, the sound of a boat motor rose again, and she watched the vessel glide out of the shadowy inlet.

They sat in silence, staring at the warehouse. Grace was almost sure they were on a wild goose chase—a wild fish chase, more accurately—but didn't want to say. She sunk into her sweater and must have been shivering.

"I'd turn on the heat, but I don't want to start the engine. It might attract attention. Do you want my jacket?"

"Of course not. You need it." She stared out her window at the beach. The tide was coming in. Waves rolled to the shore and crashed on the jetty.

"Did you do much surveillance during the war?"

"Not officially. But you needed to do some just to stay alive."

He lit a cigarette and took a long draw, then passed it to her. "Cup the tip with your hand. You'd be surprised how far a tiny light like that can be seen."

She took a puff and handed it back. He wasn't watching and nearly burned his hand, his gaze fixed on the warehouse.

"Powder your nose. More visitors arriving."

Grace scanned the water and saw another boat gliding through the inlet, smaller and sleeker than the first, dark blue on the bottom with white trim and a white cabin.

"Don't leave the car. Remember what I said about driving away." He grabbed the camera from the back seat, slipped out, and disappeared into the shadows. Grace's heart was pounding so loud, she worried they would hear it on the dock.

Chapter Thirty-Six

Alone in the car, Grace picked up the binoculars and watched the boat turn, then putter up to the dock in reverse. It wasn't as large a boat as the last vessel and disappeared completely behind the truck. Ignoring Harry's instruction, she got out to see what was going on, careful to leave the door ajar so it wouldn't make noise closing.

She crouched beside the front fender, then stumbled into the tall grass along the road's shoulder. It was hard to stay out of sight, but she soon found a spot with adequate cover and a clear view. She lay on her stomach, peaking through the grass and bramble and ignoring rocks that dug into her belly and legs.

Up on the dock, the cable used to weigh a catch hung slack from a tall metal arm while three of four men crowded at the back of the boat. They lifted out wooden crates, identical to those she'd seen at the club, and carried them straight to the truck parked beside the warehouse.

She searched the beach below the dock. She couldn't see Harry and wondered how close he'd dare to get to the activity.

But if she didn't see him, the men in the warehouse wouldn't either, she reminded herself again.

"What the hell was that?" a voice shouted. "Swing that light around. Someone's out there."

The beam swept over the beach like a searchlight scanning a prison yard. Grace pressed herself to the ground and held her breath as the area where she hid was suddenly illuminated, bright as day. Then, just as suddenly went pitch black again.

She waited before picking up her head in case the spotlight doubled back. When she looked through the binoculars, she saw two men scramble down from the dock and march along the sand. One held a flashlight. The other held a gun.

They headed toward a pair of dumpsters that Harry must have used for cover. They were going to find him. She had no idea how to help.

She snuck back to the car, slid into the driver's seat, then stepped on the clutch, and pushed the stick into neutral, as she'd seen people do. The car began a slow roll along the road, and she steered, or tried to, hunkered down behind the wheel.

If she drove off the pavement and got the car stuck in sand, they'd both pay the price. But Harry couldn't cross the open space from the dumpster to the road and escape, unless the car was closer. Even if he did have a gun and could shoot back.

She winced at the sand and gravel that crunched under the tires and hoped the sound couldn't travel far. A cluster of bushes, scraggly pines, and rocks stood parallel to the dumpsters, shielding the car from view. Grace pressed the brake and shoved the transmission into park, then searched the shadows for Harry.

The dock workers had almost reached his hiding place. Their light flashed around the metal bins.

"Over there…see?"

The beam held steady on one of the dumpsters. Grace heard the metal top slam and then an ungodly chorus of screeching as a pack of slinky, four-legged shadows scrambled out. The pack of yowling specters raced over the rocks and across the road, then scattered on the other side. More followed, yowling and hissing. Only a few daring heroes carried loot in their mouths, the remains of their stolen dinner.

Feral cats, feasting on fish guts and other tasty leftovers. She'd never seen so many at once. Maybe Harry had spooked them to cause a distraction.

The men stopped just short of the bins. The one holding the light let the beam drop and held his nose. "Jesus, what a stink. I told you to fix the lock on that damn lid. Damn, cats dragged half that crap out on the beach. Who's going to clean that mess up?"

"Don't look at me. I'm dead tired. We'll clean it tomorrow." The man holding the light turned away in disgust and headed for the dock. Then suddenly looked back. "Dirty little bastards. This will teach you."

The gun flashed as shots fired. Grace heard them ping off the metal and rocks. A few hit the ground, and sand sprayed into the air. The remaining cats raced in all directions. Grace hoped none were hit, but hoped the bullets had missed Harry even more.

"Knock it off. You want the cops out here?" the man with the searchlight said. "Christ, you're a lousy shot. You couldn't hit the broad side of your old lady's ass."

The other argued about the insult. Grace watched them retreat. The door on the back of the truck rattled down and slammed shut. A lock was clamped on. She checked the cab but didn't see a driver.

She didn't see Harry either and started to worry.

Moments later, the lights at the back of the dock went off, and her surroundings sank into darkness.

Grace was just about to leave the car to look for Harry when he appeared, slinking out of the tall grass, along with a few more cats. He limped back, careful to stay low. Grace opened the driver's door and slid to the passenger's side. He stunk of rotten fish. But it seemed pointless to mention that.

"That was close," she said. If he was shaken, she couldn't tell.

"Close enough. Good idea to bring the car down. I was relieved I didn't have to count on that guy's bad aim. Even a broken clock is right twice a day."

He dropped the camera in the back seat and peered at the dock. "Looks like they're all inside now. I'll take a chance and start the engine. We'll circle around and wait for the truck to pass, so no one in the warehouse sees us following."

Grace crossed her fingers as the car started, and Harry turned onto the road. The tires spun in the sand a moment. She squeezed her eyes shut and said a quick, silent "Hail Mary." Suddenly, they were moving.

He made a U-turn and headed away from the warehouse. Then turned again and parked at a corner the truck would have to pass, heading back to the main route west.

He cut the headlamps but kept the engine running. "I can turn the heater on now."

"That's all right. It will only make the smell worse." She glanced at him but didn't say more.

"Is it that bad?" He stared down at himself and sniffed.

"No comment."

He laughed quietly and wiped his face and hands on a handkerchief he'd pulled from his pocket. "I didn't hide inside the dumpster. But I may as well have."

They both heard the truck's rumbling motor coming closer and turned to face the road. The truck barreled past, and Harry waited a moment. When he was sure no other vehicles were coming, he pulled out and turned in the same direction.

Grace saw the truck's taillights a short distance ahead when it paused at a stop sign. They followed it down the winding road on the inlet's edge and into the village. Then onto the main route that led west, all the way to the city.

"We should be at the club around five. Unless Eddie got nervous, and his deliveryman makes a special stop."

"To hide the drugs out here, you mean?" Grace hadn't thought of that. Her heart fell at the prospect; tying Eddie to the contraband—and Mary's murder—would be even harder if that happened.

"There will still be a way to connect him. Don't worry," Harry said, guessing her thoughts.

Grace nodded and stared out her window. She was worried and wished she could speed up time and magically find herself at the end of this exhausting day and night. And soon to be, day again.

She wasn't sure how long they'd been driving. At least an hour, or more. "He's turning off twenty-seven. We'd better hang back. I don't want to be spotted."

But let's not lose him, Grace nearly said. But she held her tongue. Harry knew what he was doing. They'd gotten this far; she had to trust him.

The truck headed north on a side road. Grace found a little pen light in the glove compartment and tried to read the map.

"Do you know what road we're on?"

"I think it said eighty-five. We're going south."

She nearly pressed her nose to the map. "We're somewhere between Sayville and Bohemia?" She'd never realized that the towns on Long Island had such odd names.

"Everybody's got to be somewhere," Harry murmured.

The truck turned again. When they reached the same corner and turned, too, Grace didn't see the red taillights anymore.

It seemed to be an industrial area, with long empty lots separated by chain link fences. She could make out a few signs, one for gravel and cement, another for truck repair.

"He must have pulled in along here somewhere." Harry sounded annoyed. And worried. She didn't like hearing that.

There was no sign of the truck on either side of the road. Grace was getting upset. Then she caught sight of it, behind a high fence. Yellow letters on a black background read, "Sayville Scrap Metal."

"In that junk yard. Look, someone's closing the gate."

Harry drove past, his eyes straight ahead. A short distance down the road, he made a U-turn, drove back down the road, and parked so that they had a view of the yard.

"I'll try to see what's going on. Stay here. I really mean it this time." He glanced at her, about to open his door.

"I don't like that plan. It barely worked at the beach."

He turned to argue, but something in the rearview mirror caught his attention. He pushed her head down, and they were both huddled behind the dashboard. "Someone is passing. I want them to think the car is empty."

Grace didn't answer. She heard a car drive by and then come to a stop a short distance away. Harry sat up a bit and looked out, and she did, too.

A long, burgundy sedan had driven up to the scrap yard. It looked like two men were inside. The gate was pulled open, and the car rolled through.

Grace suddenly recognized the car and turned to Harry. "That looks like Eddie's Caddie."

"It is. I caught the first few letters on the plates." She couldn't see his face clearly in the dark, but she sensed his relief. "This is a lot better for us than the crates being dumped at this yard. Unless we sat here night and day, there's no telling where the goods might have ended up. You can put your map away, Grace. We'll let your old pals, Bernard and Dante, lead the way from here on in. I have a hunch where they're headed."

Grace agreed and felt more relieved than she'd ever admit. Less than ten minutes passed when they saw the Cadillac pull out of the yard. Harry had already positioned his car so they could follow without being noticed.

As they expected, Eddie's men drove back to Route 27 and headed west towards the city. A hint of daylight rimmed the horizon, and a few more cars and trucks appeared on the road, which had been nearly empty all night.

Grace watched out her window at the passing farms and pastures, the flat, wide open landscape of Long Island. Here and there, potato fields gave way to a construction site, where rows of identical, box-shaped houses were taking shape, like Monopoly pieces dropped on an empty board.

Did Rose really want to live out here? It looked so desolate. Grace knew that she'd never want to.

They followed the sedan over the Manhattan Bridge, onto Delancey Street, until it took a right on First Avenue. The sun was up, the streets steamy. The old brick buildings were low in this part of town, laundry lines strung across the alleys and backyards. Shopkeepers cranked open awnings and swept the patch of sidewalk in front of their store. Many signs were in Polish, and she recognized the little restaurant where she and Arty had eaten their late-night breakfast.

Mothers dragged reluctant children by the hand to school while men in work clothes, toting lunch pails, trod at a slow, steady pace. Milk trucks and ice trucks made their deliveries, slowing down the sparse traffic. But not as much as a pushcart loaded with vegetables, dragged by an old draft horse.

Grace wasn't sure how Harry kept Eddie's car in sight as it wove in and out of the traffic. He leaned toward the windshield, blinking back sleep and the sharp, fresh sunlight. Somehow, he didn't lose sight of the Caddie.

"This seems a strange route to the club," she said.

"I had the same thought." Harry didn't say more. He stared straight ahead and swung the Nash around a big, noisy street sweeper, coming so close Grace feared the fenders would dent.

"He's making a left," Grace said.

Harry did the same, turning on 5th Street, narrow and dark, lined with old brown tenements. The Cadillac double-parked. Harry drove by as Bernard emerged from the driver's side and Dante from the other.

Grace began to turn to watch. "Don't look back," Harry's tone was sharp. "They might recognize you."

Harry parked down the street, then turned the rear-view mirror so she had a view. Then picked up his camera from the back seat, twisted around, and balanced the long-distance lens on his shoulder. His window was open, and he gauged the shot with the sideview mirror.

Eddie's men had removed two suitcases from the trunk, and each carried one up a short flight of steps to the entrance of an apartment building. Dante searched the row of buzzers next to the door and pressed. Moments later, they walked in.

Harry put the camera in his lap. "Let's wait for them to come out. Their cases should look a lot lighter, if they carry them out at all."

Grace nodded. The lack of sleep was catching up. She felt lightheaded and craved a cup of coffee. But also excited in a foggy, distant way. Was this it, finally? Had they nailed Eddie Martone to a solid motive for killing Mary?

Her hands were folded in her lap, fingers intertwined. She closed her eyes to steal a moment's rest.

"Are you praying, Grace?" Harry asked quietly.

"I'm not sure...I might be."

She opened her eyes and smiled. Harry nudged her arm and lifted his camera back in place. The apartment building door had opened. Eddie's men came out empty-handed. They trotted down the steps, hat brims tugged low, then climbed into the shiny car and drove off.

Harry put his camera away and searched his pocket. He came up with a few bills and some pennies cupped in his palm.

"Can you loan me a nickel for a phone call?"

"My treat. Take a few." Grace handed him a fistful of coins. "How will the police know which apartment to search? Do they go from door to door?"

"I'm not pitching this to the police, in case one of Martone's insiders gets wind of it. I know a guy at the FBI. I already gave him a heads up." He glanced at her. "Arty Pulaski lives in that building. I doubt they'll visit anyone else."

"Are you sure?" It seemed a silly question after she asked.

"Sorry. I know you like the guy."

"I'm just surprised." She was more than surprised but didn't want to show Harry. She felt embarrassed for being taken in, though Harry had never been.

Arty had told her in so many words that Eddie had a hold on him, but she didn't think the hook went this deep. She hadn't really understood what he'd been trying to say. Or hadn't wanted to.

Grace waited in the car while Harry made a call from a phone booth on the corner. He spoke briefly, glancing once or twice over his shoulder at the street. He was soon back in the car.

"It will take a while to get a warrant. The photos should help. Someone will watch the place until the feds come to search. I need to drop the film, then I'll take you back to Brooklyn."

"That offer is positively heroic, after all the driving you've done the last twenty-four hours. I'll take a cab. And probably sleep the whole way back, and the rest of the day."

"My plan, too. After a long shower."

She sniffed the air. "An hour or so should do it. With brown soap." She felt bad teasing after all he'd been through but couldn't help it. "It will be hard not to say something to my family, but I don't want to get their hopes up."

She expected to be pummeled with questions about where she'd been and what she'd be doing as soon as she walked in the door.

"That seems smart. Keep it to yourself for now. We'll know soon enough if it was a wild goose chase."

His reply made her uneasy. It suggested the situation wasn't the sure bet she expected. But she was exhausted and sensitive, and Harry was always so circumspect. She pushed her doubts aside and told herself this was it. It had to be.

"After the warrant and the search, how long do you think it will take to connect Martone to Mary's murder?"

"It's hard to say. Eddie, his errand boys, and others at the club will be played off against each other in separate interrogations. We only need one to rat out the boss and strike a deal with the D.A."

"Call the minute you hear something. Anything at all."

Harry nodded solemnly; his gaze met hers for a long, silent moment. She remembered the way he'd kissed her on the beach and wanted him to again. Without the excuse of Mr. Quigley.

She turned and slipped out. "See you, Harry," she called back. He lifted his hand in a silent goodbye, then started the engine.

She watched the car until it turned into the traffic on Second Avenue and prepared herself to wait.

Chapter Thirty-Seven

"Grace...thank God you're back." Her mother mopped the kitchen floor with wide, sweeping strokes, as if swabbing the deck of a battleship. Grace held the side door open, waiting to be told to go through the front, so she wouldn't leave footprints on the wet linoleum.

Instead, her mother said, "Your sister came home early from the factory. Something happened with Frank. She won't say, but she's crying her eyes out. She's going to make herself sick."

Grace wasn't surprised. She'd seen this coming.

"I'll go up to her." She left her flats by the door. Right where Joe's work boots had sat each night, below his overalls. The police had taken those things away.

She tiptoed across the wet floor and into the dining room in her bare feet. She'd hoped for at least a cup of coffee before a shower, but the stove was clearly off limits and her new mission, urgent.

Her mother wrinkled her nose as Grace passed. "You smell like fishy garbage. Wrap those things up. I need to wash them separate."

Her mother reached under the sink and gave her a paper bag. "How was your trip with your boss? Did you find anything out? Did you get anything accomplished?"

Her tone was challenging, as if she still didn't believe Grace needed to stay overnight to help Joe's case. If her mother knew half of what she'd done and been through the last few days, she would have dropped from a heart attack in the middle of the perfectly clean floor.

Grace chose her words carefully. "We did learn a few things that might help

Joe. Harry won't know for sure until tonight. Or maybe even tomorrow."

Her mother squared her shoulders, preparing to attack the rest of the linoleum. "I hope Mr. Shaw was respectful and didn't take advantage."

Grace didn't answer for a moment. "He was a total gentleman, honestly."

Her mother turned the handle on the ringer. "I'll say a prayer; it was for the good. And one for your sister, too. What else is going to happen around here?"

Grace noticed that her mother wasn't asking her; she was talking to the ceiling.

She found Rose curled in a ball on her bed, still in her work clothes. Fast asleep, her fair complexion was blotchy, mascara smeared around her eyes.

Grace shut the door and went into the bathroom to shower. She took her time, washed her hair, and let the hot water beat down on her back and shoulders. When she returned, Rose was awake, her head turned on her pillow as she stared into space.

"Hey, honey." Grace sat at the edge of her bed and rested her hand on Rose's hip. "What's going on? Mom said you had a fight with Frank. Was it about postponing the wedding?"

"You don't have to worry about that anymore," Grace ached to tell her. "Joe could be free and clear by tomorrow. Frank and everyone else in the neighborhood will be eating crow."

But she couldn't. Not until Harry told her their suspicions had panned out.

Rose propped herself up on an elbow. Grace could tell it was hard for her to answer. "He doesn't want to marry me. Not ever. He said he's sorry, but he had to be honest. He says in time, I'll see it's for the best."

Grace agreed with the last part, but held her tongue. She watched her sister's expression crumble, as tears flowed. "He even took back the ring."

Grace hugged her. "Honey…that's awful. Did he try to explain at all?"

"Not really. Just that his feelings had changed. He didn't know why, but there was nothing he could do to change them back. I felt this coming. I told you. I just didn't want to think the worst."

"Because he wouldn't come to dinner Sunday?"

"More than that. A few days ago, I ran into his sister, Rita. She told me Frank's friends have been razzing him about Joe. Telling him to watch out, hot blood might run in the family. He'd better sleep with a knife under his pillow when we're married."

"They really said that? And he took it to heart?" Another man would have laughed it off or even dropped those guys. After he gave one or two a fat lip.

Rose sighed, looking sadder. "Worse than that."

"What could be worse?" Grace braced herself and tried to catch her sister's gaze.

Rose took a deep breath and stared straight ahead. "They said he'd better watch out that I didn't cheat on him with some colored guy. Or maybe I already had." She looked at Grace. "They all know I slept with Frank. He must have told them. I wouldn't have even done it, but Frank wouldn't stop pestering me. He kept saying we were almost married and what was the difference. So, one night I gave in just to make him happy." She covered her face with her hands. "He must have bragged. No one will want me now. No decent man, anyway."

Rose began to cry. Grace held her shoulders and gave her a gentle shake. "Stop that. Don't you ever say that again. It's absolutely not true."

Her sister stared back, and Grace's hold softened. "I can't think of anyone good enough for you, Rose. Certainly not Frank, or any of those *gavoons* he hangs around with."

Grace leaned back and took Rose's hand. "I know Mama and Pop mean well, but you can't listen to what they say. Things are different nowadays. A lot of men don't care a whit if they marry a virgin. Men don't come to the altar inexperienced. Why are women expected to be so innocent and pure?"

Rose wiped her eyes with a hanky. "That's just the way it is. A wife is supposed to learn about sex from her husband. That's what Mama says."

"My point is, it shouldn't matter to someone who loves you, Rose. *Really* loves you."

Grace knew that she hadn't convinced her sister but perhaps had comforted her. Rose was leveled with disappointment, heartache, and even shame. She needed time to see how shallow Frank's feelings were. And what a hollow, ignorant man he was, in every way.

"I hope Pop gets the deposit back on the hall. Mom can use the satin for someone else's dress. All the gifts have to go back, I guess…right?"

"Don't worry about that now. Everything will get sorted out." She squeezed her sister's hand. "Promise me that when you feel low, you'll remind yourself that Frank Stanco is a prize-winning idiot. If I was a millionaire, I'd rent a billboard in Times Square and write that out in big neon lights." Grace motioned with her hands, picturing it. Rose finally laughed. "You're going to meet someone wonderful, who'll love you to the Moon and back. You're going to do a lot better than that guy. I'd bet my life on it."

Rose met her gaze and gave her a quick, tight hug. "I know I'm a pain in the neck. But I don't know what I'd do without you. What any of us would do."

Grace laughed and pulled the towel off her wet hair. She crossed to the dressing table to find a comb. "You'd all survive just fine."

"I'm not so sure about that. I certainly don't want to try." Rose sat up and swung her feet to the floor. "What happened on the trip with your boss? You didn't even say where you went."

"Montauk Point…and that's all I can say for now. Sorry."

Rose stood up and slipped on her shoes. "For Pete's sakes. That's so silly. You sound like you're in the Secret Service."

Grace was combing out her hair and found Rose's reflection in the mirror. "I might like that. If they let women do more than type and make coffee."

"You crack me up. I don't know what's gotten into you lately."

Grace shrugged and fixed the strap on her slip. "Me, either. Now that you mention it."

Rose stood in the doorway and straightened out her clothes. She looked sad again. "I'd better tell Mama the wedding is off. Will you come down with me?"

Grace nodded. "Of course I will. Don't worry. She'll be too tired from mopping to make a big fuss.

* * *

Their mother refused to believe it. Mostly because Rose had blurred the fine print of Frank's rejection, sparing their mother the vulgar details.

"Men get cold feet when the date gets close. He'll come around. You'll see." Her tone was comforting and unruffled.

Rose looked to Grace for support. "I think he means it, Ma. He asked her for the ring."

Her mother didn't like hearing that. "Did he find someone else? Is that what you're saying?"

"It's not that. He just changed his mind. He says it was for the best," Rose replied quietly.

Her mother cut the air with the side of her hand, her angry, dismissive gesture. "Mr. Big Shot. It's for the best, huh? He should have thought of what's for the best before we rented the hall." She sighed and hugged Rose close. "Poor *cara*. Don't cry. We'll see what we're going to see. It's what God wants, girls. Remember that."

Her reply seemed to hold out a slim hope, but Grace knew it was her mother's way of resigning herself to a situation. Nona sat at the kitchen table, sipping demi-tasse, watching, and listening. When their mother left the room, Nona touched Rose's arm with her small, dark hand and made a tsk-tsk sound.

"Mia bellissima ragazza, un uomo così non vale le tue lacrime. Sei una perla oltre misura. Un asino ha più senso di quello."

"Thank you, Nona." Rose's voice was thick. She leaned over and kissed their grandmother's cheek.

As they climbed back up the stairs, Rose whispered to Grace, "What did Nona say? I didn't really understand."

Grace's Italian was only slightly better than her sister's, but she'd understood their grandmother's advice. " 'A man like that is not worth your tears. You're a pearl beyond measure.' She called you her 'beautiful girl'... and she either called Frank a donkey or a 'stupid ass.'"

Rose laughed. "Wow, that's some serious commandment-breaking. Nona will have to say ten rosaries to make up for that one."

Grace had to agree.

* * *

Grace felt as if she hadn't eaten dinner with her family in weeks, though it had only been five days. Still, that was probably a record, discounting the times she'd been sick in bed.

She was relieved that no one commented on her absence. Rose and Frank's breakup took center stage. Her father was livid over Frank's callous treatment of his youngest daughter. As mad as she'd ever seen him. Grace felt sure he'd guessed the real reason, though he never spoke of it directly.

"That Frank Stanco—" He practically spat the name. "Who does he think he is to treat Rose this way? Such disrespect to her…to the whole family… *Stronza…figlio di puttana…*He better not come round here no more. I see that guy, he'll be sorry…"

He was about to add a few more choice words, Grace felt sure. Until her mother touched his shirt sleeve. "Anthony, please. Not at the table. You need to watch your pressure, remember? The doctor said."

He nodded; his head heavy. Then turned to Rose, shaking his finger as he spoke, his voice low. "That Stanco is garbage. You forget him, *bella*. You spit him from your mouth, like poison, 'eh? God has a better man for you. You're gonna see, *mio bambino*."

Rose's eyes grew wide and glassy. Grace squeezed her hand under the table. "Thank you, Papa," Rose answered quietly.

Her father sat back and sipped his wine as they all started eating again.

"I'm going to close the shop on Friday and visit Joseph," he told them. "I called Mr. Kramer today, but he wasn't in." He looked at Grace. "What does Mr. Shaw say?"

Grace covered her mouth a moment with her napkin. Mostly to keep from blurting out all that she and Harry had discovered.

"I don't know if he's spoken to Mr. Kramer lately. He didn't mention it." Which wasn't a lie. "I'll ask him tomorrow. And I'll go with you to Riker's on Friday, Papa."

Grace secretly hoped that this whole ordeal would all be over by then. Maybe they'd be waiting outside the prison gate to take Joe home.

"I'll go with you, too, Pop," Rose said. "I want to see, Joe, too."

Grace was surprised but pleased. Rose met her glance a moment and looked away.

"You just missed a day of work. They might fire you," her mother said. "I'll go with your father. I hate to see my Joseph like that, but some things you have to do."

Rose helped herself to another stuffed pepper. She didn't need to deprive herself in order to look slim in her wedding gown, Grace realized. "Let them fire me, who cares. I'm not saving for a down payment anymore. I hate that job anyway. We'll all go. Joe will be surprised."

Grace crossed her fingers under the table. "He will be."

Chapter Thirty-Eight

Groucho was in fine form, but Grace hardly heard a word. She watched her father, and even Nona as they laughed at the radio, but felt as if she sat behind a glass wall.

Rose left after dinner to visit her best friend, Agnes who lived around the corner. Her mother stayed in the kitchen, talking to her sister Nina. A toll call to Rhode Island that was going to cost a fortune. Grace knew her mother needed a sympathetic ear, but desperately wished she'd finish up and leave the line clear.

When the rest of her family went up to bed, she lingered downstairs, claiming she wasn't tired and wanted to read. She was sound asleep on the couch when the phone rang around midnight. She stumbled into the kitchen to pick it up.

"Sorry to call so late. But I knew you were waiting to hear."

She heard muffled voices and tinkling glasses in the background. Harry was calling from a bar. "What happened? Did it take a long time for the police to get the warrant?"

"Not unusually long. They knocked on Arty's door about three this afternoon. The suitcases were under his bed, barely hidden. Packed with cigarettes full of dope. Arty gave up the whole crew before the cops got the cuffs on him. Eddie, Dante, Bernard, along with everyone who works at the club."

"Did the police ask about Mary's murder? Did any of them tell who did it?"

Harry didn't answer for a moment. "Not yet, Grace. The thing is all the alibis for that night are holding tight. Including your friend, Arty. A witness places him at the Indigo Club during the time of the murder, just as he said."

Grace was relieved to hear that, though she knew Harry had called him her friend just to needle. If she didn't know better, she'd say Harry was jealous. But that was just… preposterous.

"I've been checking and double-checking all day on the others," he continued, "hoping to catch one of them with a foot off the bag."

Grace felt confused. This was not the conversation she expected to have with Harry. Far from the good news she'd immediately share, waking everyone up to celebrate. She felt as if someone had just pushed her off a cliff. And punched her in the gut first.

"Maybe you're wrong. Maybe the people you're talking to about these alibis are lying. One of Martone's men still might tell the police he was ordered to do it. You told me that yourself."

"That's the way I thought it would play out. But that scenario is starting to look unlikely."

His tone was quiet and even, but she was sure Harry knew how painfully disappointing it was for her to hear his admission. After all they'd been through, they'd hit a wall. He just didn't want to say it so bluntly. Maybe couldn't even admit it out loud to himself yet.

He waited for her to speak, but she didn't know what to say. She heard ice in a glass and pictured him sipping his bourbon.

"We must have missed something," Grace said finally. "If it wasn't someone from the club, who could it be?"

"Come in tomorrow. We'll lay the pieces out again and see what we've got."

"I'll bring my notebook." She planned to dissect every word before they met. Even if she had to stay up all night. "And the record jacket. You haven't seen that yet."

"Record jacket? What are you talking about?"

Grace's heart skipped a beat. She realized she'd never mentioned the souvenir.

"I found it in Mary's apartment. It slipped behind the cabinet that holds the record player. There's a fingerprint on it. A fragment of one, anyway."

She braced herself for his reaction. "For Christ's sake, Grace—you took even more evidence out of that apartment than the book? Is that what you're telling me?"

"I put it away and sort of forgot about it. Sorry." She whispered, afraid to wake the house. Though Harry was the only one shouting. "It might show that someone else was in the apartment that night, besides Joe."

"I realize that," he said angrily. "But I'd rather forget you even told me about it."

"I know I shouldn't have taken it. But there must be some way to bring it forward if it can help?"

"Did you ever stop to think it could hurt him? If that's Joe's print, it gives the prosecution more ammunition. He's never denied he was there. But a bloody fingerprint found on the scene never helped anyone prove their innocence in a courtroom. Not that I know of."

She had thought of that. But if it wasn't Joe's and showed that someone else was there, it could be his last, best hope. Otherwise, his fate would end up in the hands of twelve fellow citizens who may not like the look of his face, or may not like Italians, or may not think white men should sleep with colored women. Or any of a thousand and one reasons a jury might fail to find reasonable doubt and decide he was guilty of murder in the first degree.

"The problem is," Harry said, "even though we don't know if it helps him or hurts him, I can't suppress evidence in a murder case now that I know about it. Even if the fingerprint belongs to Joe. I can lose my license and get thrown in jail, too."

The rebuke stung, but Grace didn't call him on it.

"Isn't there some way to find out if the print belongs to Joe before you turn it in? We can ask him if he remembers handling it. That could eliminate him. Then it will prove someone else was there."

"Maybe. Maybe not. You heard Joe describe his state of mind when he found Mary's body. He nearly blacked out. He may not remember. And what if he does? The prosecution will blow up that scrap of paper the size of a movie poster and put some expert on the stand who looks like Einstein to give a lecture about it. It won't prove Joe murdered Mary. He's never denied he was there. But it's some beautiful stage prop."

His words were sobering. "You're saying it's too risky and we should just forget it."

"I'd love to say that. But it's too damn late. Bring it tomorrow. I won't tell Kramer about it for now. Even if the print doesn't match Joe or any of our pals from the club, that still leaves Gem Washington and Reverend Holmes. I haven't confirmed their alibis yet, but I should have that nailed down by tomorrow."

She forgot that Harry was still working and might not be done for hours. "I'll be interested in what you find out."

"Gem probably dumped his friends for Dolores as soon as they got to the Indigo Room. I just spoke to the guy at the door who saw them leave together. Reverend Holmes is harder to track. Did you know that he works at Harlem Hospital?"

She recalled asking him, but they were interrupted. "That's just a few blocks from Mary's apartment."

"He had a shift the night of the murder. Now I need to find out if he was in the hospital the whole night. We know that he went to the club to see Mary sing. It could have been the Saturday night that Joe's jacket went missing."

"I know it fits logically. But I saw him preach. I sat at his kitchen table and met his family. I heard the way he spoke about Mary. He was worried about the fate of her soul, and that she hadn't reformed," she said bluntly. "I don't believe he would have knowingly risked that she might end up…well, in the wrong place."

"Theology is not my beat. I do know that no one on this green earth is all good or all bad. Practically everyone is capable of an unthinkable act if pushed too far. I've seen it with my own eyes, Grace."

He sounded tired. Even more tired than she felt, a weariness that seeped down to her bones.

"I should be in by ten," he added.

"I'll be there before you."

"I'm sure you will be. Good night, Grace. Sleep well."

She heard a smile in his voice and had a warm feeling, despite their bickering.

"Good night, Harry. I doubt I'll sleep much at all."

* * *

Grace was at her desk, sorting through a pile of mail and message slips, when Harry walked in. It might have been any other day, except that her pulse was racing. The day was anything but ordinary.

Her notebook sat on her desk, pushed to one side along with a manila envelope that held the record jacket.

"Good morning, Grace." Harry removed the gray Fedora and draped his suit jacket over a chair. "I followed up on those leads we talked about. Washington was with Delores, no question. She has—or had?—a boyfriend, so she and Gem had to sneak out of the club. But a neighbor saw them going into Dolores's place at the time of the murder."

"What about Reverend Holmes?" Grace had been working her way through the mail, stacking utility bills and other important-looking pieces in one pile, and making a second she knew Harry would ignore. Though the same fate often met the envelopes in the important one.

She paused to give Harry her full attention.

"Holmes did punch out early Monday night. But he went straight back to Brooklyn, to the bedside of a dying church member and stayed there until Tuesday morning."

She felt relieved to hear that. "So, that's that."

Harry sat on the edge of her desk and offered her a cigarette. He lit hers, then lit one for himself. "We're down to the bottom of the list. Back to Martone and his flunkies, I guess."

His way of saying a dead end. She pushed the stacks of mail aside and placed her notebook in the center of her desk, along with the envelope.

"I couldn't sleep and went over my notes again last night. I noticed something. You're going to think this sounds a little desperate, even crazy.

But hear me out."

"I've got nothing else up my sleeve. It's the perfect moment for desperate and crazy."

"It wasn't anything I wrote down. But something I noticed on a page where I'd used a fountain pen." She had marked the page she needed to show him and spread open the book so he could see it clearly. "The pen started to leak, and my fingers got inky. They left prints. And right above that, these little curved marks. See?"

He peered down at the page, then back at her. "What of it?"

"Those are marks from my fingernails." She held her hand out. "My nails aren't very long, but long enough, I guess." She opened the envelope and slipped out the record jacket. "Here are the bloody prints on the jacket. And the same marks above." She met his gaze and held it. "A man didn't kill Mary. Unless he had long fingernails. Most likely, it was a woman. I'd bet anything it was Judy Stemple."

Harry leaned back, clearly surprised. And not buying her theory. She could tell by the way he sighed and squashed what was left of his cigarette in the ashtray on her desk.

"I know she was a bitch on roller skates to work for. But isn't murder taking it too far?"

"Is it? Think about, Harry. She had every chance to steal Joe's jacket, and with her height, she could have easily disguised herself as a man. That's why Louis Robillard heard Mary laugh when she opened the door, and she sounded surprised, as if it was someone she didn't expect. That's why she said, 'Oh, it's you.'"

Harry frowned but didn't interrupt. "Judy and Eddie Martone had a long, twisted relationship. A sick sort of bond I saw with my own eyes. I bet she hated being pushed aside for Mary, a glamorous, younger woman. Mary's star was rising, and Eddie would prize her even more when the record was released and she became famous. Judy must have hated watching that, especially when her own career had ended so abruptly. And sadly." Grace paused. Harry was listening, though she couldn't tell from his expression if he was buying or not.

"Add to that, Judy's blatant disdain for colored people. She talked about Sylvie as if she was dirt and told me to 'stick to my own kind.' Being dumped for a colored woman must have stung horribly. It must have infuriated her. She flaunted her fiancé, Carter, to make Eddie jealous. But even she must have realized Carter would never marry her. She must have believed that if Mary was out of the way, she could win Eddie back."

"I'll grant there was a triangle. But if Judy knew about Mary and Joe, why not just tell Eddie that Mary was cheating and let lover boy's vicious nature take its course?"

"I wondered about that, too. But if Judy told Eddie about the affair, he would have killed Joe. Not Mary. She would have still been around to taunt Judy, and Eddie's grip on Mary would have been even tighter." Grace paused, thinking back to the vicious argument she'd witnessed at the club. "One night Judy got drunk and put on quite a show with Eddie. The two went at it like an old married couple. Unhappily married," she added. "Judy said, 'I know how to get you where it hurts.' And 'I can fix your wagon for good.' I thought she knew he was behind Mary's murder and was threatening him. But now I realize, she knew how much Eddie prized Mary and how much it had hurt him to lose her. She was practically confessing."

Harry lit another cigarette and sat quietly a moment. He picked up the record cover and studied it. "Why play the record? It seems someone put it on the turntable after Mary was stabbed. And it wasn't to cover her screams."

"Maybe Mary wasn't dead yet and still able to call for help." Grace glanced down a moment. It was hard to say that aloud, and even more painful to picture it. "To tell you the truth, I think Judy did it for spite. Mary gave up so much for that recording. But it was never played on the radio or sold in stores. Who knows what Eddie wanted from Mary for that next step? Judy played the record to cause Mary even more agony. To remind her that all her efforts and high hopes, the compromises she'd made in exchange for Eddie's help, had been in vain. She would leave this earth with her wonderful talent mostly unknown."

Harry answered with a somber gaze, then carefully slipped the record jacket back in the envelope.

"Women don't commit murder much. But I know a few I wouldn't turn my back on. I guess I'd include Miss Stemple on that list."

"She's no dumb blonde. She had it all figured out and had everyone looking for a man."

"Including me," Harry admitted. "Stemple was brought in and questioned yesterday, with the rest of the crew. She claims to have no idea of Eddie's sideline business. The same for Clara Trento. Eddie backed them up, of course. Honor among thieves. There's no evidence to link either of them to the drugs, so the cops had to let them go. Let's hope they got Stemple's prints, and she didn't wander too far."

Harry had slipped on his jacket and picked up his hat. He stood at her desk with the envelope in hand, his expression impatient.

"Well? What are you waiting for? Get your things, Grace. Bring that notebook, too. You need to explain all this to Kramer. I could never do this drama justice. We'll see how he wants to handle the record jacket with the D.A. It's going to be tricky."

Grace grabbed her purse and stuck her hat on. She was surprised to be included in the visit to Joe's attorney but tried not show it. Harry opened the door and stepped aside, allowing her to precede him into the hall.

Standing side by side, they waited in silence for the elevator. Grace watched the slim brass hand on the dial above the doors glide over the Roman numerals as the car came closer.

Just before the bell rang, Harry said, "I'd call it beginner's luck with anyone else. But the plain truth is, you're awfully good at this racket, Miss Russo. Damn good, I have to say."

His simple, blunt praise warmed her. She could only guess how hard it was for him to admit.

Even if he'd never said a word, she already knew she'd done a good job; that much was true.

Chapter Thirty-Nine

Grace returned to Sackett Street at half past three. The house was empty, and she went straight to her room, pulled the shades down, undressed to her slip, and slid under the covers. She'd left Harry and Martin Kramer downtown, in front of the D.A.'s office, after they'd turned in the new evidence, and Grace again put forth her theory about Mary's real killer.

It was late in the day for a nap, but she felt as if she could sleep for a hundred years.

When she woke up, the room was dark. Rose stood over the bed and shook her shoulder.

"Let me sleep, will you? Tell Ma I don't want any dinner."

"Mr. Shaw is here. Are you going to sleep through that, too?"

Grace still didn't open her eyes. "Good one, Rose. You nearly got me."

"He's sitting in the living room. Mama just gave him coffee and biscotti, though I think he said he didn't want any. Pop was going for the anisette bottle. Your boss looks like the nervous type. He might make a run for it any minute."

It really was Harry. He was down there. With good news, or bad?

At this stage, he might feel he had to tell her about the outcome in person, no matter where their latest, and likely last, Hail Mary pass had landed.

Grace slipped out of bed and looked around for her clothes, which were scattered in all directions. "Tell him I'll be right down. Whatever happens, don't let him leave."

She pulled a comb through her hair but didn't bother with lipstick, then tucked her blouse into her skirt as she trotted down the steps.

Harry stood up when he saw her. Their eyes met, and he smiled, and she felt lightheaded with relief. She could see it in his eyes. It was good news, and she was glad that he was here, with her family to celebrate.

"Sorry to drop by without calling. I won't stay long. I wanted to tell you in person, Grace, after all the work you did and what you went through. A little while ago, Judy Stemple confessed to killing Mary Delmore. She's been charged with first-degree murder. Her motive was just as you guessed." She was surprised to find genuine admiration in his gaze. "Add to that, but not surprisingly, she was a big fan of Fritz Kuhn and Father Coughlin before the war. Our high-stepping showgirl has pure poison running through her veins."

Grace saw the baffled but vaguely hopeful expressions on the faces of her parents, Nona, and Rose.

Harry turned to them. "Joe is free and clear. He'll be released from prison as soon as the paperwork is processed, definitely by tomorrow."

Her mother and father stood speechless. Rose hugged Nona, who had started to cry, her rosary beads gripped in shaky hands.

"Mr. Shaw, God bless you." Her father stepped forward and pumped Harry's hand. Then impulsively hugged him, squashing his hat. "How can we ever thank you? How can we ever repay you?"

Harry shook his head and glanced at Grace. "Don't thank me, sir. It was all your daughter's doing. I nearly gave up. But she kept going on her own until she figured it out."

Her father's smile was full of affection, but Grace could tell he didn't believe that his daughter, a mere woman, could have possibly done this marvelous thing. "Grace is a good girl. She has a good head on her shoulders."

"More than that. Much more." Harry didn't look at her, but his praise made her self-conscious.

"I'm just happy it's over. It's like waking up from a bad dream," Grace said.

Her mother nodded, holding back tears. "God is good. He answered our prayers. I can hardly wait to tell Father Dom."

"What time will Joe be out? Do you know?" Rose asked Harry.

"I'm not sure exactly. Mr. Kramer will call with the details." He smiled and backed up towards the door. "I guess I'll leave you folks to celebrate."

Her parents exchanged panicked glances. "You stay, Mr. Shaw. *Veneca.* You stay." Her father gently took Harry's arm and urged him back into the room. "You drink with us. For luck. What do you like? Rye? Bourbon? Some sherry?"

Harry's eagerness to leave melted under her father's adamant hospitality. "Bourbon is fine. Just a short one. Straight up."

"Just as you like." Her father hurried to the liquor cabinet as her mother trotted in with a tray of glasses. Grace would have preferred to join Harry in a real drink but settled for a glass of sherry with the rest.

Her father carried a shot glass to Harry, filled to overflowing. "You come by my shop, Mr. Shaw. I make you a beautiful suit. No, two suits. Hand-stitched. Merino wool. You know what's merino? The finest cloth," he explained before Harry could reply. "You'll look like a prince in a good suit, a nice tall man like you."

Harry laughed and took the glass from her father's hand. "A prince, huh? I might take you up on that, sir."

When everyone had a glass in hand, her father raised his for a toast. "To Mr. Harry Shaw. God bless you for this gift to our family. *Salute!*"

Harry nodded his thanks. He turned to Grace; his glass still lifted. "And to Grace…She's one heck of a gal." He paused, and she worried about what he might say next. "Long may she wave," he added.

Everyone laughed at the tribute and shared a private smile

Her grandmother raised her glass, too. *"Dio benedici la famaglia."*

"Here, here, Nona. *Alla famaglia,*" her mother said.

"Si, la cosa piu importante," Grace's father added.

"It *is* the most important thing, Poppa. *Sempre,*" Grace said. *"Sempre."*

Chapter Forty

Joe would have left the day after he was released from Rikers, just enough time to pack his things and pack in a few of his mother's home-cooked meals. But he stuck it out until the end of June. He earned money house painting, so he could pay their father back for Kramer's bill, and to put towards the annulment from the Vatican Camille had demanded.

A plain divorce would have been cheaper and faster, but it didn't wash with the church or the Ricci family. Movie stars divorced all the time. But Camille was no movie star. Joe had ruined her life. She couldn't even take communion or marry again at the altar, her parents complained. What kind of future did their daughter have now, a divorced woman with no husband or children?

Joe could not refuse the request after all he'd put her through.

Her brother had changed. He'd become quieter and inward-looking, even more than after his return from the army. But the brooding anger had been burned away, along with his highs and lows. Sober was the way Grace would describe him. Sober and settled into himself. Mostly, more mature.

There was no question he mourned Mary and always would. He told Grace it was hard to go through with their plans, but it made him feel better in a way, too. As if they really were running off together. He told Grace he talked to Mary in his head all day, and out loud in the middle of the night.

The night before Grace moved into the city, she and Joe sat together in the basement apartment, passing a bottle of whiskey. Camille's things were gone, along with the white satin bedspread and the heart-shaped pillow. The rooms were bare, except for Joe's instruments, records, and piles of clothing on chairs.

Grace apologized for the night she'd tracked Mary down and outlined all the reasons why her romance with Joe would come to no good. In her well-intentioned, "know-it-all" way. She knew now she knew nothing at all and never had.

"I had no right to do that. To corner her that way. I should have helped the two of you, the way you expected me to. Instead, you and Mary argued. If you hadn't, maybe you would have gone uptown sooner. Before Judy Stemple knocked on Mary's door."

Her brother bowed his head as if she'd piled stones on his shoulders. "You can talk about 'what ifs' until you're blue in the face. Until you drive yourself crazy. What if Stemple had decided to kill Mary just a day or two later? We would have been halfway across the ocean, and that bitch's problem would have been solved."

"I thought of that, too," Grace admitted. But she had to continue. "I'm sorry to dredge this up, Joe. But you're leaving, and I need to get it off my chest. The thing is, sometimes I feel that Mary's death was my fault… I need to know if you do, too."

Joe stared at her, then shook his head. He was crying, and Grace realized she was, too.

"Don't say that. What you told Mary was true. We would have had a hell of a time with all of them upstairs. And Mary's family. I never blamed you, Grace. Not for a minute. It's my fault Mary is gone. As if I stuck that blade in her heart with my own hand. Not because I dragged my ass that night, either. I should have married her when I got home. Instead, I let everyone tell me what to do and who I'm supposed to be in this world."

She knew that was true, but she hated to see him so hard on himself. "You were tired when you got back, Joe. You were worn out. You needed time to clear your head."

"Don't make excuses for me. I hated the army. I hated being out in the field. But I got through it. All those months. Day by day. Hour by hour, sometimes. I don't know where the grit came from, but I found it. But when I walked back into this house, I went belly up. I turned into a sad, confused

S.O.B. who didn't know his ass from his elbow. Who didn't know his own mind, or what he wanted from the life God spared. I should have told all of them—Camille, the families, Father Dom. Even you. All I want is to be with this woman and my music. If anybody doesn't like it, the hell with you. That's why Mary isn't here now," he added in a harsh whisper.

Grace didn't answer. She knew it was true.

* * *

"Time for another round?" Harry pushed his seat back, ready to fetch more drinks from the bar.

Joe checked his watch. "I'd like that, but I better go. I don't want the ship to sail without me."

Short on cash, as usual, Joe was working his passage. He tossed back a swallow of rye and reached for the bag under the table.

There wasn't much left to say. Many toasts and well-wishes had already been dispatched. And they'd heard his vague plan of where he'd stay and where he'd find work once he reached Paris. He'd packed just his G.I. issue duffel, though there were plenty of boxes of music and records Grace had been instructed to ship once he was settled.

Out on the street, Grace took her brother's arm. "Can we walk you to the dock?"

"I'd rather say goodbye here if you don't mind, honey. It will just get harder."

Grace thought so too, but was willing, if it meant a few more minutes with him.

"This is it, I guess." Joe turned and shook Harry's hand. "Take care of my sister, old man. Keep her out of trouble."

"That's a tall order, but I'll try." Harry slapped Joe's shoulder. "So long, Joe. Take care of yourself. Let us hear from you."

Joe turned to Grace, smiling nervously. She hugged him as tight as she could, and he hugged her back, lifting her off her feet.

"Send a card when you get there, just to let us know you're all right and where you're living."

"*Con arriva, scriva?*" Joe imitated their father perfectly as he let her go. "When you get there, write," he'd instructed Joe a few times. Grace had to laugh, though she felt more like crying.

The light turned green. He stepped back and slung his bag over his shoulder, then waved as he dashed across the street towards the pier. Grace waved back and watched until he was out of sight.

A warm breeze rose off the river. The flat, metal buildings on the pier and the outlines of massive ships loomed against the sky.

She looked up at Harry but couldn't speak. He brushed a strand of hair off her cheek.

"Should we get a cab or walk awhile?" he asked in a quiet voice.

"Let's walk."

He took her hand they headed east.

Saying goodbye to Joe made her think of her family and how much had changed. "Tomorrow was supposed to be Rose's wedding day."

"How's she taking it?"

"Surprisingly well. Unless she's putting on a brave face. That ploy can get you through a lot of things, too. I think she felt worse about returning the gifts than she did about Frank. Once she got past the shock." She glanced at him. "He tried to patch things up, but she wasn't buying."

"Good for Rose. She'll get her china someday."

Grace laughed. "I think so, too. She's going on a date tonight, someone she met at her new job."

Rose had found a new job at a company that made medical supplies. The line work required special training and was far more precise than the box factory. The hours were decent, and it paid better, too.

They'd reached Seventh Avenue South and stood across from Waverly Place. "Feel like a bite to eat?" Harry asked.

"It's Sylvie's birthday, we're meeting later, when Lucille gets off her shift."

She shared an apartment on Cornelia Street with Lucille and Sylvie. Lucille had been reluctant at first to include Sylvie in their plan, claiming she didn't want to live with "someone she didn't know." Code perhaps for a colored girl. But when Lucille saw how adamant Grace was, she'd agreed to try. Sylvie turned out to be quieter, tidier, and a better cook than either of the Brooklyn girls, and the three had become fast friends.

After The Starlight Room, Sylvie had found work at a Horn and Hardart's and was soon promoted from dishwasher to loading the little windows with sandwiches and dishes of pie and pudding. She said she was treated decently, and it was a far nicer place to work than the club. But Grace knew it was just a lily pad where Sylvie could get her balance. She knew her friend could find a better job and even had one in mind for her.

Fully recovered, Mrs. Pfeiffer had decided to retire and spend more time with her grandchildren. Grace had already begun going out on surveillance with Harry and even working on her own cases. She was taking classes in psychology at the New School and to earn a private investigator's license. The process didn't take that long, but as she'd expected, female applicants were frowned upon.

It was Grace's idea to hire Sylvie to do all the things she used to do. Sylvie's typing was rusty, but she had an incredible knack with figures. She'd once told Grace that the only way she kept sane at her kitchen jobs was to play with numbers in her head—to add, subtract, divide, and multiply the number of plates she washed or potatoes she peeled. She quickly whipped the bookkeeping into shape. Harry, who rarely knew what he owed or who owed him, appreciated that.

"Now you really have associates," Grace had told him. "When do our names go on the door?"

Harry had laughed. "You're kidding, right? If anyone figures out that women are working on my cases now, we're sunk."

Grace had decided to table the discussion for another day.

"Where are you meeting up? I'll walk you there," Harry said.

"Minetta Lane Tavern. I have time. Let's have a drink."

"How about my place? Want to come up a while?"

"That would be fine."

"Good. I want to talk to you about something."

His tone disturbed her, but she held on to her questions. At first, she'd thought he just wanted to be together. She did, too. It was far from their first time, though it hadn't happened so often; it felt routine. She didn't think making love with Harry could ever feel that way.

Harry lived on the second floor of a row house on Washington Square. The front room had a wonderful view. Grace stood by the shuttered window and looked out at the park, filled with his neighbors, enjoying the mild summer night. Children playing, young couples courting, old people, and students. Street musicians and ragged bums. Noisy and full of life, it would stay that way long after dark.

Harry handed her a drink and put his arm around her shoulder. They stood together watching the world outside as the shadows deepened.

She lit a cigarette and turned to him. "What's up, Harry? I have a feeling I'm not going to like this news."

He left her at the window and sat on the couch, confirming her intuition. "I have to go out of town. I'm not sure how long I'll be away."

"And you're not going to tell me where or why, right?"

He met her glance and looked away. "It's best that you don't know. It's safer for you and Sylvie."

"You know I'll find out, sooner or later." When he didn't answer, she added. "I hope you don't plan on closing the office. We have cases going on. That won't be good for business."

"I'm of two minds about that."

"This is about White Lake, right?" She knew she'd guessed from the expression on his face, one that passed in a heartbeat before he was able to hide it.

"No, it's not. Good try, though."

"You can't fool me, Harry. Aren't we done with that?"

Harry sipped his drink and set the glass on the table. "You're like a dog with a bone sometimes, Grace Russo."

"I love dogs. I'll take it as a compliment." She sat on the couch and turned to him.

Soon after Joe's release, Harry had called her at home and said that he had to take care of some family business and would be back in about a week.

Grace had no idea he had a family. He'd never mentioned anyone.

A few days later, she'd been checking the death notices in *The Journal American* for Nona. There was a wake for Mrs. Costello's brother at funeral parlor in the neighborhood, and Nona wanted to know the visiting hours. Grace saw a notice for Laura Shaw—age twenty-eight, survived by her husband, Harry, sister Katherine Cooney Flynn, and mother, Eileen Cooney. Visiting hours were listed at a funeral parlor in Queens. In lieu of flowers, the family asked for donations to St. Christopher of Otille Convalescence Home, Tarrytown, N.Y.

She remembered the story about the naïve cop who stuck his neck out to do the right thing and how his car was rigged, and his wife became an invalid. And she knew that cop was Harry.

When Harry got back to the office a few days later, she told him that she was very sorry about his wife and explained how she'd come across the notice.

He seemed confused and even angry. He stalked into his office and slammed the door. She heard him crying behind the frosted glass.

She went in and put her arms around him. And he didn't pull away.

Afterward, he told her why and how Laura had been hurt, her body and mind ruined. The man who'd rigged the car had been apprehended, but there wasn't enough evidence to charge him. He'd walked free and disappeared.

But right around the time Joe got in trouble, Harry got a tip that the guy who'd hurt Laura had come back to New York and found a hiding hole upstate. Ray Tedesco was his name. Harry found the cabin, intending to kill him, but someone had beaten him to it. Tedesco had been shot in the gut and head, gangland style, and the farmhouse set on fire.

The police believed the hit was ordered by a rival gang. An informer had even slipped them a name, but they failed to apprehend the man.

Grace finally understood the reason Harry had disappeared during Joe's case. It was a darker and graver reason than she'd ever imagined.

"It's too bad the police can't find him," she'd said. "But you're well out of it."

"I hope so," Harry had replied, his tone not entirely comforting.

"It's pretty simple," he said now as he touched her hair with his fingertips. "Tedesco's friends don't buy the conclusion of the Sullivan County police. They decided I'm their man."

The explanation was simple but just as troubling. "Can't the police protect you?"

"Not likely. Besides, some cop breathing down my neck would drive me out of my mind. I need to find the guy who skipped town. If he really didn't do it, I need to find out who did."

When she didn't answer, he added. "Now do you understand why I didn't want to tell you?"

"Not really. I can help you."

"I know you can. But I don't want you to. Not this time. I didn't even want you to know this much. It puts you in a tight spot. Promise me you'll forget we ever had this conversation."

When she didn't answer, he took hold of her shoulders and made her look him in the eye. "Please, Grace, promise. I mean it."

She'd never heard Harry speak in that tone before. Frightened and upset. "I don't know where you are or what you're doing. You told me it was a family matter and haven't been in touch since."

"Not bad. But I'll still worry."

She'd worry about him, too. But he already knew that. "When will you leave?"

"Tonight. After you go." His hands slipped down her bare arms, and she moved into his embrace.

"I'm not going anywhere yet."

"Not if I have anything to say about it."

* * *

When she woke, it wasn't quite dark. The sounds of traffic and voices in Washington Square drifted through the window.

She found her slip and pulled it over her head. Then sat on the edge of the bed and watched the streetlights come on. She heard the spurt of a match as Harry sat up and lit a cigarette.

"Thinking about Joe?"

"A little. Who knows when I'll see him again?"

She felt his hand on her back, gliding down her skin. "He'll be back, sooner or later."

She turned to face him. "Will you?"

"I'll be fine, Grace."

"I'm tired of saying goodbye to people, Harry. I thought that was over when the war ended."

"I know. Me, too…Let's just not say it." He urged her down to the tangle of sheets, and she moved back into his embrace.

It wasn't an answer, but she knew it was the best she'd get. All she could do now was wait and watch, to see how the pieces fell together.

Author's Notes and Acknowledgments

First, my heartfelt thanks to my husband, Spencer and my daughter, Kate for their unflagging encouragement as I traveled a surprisingly long and often daunting road. I'm also thankful to my dear sister, Donna, a one woman cheering squad, always armed with champagne, who makes it impossible to doubt a happy ending. We aren't much like Grace and Rose, but growing up, we did raid each other's closets.

And many thanks to so many friends and fellow writers for their good cheer and insightful comments on early drafts; particularly Ellen Stieber, Alan Weiss, Val Pedersen and my sister-in-law, Martha Vibbert. I'd also like to thank the editors who couldn't find a place for this project but pushed me along with heartening words that filled my tank, Kathy Sagan, Michaela Hamilton and Tara Gavin.

If I'd ever known in advance the amount of work and time required to write a historical, I probably wouldn't have attempted it. But once begun, the process had an irresistible pull that carried me along.

Much of the Russos' domestic life is drawn from stories I'd heard as a child about my mother's family. Grandma Cavaliere was a born storyteller with no qualms about exaggerating the facts to pump up a punchline. I'm sure my writing DNA can be traced to her directly and just as sure she's pleased to see her recollections put to good use.

Researching this era, the story's settings and events, entailed endless hours surfing the internet and piles of books. Two titles that stand out are *Over Here!: New York City during World War II* by Lorraine Diehl, which helped immensely in creating the post war world of Grace Russo, and Harry Shaw. And *The Street*, a novel by Ann Perry, published in 1947. The first book by a female Black author to hit the *New York Times* bestseller list, Perry's vivid portrait of Harlem in the late 1940's helped me depict Mary Delmore's life, away from the Starlight Room.

Both *The Good War* and *Working,* by Studs Terkel were also important resources that helped me create the backstories of many characters.

I'd also like to thank Mark Carpentieri, president of MC Records, for sharing his knowledge about the music scene in New York City in the late 1940's.

Many early readers have asked the same question about the plot. Perhaps you do, too. "How could Grace and Mary have met in high school if the New York City schools were not integrated until 1964?"

Studies of the New York City school system, and high school yearbooks of the 1940's as well, show that their friendship was definitely possible. The racial make-up of New York City schools in predominately white neighborhoods at that time, such as Red Hook (later called Carroll Gardens) was typically 85% to 90% white, with the rest of the students Black, Puerto Rican and other races. Schools in predominately Black neighborhoods, like Fort Green, had a 90% to 95% Black enrollment, with the rest of the students white, and other races. After WWII, when redlining became widespread, these proportions grew even more imbalanced. But Mary and Grace had finished school before that period.

Finally, it's hard to put into words my gratitude to Shawn Reilly Simmons, an amazing, multi-talented publishing guru who wears many hats. Mainly, that of an insightful, outstanding editor. From the start, she thoroughly "got" this story, believed it had merit and took the bold step of including it in the Level Best/Historia list. I'm very grateful to her and the staff at LBB for the many hours it took to deliver this book into the hands and hearts of readers.

Discussion Questions

What was your experience reading about life in the 1940's in New York City. Did the author successfully evoke that time and place? Do you feel any connection to the era? Were there advantages of living back then, over today? What were the disadvantages? Would you ever trade living in this era for that one?

The story depicts an era where there were very strict gender roles for men and women. Which characters accept and even embrace those roles? Which balk against them? How do they rebel, suffer or make compromises?

The story looks at social taboos around race. Legally, many of those taboos have relaxed since 1947. Do you think the root prejudice still exists? If so, what form does it take? How did the interracial relationships (love, friendships, employer/employee) in the book reveal the time in which it is set? Can you relate to Grace's feelings and reaction when she discovers Joe and Mary's relationship?

One prominent theme of the story is the pressure of the status quo and social expectations. Which of the characters are engaged in his struggle? Do they resist the pressures, or compromise? What is the cost of their choices?

All the characters have survived WWII, either on the homefront or the battlefield. How do wartime experiences and memories impact their personalities, decisions and values? How does their personal histories effect the story? What were the ways that the characters submitted to, or transcended their personal histories?

Women of the era were labeled the "weaker sex" and "less intelligent." How did those labels restrict Grace? How does she push against these labels? How does she use them to her advantage?

Harry Shaw initially seems the typical mid-century private detective. How is he different, if at all? Does this make him more, or less appealing as a character?

Harry and Grace share the trait of loyalty, especially family loyalty. How does this trait motivate them and drive the story? Does either go too far trying to honor that value?

In what ways does Grace change over the course of the story? Did you see any key turning points? Did you see a moment when she realizes she's changed and expresses it? In what ways is she different when the story ends?

Why is Grace so determined to solve this case?

Mary only appears in a few scenes and yet is central to the story. Even though Grace doesn't get a chance to rekindle their relationship, how does Mary influence her? Did Mary's character surprise you in any way?

Religious and spiritual belief is threaded throughout the narrative. Which characters are believers? Which are not? How does belief help or hurt them? How do questions of faith resonate in the story?

When Grace begins working for Harry, he tells her that she'll need to learn how to lie a bit. How does lying work into the narrative? Who is lying and why?

The meeting between Grace and Mary at McNulty's might be the most important scene in the book. Do you think it's the most important? If so, why? If not, why not?

At the end of the story, Grace confesses feeling responsible for Mary's death. As does Joe. Do you think she bears any responsibility? Do you think that Joe does?

About the Author

Anne Canadeo is the author of over forty books, including *The Black Sheep & Company Mysteries,* and the bestselling *Cape Light* and *Angel Island* novels, written under the pen name Katherine Spencer. Away from her desk, she's a gardener, cook, and ardent dog lover. Active in her community, she's been recognized by New York State for her volunteer service. Anne lives on Long Island with her husband and a wacky rescue dog. She loves to hear from readers. Contact her at: anne@annecanadeo.com and follow her on Facebook, Instagram, Threads, and Blue Sky.

AUTHOR WEBSITE:
  annecanadeo.com

SOCIAL MEDIA HANDLES:
  Facebook: AnneCanadeoAuthor
  Instagram: @AnneCanadeo
  Threads: annecanadeo
  BlueSky: @AnneCanadeo

Also by Anne Canadeo

The Black Sheep Knitting Mysteries (published by Simon & Schuster)
While My Pretty One Knits (2009)
Knit, Purl, Die (2009)
A Stitch Before Dying (2010)
Till Death Do Us Purl (2012)
The Silence of the Llamas (2013)
A Dark and Stormy Knit (2014)
The Postman Always Purls Twice (2015)
A Murder in Mohair (2015)

The Black Sheep & Company Mysteries (published by Kensington Books)
Knit to Kill (2017)
Purls and Poison (2018)
Hounds of the Basket Stitch (2019)
Strangers on a Skein (2021)
Death on the Argyle (2022)